Helens

NOT NECESSARILY ABOUT SEX

Charleston, SC
www.PalmettoPublishing.com

Helens: Not Necessarily About Sex
Copyright © 2021 by Matthew Louis Kalash

First Edition

Hardcover ISBN: 978-1-63837-965-2
Paperback ISBN: 978-1-63837-966-9
eBook ISBN: 978-1-63837-967-6

There are only two ways to start a story:
A man goes on a journey, or a stranger arrives in town.

—Literary axiom variously attributed to Tolstoy,
Dostoyevsky, Ernest Hemingway, John Gardner,
and everyone's high school English teacher.

Contents

Pretense
The Unfinished Work   1

Irony
En Passant   21

Destiny
Helens   47

Identity
The Italian Manuscript   95

Fidelity
Oral Sex in the Communication Age or
The New Pygmalion   239

Security
The Confectioner's Mistress   283

Reality
Ibid., a Symposium   309

About the Author   337

The Unfinished Work

Art is never finished, only abandoned.
—Leonardo da Vinci

*P*aris. A heavy fog covers the city like a suitor, hiding her from the eyes of God and Flight 434 from New York. By nightfall I'm deep inside Italy, the womb of Europe, seated in a train box with a man chattering breathless trochees in his cell phone; lost beneath a thousand miles of clouded sky, eclipsed from the winter moon, settled even beyond reach of the words spoken right in front of me.

"We're going to my parents' house for Christmas," she'd said.

"What?"

"Don't pretend you didn't hear me. They invited us for dinner."

"Didn't we just see them?"

"What's that supposed to mean?"

I gave her a blank look. We were in the kitchen fixing separate meals.

"Let's talk about *your* family," she said.

"We haven't seen *them* for years."

She said: "Thanksgiving wasn't that bad."

"Thanksgiving was a disaster. Why don't we go away for a while?"

"Because Christmas is supposed to be a nice, family holiday."

"But you don't have a nice family."

Hurt, she stalked out of the kitchen.

"That was a joke," I called after. But I couldn't stop myself. "Jesus, Lil. For Thanksgiving she threw crockery. Christmas, by rights, can only be more violent—especially if there's no yams."

1

"Yuck it up," Lily said, returning. "But I won't tell my parents we're skipping Christmas dinner because you want to run away. If you want out, do it yourself."

As my train kisses to a stop inside the bright cavern of Central Station in Florence, I consider phoning Marco Rinaldi again, as I'd done once from Milan without success. But on second thought I figure an old friend showing up at your doorstep unannounced is, by some small margin, less imposition than an unexpected old friend who needs a ride from the train station. I get a cab.

In the city center, the lights of Florence glisten off a thin finish left by the day's rainfall, lending the granite stonework a bronze façade. For my mind, there's no other city in the world where structure so utterly occupies the eye; like an unwanted guest, Florentine architecture overwhelms the senses, warping gravity with a mass that's intimidating in the light of day—to say nothing of a rainy night, when its effect can be perfectly vertiginous. In fact, there exists an inner ear condition called Stendhalismo for the French novelist who suffered dizzy spells on his first trip to the city. Florentine doctors, it is said, treat up to a dozen people each year whose equilibrium is disrupted by the city's tantalizing grandeur.

Moments later, Marco Rinaldi answers his door sporting an enormous grin. His wide Roman forehead, now wrinkled like the tides, has overrun a jetty of hair that once connected either side of his brow. The pounds he's gained since college give him, like the city's buildings, an arresting presence. I realize for the first time what a consummate Italian he is, how foreign he'd seemed in the States.

Over dinner and two bottles of Chianti, Marco and I reminisce about our years in America and the years since. I catch him up on mutual friends—who is successful, who is married, who has fallen off the face of the earth—until finally he comes round to Lily. I'd forgotten that Marco knew her before I did; we'd started dating just weeks before graduation.

"What happened with you and her?" he asks in accented English.
"We split up years ago," I lie.

I met Lily in the spring of 1998, sitting by a linden tree reading one of those trashy novels she loved so much. It was a month before commencement and my world was a blur; the first warm breeze of the season filled my nose as I rushed across the quad to meet my I-don't-know-what... One look at her stopped me dead.

She leaned idly on the trunk with her feet tucked neatly beneath her, revealing a dark beauty mark just below her right knee. Sandals and a cardigan rested in a pile at her side and she read intently, carefully tucking and re-tucking a stubborn strand of hair that kept falling from behind her ear. That simple, sensuous gesture seemed an odd note of self-consciousness amid the muddle of vines and lindens, plans and expectations; it shot through to me like a light in the fog—kind of thing that makes a man change course. I can't actually recall how we got together, but that moment I remember clear as day, and by the time the lindens had their sap up Lily and I were a couple. I gave up my summer plans (a trip to Europe with an old friend returning to the city of his birth) and indulged myself in sweet infatuation.

That was easy enough—everyone loves beginnings. In the beginning, every gesture is a revelation, and each revelation is a little miracle, novel and inevitable, like destiny or cable TV. I made her laugh and the sound of her laughter added dimension to my fickle soul. I admit that a part of me felt the need to turn from her bright light, but in the end I was helpless to resist. Of course we fell in love, though I can't say how it happened or when that reality first dawned on me. It's an awful phenomenon, love: Few people see it coming, fewer see it leave; most, with silliness and pleasure just step in it, and one day the mole below her knee seems like the most precious thing in the world.

We finished college, found jobs, and lived together on a tree-lined street in Brooklyn, much to the chagrin of Lily's traditional parents. We adopted a puppy and had dinner parties, spent weekends with friends on Long Island. Though we'd been together more than three years, we deliberately avoided the issue of engagement. As a result, being a couple remained a precious balancing act between the reality of here and now and the ideal of happily ever after—pretending, as we were, to be a married couple without the sanction of rings or ceremonies.

Nevertheless, there were pressures. Her parents, especially, were full of questions about my "intentions." What could I say? To my mind, we were too young for vows. Perhaps it was the heretic in me, but it was easier to believe that our relationship would always feel novel if we didn't consecrate it. Nothing could come between Lily and me. Why screw it up with all those rules?

And consider our examples. My parents stayed married barely long enough to conceive me, and my father was a diminishing presence throughout my childhood, disappearing altogether when my mother married someone else—the first time. Lily's folks, on the other hand, maintained a bond of unrelenting hostility sanctioned only by a simon-pure fear of hell. Indeed, Lily is still the only single child of a Catholic family I've ever met, which seemed odd only till I met her folks. She was mortified by them. I couldn't imagine she'd want to follow those footsteps.

Yet as time went by, it seemed that no more than inertia was keeping us together, that without the foundation of matrimony our relationship was built on sand. Intercourse soon became a ritual she countenanced more than actually enjoyed. What, I wondered, had become of the nymph I'd seen beneath the linden tree—not to mention the girl who used to greet me at the door wearing nothing but a smile? That just wasn't Lily anymore. Fidelity was never an issue, nor trust, nor love for that matter. It wasn't necessarily about sex either. I just wasn't drawn to her the way I'd been that first day on the quad, and frankly I worried that my youth had somehow withered on the vine.

Eventually the only heat in our relationship came from disagreements. Lily didn't like the hours I kept; she said freelance writing was probably the worst job on the planet. In return, I hassled her over trifles such as curtain rods and petty cash. Though such quarrels were little more than pinpricks, they became more pointed over time. And that's not even speaking of the big-ticket items—romance, communication, fringe benefits—all of which were lacking according to one or the other of us.

Of course, we periodically visited Lily's parents, which was always a harrowing experience. Her mother, Pat, was a drunkard who hounded her husband about twenty hours a day, near as I could tell. Spiro, Lily's dad, had had the life hectored out of him; the creases in his face seemed to mark out years like rings in a tree. To see them together you got the feeling that each wished they'd done something better, but they were bound by circumstances and the Holy Church. Still, Lily was scrupulously loyal, and suffered no criticism of her family, especially from me.

One late summer evening, as we were getting ready to leave (Lily's mom was face down on the couch, Spiro had retired to the garage to fiddle with his fishing lures), I came across an old photograph of the couple when they still had their polish on, probably thirty years earlier, posing on the boardwalk at Coney Island. She was bright and beautiful, he had a gleam in his eye and a smile so wide it was a wonder he could breathe. They were young, happy, hopeful—they didn't resemble the people I knew.

I went to the garage to say goodbye to Spiro, who I found peering listlessly into a rusted tackle box, his glasses hanging at the end of his aquiline nose. He remained still as an effigy till I spoke.

"Mind if I ask you a question Mr. Ginetti?" I said, stepping through the doorway.

Lily's father did not look up, but raised a hand in one of his oft-used Italian gestures that meant for me to proceed as I wished, it was no skin off his nose.

"How'd you and Mrs. G. meet?"

At that Spiro raised his head, tipping his glasses a fraction back on his nose. "I don't remember how we met," he said with bland annoyance.

"You don't remember at all?"

Spiro shook his head. He looked at me as though I'd just asked him how to split the atom. "What's to remember the first day? That's my wife. You think bombs go off? You think lighting strikes then it's happily ever after?" Spiro asked, using his hands, as usual, to illustrate. "That's a myth." And then, for perhaps the first time in my presence, he laughed: a low, whispering chuckle that wouldn't shake a dead leaf off a tree.

"Love just happens," he went on. "Marriage is an act of will, an act of faith that takes a little piece of you every day. What you got to do is decide you've got enough pieces to give."

Then Spiro did something awful. He came toward me and placed both hands on my shoulders. As he held me there, both within his grasp and at arm's length, I saw for the first time the man he was, and the man he might have been.

"Son," Spiro said softly, "Love is like a day at the beach." A phantom smile passed briefly on his mouth before his face turned grave. Then he said, "Marriage is when you go back to work."

At that, he lifted one hand from my shoulder and patted me gently on the face. Spiro then turned and resumed his practiced statue above the tackle box.

"Why?" I asked, suddenly wanting to help this ruined old man. "What do you get in return for all that work?"

Spiro raised neither his voice nor his head as he answered, "Marriage is the homage we pay to love. To expect a reward is a betrayal of that love, you nitwit."

I sputtered and stared at his hunched back, confused and dismayed by the man in that garage—a man who'd surrendered himself to an unworthy cause, in my opinion, leaving an unfinished picture of what his life might have been. At that moment, I never wanted to see either of Lily's parents again.

Yet I couldn't stop wondering what had happened to that bright young couple to turn them into such dark old people. Was it just the ruin of time, the accumulation of petty criticisms that did them in? Or was it something fundamental? Can two people really be together for twenty, thirty, fifty years and not develop resentments that turn the blush of love blood red? If not, marriage seems an unhappy task, recasting ardor as the first symptom of a malignancy.

Ironically, one day soon after that Lily went to the dermatologist and had the mole removed from her knee. Better safe than sorry, the doctor told her. But I'd never told her (I never really knew until the little spot was gone) that it was the first part of her I fell in love with. And I couldn't tell her she wasn't the same without it, so I mourned the lost beauty mark in secret, all the while taking special exception to the idea that the initial object of *my* love could be tainted.

And then came Thanksgiving.

It was a typical evening, really, though tensions were magnified by an increased contingent of Ginettis in the house on Court Street. Despite the holidays, and seemingly oblivious of company, Lily's parents were at it from the moment we walked through the door. Pat was grousing in the kitchen, where she nursed bourbon and a cigarette over a steaming crock of sweet potatoes, which, amazingly enough, were the source of the quarrel. Apparently, Spiro had got the wrong thing.

"God*damned* worthless old goat," Pat said at high volume, stubbing her cigarette to give Lily a hug. "Twenty years we've had yams at Thanksgiving. But stupid over there can't handle a simple thing like that." She picked up an empty can labeled "Sweet Potatoes" as an emblem of her righteous anger. "I send him to the store for yams and he brings back *this*. No wonder he never made anything of himself. Now Thanksgiving dinner will be as much a failure as your father," she said with blatant rancor.

"It's okay mom," Lily answered gently.

I was next, and as I leaned in to hug her, Pat's smoke-fouled hair enveloped my face. I winced. "God forbid I had a heart attack," she continued over my shoulder. "I'd send him for an ambulance and he'd bring back a tugboat."

Spiro walked softly into the kitchen and took Lily in his arms. "Don't worry," he said, looking his wife in the eye as he held his little girl against his shoulder, "When you have a heart attack I'll know just what to do." He released Lily and shook my hand. "I've got a shovel in the garage," Spiro said, turning to walk out of the kitchen.

Lily's mother's eyes flashed past me, and in a second she'd put down her drink and picked up the crock pot. With a flip of her wrists she sent the sweet potatoes flying in the direction of her husband. Luckily—and I can't say it was anything but luck—the crock pot whizzed past Spiro's head, exploding on the wall beyond him with a crash; it fell to the floor a mixture of jagged Corningware and searing mush.

Spiro stopped and looked down for a beat before his gaze shifted vaguely toward his wife. "Yams and a sweet potatoes are the same thing, you bitch," he said blandly.

At that Spiro turned and left while Pat lit a cigarette with a loud huff. In another second, she too escaped through the side door. Without a word Lily went to the pantry, gathered up the broom and dustpan, and in a few moments the remains of the quarrel had disappeared. Worse yet, after a short lull the Ginettis returned to the kitchen as though nothing was amiss; despite the recent occurrence of flying crockery, dinner went on without a word about the incident. I swear it scared the shit out of me.

The next morning, still dazed from the holiday, I took a long look in the mirror, where lines were beginning to deepen and spread. What was I doing? I had a mortgage, a joint checking account, insurance policies, bank loans, and sundry other mutual credit concerns; Lily and I were already as good as married, tied by laws too intricate to unstitch. But she wasn't the same girl who once took my breath away. Where was my linden nymph? Where, after all, had my favorite beauty mark gone? I had to face the facts: Little by little, Lily was dying—and so was I. While the former prospect was sad, the latter was a shock. Because in coming to terms with my own mortality I realized one thing above all: I had to get the hell away from these people, or face thirty years of Thanksgivings like that. And flying crock pots can, in fact, kill you dead.

"So you and Lily," Marco asks again, sipping Chianti in his kitchen in Florence. "What happened?"

"Just didn't work out."

As if on cue, we fall into picturesque silence—wine glasses half-emptied on the black lacquer table beside a bowl of clementines and a sliced baguette. I love Italy for such moments, the moments when life slips glibly into figure.

"Alora," Marco sighs. "Tomorrow I must work."

He gives me linens and a pillow, and directs me to a spare bed on the ground floor. I flip a switch throwing white light on an unfinished room, the cement floor and plaster walls as bare as the day they were made, except for a lone, arched doorway, around which, frescoed perfectly in the plaster, is a portico like those that surround the old city of Florence. Beyond the portico, witless phantoms queue against the walls, tucked loosely under sheets to keep away dust and concern. There are easels and canvas, spare wood for framing, brushes, paints, medium, knives, a palette or two—the anonymous vestiges of a painterly life.

I find an old cot buried in a corner behind the only erect easel in the room, which hovers under a white sheet. A bit tipsy from the wine, I stumble toward the bed, catching the standing easel with a stray elbow and send that ghost crashing to the floor. A bolt runs down my body at the sound. As I stoop to pick up the easel, I find that what I'd knocked over is the portrait of a pretty girl lit seemingly from within, her background cast in shapeless shadow. But no. Upon closer examination, I realize that the painting remains unfinished beyond her perfect aureole.

I reset the easel and the picture atop it and sit on the edge of the bed, gazing at the canvas, reluctant for some reason to surrender the day. The girl's top shrugs temptingly off her shoulders, which, like her back and neck, appear livid with sweat. The neckline clings tentatively to her breasts, poised to swoon into the nervous space between her legs, where her skirts are gathered in clinging fingers. Delineated thighs beneath the dress, haughty calves at half-angle, and the merest glimpse of her left knee. She trembles, almost; *amity, lightly dressed*; inertia and the gravity of the moon. I have the sudden urge to touch that limned face, if only for a moment, to feel real life behind the rough canvas.

Instead, I undress and throw the linens on the cot. The chill sends another shiver up my spine. I shake, lay down, and in a fit of panic, discovery, and abdication, with an eye on my Galatea, ejaculate on the cold stone floor.

The next morning I awake to the ringing of church bells in a nearby campanile. Marco is already gone, but has left a pair of house keys on the kitchen table labeled *tempo* and *moda* with scotch tape over the words cut from a glossy magazine, along with a note and a legend wedding the keys to their respective locks. I pick them up and leave directly, verifying both the *tempo* and *moda* behind me as I set out to walk off my hangover in the birthplace of the Renaissance.

I'm struck immediately by the simple vista of daily life in Italy. Every scene seems a living image; the air, the people, even the earth affect the senses with their subtle brilliance. One can surely understand, on a radiant December morning in Florence, the inspiration that has lived there for centuries.

I spend the next few hours wandering the narrow byways of the old city, lost in the tranquilizing confinement of a place where most buildings are no more than four stories high. Marco once told me, in fact, that there's an ordinance prohibiting any structure in Florence from rising higher than Brunelleschi's dome on the church of Santa Maria del Fiore. Yet because of the close streets, it's possible to pass within yards of the Duomo and not have caught a glimpse of it over those simple, four-story buildings—so intimate is Florentine architecture.

Consequently, when at last I stumble across the Duomo—the pith, the umbilicus of the city—I'm overwhelmed as much by the suddenness as its tremendous mass, augmented by marble fascia and cornices hovering a hundred feet above the cobblestones. It's a breathtaking sight. One can argue that the church's reverence has been sullied somewhat by the constant, ungodly presence of tourists, but the Duomo itself remains a wonder to the senses: exquisite, infinite, witherless. It's then that am I dizzied with the pilgrim's vertigo, my eyes allured forever upward to the lantern summit seemingly leavened by the light of the piazza. As though lifted by that queer radiance, I float forward, enraptured by its strange beauty, lost in my own epiphany... Until I stop short on a squish, and a gamy odor rises from the sidewalk.

Dogshit. Italians have an abiding love of dogs. However, they're far too urbane to consider curbing their animals. Ergo, when in Florence you'd best watch your step.

I'm still scraping my sole on the cobblestones when a procession celebrating the Feast of the Virgin Birth enters the piazza in full throat, singing hymns with singularly Italian passion. The group is led by clergymen in rose-colored tunics, bearing gonfalons; they're followed by women with armfuls of cut flowers and children dressed like tiny *amorini* waving wooden crosses over their little heads; behind the children come drums and trumpets and a huge depiction of the Nativity, complete with real animals borne on a litter carried by a dozen men. The scene is marvelous, a testament to the strange and sanguine vigor of the Italian people, a joyful witness to two thousand years of daily faith—an act both extraordinary and quotidian at the same time. I am overwhelmed, and in moments find myself crying like a child in the middle of the piazza, shit still hanging on my shoe.

When Marco returns that night, I'm lounging on the couch, lost once again in a fog, contemplating, for lack of a better word, my fate. I considered religion, destiny, and the duality of man; sex, youth, and loneliness. I thought of Lily's dearly departed beauty mark, and the unending labor of love, so different from the first gasp of rapture. Spiro was right: No matter what people think, moments don't truly breathe life into the heart; love at first sight is as mythical as Sisyphus. Rather, it takes time and diligence, for emotion is nurtured by experience and animated in reflection. Hindsight is the looking glass of love, which is a work of art that is never finished.

The display of bona fides in the piazza had shown me the subtle substance of devotion. One day in Florence, where the rarest beauties fuse immaculately with the everyday dirt of the earth, puts life in a new light; suddenly, I want to go back to Brooklyn and marry Lily, if she'll have me.

Turns out it's no fun being a faithless bastard.

"*Stai stanco?*" Marco asked.

"I think you could say that."

"You did not sleep well last night?" He makes a fickle Italian gesture with his shoulders. "You know, no one has went to that basement for many years, not since my uncle died. It was his studio, he was an artist."

"Don't tell me he died there," I say.

"No, no," Marco avers, also with his hands. He grins impishly. "Did you see his mistress?" His eyebrows rise, creasing his thick forehead. "The painting."

I don't answer.

"Did I not ever tell you of my crazy uncle? For ten years his only companion was a portrait he had painted years before. Most of the family thought he was only making eccentric, but some believed he was truly *fuori la testa*—out of his head, you know?

"Uncle Luca never explained. But once, at my mother's house, he said something of inspiration and sex and the Holy Ghost. He was stopped for good when he mentioned the Virgin—you don't talk sex and La Madonna together in my mother's presence, you know?" Marco shakes his head and laughs quietly. "She called him a dirty *communista* and a whore-lover, and never let him back in her home after that day."

"Who is it?" I ask.

Marco shrugs. "*Boh*. Some Polish bourgeosie, I think. I never knew her name. I wish I could sell the portrait; my uncle was, after all, an artist of some reputation. But Uncle Luca left the picture unfinished. He claimed that to finish it would be a betrayal." Marco gave a shrug of incomprehension. "Probably he was just spent as an artist, and as a man," he concludes sadly. "Is too bad, you know. My uncle could have been a great artist. The kind Giorgio Vasari wrote about."

He looks at me strangely. "But I am sure I have told you this story. You don't remember?"

True genius, it is said, lies beyond the ken of mortal man, and comes to this world only by the divine will of the Father of all things. Thus, we can be sure that it was no less than the hand of God that delivered into the ancient Etruscan village of Fiesole, mere kilometers north of grand Florence, the seat of the Renaissance and indeed the beating heart of artistry to this day, the babe Andaluca Rinaldi, who would resurrect the legacy of Giotto with his breathtaking representation of the human form, his heartrending delicacy of expression, and the supple relief in his figures. Indeed, no true lover of art can resist the vivid skin tones or the brilliant sensuality of his canvas. His gifts, truly, have become the world's.

As a child, the artist was noted mostly in his village for the strangeness of his Christian name (the story goes that Andaluca's father, a leather merchant, was in Andalusia at the time of the boy's birth), but like all men of real genius, his talent burgeoned early, and could not be suppressed. Andaluca's father grew hoarse from scolding him at the workshop for drawing in the dirt or on spare—and sometimes not at all spare—scraps of hide. By the time the boy was in his teens, his father could see no reason to keep him in the workshop, having disciplined him to the point of a weary hand and a worn belt. Hence, the father looked to Florence to have his son apprenticed to an artist, and he felt fortunate to strike a deal with the Sicilian Giovanni Viola, a painter of some renown, who in return for Andaluca's service at home and in the studio would teach the boy to improve upon his gift.

Yet in little time the pupil's talents grew equal to, and eventually surpassed, those of his mentor. When he was only seventeen years old, Andaluca secretly applied for and won a municipal commission over his master. That incident put an end to his apprenticeship, and for a long time soured Andaluca's fortunes in Florence, for Giovanni Viola was still a powerful influence, and his disfavor made it nearly impossible for a young artist to earn a living in that city. Andaluca was forced to abandon Florence altogether, and make his reputation elsewhere.

Fortune finally smiled on the young man some eight years later, when he was living in a one-room flat outside the city of Parma, selling drawings in the local market to make a meager living. By chance, he was introduced to a certain Polish merchant, M___, who was then vacationing at a summer home he'd recently purchased on Lake Como. Upon seeing the artist's work, the Polacco (who despite courtly shortcomings typical of the nouveaux riches, did have a fine eye for painting) commissioned Andaluca on the spot to fresco the interiors of his huge new villa. This project, undertaken in stages, occupied Andaluca for more than six years. When he finished, the artist was summoned to Warsaw to paint portraits of his patron's family—which by that time included a daughter and a son—for which commission he spent eight months living in Poland. When those portraits were finished to his patron's satisfaction, Andaluca was at last rewarded for his work, and at a handsome price, making him, when he finally returned to Florence, wealthier than he had ever dreamed.

With time and the continuing influence of his patron, Andaluca soon developed a reputation among European collectors, earning enough from his paintings to purchase an atelier and apartment on the Borgo degli Albizi. In fact, Andaluca was rich. His work was featured in exhibitions, where galleries and private citizens bid for his paintings. Aristocrats and industrialists wanted his canvases in their homes; their wives wanted him in their beds. Everything Andaluca had ever wanted, more than he'd ever dared hope for, was his—and he owed this great good fortune, in large part, to his original benefactor. So even though Andaluca was by no means fond of the overbearing old Polacco, he remained grudgingly grateful to his original patron.

Because he was beholden, Andaluca could not refuse when asked to lodge the Polacco's daughter while the girl herself studied art in Florence. The patron also arranged to have his daughter assist his artist in studio, as similarly (the Polacco said) Andaluca had been apprenticed to Giovanni Viola so many years before in exchange for room and board. Andaluca groused openly about this old custom, long since discontinued in favor of formal schooling, and assured his patron that he would gladly offer the room to the daughter of so great a man without any talk of compensation. But the Polacco insisted. And so Andaluca consented, not without chagrin, to the notion of an "assistant" in his studio.

The daughter of Andaluca's benefactor came to stay in the spring of 1973. Upon her arrival, he installed her in the dungeonous unfinished basement of his flat, with nothing but an old cot on which to sleep. Privately, Andaluca supposed it to be a fine revenge to put this Polish princess in a bare room on a narrow bed. He was sure that as soon as the girl told her father about the accommodations, the old man would give up his charade and buy her an apartment of her own, thus removing this ridiculous imposition from Andaluca's life.

It was then some five years since Andaluca had lived with the family in Warsaw, and painted a portrait of the Polacco's daughter in her *primavera*. The daughter-girl (as Andaluca called her) had been just twelve when the portrait was finished. She was now a fully grown, radiant woman. When he spoke of her, years later, Andaluca noted her elegant gestures, her fulsome hair, and the walnut skin on the soft part of her arms. Her eyes danced bossa novas, he said, brimming aphrodisia. And when she smiled, the daughter-girl revealed a charming gap between her two front teeth. Some would have considered this an imperfection—not so to the artist's eye.

Under the circumstances, however, the girl's budding sexuality presented potential problems for Andaluca, whose taurine exploits were legend on Europa. Now he would be responsible for the well-being of his patron's only daughter, and no flight, not even of an artist's fancy, could interpret that charge as an invitation to liberties.

Indeed, the trust that the Polacco showed in Andaluca was something of a mystery, for he was surely acquainted with his protégé's character, having hosted the artist those months in Poland, in which time Andaluca became intimate with literally dozens of Warsawian women. Andaluca himself enjoyed retelling the story of a particular evening during that stay when he held forth on the subject of rapture for almost an hour at the dinner table, to the point of disregarding his meal, and to the acute displeasure of the lady of the house.

But perhaps the Polacco supposed he could buy Andaluca's good faith, for he'd sent a letter with his daughter commissioning a canvas depicting the Annunciation to Mary. And therefore, whether it was out of a feeling of loyalty or the promise of payment, Andaluca resolved that his behavior toward the daughter-girl would be above reproach.

The story continues in the late afternoon of a typically sweltering July day in Florence. Andaluca was at his studio pining over the

Annunciation, completely dissatisfied with every idea he presented in cartoon. He worked that day, as was his habit, shirtless, absorbing the light of Tuscany, the womb of art, through his pores. He liked to paint naked to the waist, he said, to allow the light to infuse his skin.

The daughter-girl—that assistant imposed on him by his most important patron—was late arriving, and Andaluca hadn't eaten since morning. *Aveva famissimo.* Yet there wasn't a morsel in his studio, save for a few clementines he'd bought the week before in order to imitate their color. But he could sense, if not yet see, the flies gathering round the overripe fruit. He wanted his assistant to retrieve supper.

She was eager. Despite his reluctance to take an assistant, Andaluca couldn't help but appreciate the girl's zeal. But he had in no time determined that she was artistically bereft; composition was lost on her and she was blind to color, yet her draftsmanship was the worst of all. The poor girl just didn't have a ribbon of talent. In addition, she was frustrated to tears by isolation, muteness, and the adamantine rebuff of the Italian language by her Polish psyche. Most days, Andaluca could sense, as he did the perceptible gathering of flies over old fruit, welling fear and desperation in the atmosphere around her. Thus his self-restraint, always a deficit in sexual matters, was hard-pressed to restrain him from giving comfort to flustered beauty. But for the moment, his most compelling need was some six inches above that impulse, and grumbling like a galley slave.

Where was that girl?

As Andaluca stood at the entrance to his studio, beaming into the shadows after his assistant, the melancholy sky announced one great clap of thunder and shed a torrent into the city. He stepped outside to take in the shower. Down the block, a man on a Vespa strayed too close to the curb and was toppled onto the street. Andaluca laughed from his bare belly as the man rained blows on the machine.

Just then he heard the splash of feet on wet pavement, and turned to see the daughter-girl running up the avenue, pensive and damp, one hand crossing her brow to shield the raindrops. His hunger, her tardiness, and the variety of frustrations fermenting on him like sweat in the evening reaffirmed themselves in Andaluca's mind.

She froze upon seeing him outside the studio, not yet ready to explain. "*Non e*—" began the daughter-girl in a breathless, awkward tongue. Her mentor batted at his throat with the blade of his hand. Fed up.

Andaluca knew that the language of Italian hand gestures had come more easily to her, but when the girl seditiously flicked her chin back at it stunned him to the core, redoubling his anger. He thrust out an arm, pointing her to the studio. There, he spread layers of epithets and detailed lamentations on the daughter-girl. And she, having exhausted her mutiny in the one gesture, fairly crumpled under an authentic Italian redress—no matter that she understood hardly a word.

The tirade, which lasted nearly ten minutes, had reddened Andaluca's face and neck and the bared skin across his shoulders. The daughter-girl endured it bravely, but when the artist paused to clear his throat, she began at last to sob, standing rigid in the center of the room, arms pendent at her sides, looking every bit as awkward as her Italian—a weeping child as certain of the need for help as the fear of asking it.

He paced away, pulled at his hair. Guilt frustration hunger choler bother…godawful lust. And she's crying pitifully, hands clasped, feet together, proud, rich chin beginning to bow, dewdrops on her shoulders, moist dress of perspiration and rainwater, spattered mud along the hem and up her bare calves, hips quivering with each sob…and the buds of her young nipples. The poetic space between her front teeth.

He brought her a stool and slipped the damp sandals from her feet without so much as brushing her skin; brooding, retreated to a corner.

She wept.

Peculiar thrill it is to see a woman cry—fragile, like a child, but charged with a borealis of inevitable sexuality. Sadistic empathy. Like Leda cowering before the queer might of a swan, She trembles before the Spirit. A pitiful seduction. The soul of mythology. The thesis of literature. Future events cast shadows in the present, auguring vast consequences. Yeats asks: Could she have known? And the wind cries "Mary." He circles the room till he finds himself behind her at its center; without words, the golden aura of a woman draws the artist. He lays a hand on her head.

"Non piange," Andaluca says softly.

He unlaces the ribbon from her hair, which falls damp across her shoulders; his thumbs, of their own volition, make circles at her nape, distending the muscles of her neck. The girl rises instinctively to his touch as her hands grasp at the folds of her dress. Steadily, he kneads down her back, her skin kindling beneath his fingers as her dress falls past her shoulders, allowing his caress to ramble across her virgin flesh, pure even as it redampens with sweat.

The daughter-girl breathes shallow puddles, tugging at the material between her thighs; sniffs, bats her lashes against the tears yet welling in her eyes, lost in the space between her shoulders where her chimeric lover—the mad, omni-potent man who painted the portrait of her adolescence—permeates every cell of her body.

Andaluca waxes heavy, breathing her scent as he measures the sordid valley of her spine with his fingers, remembering the girl in her youth, the seeds of her mother's sex coming to fruit on her body. He'd wondered then if she would be a pleasing woman, perhaps even more than the mother. She is, at that. This girl is a corporal parable; her body hums like a siren, God himself hidden in the strain of her skin.

Too close, lost, he billets one kiss in the cave behind her ear. *"Sta cosi, bellina."* Andaluca paces away in a long arc, shuffling his feet and rubbing his hands gently against his pursed lips, which is his habit of nervous thoughtfulness. He keeps his back toward the girl to allow himself to think, for he is distracted to epiphany by the sight of her.

But he knows what he must do to still the wind within him. Andaluca tosses aside the heartless canvas he'd been working on, and replaces it with a naked one. He then eyes his work and sets to beauty, scrutinizing, lingering on hip's curve with his palm, cheek, mouth, sex—still poised before the canvas across the room from the daughter-girl. He coaxes the oils, dissolving into the pity of her fingertips and the pastel glow of her torso while she, stunned immaculate, remains perfectly still aside from the creeping poignancy in her forehead and mouth. Two hours.

When he was done, the artist reclined, numb from the pulse that had gone through him—the only time in his life that such inspiration, which could only be the breath of God, had filled him so fully and spent him so completely. He didn't move, think, hear, or speak, but melted into the cold stone floor: post-coital, famous, indigenous, brilliant.

En Passant

Chess is as much a mystery as women.[1]

uck these fucking people.

You know who I mean: these sheep, these groupies, these bandwagon-jumpers, these dry-humpers, the droll, the indistinct, the undecided, the undeclared, the committed, the enthusiastic, the earnest, the plain, the bad, the dullstupidbeautiful, the "extreme," the smelly, the normal, the nuts, the sluts, the jocks, the mods, the rockers, the mockers, the Boomers and their coddled broods (separate or en famille, always an unpardonable lot), addled oldsters, brainless teens, newly affluent, old and penniless, beggars, thieves, past-their-primes and prime-time wannabees, the weird, the wicked, the stunning, the dark, the pierced, the painted, the impressionable, the idealistic, the socialistic, party-goers, potheads, activists, professoria, studentdom, college dropouts, anachronisms, guitar players, couples, singles, divorcees, their babies, their dogs[2]... Because they're all here all of a sudden with their happy chatter and their day-glo teeth. These people. They're disgusting.

And I'm huddled in the corner of Boccaccio's Café, riled out of my mind by this teeming Volk, trying not to ponder murder while I drum my fingers on a great, graying, faux fresco[3] of a woman in red, which was apparently slapped on the wall by some poor shlub under the impression that there should be a little bit of beauty in a dingy

---

1 From *The Search for Chess Perfection* by Cecil John Seddon Purdy (1906–1979), Australian Grandmaster, book author, and inaugural World Correspondence Chess champion.
2 Categories are not necessarily mutually exclusive.
3 fres • co 1. *v.i.* The art of painting on fresh, moist plaster with pigments dissolved in water, 2. *n.* A painting executed in this way.

spot off the beaten path. But of course he was an idiot, and the fucking fresco is crumbling like stale bread, just like the atmosphere in
here, which has become, for the record, far too trite to abide.

Because Boccaccio's is vintage, magnificent—a strange mélange of
Art Deco, Ed Hopper, and *fin de siècle*, complete with goofy decor, full-
tilt filth on the ceiling, insupportable plumbing, and the odd wobble under every table, chair, glass, and saucer, compliments of the staff, which is
so indifferent you can't help but admire them. On top of that, the food's
as dull as monks' pate, yet somehow (somehow!) the coffee is *fantastic.*

All this is lost, of course, on the horde of morons already malin-
gering over every inch of the café's worn checkerboard floor—and
this not yet 10 a.m.—as though they belong in such a sublime place.[4]
They certainly don't. Somewhere in their pre-fab, decaf, Styrofoam
souls, these people (these people!) must know that they're encroach-
ing, that there are yet left nooks and crannies of the livable world
where their demographic asses are not wanted—are, indeed, strictly
prohibited. These people: Why are they here?

I look into their stupid faces for a trace of conscience, some clue
to the racking banality of it all… But they're as flat as a one-note
band; I'm not getting a bit of relief from these people. They're just
here all of a sudden, with their fancy demands and their Blackber-
ries, their faddish opinions and spontaneous sameness, glamorous
shoes, name-brand chinos, and market-tested hair, utterly oblivious
to the subtle idiosyncrasy of what it means to be *here.*[5]

Meanwhile, I'm beveled like Catfish fucking Hunter,[6] peering
into the chessboard for some kind of sign, a little glimpse of kismet

---

4 They don't.

5 Not *earth*, not *alive*, damnit. Fuck Sartre[a], I'm talking about Boccaccio's.

    a. Sartre, Jean-Paul (1905–1980), French philosopher, playwright, and novelist; a
leading exponent of 20th century existentialism whose writings examine man as a responsible but lonely being, burdened with a terrifying freedom to choose, and set adrift
in a meaningless universe. First class prick.

6 Hunter, James Augustus "Catfish" (1946–1999), prolific right-handed starting pitcher
who earned five World Series rings with the Kansas City and Oakland Athletics and the
New York Yankees; threw a perfect game in 1968 and was inducted into the Hall of Fame
in 1987. Helluva ballplayer.

or whatnot. I'm Delphic, I'm neurotic. I genuflect to the chess pieces like it's Sunday morning.[7] I love this game, I hate this game. I need my coffee refilled. I have to win. Because I'm invincible—I must be.

And yet I'm getting my ass handed to me, no doubt about that. In my defense, however, this shit ain't easy. It was once calculated that the number of possible moves in a game of chess can be represented by a one followed by fifty zeros (10^{50}). By comparison, it was once reckoned[8] that the number of grains of sand it would take to fill the universe is 10^{63}. Those numbers are far too close for my comfort.

For his part, Chas waits impassively on the other side of the board, steady as the sea, unmoved by human things like dread, hubbub, smallness, neurosis (etc.), hands folded in his lap, posture rigid as a battleax while he peers across the coffee shop like it's a train station. Indeed, he's hardly glanced at the table in the course of beating me twice already. The first game was all derring-do and mindless hubris. Story of my life. The second game was pathetic: mated in less than twenty moves.

As a new tactic, I've introduced a veritable sideshow of tics into the ridiculous theater of the café. To wit: I'm rubbing my chin, tapping the table, whistling a tune, cracking my knuckles, scratching my femur, picking my nose, twiddling my thumbs, breathing deeply, sipping shallowly, hiccoughing, burping, chortling, wheezing, sighing, fidgeting, and spying over Chas' shoulder at a Great Dane in the corner that's found an interesting spot on his balls to lick[9]—all the while maintaining a perfect knee-jerk shiver with both legs. Ah caffeine! I am dexterous. I am agile. I am the epitome of human inertia, set off on a grand mal joyride. Meanwhile, these people are starting to look a bit crosswise at me—my first real pleasure of the morning.

"Are you planning to make a move anytime soon?" Chas asks, still peering past me at the dull multitude.

---

7 It's Sunday morning.

8 In *The Sand Reckoner* by Archimedes (287–212BC), Greek mathematician, physicist, and inventor. Tough name to pronounce.

9 Old joke: Guy says, "Wish I could do that." Another guy answers, "Well, maybe if you pet him nice he'll let you." Old joke, old joke.

I shift my chair, wave erratically at a phantom fly, hiss in his general direction. Chas rolls his eyes.

I play my queen's knight; he quietly shifts a pawn. "You think she's in the kitchen?"

"Yeah," I answer, closing with a bishop, probing for a soft spot. He pins me with another pawn. I brood and kick up the epilepsy once again.

Of course, I want to pretend that all this fidgetry is meant to bait Chas. But I'm painfully aware[10] of the underlying psychosis. I am jealous. I am resentful. I am narcissistic. I need to stand out in the crowd, even this crowd. *Especially this crowd.* I am a superstar. I am a martyr. I am a pathetic shell of a man. However, all things being equal, a good twittering scene might just embarrass him into making a bad move. I'm not above that.

Chas casually skewers my queen's knight with a bishop. Prick. He's untouched by my histrionics. Chas is a rock, Chas is an island. Chas is handsome, Chas is affluent. Chas is a vanilla fucking milkshake. And Chas sees the field three, six, ten moves ahead, intimating the discrete geography of a game played within a semigoogleplex of possible combinations. The bastard.

Chas is a resident med student at St. Agnes Hospital.

He fondles his collar, trying to catch his reflection in a picture frame. "You're sure she works today?"

"No."

"Then why am I here?"

"For the pleasure of my company."

---

10 Oh too aware.

_ᏊᏉ_

Yes, I've got issues. But that's not what's important here.[11] What's important is to see to the issues on the table, so to speak, address the situation at hand, maybe even beat Chas at his own game. All the other stuff is just sweet-lovin' bunk and petty eccentricity—plenty of time for that later.

So: Issue Number One is the startling appearance of so many of the city's mind-numbingly yuppified, faux-hip constituents[12] at Boccaccio's, a place that's always been, for the record, way too cool for these people. So what gives?

Of course, coffee houses have always been important institutions of social, cultural, and political life,[13] or at least since the introduction of this lovely beverage in the western world. Indeed, at a time when journalism, as such, was still in its infancy, the coffee house served as a forum for discourse of the highest type, a place where intellectuals, artists, poets, and wits gathered to exchange ideas—and where revolutionaries gathered to foment big-m Movements.[14] But these people? They pale in comparison.

And there's the rub. For, in the interest of full disclosure, I have to admit it's probably my fault they're here. As designer, writer, and co-founder of the *City Reader*, a diacritical arts and entertainment rag that's the very lifeblood of ironic hipsters in our spiffy little Midwestern ex-urb,[15] I may have personally (though inadvertently) drawn this hoard of interlopers to my favorite, if previously undiscovered, cafe.

---

11 Never trust someone who makes a statement and then says it's not important.
12 See above.
13 "It might indeed at that time have been not improperly called a most important political institution." Thomas Macaulay, *History of England*, vol. I, ch. 3, part 5
14 "Nothing resembling the modern newspaper existed. In such circumstances the coffee houses were the chief organs through which the public opinion of the metropolis vented itself....Every coffee house had one or more orators to whose eloquence the crowed listened with admiration, and who soon became, what the journalists of our time have been called, a fourth Estate." Ibid.
15 Pop. 75,683 (2000)

How did this happen? I'll explain. But first, a little background.

While the *Reader* (which Myron Fine and I conceived in a fit of chutzpah soon after the departure of his would-be fiancé[16]) is a cause that's near and dear to my fickle heart, it can't be denied that the magazine has been both a labor of love and a labor of loss.[17] Mostly, it serves as a convenient outlet for Myron and I to look down our postmodern noses at people who are richer, smarter, prettier, have better jobs, and get laid more often than we do. Yet in that respect (and perhaps in that respect alone) it's a tremendous success.

Did we ever expect to turn a profit? Officially, the answer is no. Because that would be passé—exactly the kind of thing we expend countless hours and gallons of ink mocking. But unofficially, a little bit resentfully, in some dim bar at happy hour when we're trying to scrape together enough schmundo for another pitcher of beer—because the Reader didn't have the manpower or the wherewithal to collect Accounts Receivable—yes, profit would be nice.[18]

Anyway, for most of its charming young life, the Reader's been pretty much a push, neither fully supporting nor finally breaking us. In general, we bring in just enough each month to pay the rent and print the next issue. Still, the magazine has dictated certain "lifestyle changes" for Myron and I, like consolidating our offices in the unfinished basement of our house, and sacrificing the World-Famous Wild West Game Room-cum-Alehouse[19] to a third tenant.

---

16 She ran off with a traveling salesman for a hedge fund, the bitch. Said he was "more stable." MF was crushed. Her name is *verboten* in our home.

17 To wit: Myron and I love the street cred, the approbation, and the sometime sexual facilitation associated with owning a magazine (complicated by the fact that it is published under a veritable rouges' gallery of *noms de plume*; my favorite: Nick Taint). On the other hand, we've lost a lot of money and a most of our sincerity producing it.

18 No one said it was a well-laid plan.

19 I shit you not. Both of these silly functions actually arose from stories the *City Reader* published in its salad days, when we still had enough savings (and credit) to get by. The first was a headstrong gonzo piece on a fledgling paintball outfit, for which I was pelted mercilessly by a gang of blue-collar thugs from a local Post Office branch. Though the paintball company quickly went out of business, they were so thankful for the happy review (despite the bruises) that they willed their equipment to us, at which point we initiated a weekly quick-draw contest in our basement, complete with a wager scale and an elaborate ranking

(A certain well-groomed med student from Hartford, Conn., as it happens. More about that later.) But recently, defying all expectations, the *Reader* has shown unlikely signs of growth; Myron and I even skimmed enough profit off it last June to surprise ourselves with a trip to Caesar's Palace for the magazine's third anniversary.[20]

Still, do we really know that people are reading the *Reader*? After all, a couple of healthy months (by no means fat, just not starveling) don't exactly spell success. Where's the proof? Once again, there's the rub.

---

system, which provided oodles of entertainment and a little extra cash during the *Reader's* first year. (The house always wins.) The second feature, strangely enough, came from an article Myron did on home brewing. Pretty soon we were straining, fermenting, and bottling like Medieval monks. Go figure. Unfortunately, the two elements made strange bedfellows, as combatants, if missed on the first shot, often ducked behind a working brew pot, rendering its contents unfit for human consumption.

20 We promptly blew the money on keno and strippers, but the "Vegas Issue" was a gem, exploring the ridiculous, irresistible pretense and bravura of America's Playground. It included, among other items, Myron's tribute to the city's quicky wedding scene and casual divorce laws (last line: "Yes, love is gamble—but in Vegas it's the easiest debt to pay back."), and my extended digression on the flamboyant infidelity of Las Vegas architecture, from the decadent spectacle of fountains in the desert to its latter-day fondness for rank shammery[a] (first line: "Diogenes is dead.").

a. I don't know exactly when the theme park concept took hold of Vegas, or why. My personal opinion is that it started with the fantastic (in both senses of the word) extravaganza that is Treasure Island. From there, an historical leitmotiv spread through the city, encompassing Roman times (Caesar's Palace), Pirate days (The Barbary Coast), Medieval times (Excalibur), even ancient Egypt (The Luxor). In the 70s and 80s, irony definitely had a temporal aspect on the strip. Nowadays, Vegas is even more blatant in its pretensions, abandoning the time-machine quality of its previous whimsies for the mantle of an Everycity. The additions of New York New York, the Paris Hotel, The Venetian, and the Bellagio make Vegas not only a city for all times, but all places as well. So if you want to see the Eiffel Tower and the Chrysler Building, you can spend tens of hours and thousands of dollars traveling to France and Manhattan, or you can see them within minutes on the strip. The point: You don't have to waste time and money on travel—better to gamble it anyway.

The Bellagio is the *piece de resistance* of Vegas mendaciousness, taking pretense to previously unknown levels by effectively replacing the object of mimesis as the primary signification of its name. (How's that you say? Let me explain.) Seriously, did you know there was a resort town on Lake Como called Bellagio? Of course not, And probably not 1 percent of the tourists who stream through the hotel know it either. Hell, I'd bet less than 10 percent could even place Lake Como by country. But they've heard of the hotel in Vegas. The Bellagio is, in fact, more recognized than the place it's named after. And that's just weird, if you think about it—conceptual back-formation, as if someone eating Rice Krispies had never heard of rice before.

(continued)

Because, you see, about a month ago, being completely strapped for ideas, the *City Reader's* clever editors came up with the notion of printing a "City's Best" survey issue, primarily in order to ape the kind of dull folderol inevitably put out by more reputable publications. Secondarily, it offered us the chance to thumb our noses at the places that normally appear on such lists (and by extension the people who habituate the most popular bars, restaurants, nightclubs, etc. in town). To a couple of wisenheimers with their own magazine and a little bit of recognition, this seemed a grand plan. And naturally there was no question which coffee shop would be rated best in the city, mostly because I spend about thirty hours a week here feeding my wicked caffeine habit.[21] So despite the bad service, the dissolute ambience, and a perplexing smell—and the fact that two weeks ago hardly anyone knew it existed—Boccaccio's was named (unanimously, according to the story) the best coffee shop in the city.[22]

That issue came out a week ago and already the place is overrun with the very same jackasses we meant to ridicule. And yes, I recognize the irony. But in my defense, I was blinded by a pathological need to seem witty. Story of my life.

And that's just the start. Granted, the hotel itself is beautiful—all marble archways and gold inlay—but it's a beauty that's so self-aware that it borders on being creepy. For instance, the boulevard in front of the hotel (or, more specifically, in front of the four-acre, three-foot-deep "lake" that stands in front of the hotel) is designed in exquisite Mediterranean style, with stone rails and beautiful cast iron street lamps. Landscaped with trees and paved with amazing cut stone, the boulevard makes walking itself a fond experience. And because nothing should be left out, there's a constant stream of music piped in your ear as you walk past the Bellagio. But I got to thinking: "Where the hell is that music coming from?" I searched for five minutes, high and low, even looking up into the branches of the trees, before I finally found the speakers—embedded in the high-design, cast-iron street lamps. Like everything else in Vegas, the beauty of the sidewalk is just a prop.

Which is exactly why it was the perfect place to stage a special issue of the magazine. After all, with its baroque sense of irony, no city in America comes closer than Vegas to matching the facetious ethos of the *City Reader*.

21 Hence Myron's contention that I am an unreliable arbiter.

22 Criteria for the awards were inconceivably arcane, categories absolutely random. For instance, the second-best nightclub in the city was Myron's parents' bathroom, and a highly recommended eatery was a birdhouse on the south side of town ["Always busy"]. We included citations for Best Spoon, Best Dust Jacket, and Best Prefix (as opposed to prix fixe) in the city. A special lifetime achievement award was given to glass.

This is, of course, an unforeseen hazard of being too hip and publishing it: The irony just keeps spilling into real life. You see, the *Reader* can't possibly mock the suckers of the world without enlisting the complicity of its readers at some point. The reader, in turn, assumes reciprocal complicity from the *Reader* (unless, in the best of all possibly cases, he is utterly offended), thereby imagining that he (the reader) has achieved cultural parity with the *Reader*. To wit, the reader feels he's privy to the joke, not part of the punch line. He (the reader) seeks to partake of the satirical gaze, rather than being lumped with the object of the *Reader*'s satire. You dig? He wants to be us, not them; to do what we do, think what we think, go where we go—because in his mind the *Reader* and the reader are much hipper than the slobs that don't get the joke. Unfortunately, it doesn't always work out that way.

Because, of course, it's all an act. The *Reader* itself is less a periodical in the typical sense than a platform for Myron and I to spin out bullshit. I mean sure, each story has a premise, thin though it may be. But unlike "real" journalism, the premise isn't really the point. If there is a point—and often there isn't—it's usually hidden in seemingly trivial information or meta-data that pretends to have no purpose, other than in passing. But more often than not, there's no purpose but to pose—which is a different kind of purpose entirely: the difference between a stripper and a whore, a model and an actress, a wedding cake and pot brownies. You get the picture. Because the *Reader* isn't satire, it's pure irony. Pretense for the sake of pretense: the modern-day reiteration of "art for art's sake."[23]

Anyway, Myron's going to love this shit. He'll go absolutely off his gourd over suckering these people into thinking that Boccaccio's,

---

23 Granted, writing as performance is a more awkward posture to uphold, intellectually speaking, than other forms of performance that are deliberately confrontational (see Lenny Bruce, Andy Kaufmann), because real performers have to look their spectators in the face. The relation between a writer and his audience, on the other hand, is always vague and extra-temporal. As a result, excessive irony leads to a lot of solipsistic pomo nonsense that tends to be high on self-regard and low on sympathy (see David Foster Wallace, et.al.). Still, it's the form that's in fashion—the language of my generation, for better or worse.

which he detests as a "fantastic dump,"[24] is in fact tres chic.[25] Granted, he'll also be pleased to learn that the magazine seems to have an
audience, and as publisher pro tempore will likely raise ad rates. This
is just peachy with me, since general penury is the reason I'm at Boccaccio's with my roommate. Which brings us to:

Issue Number Two. Chas is really kicking my ass. No matter how
many times he beats me at chess, no matter how predictable the outcome, I continue to find this insupportable.[26] His mere presence in
our home/office is the epitome of the irony/reality paradigm that so
bedevils the editors of the *City Reader*. For you see, Chas was the
only person to answer the ad Myron and I placed in the *Reader* for
a roommate.[27] Naturally, we assumed that anyone reading our magazine would at least make a suitable roomer. However, to this day Chas
claims he hasn't seen more than a page or two—notably that ad-
vertisement and the previous issue's piece on Boccaccio's, which, for
reasons that will undoubtedly become clear, has brought him to the
coffee shop in lieu of some money I owe him.[28] He alternately con-

---

24 So true, yet all the better.
25 The inference being that the readers didn't get the joke. Get it? We still win. Myron will
find this priceless.
26 Charles Nelson Vandermier (1971–), only son of Dr. Nelson and Mrs. Bippy (nee
Nelson) Vandermier, Presbyterians of Hartford, Connecticut. One sister, Jane, two years
his junior. From an early age, Chas was directed toward pursuits that fostered socialization
and discipline of thought, habit, and manner; thus, piano lessons and Webelos occupied his
preteen years. Attended regular church services; summers, was tutored in sailing, golf, and
bridge, and became a regular member of a respectable chess club. Prepped at the Urbana
Academy, college at UConn (Go Huskies!), where studied pre-med and became a brother
in the fraternity of Delta Tau Epsilon (the insignia of which is rumored to be tattooed on
his hindquarters). Graduated cum laude and was admitted to medical school on the first
application. Height: 5'11". Weight: 185 lbs. Hair: Black. Eyes: Hazel ("his best feature," say
some factions; others insist they are "piercing"). Chin: Solid. Voice: A dense tenor. Eats:
Rice Krispies. Drinks: Microbrews. Smokes: No data available. Hobbies: Bathroom humor,
his looks, platitudes, and napping. Fetishes: Hair gel. Notable quotable: Once referred to
his 24th unique lay as "the case." Impressive statistic: Claims he made "the case" by the time
he was just 21 years old. A genuine, latter-day Casanova.
27 "Roommate needed to share three-bedroom house with a family of badgers. Must be
clean, gullible, and own your own pants." In retrospect, I don't think anyone took us seriously.
28 Predictably, the Wild West Game Room-cum-Alehouse was not quite fit for full time
human habitation when Chas moved in. Since then, he's been gradually making improvements
for which I repay him. But I don't have the money, damnit, so something had to be arranged.

siders our magazine (when he considers it at all) a "waste of fuckin' time" or a "fuckin' waste of time."

Chas straightens his stiff collar and runs a hand through his hair. "I'm going to the bathroom," he says, "Don't try to cheat, Jack."

Deadpan answer: "I wouldn't do that."

Chas trots off past the dogs and the dudes, the babes and the Boomers, making his way toward Boccaccio's awful bathroom, presumably to refine the already perfect part in his hair, and before he's out of sight I've taken his chair on the pretext that from that vantage I should be able to magically understand his strategy and foil whatever the putz is cooking up. But the whole thing just looks backward.[29]

Honestly, I'm not a complete patzer. I know my way around the chessboard. On top of that, I've got style, damnit. My chess may not be GP material, but at least it's exciting: a whirlwind of attack and capture, sharp gambits and snatching tactics. Such theatrics make me what experts call a "romantic" player, as opposed to Chas, who could bore the paint off the wall. But that ain't the way the game should be played. Chess, like love, is about pretense and deception, irony and artifice.[30] In either case, your opposite can never know exactly what you're thinking, or you'll not only lose your advantage, but ruin the subtle poetry of the game.

At least that's the way I see it. Chas, on the other hand, has no sense of poetry—and that's what insults me so much about his regular, centralized game. He doesn't win with artifice, but by transparent

---

29 Chas and I have, in fact, played chess some two dozen times, always in our living room, and always on a cumbersome slate game board that his parents brought back from the Yucatan. The overall avoirdupois of the pieces jibes perfectly with his enervating style of play—no feints, no surprises; just a steady push, like the tide, clubbing me with probity. I've never even come close to beating him, and I take it as a personal affront that even though I know exactly what he's doing, *there's no way I can stop it.* The mere fact that I keep trying is testament to the obsession the game engenders.[a]

    a. Grandmaster and noted chess writer C.J.S. Purdy actually died of a heart attack while playing in a tournament. His last words were, "I have a win, but it will take some time."

30 Which is why I despise pawns. All they can do is move one forward or one diagonal, and that only in special cases. Such monotonous, honest little pieces. Generally, I try to get rid of 'em as quick as possible.

craft. That I cannot stand. Chess is a performance, after all, and even though I always lose to Chas, I do it with panache. Still, I cling to the idea that one day, when stars align just right, I'll beat this cheesy bastard. Then I'll lord it over him like a Jacobin. I'm not above that.

[But I digress. Where were we?]

So I'm leaning over the chessboard, trying to get some hint of the mysteries to which Chas is privy,[31] and despite his last admonition and my cheap demurral, I'm seriously considering a nudge of his king's bishop, if only to piss him off… when a voice buzzes in my ear:

"Oh, he *must* be up to no good."

At which point, my maximally caffeinated nervous system does a full-tilt boogie and I knock the bishop sideways, dominoing most of the board and my empty cup in the process. It falls on the floor and breaks cleanly in two pieces. Odd, that. I stare at it with pitched ennui.

Behind me, the waitress is failing horribly to suppress a laugh. "Now I *know* he was up to no good," she says, more than a little amused by the mess she made of my mean iniquities. "Another cup, Francis?"

"Yes, black," I answer, shifting my vague gaze to the chessboard as I think of a lie to tell Chas. "And please," I say to the waitress, "Call me Jack like everyone else."[32]

"But I like Francis. It's old-fashioned," she says.

I look at her critically, weighing the irony in her speech as she smiles back at me, sweet as molasses. "And the other," she asks, gesturing at Chas' chair.

"Vanilla milkshake."

---

31 And I am not. Q.E.D.

32 Full disclosure: Though I go by "Jack" Tuckwell, my Christian name happens to be Francis. It's horrible, I know. And I know it's hard to believe when I say my parents weren't cruel to me in any way *after signing my birth certificate*. As for their actions of that day, they tell no tales. I've never been able to pin them down on the origin of the awful moniker, which I carried like an albatross through childhood and high school. Luckily, college in an unfamiliar city allowed me the option of changing my name, and with it the chance to fashion an alter-persona. Indeed, I've even managed to get my mail delivered in the new name, and only a handful of people, either by happenstance or (in a few cases) some late-night confession, are aware of the original. In the case of the waitress at Boccaccio's, an unfortunate incident with a lost wallet blew my cover. Now she holds it over me like a loan shark.

With that, she tips her dyed-blond head preciously and disappears as suddenly as she'd appeared, executing a perfect a fianchetto toward the bar. She is, of course, the one Chas is looking for, though he's never actually met her. Naturally, Sasha[33] is more familiar to me, owing to the fact that I stop at Boccaccio's at least twice a day. She's been working here for about six months, in which time we've developed a regimen of mild flirtation—about all a healthy patron/waitress relationship can stand, IMHO. And even though my eyes tend to linger when she turns (wondering idly about that fabulous chain around her waist), the idea of a romantic pursuit on the grounds of the coffee house immediately sets off warning lights. After all, if something should go wrong (as it always does), I'd be forced to alter my coffee program. That's just out of the question.[34] Besides, whatever passing fancies I might have, chasing Sasha would clearly be futile. I'm not nearly punk enough for her, nor chic enough—which is, of course, pretty much the same thing these days.

Nonetheless, she's gorgeous as hell, a dagger right through the heart. I even convinced Myron to photograph her for the City's Best edition of the *Reader*, the cover of which features a candid shot of Sasha seated neatly on Boccaccio's Art Deco bar, beaming over her shoulder at the astonished lens, her exquisite back in quarter-profile, bosom like a continental shelf in a robin's egg halter top, and a lush smile that's no doubt getting double-takes all over the city.[35] Indeed, the cover's so striking that even young Charles Vandermier took note of the *Reader* for the first time in months. Thus, he insisted I introduce him.

---

33 That's what she calls herself, though I secretly suspect she's really a Susan or a Sara transplanted from the rural surrounds, and the quasi-exotic name is just another part of her current reincarnation, along with the nose ring, darkish makeup, and a pretty belly chain that snakes along her waistline.

34 Can't traffic with the rabble at Starbucks; even worse than these people.

35 The backlight is amazing, not least because it emphasizes Sasha's torrential bosom. Myron's no professional, but that's a helluva snapshot. One in a million, really. No idea how we got so lucky.

And yes, I realize there's something unsavory in this business. First of all, for the first time since we started the *Reader*, Myron and I explicitly used sex to move issues. Yet clearly it worked, and I'm not above that. But even more fishy (you're no doubt thinking) is the idea of introducing my roommate to Sasha in lieu of money. Luckily, I've rationalized the matter with terrific aplomb. After all, if I'm too square to raise Sasha's interest above passing banter, Chas ain't got a chance—because compared to him I'm as rounded as a red rubber ball. There's simply no way he'll make headway with this hipster nymph. Ergo, I'm less pimping her than setting him up for rejection. Which, all things being equal, should give me a little bit of amusement.

Chas has yet to return from the bathroom[36] by the time Sasha smuggles back my second cup. In the meantime, I've done nothing about the wreck of the chessboard, or the broken coffee cup.

"We believe you've made quite a mess here," Sasha says impassively, standing beside the table sipping her own coffee with a serving tray cradled thoughtfully against her abundant breasts. She looks fantastic, of course, in a white buttoned-down blouse with a black push-up bra playing peekaboo through the thin cotton, and a knee-length black skirt that reveals a good deal of thigh in exquisite *contraposta*.[37] We both stare blankly at the table, like it's a campfire, or the tide.

"Yes, a mess," I repeat with perfect apathy.

Yet just when Sasha should scurry off with her own blasé turn of phrase, she remains, sipping, staring, sexy as hell. Though we don't speak for half a minute or more, we seem to be having a moment.

---

36 One quirk in Chas' otherwise nondescript character is the inordinate amount of time he spends in the bathroom. At home, he's been known to occupy up to 45 minutes, at midday, for reasons that defy comprehension. He always emerges happier, though to all appearances no more spruce than when he entered. Odd, that.

37 Along with four-inch heels, the look suggests late twentieth century slutty office temp. This, in a dumpy small-town coffee shop on Sunday morning, suggests something intriguingly theatrical about the girl's character.

Frankly, I don't know what to make of this. Certainly, wit and its attendant pretensions[38] are expected, *in passing*, but there's suddenly something less affected in this interlude we share over the wrecked chessboard. Then again, maybe she's just waiting for me to clean up the mess—which, of course, is what I'm waiting for her to do.

"Saw your picture in the paper," I say without commitment.[39]

"Ugh. Don't remind me." [Sip. Sigh.]

"You mean it's not a good thing?" [Sip. Angst.][40]

Sasha shrugs; her breasts waggle marvelously. "It's a pain in the ass. Now all these guys come in here wanting to *get a look* at me," she says. "Like some picture gives them a reason to hit on me. It's bullshit, you know, because I never said anyone could take my picture." [Sip.]

[Gulp.]

At that, Chas returns from the bathroom, no doubt feeling fresher and handsomer than when he left. He smoothes his hair and proceeds to stand on my right, shifting an eager gaze from Sasha to me, and back.

"Sasha," I say, "This is —"

"Vanilla milkshake, I presume." She flashes me an inside look, and I can feel a puzzled stare boring into my other ear.

"Charles Vandermier," says Chas, hand extended; he asks Sasha for an herbal tea (the whelp). As she leaves, he picks up the broken cup and gathers the chess pieces, tossing a rook at me, grinning sophomorically, and raising his eyebrows a little too eagerly for my comfort. Normally, of course, this wouldn't bother me at all, being of

---

38 For instance, the occasional detour into the third person, a habit that Sasha has displayed, charmingly, from her first day in the café.

39 I'm sure Sasha knows nothing of my connection with the *Reader*. She's too cool to ask what I do for a living, as befits the indifference of Boccaccio's entire staff.

40 I've got to say, I'm genuinely surprised by Sasha's response to her (albeit trivial) fame. No matter how jaded a person seems—or even claims to be—seeing your picture on a newsstand tends to bring out the unabashed egoist in us all. And it's such a great picture(!). I'm at a loss, damnit, since only a moment ago I was thinking of revealing the backstory to her (viz. my fundamental connection to the *Reader* and the provenance of the photo). Not so sure about that now.

a piece with Chas' cartoonish sobriety. Yet now, unaccountably, I'm feeling complicit, and a little protective. This cannot be good.

Within seconds, Chas has taken his seat (formerly my seat) and reset he pieces for a new game,[41] though curiously he hasn't mentioned the mess I made of the last. A stickler for the rules (any rules), Chas has somehow let this obvious transgression pass. Odd, that.

"What should I say to her?" he asks, opening with a pawn (e3).

I counter with a long pawn and advise: "When she brings you the tea, just say 'Thank you.'"

Chas huffs. "Jesus, Jack, no wonder you're single." (c3)

"Leave it at that, Chas." (queen's knight to c6) At which he baits my knight with another pawn (d5), and I, impatient as usual, hurl myself two moves from his king (Nb4), in the process allowing Chas to backdoor me with his king's bishop (Bb5).[42] He threatens my knight with yet another goddamned pawn (a3). The game, as they say, is afoot.

We trade a half dozen more moves in silence before Sasha arrives with a steaming cup of herbal tea, as well as a tall, thin vanilla milkshake. Once again, she and I share a smile while Chas pipes in brightly, "I saw your picture in the paper. You look hot."

Sasha rolls her eyes and walks away.

"What's that?"

"I thought you'd like a milkshake."

"You know what I mean, Jack. Did you say something while I was in the bathroom?"

"No."

"Then what's going on?"

"Honestly, nothing. Are we playing here?"

"You haven't got an honest bone in your body," Chas says. "What did you say to her?"

"I didn't say anything."

---

41 Chas white, me black—natch.
42 An uncharacteristically aggressive move.

Suddenly, Chas flies at me with his king's bishop, taking a stray pawn off the sixth rank.[43] This leaves me just three moves to pinch the bishop with my queen, a circumstance that makes Chas even more uncomfortable than Sasha's mild rebuff.

Mind, he won't whinge or fidget (like some people); he won't tap his foot or make a face or spill even a drop of his herbal tea—but I can see it, I'm under his skin. And when the pretty waitress returns with a moist towel, takes my face in her black-lacquered fingers, and wipes a spot of coffee off the side of my pliant mouth, it's not only the sexiest thing that's happened to me in months, it also drives Chas nuts. She tuts cutely, winks at him, and leaves without another word. Zounds.

Now he's angry. We stare at the board, trade a few moves.

"What are you doing?" he asks eventually.

I shrug and look up. "I'm not doing anything. She's not spoken for, Chas. Christ, this is the first time you've met the girl."

"But you owe me."

"Keep your money."[44]

He slams an innocent pawn on the table to underscore his anger.

This is ridiculous, of course. I'm still not Sasha's type. And despite the rise I got when she held my face, the security of my caffeine habit is at stake in even considering the notion of pursuing her. It's just not a good move. On the other hand, Chas is clearly rattled. The thought of Sasha preferring me has (finally!) put the ants in his pants. This is a perfect opportunity to stick it to him—and I'm not above that.

"Fine," Chas mumbles, looking out across the coffee shop, "We'll see who she goes for."

"All's fair in love and war, babe," I say. "Check."

Chas looks stupidly at the chessboard to find that I'm threatening his king with my bishop. Sullenly, he castles to escape—

---

43 Weird move.
44 I'll regret that, I'm sure, in many ways. But I couldn't resist.

not a move he'd planned at the outset, and Charles Nelson Vander-mier likes to see things go as planned.[45] But what can he do? For good measure, I take a pawn.

Chas wastes a move in retreat, shifting his king; I check him subtly with my queen. Now he's flustered as hell, and all at once it dawns on me: This is it, I've got him on the tenterhooks. Once again, he grimly pushes his king out of harm's way and for a long moment I gloat, sipping coffee rather more loudly than etiquette permits. He doesn't look up. That's fine. I take time to smell the roses, rocking back on the hind legs of my wooden chair, which creaks teasingly along with my invidious mirth. At last, clearing my throat I begin the endgame with a pawn to f4,[46] confident now as never before in the command of my talent, the vigor of my iron-clad, manly will.

Oops. Shit.

Chas calmly takes my pawn *en passant*,[47] mucking up my end-game while simultaneously putting my king in check. Bastard. This is not good. I'm squirming like a worm on a hook. If I want to sal-vage my advantage, I need to think carefully through my next move, reconstruct the staggered structure of my endgame.

Instead, of course, I lash out at the offending pawn with my queen (Qxd3[48]), forgetting about his castled rook, which swoops down like a horde of Huns to relieve me of my queen and really, my balls in the process.[49] After that, there's no point, really. Chas executes a

---

45 viz. the situation with Sasha.

46 This nifty little move protects my bishop, still harassing his king from e5 against Chas' queen on h5 while simultaneously opening the way for an across-the-board parry at his queen's rook with my queen. After that, I'll plow across his back rank like Sherman on his way to Atlanta. This is my endgame. All I have to do is remove the pesky pawn on e4.

47 En passant (from French, lit. "in passing") In chess, a method by which a pawn that is moved two squares can be captured by an opponent's pawn commanding the square that was passed.

48 Actually, my notation is almost entirely unreliable—there might be something com-pletely different going on here

49 Though in theory the king is the most valuable piece (capturing it is the object of the game, after all), in practice it's the queen that holds sway over the chessboard. Capture your opponent's queen and you pretty much rule the field. Ergo, I'm fucked.

three-move combination to take my remaining bishop, then forks my king's rook with his queen. Whereat I resign in disgust.

In another moment Sasha's back at the table with more re-fills.[50] She takes a chair from the next table and sits between us, cradling a cup atop her crossed legs angled in my direction. I can't help but glance at the tea label resting on her bare knee. This is very, very good.

Chas is...Oh, who cares.

"So Charles," Sasha says, apropos our cozy triangle, "How do you know my friend here?" (It's the same purring tone that crept inside my ear some moments ago, scaring the bejesus out of me.)

"You have a great voice," I break in. "Do you smoke too much?"

"My father thinks so."

"Yeah, but he's back in the sticks," I say smiling wryly.

Sasha smiles back, dips a finger in her tea, and casually bites the pinkened tip. "Chicago, babe." She wrinkles her nose coquettishly. "Et tu, sport?"[51]

"Just around the corner," I lie.

"I'm from Hartford, Connecticut," Chas says.

"Really?" Sasha sings, turning at him with mock-curiosity. "Francis didn't tell me that."

Chas cocks his head.[52] "Who's Francis?"

Double shit.

Sasha turns to me, amazement veiling her lovely face. "He is, dummy."

Chas laughs. "Is that what he told you?" Looks at me. "His name is—"

"Francis Tuckwell," I groan, scowling at Sasha.

Chas is struck dumb. This, at least, is a good thing.

---

50 Odd, that. Like I said, the service at Boccaccio's is chronically blasé. To receive such attention—and on a busy morning, no less—is almost epochal. Is this girl hitting on me?

51 Did I mention that she's charming? And I think she's hitting on me.

52 Cheeks, eyes, hair, all perfectly cast, command the dim light of morning like a fucking Vermeer. Shit.

"So how do you know Francis?" she asks again, deliberately repeating my humiliating name.

"I found him on the street," I answer.

"Awe-fully well dressed for a vagrant," she says haughtily.

"I'm Francis' roommate," Chas answers. He, too, clearly enjoys my dippy name, and I know it's the end of my anonymity, or later-onymity, or whatever. Francis, it seems, shall rise again.

Sasha, meanwhile, proceeds to look satirically from one to the other of us, clucking under her breath. "Talk about an odd couple." She sips, smiles, shakes her pretty head pensively.

"I just moved in a little while ago," Chas says with first class banality. "I'm in med school."

"Doctor," she says, and that whistle's either mocking or honestly impressed—I can't tell which. Once again, the pretty waitress flashes me a quick look, and lays her hand palm up on the table. "What do you think of that, doc?"

He examines a cut of the soft pad of her index finger.

"Broken glass." She shrugs.

I'm waiting for Chas to say something crass, but he's now confidently on his own turf. "Superficial subdermal laceration. Nothing serious. My prescription: peroxide, band-aid, repeat." He smiles, yet holding her hand.

"I bet you say that to all the girls."

"I do."

She winks. "Save the 'I dos' for later."

"I will," he answers.

Well. This isn't good.

"So what brought you all this way from Chicago?"

"I just love waiting tables."

Chas smiles, his teeth beam like the sunrise. "Do you ever say anything you mean?"

"Yes, But I never really mean anything I say."

"Come on," he says, touching her elbow and holding her with

his piercing blue eyes. All at once Sasha seems to freeze, disarmed by that goddamned handsome gaze.

"Well," she hesitates, swallowing and fidgeting as her defenses fall. "I'm studying art at the university."

"That's great! Did you know that, Jack?"

"No I didn't."[53]

"Why not?"

"You know," I redirect, trying to stifle that damnable charm. "Sasha says there's been a lot of strange people in here lately. You haven't seen anyone *strange*, have you, Chas?"

Chas just shakes his head, muttering "Francis," as though I'm a fibbing child.

Sasha, on the other hand, rolls her shoulders gorgeously. "It's that damned newspaper thing," she says, and actually gives her breasts a smart lift with her fingers,[54] indicating the photo on the cover of the *Reader*. "Before that, it was a nice, quiet place to work. And Francis here was the only man in my life." She takes a languorous sip of tea, crossing her legs again. "I wish I could find the bugger that took the picture."

As Chas' eyes meet mine meet across the table, his face explains a wave of confusion; he can't quite judge the situation. Is Sasha's being typically ironic, knowing the culprit's right beside her, or does she actually not know?

"By the way, Chas, how many times have you been to Boccaccio's?" I ask, probing for a soft spot.

"You know it's the first time I've been here."

"Why'd you come today?"[55]

"Actually," he answers with ridiculous candor, "I saw your picture in the paper, and I thought it would be nice to meet you."

And that should put an end to this nonsense.

---

53 No, I didn't.
54 Zounds!
55 That oughta wipe the smile off his face. (Right?)

But when I look at Sasha, all the ennui I was expecting—along with a cold shoulder, a few biting words, maybe even a cup of tea on Chas' trousers if she's feeling particularly dramatic—has failed to materialize. Rather, her cheek shows the flush of a well-flattered woman.

"It's nice to meet you too," Sasha answers in a voice disarmed of sarcasm. "You never told me you had such nice friends, Francis."

"Call me Jack."

"No boyfriend then?" Chas asks.

Sasha wrinkles her nose.

Then, apropos of nothing, she scoots her chair away from the table. As she slides back, I'm so caught up in the sight of her—the legs, the eyes, the lips, the breasts—that I don't even notice at first that she's actually hiking up her skirt (!).

"Look at this." She raises an eyebrow while gerrymandering the skirt upward; the scent of some quasi-exotic body oil hits me like a warm drizzle.

The rising hem eventually reveals a tattoo of two blue Arabesque figures cutting an erotic image on her thigh. Sasha arches her back, striking a pin-up pose for better viewing; in the corner of my eye, I see Chas leaning in to get a better look.

"You like?" she says, girlish again.

"It's completely indecent," I answer, hoping to God she won't move. "Where'd you get it done?"

"Tattoo Seen on Pleasant Avenue. The owner's son is a friend of mine."

"Really? He do your nose too?"

"No," straightening in her chair and lowering her skirt. "Did that myself. I'll do yours, if you want. You too, Charlie," winking in his direction.

"No thanks. Chas?"

But he doesn't answer, distracted as he is by Sasha's momentary exposure. This is good.

"Do you really know Magoo's kid?" I ask. I'm indifferent to a piercing, no matter how pretty the girl. But the Magoo thing is interesting, if true. That is, however, a big if.[56]

"Sure," Sasha says like it's the most natural thing in the world to know the younger Magoo. But now I can't tell if she's tying one on (which would be cool enough, because it means she understands the whole cock-and-bull principle we're touching on), or if she's really serious. Either way, it doesn't matter now—a gauntlet's been thrown. Besides, I've got to divert her attention from the WASP god on the other side of the table, and it's gonna take all my wits to counter those damned cheekbones. If I want to get the girl (and yes, now I do), I must magoo.[57]

"Well," I begin, settling back and raising my hands in perfect Homeric mode, "Have I got a story for you.

"About a year ago, after his thirteenth divorce was finalized— or, to be more specific, after the weeklong celebration of the event ground to an end—Magoo, the great man himself, comes to me with a personal ad he wants to place. Of course, I don't know why he needs it, because even at age eighty-five or whatever, he's still the most eligible bachelor in town, right? The guy's got a black book like the Bible; there was a line of women, most of whom could be his granddaughters, waiting to service little Mr. Magoo—if you get

---

56 Magoo (first name unknown) is the owner of Tattoo Seen, acknowledged by one and all as the best place in the tri-state area to get inked. (That's actually true.) But that ain't the half of it, because you see Magoo also happens to be a quasi-mythological figure, a sort of Midwestern Finn McCool. The facts of the case are that he's a charismatic old beatnik dude known far and wide for his wholly painted body (some 250 tats, at last count), his handiness with a needle, a Don Juanish way with the ladies, and a penchant for epic drinking jags. Magoo himself is also a treasure trove of first-person Americana, with a stock of tales ranging from the Haight-Ashbury to the Algonquin Hotel. And that ain't even the half of it, for while the old man's stories about himself are amazing, the lies that the man engenders from others have become far more plentiful, and far more baroque. A good Magoo tale is, among a certain tragically hip sub-society of our little burg, a sure sign of rhetorical éclat: cock's plumage for the ironically modish. (Exactly the type of people who follow the half-ass gonzo crap we publish in the *Reader*.) Ergo, we've segued into *my* arena.
57 ma·goo [ma gū'] *v. i.* To tell fabulous, ironical, and mostly apocryphal stories detailing theexploits of a certain impish tattoo artist living in a nondescript town in the Midwest.

my drift—once the divorce was finalized. The guy's an animal. And
everyone knows that his latest ex, the twentieth-or-so Mrs. Magoo,
left on account of his philandering."

Here I pause for effect.

"Why would he come to you to place a personal ad?" Sasha in-
terjects. "What *do* you do for a living, Francis?"

Oops. Shit.

"Francis writes the *City Reader*," Chas answers helpfully. "Didn't
you know that?"

"No."

"Yeah," Chas continues, using probity like a club. "It was his idea
to put you on the cover."

Sasha glares at me with withering disdain, her face suddenly
drained of its wonderful irony.

"That's not entirely true," I say. "You see…"
[58]

"Christ, Jack!" Sasha snaps.

"What?"

"Oh come on! I thought we were cool! And then you send that guy
in here to take a picture of me all slutty boobs on top of the bar like that?"

"Well, that's not entirely true. You see…"

"Oh shut up! Just shut up! I can't believe you did that."

"Did what? All we did was take your picture."

"You made me look like a tramp."

"We didn't *make* you look like anything."[59]

"Fuck you! What are you trying to say?"

Chas, too, is curious. "Yeah, Jack, what are you trying to say?"

"Just wait a minute," I say raising both hands in defense. I turn
to Sasha,[60] appealing to the intimacy we'd had, oh, fifteen minutes

---

58 Here occurs an excruciatingly long silence wherein I rack my brain for a lie that might
extract me from this situation.
59 Oops. Shit.
60 Beautiful, clever, inestimable Sasha.

ago.[61] But she's a blank slate. This is not good, not good at all. If I want to salvage this, I need to play it cool, think through my next move, wait for Chas to make a mistake—because that's my only chance to get back in the game, right? Right.

"What about him?" I blurt out instead. "Did you know he paid me to meet you today?"

She looks at Chas, who shrugs. "He owes me money. I said he didn't have to pay if he introduced me. No big thing."

"What are you, a pimp?"[62]

I pause, taking a long sip of coffee that seems to have lost its flavor. And by the time I swallow, there's no point in going on, because Chas already has a gentle hand on Sasha's back, executing textbook empathy with polished precision. Once more, I resign in disgust.

As I get up to go to the bathroom, I'm reminded of Purdy's anecdote of the lesser chessmaster al'Mawardi, a court favorite in the early tenth century caliphate. When the caliph heard mention of a certain man in his kingdom renowned for his brilliant chess skills,[63] he invited the challenger to his palace for a game against al'Mawardi. As the exhibition began, the caliph made no secret of his preference, and in the early stages of the game, as'Suli, the challenger, even feared that should he defeat al'Mawardi it would be seen as open defiance of the sovereign—a thing that could mean death. But because he was a pious man and could not lie, as'Suli put aside his discomfort and dispatched the lesser master al'Mawardi with ease, thereby disgracing the caliph, who had backed his favorite shamelessly. Yet as'Suli had no fear of punishment, having done what was right. When asked his opinion of the game, the caliph congratulated as'Suli with a gracious salaam. Then turning to al'Mawardi, the commander of the faithful noted grimly, "Your rosewater has turned to urine."

---

61 Did we?
62 No. I explained that, didn't I?
63 The man, as it turned out, happened to be the legendary Arab chess master As'Suli.

Indeed.

But, really, how can I complain? The best man won. Merit beat cynicism; honesty is (believe it or not) the best policy. And the prince gets the girl while the court jester—beautiful loser that he is—fades into obscurity. Corny as it is, maybe probity has real value. Chas, after all, is what he is, without pretense or performance, and such a thing has powerful appeal, even to a girl with a Byzantine sense of irony. Indeed, one ought to stop and salaam, at least in passing, when righteousness shows its face in a spurious world, and somehow, by miracle or design, the pieces all fall neatly into place.

But, of course, I won't.

Returning from the restroom, I see that Chas and Sasha have performed a kind of castling maneuver, and she's now seated in a cozy nook beneath the old fresco, his posture hemming her neatly between the table and the wall. Likely right where she wants to be.

I head for the coat tree to retrieve my jacket; no need for good-byes. As I do, I hear her ask cheerily what made Chas want to become a doctor.

"I've just always wanted to help people," he answers with perfect earnestness.

But that's not the worst part. The worst part (I realize as I slink toward the door) is that from now on I'll have to take my caffeine with *these people* at Starbucks. That is, once the novelty—the irony— of Boccaccio's wears off.

Helens

If love, a god, prevails over the power of the gods,
how could a lesser being reject and refuse it?
But if love is a human disease and an ignorance of the soul,
it should not be blamed as a mistake but regarded as a misfortune.
—Gorgias in "Helen"

I first met Kent Flickinger when he was working as an "intern" at my prep school, the Urbana Academy. That's what they called student teachers at Urbana—interns—frankly because they had the status of neither the students nor the teachers, and calling them either would have gilded them with a privilege the administration didn't think they deserved.

That was just one of the prosaic observations Kent made to our eighth period World History class in the first days of the semester, speaking with a big a grin utterly naked of ceremony. And at Urbana, in the late-1990s, ceremony was imperative. Kent's manner, on the other hand, was so staggeringly natural that most us—who took formality as rote—had a hard time taking him seriously. He was just twenty-three then: risible, unwrinkled, and unrelentingly boyish, with a habit of chatty plainspokenness that belied every prep schooler's conception of the teacher/student relationship. But of course Kent was neither a teacher nor a student; he was an intern, as he was at absolutely no pains to point out.

All in all, he was a rather nondescript presence in the classroom: robust rather than handsome, friendly instead of charismatic, and much more endearing than interesting in character. Good teeth, strong swimmer, never spent a day in jail. He was prompt, didn't litter, polite to elders, a nonsmoker, registered voter (Democrat) with a solid credit rating and his own middle-of-the-line set of golf clubs. He was, in his own engaging way, a thoroughly dull, unromantic soul—and to a man (though we were only boys) the whole class was drawn to his damnable good nature, as pupils as much as friends, and contrary to our experience, as equals. Amid the tight-lipped tuition of Urbana, the camaraderie between Kent and his class was as rare as the weathered pair of Reeboks he slipped on with an auspicious smile at the end of each day.

Before a week had passed, our class was ceded completely to him by the tenured instructor, Mr. Overton, who took the opportunity of having an intern very seriously: It was an opportunity for him to leave early. Of course, that kind of thing wasn't unusual at Urbana. "Interns" were regularly welcomed with a pat on the back and a syllabus, then promptly left to make their own way in the classroom. Yet if it was odd that one of the best prep schools on the eastern seaboard took such a lax attitude toward education, none of us noticed the irony—at least not until Kent Flickinger pointed it out.

Still, no one complained, because the corollary benefit was that eighth period World History class became buoyant, even enjoyable. Spared were we the canons of memorization; not one student was asked to write on a blackboard, and the penalties for tardy work were incredibly gentle. It was a revelation for some—for me—because the scholastic atmosphere at Urbana was generally intense. After all, students there were groomed for, and contended for, Ivy League placements from the day they arrived. Drilled by demanding instructors while competing with nasty adversaries, we were like trained seals let loose in a shark tank.

But not in Kent's class. There, we were introduced to the idea that what we learned meant something more than just a number on our transcripts. For one semester, World History was a breath of fresh air within the stuffy confines of boarding school—an experience that recommended a new way of thinking, a new way of life.

Some days, as his pupils filed into the classroom, ready to tackle the Punic Wars or the fall of Rome—or whatever—Kent would survey the class with an air of impish mischief. And when we'd all settled in our desks, staring for a long moment at his expression of genial blandness, Kent would suddenly throw out his hands and declare: "To hell with it."

Huh?

Then something truly strange would happen: We'd put our books aside and *talk* for the whole period, "shoot the breeze" as they called it in the provinces—North Dakota or Missouri or wherever the hell Kent was from—as though whatever we had on our minds that day was every bit as important a chapter in history as the words in our textbooks.

And Kent loved to tell stories—about his first car, about the night he and his friends jumped a freight train to a neighboring town, the first time he got laid, the idiosyncrasies of his family, the crude rubric of a university education, baseball, movies, taxes, love—his whole life. Yet every anecdote Kent told was tied to life by relating it to some benchmark in history. During the Clinton impeachment hearings, the boys in his school couldn't get dates for the prom, when the World Trade Center was bombed, Kent's father had been sent to the hospital after hitting a deer with his Buick. Elections, earthquakes, revolutions, records, watersheds, millennials, Moammar Quaddafi. Everything in the framework of Kent's life had an analogue in history—and vice versa.

Of course, this is true for everyone. After all, the world turns on just one axis, time is yours and mine, reality is singular. Yet until Kent Flickinger came into our history class with his ridiculous grin and his battered Reeboks, I for one had never considered the implications of History so personally. Suddenly, I was being told that the most insignificant life represents a thread in the pages of history, even if it's not recognized in the writing.

For Kent, on the other hand, the correspondence between history and life achieved complete agreement—sometimes mystical, sometimes trite, sometimes touching, but never irrelevant. Because of that fact, he was able like none before him to teach us the primal meaning of history: It's happening *right now*, to each of us. In Kent's hands, the record of mankind wasn't just a series of dates to be memorized or names to be learned. To him, the book of time was a living, breathing organism, every bit as unified as a person. Culture isn't an echo; we don't discard our memoirs, neither singly nor as a society. That's a novel concept at age sixteen.

As a result, I realized for the first time that Urbana could offer me more than just a diploma. Of course, college had always been waiting, vague and spiritless, somewhere on the other side of commencement. But in truth it had always seemed more like a chore than an opportunity. Yet when history and life combine, time opens a field of possibilities that are inspiring and exhilarating rather than merely unnerving or enervating. I grasped then that there was a big world out there waiting for me, and now I had the attitude, if not yet the tools, to make use of that opportunity.

In that semester, my purblind adolescence was enlightened by a real teacher in the guise of a student intern.

Yet despite Kent's amiable nature, and the fact that he'd essentially opened my eyes to a new way of looking at the world, in the end I couldn't help but despise him. It shouldn't have been so. But there was one thing his ridiculous bonhomie could never overcome, an insurmountable obstacle between my fondness for him and the esteem he surely deserved. That obstacle was his girlfriend, Moira Apple.

As an intern at Urbana, Kent was encouraged to attend school functions such as choir recitals, faculty luncheons, and the odd soccer game if he happened to teach any students on the team. He did so reliably, perhaps even gladly, and most often when Kent turned up Moira attended as well, ringed by the arm of her spectacularly affable, inordinately ordinary boyfriend. And from the moment she appeared on campus, willowy as idealism, all of Urbana was abuzz.

Because she was, dare I say, splendor made flesh, Venus in the springtime, able to woo with a glance or kill with a gesture. Or vice versa. At twenty, she was still in the shadow of her own adolescence and carried her girlishness playfully, enjoying the attentions of men both young and old. Long, dark curls fell like ivy across her cheeks and slender breasts, trailing away near her narrow waist. Her eyes shined like marble in the moonlight, holding the whole world in her gaze. The poise of a princess, the finesse of a benediction, grace as though floating on water, bespeaking rarity with every step. It hurt to look at the girl, goddamnit, yet no one dared turn away.

And beyond her physical attractions, Moira proved as charming as a song. Among faculty, a quiet, beguiling listener who showed no signs of disinterest when faced with pedantry. Yet removed from such saccharine ceremony, the elegance gave way to laughter as perfect as the first reckless rays of dawn. For a prep school boy, that kind of charisma was exotic and intoxicating. I flushed with chaste adoration every time I laid eyes on her.

Others, of course, were less modest, and in the hormonally charged atmosphere of an all-boys' school, Moira quickly became an object of admiration in forms both high and low. For instance, there were rumors that Mr. Genry, the English professor, had written a series of poems in her honor, and had tried, rather baldly, to seduce her at one faculty dinner. He failed of course, but the poems were supposedly quite good.

Moira also became a hot topic in the locker rooms, and a series of pornographic drawings soon appeared, making their way cross-campus through furtive adolescent hands. Kent even managed to see a few, but just grinned and shrugged it off in his excruciatingly good-natured way, complementing the artist with the unbiased rise of his eyebrows. I too had seen the drawings, but never deigned to compliment them, because I (who couldn't even dream of asking Moira the time of day) considered myself deeply offended.

It was an impotent kind of chivalry. But God, I adored her—painfully, uselessly, invisibly. Kent had introduced us on a few occasions, but each time her eyes met mine or I took her hand, I froze in cold sweat and, I'm certain, uttered something dumb. I've mostly blocked the memories. What I do remember is feeling the most pathetic creature on earth, powerless with wanting. I'm sure, however, that I wasn't the only boy at Urbana Academy in whom Moira Apple excited the first pangs of awful love.

Naturally, my infatuation affected my attitude toward Kent, to the point that I became confrontational in class, taking advantage of his lax discipline in an effort to rouse his anger. I became the class gadfly, hoping to raise his hackles so I'd have a reason to hate him. But of course Kent couldn't be goaded. He just shook his head complaisantly, which aggravated me even more.

How, I wondered, could Moira be with a man whose passions ended with a shake of the head or a slim uptick of his trivial smile? In fact, it was exactly the traits he displayed in the classroom—dispassionate, indulgent, not governed by pride—that made Kent, to my mind, too much a schmuck for a woman like Moira. She deserved more. I had fantasies of gondolas and Dom Perignon, moonlight and violins; given one opportunity, I'd show her romance. Kent, on the other hand, squired her to mid-term debates at the Urbana gymnasium. Whatever their relationship was, it couldn't be love. It was a travesty of love as far as I was concerned. I was indignant for her; a man like Kent was better suited to be her butler than her lover.

On the last day of spring semester, Kent invited our class to have dinner with him at a bar and grill not far from campus. Moira was there. Gathered around a large table, we discussed current events, future plans, sports, television, and at Kent's gentle suggestion gossiped idly about the faculty. Moira was, as usual, uncommonly gracious, and seemed perfectly at ease as the belle at a table full of young admirers. Unfortunately, I could muster no more savoir-faire than to quietly eat my cheeseburger and offer good wishes to both of them as they left.

"It was very nice to have known you," I said, touching her hand for just a moment.

"It was nice to meet you too, Dwight," she said with a smile, then walked out the door.

My God, I thought, she knew my name.

Five years later, again in the springtime, I found myself roaming the softly perfumed streets of Haber, Virginia, in a borrowed car, belatedly seeking the campus of Haber College where I'd scheduled an interview at the graduate school of History. Miles of congested highway out of Philadelphia had already threatened to make me miss my appointment with an assistant professor who'd agreed to be my tour guide. But it had been a long time—since my days at Urbana, in fact—since I'd witnessed a spring bloom unencumbered by asphalt, and my pleasure in taking the scenery got the better of me, making me enormously overdue for my rendezvous at the university.

As a result, when I finally reached the main office of the History Department, in a building called Smyrna Hall, my faculty tour guide was already gone. In his stead stood an unconcerned undergraduate named Chuck, who had an odd habit of covering conversational silences by clicking his tongue.

"I was just about to leave," he said. *Click, click.*

With only that greeting, Chuck turned and led me toward the faculty offices to see which of the instructors we might yet find; likely he (too) figured they'd have something more interesting to tell me than his own indefinite impressions of Haber. It was just barely possible, he said (click) that someone was still around at that hour, though I had to be a fool to think I could show up at five on a Friday and find a professor still in his office. Indeed, the long, silent vault of Smyrna's south wing (resounding with the echoes of odd clicks) was less than encouraging.

But as we entered the offices, something happened. As if out of a dream, a familiar name caught my eye, and without excusing myself I broke from Chuck mid-click and knocked lightly beside the rose-water moniker on one of the doors.

A man's voice answered: "C'mon in."

And there he was, the very same Ken Flickinger, sitting at the farthest of four desks arranged in motley formation around the room, the only person present, hidden behind a melee of papers so high that from the doorway I could see nothing but the dirty pair of Reeboks that rested gently on the edge of the desk. Still, I was familiar enough with the posture to be absolutely sure who I was dealing with. I wasn't certain, however, that he'd remember who *I* was. But then Kent looked up, and with the same homely, amiable air I remembered, greeted me without a stitch of hesitation, chatty as a magpie or a peanut politician. He immediately dismissed Chuck, and the grateful undergrad walked off down the empty hall, clicking like a metronome all the way.

I gave Kent a summary of my four years at Penn, that I would be receiving my B.A. in History in a couple of months, and that I was looking for a graduate school to continue my studies next year. He asked me about long-term plans. I offered none. For his part, after Urbana Kent had declined a position in secondary education in favor of working toward his Ph.D. at Haber. Apparently, Urbana had turned him against prep schools.

"You remember Overton?" he asked. "Do you know the reason he was never around was that he was sneaking off to spend the afternoon with the math teacher's wife at in the Pine View Motel? It was right off the highway. Hell, I used to pass him half the time on my way back to the university." Kent ended with a gingerly chuckle, which was still just about the most callous expression he was capable of.

After talking for a few moments, Kent led me downstairs, and we slipped quietly into a room on the ground floor, where a lecturer stood at the blackboard with his back turned to the class. He held a book, partly ajar, cradled at his diaphragm, swaying softly on the balls of his feet. There was something almost coiled about his posture, as though any second he would spring up like a jack-in-the-box. Kent and I took chairs in the back of the classroom, trying to get settled before he popped.

The lector, I would soon learn, was Dr. Vincent Pria, professor of Classical Studies at Haber College. I'd also learn that it was he who'd convinced Kent to stay on at Haber when my old teacher was seeking a position in academia. One day, I would think of Pria as perhaps the most brilliant mind on the faculty, as well as a contemptible prick. Yet at that moment, I, like the rest of class, sat bristling with anticipation of what the small man in the tweed jacket was about to say.

And he was small, no doubt—nothing over five-eight—yet there was something in his shoulders, thrown back in kingly manner, along with his trim build and perfect, circular head that made Pria seem bigger than life. As though stature was merely a manner of speaking. Both his beard and the parabola of pattern baldness that spanned his head were close-cropped salt and pepper, and his roughly Mediterranean complexion showed signs of an early season tan. Though in his late forties, Pria seemed as vital as a teenager, and when he turned from the blackboard, placing the open book on a podium, a wave of unwashed gusto swept to the back of the class.

"And godlike Alexandros, husband of lovely haired Helen, put on his fine armour. First, he placed greaves on his legs, a fine pair, fitted with silver ankle pieces. Next, he put a corselet round his chest: it was his brother Lykaon's, and it fitted him..."

Pria took up the book and walked down the aisle, looking up abstractly, dramatically, from the page at odd intervals, glancing past his students with fugitive excitement.

"Over his shoulders he slung a bronze sword, the belt nailed with silver, and then a great massive shield. On his mighty head he placed a

well-made helmet with a plume of horse hair, and the crest nodded fear-fully from its top. And he took a strong spear, well fitted to the grip of his hand. In the same way, the warrior Menelaos put on his armour."

At the back of the room, he winked at Kent, then turned and looped back around toward the front, reading all the while. Finished, he tossed the book on the desk at the head of the class and again paused with his back to us, drinking our gaze like Beau Brummel, grandstanding like Patton.

"Mr. O'Riley," Pria said, turning to a student in the front row, "What are these men doing?"

"Well, they're getting their armor on to have a fight," O'Riley answered.

"A fight?"

"Yeah. Like a duel."

"A duel?"

"Yeah."

"Why?"

"To end the war?" O'Riley answered in a questioning tone.

"Yes," Pria confirmed. O'Riley smiled with relief.

"Mr. O'Riley, how long has this war been going on?"

"You said it was ten years when the book starts, sir."

"Yes, yes," Pria mumbled, fingering the bristles on his chin and turning his attention to the class at large. "Why would the Greeks and Trojans waste ten years of war only to settle it with a duel? Seems a bit foolish, doesn't it?"

"I'll say," murmured Mr. O'Riley, seemingly unsure of the question's trajectory

At that Pria leaned close to the young man, staring him straight in the eye; he tapped his finger on O'Riley's desk and asked: "*Why* would they *do* that?"

The poor young man was suddenly crestfallen, likely cursing himself for having answered the last rhetorical question, which only focused more attention on him. Now he was trapped. Pria's eyes glowed, enjoying the brief drama he'd staged—which scene, in fact, seemed to entertain all the students but one.

Suggested O'Riley: "They wanted to get it over with?"

Pria shrugged. "Yes, certainly, they wanted to end the war. After all, these men have homes and families, estates and kingdoms back in Greece. So of course they wanted to 'get it over with,' as you so eloquently put." Pria straightened, patted O'Riley paternally on the shoulder, and sauntered once more toward the back of the room—the man simply couldn't keep still. "But it doesn't make sense, does it, that the Greeks and Trojans would wait ten years for so simple a resolution? *Mano* (offering his right hand) *a mano* (his left) for the girl?"

From the back of the room, I saw O'Riley consciously check himself rather than answer again, and Pria's question hung in the air as he drifted back toward the chalkboard.

"And so, my hungry young sages, can anyone tell me just what the hell is going on here?" He looked around the room, but no student dared to speak up. After a moment, Pria resumed, "Homer is using this duel—the very first instance of violence in an exceedingly violent book—as a reminder of the singularly personal nature of the conflict. Alexandros—better known to most of us as Paris—has *stolen* Menelaos' wife, literally as well as figuratively. Menelaos has been expressly humiliated. Wronged!" exclaimed Pria with his fist in the air, once again gauging his students' reaction, and basking in his own melodrama.

"And for this, thousands of Greeks will be killed and the city of Troy razed to the ground. This duel, this skirmish, this *passage d'arms* between two warriors who turn out to be really rather minor characters in *The Iliad*, inaugurates the grand and truly gory battles to come. And in relatively short order the duel between Alexandros and Menelaos fades into the fabric of the poem. Why?"

Coming to the podium once again, Pria stopped and bowed his head, hands clenched close against his breastbone as though conducting a taut *breve pausa*. A veneer of sweat shone on his olive-colored forehead.

"Because it *is*, people, the fabric of the poem," he said, coming back to life. "It's a tool of the poet, like the quill or the scroll or the instrument that was played when another singer sang to Homer. He sings 'of the anger of Achilles.' Yet the dread, mortal, cuckholded anger of Menelaos is left a stalemate!" Suddenly Pria, who'd just decrescendoed, seemed ready to burst, and the whole class—me included—eked up in our chairs in anticipation of the next word.

But all at once he broke the momentum, and with almost comic calmness wondered: "Does Homer really need to remind his readers of the *reason* for the Trojan War?" He screwed up his dapper face, pantomiming along with the question for the benefit of all of us watching. Stepping forward, the professor snatched a moving pen from the fingers of a student in the third row, who had the audacity to take notes rather than watch his performance.

"Quick: What were the names of the two people in the Garden of Eden?" he quizzed.

"Adam and Eve," she said with a shrug.

Pria mimicked the student's shrug as he handed back her pen. *"Exactly,"* he said. "And Homer needn't remind his readers of the cause, the players, or the end result of the Trojan War. It's their mythology, as intimate to the societies and psyches of the Greeks as the story of Adam and Eve is to you.

"What else does the scene do?"

Once again his question rose and fell like an ellipse in the quiet room. None would meet his gaze, and Pria took the opportunity to smile delightedly over their heads at Kent; he even acknowledged me with a nod.

"It's just a few words, guys. Not even a full page. Here, Homer links history and mythology, his poem, with the hundred other songs written about the Trojan War. Here, Homer plugs his readers into the influences of past, present, and future in a single motif near the outset of his huge symphony. And in this instant, Alexandros and Menelaos feel that force at work. They exist in the past and the future as well as in the moment when they decide to reconcile the greatest war the world has ever seen in single combat, placing themselves squarely in the path of mythos." Finishing the last of this homily, Pria once again hushed, as though troughed in the waves of his own oration. And now every eye in the room was on him, waiting with baited breath for the next word.

"And yet–"

But at that moment the bell rang. Pria stopped dead and threw up his hands in deference to fate. The whole class sat silent for a beat, during which I half expected him to take a bow, for he was easily that theatrical. Instead he turned and gathered up his books without another word, and the students dutifully filed toward the door. Meanwhile, Kent and I met Pria at the front of the room, and Kent introduced me as a prospective grad student.

"You've taken up recruiting now?" Pria asked archly. "Do you have so much time on your hands in the History Department?"

Gently, Kent grinned at the quip. "Dwight was a student of mine at Urbana. Besides, everyone can use a push in the right direction. Isn't that what you said to me? I'm just passing that encouragement along."

"Let's be clear," mocked the older man, smirking, as he led Kent from the room with a warm grasp above the elbow, "I won't have you blaming your decisions on me."

I followed the two of them to Pria's private office on the first floor of Smyrna, at the opposite end of the building from Kent's shared space on the third floor. Whereas Kent's office had a view of the faculty parking lot, Pria's bay window peeked out on a quaint walking bridge over the shallow creek that meandered across campus. An exotic potted tree yawned in the sunlight beside a filing cabinet sporting an overhead photo of what looked to be the Aegean.

But by far the most remarkable feature of Pria's office were the books lining the walls. And these weren't just any books. Many were rare, arcane, outrageously expensive manuscripts. In a glance, I saw the *Introductorium in astronomium*, an edition of Aesop's fairy tales with a Venetian watermark, and a first edition of Macaulay's *History of England*—the three of which alone cost more than I spent in a year. And that was just what I saw on the walk in; surely there were dearer treasures buried in the stacks. It seemed a mark of either great arrogance—trusting the ignorance of his colleagues—or great foolishness that anyone would dare keep such objects in the thorough insecurity of a faculty office. Suddenly, Vincent Pria seemed intriguingly eccentric.

He took his seat opposite us, nearer the window than the desk, actually, and crossed his legs casually at the knee. His shoes were Bruno Magli. Kent and I sat with our backs to the door. Half a dozen papers were fanned dramatically across the desk between with two antique penholders manned by handsome, modern stylographs; a bearded bust and a simple, leather-bound calendar filled the remainder of the desktop along with a gilded name plate that read: V.I. Pria, Ph.D.

While he and Kent chatted about their academic projects (a book and a dissertation, respectively), my interest was caught by a painting balanced on the bookshelf behind Kent's head. It showed a plain of swaying amber grassland, punctuated by shoots of green shrub and a lone stone tower that overlooked the serpentine river spanning the canvas. At center, to the left of the river, two small but finely drawn figures faced one another with spears. One, with bulging arms and iron mail, was posed to lunge; the other, in sanguine repose, was arrayed in splendid golden armor.

"Paris and Menelaus," I said absently.

"Book Three," answered Pria.

In a second he'd hopped around his desk and stood over Kent's chair scrutinizing the painting with his hands and eyes. "Two men," he said, "Very different. Yet each is, in his most enduring capacity, the husband of Helen.

"Menelaus," Pria went on, zeroing on the figure, "Is strong and sensible, a man with a kingdom to administer, a son of Atreus, and brother of the most powerful man in the world. A veteran of many wars, he is practical to a fault: He wears armor made of steel.

"Paris, on the other hand, is a dandy, the *son* of a great king and the *brother* of a great warrior." Pria's winked at me: "Lover not a fighter. In his vanity, he prefers a suit of gold to a suit of armor. The devil's in the details, my young friend."

"Menelaus will kill him," I said.

"Will certainly," Pria concurred, squaring his shoulders and resuming the emphatic vitality that had bled off since he left the classroom. "He's a brute, really, a farmhand. A rich farmhand no doubt, but a vulgarian nonetheless. Certainly not a son of Priam. Paris, on the other hand, is brimming with Romance—with a big 'R.' That's exactly why he goes out to fight the Neanderthal, which, as he knows, will surely mean his death. Paris has style. A knack for seducing women has made him a scapegoat, but dying to save the kingdom will make him a hero.

"Besides," he said, stepping back to appraise the painting from a more philosophical angle. "I think he likes the attention."

"You seem to favor Paris."

"Never!" exclaimed Pria, throwing a hand in the air, caught up as ever in his own histrionics. "I prefer Helen. Always. Only." His shoulders dropped, ebbing like lost love—exactly the kind of dramatic volte-face that made him so fascinating in the classroom. "But of the three, Paris is surely my second favorite."

I gained from his grin and a thin shift in posture that the show was over, and indeed Pria patted my shoulder briefly as he passed back to the other side of the desk. But I couldn't help being ingratiated by the private lecture, and pressed further.

"But she's married to Menelaus," I said.

"She's married to both."

"Is there no priority to her first commitment?"

"Perhaps," he mused, wistfully, to the ceiling. "I suppose Helen has taken a lover. Then again, *it is better to take a prosaic husband and have a romantic lover.*"

"And why didn't you mention any of this to your class?" I asked, challenging.

"Principally because it's not germane to a survey of classical literature. I have only two weeks for the *Iliad*, Dwight. I can't really justify bringing Gorgias to the classroom for a recounting of his "Helen." Besides, Homer rationalizes her attraction to Paris through Aphrodite's influence. No need to confuse students with such affairs."

That summer, I received two letters posted from Haber. The first was from Kent.

Dwight,

I was happy to see your name on the list of graduate students for the fall term. I assure you that you've made a wise choice. The History Department at Haber will be a great fit, and I know that the faculty here will treat you as one of their own. You can trust that I've already put in a good word for you. Unfortunately, I won't be here to meet you, as, at Vincent's suggestion, I'll be headed to Florence for the fall term to do some research on my dissertation. I dreaded going at first, but now I'm quite excited, as I've never really been overseas. Of course, I'll miss Moira, as she'll be staying here in Haber. That's one of the reasons I'm writing you. I'd like to ask you to keep Moira company if you can find the time. She seemed to take a real liking to you when you visited, and I know that she gets lonely. Anyway, Dwight, I'd appreciate if you could visit her from time to time when you come to Haber, just to keep her spirits up. I've promised to be in touch as much as possible, and I hope to schedule some trips, but there's going to be a lot of empty time for her. So please do what you can. You have my many thanks for it. I look forward to seeing you again in the spring.

Best wishes,

Kent

I did not reply to the letter. Though in truth, an invitation to keep a man's wife company in his absence seemed strange. But surely Kent, in his limitless innocence, couldn't possibly have known that he was asking me to comfort my first true love.

Besides that, I'd only spent a few hours with the Flickingers; there certainly should have been someone else in Haber to whom such a request would be more fitting. Most likely there was. In fact, a certain sense of urgency suggested Kent had written at the last minute. In that case, I supposed it was more likely for my sake than his wife's—a final, cordial remark from Kent, who still considered himself my host at Haber.

I'd had dinner with the Flickingers that day in the spring. Moira was a vision, of course, her beauty only improved by the years, like a song sung in a different key, she having matured from a fresh-faced coed into a striking woman. In the interim, she'd shorn her pre-Raphaelite ringlets in favor of a smart mop that clung to her forehead like laurel, gaining her face (who would have thought it possible?) even more warmth by exposing her broad brow and siren's eyes. And somehow she seemed taller than I'd remembered, more regal. True, she no longer laughed with the candor of youth—that rush of pure mirth that once made me weak in the knees—but her every gesture now seemed tempered with sensuous assurance.

Of course, even then I knew that the differences were more clearly marked for the changes in me. After all, when I'd seen Moira at Urbana, I was just a schoolboy, pitifully limited by my insecurities. Five years later, I was seeing her as a man who'd been with women. All at once, as though grasping the meaning in a long-forgotten dream,

I understood the lusty undertones that had surrounded Moira at Urbana. And suddenly I sympathized with the boozy instructors who were intoxicated by the rise of her hips, the current of her skin, and that incredible scent of jasmine that seemed—somehow—to actually *precede* her into a room. In retrospect, the passions of a man like Mr. Genry, who'd composed the book of poems in Moira's honor, seemed less creepy than bittersweet.

As for me, the heat of desire combined with the light of my first romantic love had all the effect of throwing gasoline on a candle; I struggled all evening to keep my eyes from wandering toward her skirted thighs and aristocratic breasts. Because, of course, she was married, and her husband—an old friend—was sitting not ten feet from me.

To complicate matters even further, as Kent later said in his letter, Moira indeed seemed to take a liking to me. She was wonderful company, by turns cordial and dear, then familiar and kind. Composed and perfect. Kent was, as expected, faithfully genial. We had a fine night.

Halfway through the evening, it occurred to me that being near Moira again, and sensing for the first time her powerful sexuality, marked the true end of my adolescence. Leaving the Flickingers' home that night, I felt like a man.

The other letter I received from the college came in a manila envelope with no return address. Opening it, I found a stack of Xeroxes with a note attached on five-by-eight Haber stationery:

Duped these from my personal collection for your benefit.

VIP

They were copies of the "Helens" of Gorgias and Isocrates, rhetorical dissertations written by Greek sophists to exonerate Helen of blame for the Trojan War.

By mid-August, I'd installed myself in a two-room studio amid the ten square blocks that make up downtown Haber, a small congregation of quaint brownstones near a scenic bend in the Appomattox River. At the college, I registered for classes in Contemporary Moral Issues, the History of the Mediterranean, Baroque Art, and Greek Tragedies—the last of which was to be conducted by Dr. Vincent Pria, who'd contacted me upon my arrival and warned that he could have my financial aid revoked if he didn't see me in one of his classes.

As it does in that part of the country, August passed in stately leisure, the sweltering air permitting little real work to be done. I spent much time walking or riding my bike slowly around the town, surveying miles of river and occasionally feeding ducks in the Brandon Coulee (the stream that was visible from Pria's office window). I vowed to get a head start on the semester's reading, but I did none, of course, preferring instead to lose myself in the panorama of the Virginian landscape, worlds apart from Philly, where I'd spent the last four years. Cities have a tendency to shrink on themselves, decreasing dimension to sharp corners and demarcations. The countryside, on the other hand, grabs your senses, demanding notice like a child. Virginia was florid, pastoral, serene—just the kind of place I'd imagined in the stories Kent Flickinger told of his youth.

When classes started, I managed to channel my wandering mind toward graduate studies, and satisfied my wanderlust, at least intellectually, by lunching with Pria three times a week, whereat we explored trends in theory, culture, history, literature, mythology, and every other subject that crossed his overactive mind. Pria revealed himself as a man of brilliance and dalliance, both owing largely to his wildly affluent background.

The son of the principal owner of Plymouth Shipping in New York, Vincent Pria was raised in the aerie of outrageous fortune. "Home" for him had been a 12,000-square-foot townhouse on Central Park West.

In addition, the family owned a 20-acre Palm Beach estate, smaller homes in Barbados and Rome, and what amounted to a small county in the south of France. Of course, there were also yachts and helicopters, limousines and servants…all the trappings of fabulous wealth.

When his older brother died young, Vincent became sole heir to that fortune. But business—especially the shipping business—held no interest for him. Vincent had attended boarding schools on both sides of the Atlantic, then Yale, Cambridge, the Sorbonne; he spoke five languages, had lived on six continents, still owned homes on three; he served on the boards of half a dozen artistic and philanthropic foundations, and generously supported causes from Greenpeace to the local cathedral. Though he still served, nominally, on the board of directors of Plymouth Shipping, he rarely if ever had contact with his father's business. Indeed, the only relationship he had with Manhattan was the bank that kept money flowing inevitably, enigmatically through his hands.

He'd been enrolled at the Art Academy in Florence when he made his first trip to Athens. And though Vincent had traveled widely, and knew the classics by heart, it was something altogether different to feel the antiquity of Greece in your bones, in your bowels—the weight of an atmosphere so layered with civilization that your feet seem to sink in the earth.

"It's overwhelming," he explained at one lunch, fork waving about dangerously, his voice infused with wonder—perhaps this once more than just for show. "An otherworldly kind of power, but incredibly profane. Those ruins…They're the bones of humanity, exposed to the harsh light of being. Weather-beaten, ruined, of course, yet emanating gravity as intense as the sun. It's the wisdom of the ages radiating through you, making you forget the 'when' of your existence; removes all sense of time from your life." Pria shook his head in retrospective astonishment. "I was struck dumb in Athens." He looked puckishly across the table at me. "And you understand that's no small feat."

"There's a lot of history there," I said.

Pria waved a hand dismissively. "Not history, nothing of the sort. History is a fraud, Dwight, an arbitrary conception. Man is a gnat on the back of an elephant, and history is his meager attempt to index a little stretch of skin. In the larger sense, there is no such thing as history."

"I think you're drunk," I said, defending my discipline.

"That may well be, my gnattish young friend. But I still speak the truth."

"Ten seconds ago you were awestruck by Athens. Now you say that history itself is some kind of lie. There must have been some truth there to make you speechless."

"Of course there was: the truth of myth."

"That's a contradiction in terms, Vincent."

"Not at all," he said, shaking his head. "Myth is the soul of truth. Think of Atlas, Prometheus, Minos, Orpheus—these are the things that get to the essence of what it means to be human; the fundamental truths; the eternal verities, my friend. Sure, the finer points can be mixed and matched, but no matter how you tell it, the vital heart of myth is as compelling as an orgasm."

I stopped short, almost choking on a piece of beefsteak at the sudden vulgar turn of phrase.

But Vincent plowed forward without the slightest hesitation. "That's why the truth of myth is so much more real than the flimsy trivia of history, which is just a certain person's version of events, affected by perspective and muddied by everyday details—far too trite to be reliable, far to arbitrary to be taken seriously. History's tendency is to get the facts straight and muck up the essence."

"But isn't that the point?" I protested, drawing on the lessons I'd learned at Urbana. "Myth is the musing of a solitary poet. History is a living discipline. It parallels life. It gives human beings a place in the world. People live within the context of history, and add a little bit to the fabric of culture in the process. Vincent, that's the point of history."

He huffed. "Well, perhaps that's the *point*," he said. "But it's not exactly an interesting one. Not every point is critical, you know. Every day, people eat, sleep, shit, cry, and fornicate—most of them badly, no doubt—and with no more or less significance than most of what is written as 'history.' History is temporary. Myth is timeless.

"For instance," Pria went on, settling into his banquette chair, "Take our lovely haired Helen of Troy. Now *there* are some verities, if you know what I mean." He raised his eyebrows playfully, busying himself with the pretense of taking a leather cigar case from his inside coat pocket. "You want truth? I give you beauty, love, war, betrayal, death. All the biggies, kid, the stuff that sticks in your guts. Why do you think the *Iliad* was the first work ever written? Why do you think it's lasted so long? This is the essence of culture, my young friend, the seed of every piece of art ever produced.

"And of course Homer wasn't the only one fascinated by Helen. Gorgias and Isocrates, you saw. So too, Euripides and Steischorus, Aeschylus and Theocritus and a thousand others wrote passionately about her. Hell, every solitary romantic fool who ever took pen to paper was, in some way or another, writing about Helen.

"Why? Because the impulse behind writing Helen is the desire to reveal her—and thereby know and possess a beautiful woman. And that's the burden and the purpose of manhood, the stuff deep down in your psyche in the part of your brain that's as old as the seas. That's what drives men to write. You—the historian—may think myth is just the musings of some solitary romantic fool, but you can't escape its implications. Biology is destiny, my young friend. You can only hope to satisfy, or at least appease, those needs with whatever tools you've got at your disposal. Rich men acquire Helens with money, strong men subdue them with brawn. Poets animate Helens with myth, giving rise to the cult of love."

"What about women writers?"

"Evolution of the principle," he said with a wave of his hand. "*Homo sapiens* didn't drop back on all fours when it was selected over *Homo erectus.*"

"Okay. So what do historians do?" I asked.

Pria raised his eyebrows and pulled staccato puffs from a lighter that danced at the end of his cigar. After a moment, he took it from his mouth and examined the cherry tip, then said to me flatly: "Not my area."

Of course, I wasn't at all sure I believed him, but it made for great entertainment, for when Vincent got going he could spend hours spinning out every thread of an idea *con brio*—sometimes absurd, sometimes profound, sometimes a complex combination of both. But never boring. Indeed, sometimes he'd get so involved in a topic that when I finally drew him out of his musings we'd discover that we were both late for afternoon classes. In those cases, of course, Vincent would order another bottle of wine, and the conversation would continue apace, regardless of schedules.

On the other hand, though I thought of her almost constantly I did not contact Moira Flickinger during my first month in Haber—mostly because I couldn't shake my guilty sense of expectation. Why? Because I thought, given no further encouragement than the brief hug I'd received six months earlier, I had a chance with her. The burden and the purpose of manhood, as Pria would say. No matter how circumstances inveigh against us, men by nature seek requital for our feelings. Biology is destiny, right?

And despite my high regard for Kent, I still maintained (privately) that Moira deserved more than he could offer. To me, she was wasting herself on a hopelessly dull man. So with feelings of conflicted nobility, I put off calling on her. After all, the only logical consequences of seeing Moira again were a high likelihood of heartbreak or a small chance of adultery. Not good prospects, either one.

Nonetheless, Haber was a small place, and eventually we found each other one Saturday at a farmer's market near the riverbank. I actually spotted her first, browsing the selection of honeydew melons, long before she saw me. Despite my good intentions, I froze—a blushing schoolboy once again—upon seeing Moira for the first time without Kent at her elbow. And though I should have beat a hasty retreat, I lingered instead among the cucumbers, waiting for her to see me. I was bowed over a squash when she called out.

"Hello, Dwight." She approached holding a honeydew melon high in her hand. "What do you think?"

"I don't know," I answered, my ears filling with hot blood.

"I *thought* you were going to come see me."

I managed a shrug. And just like that she dismissed the illicitness I'd imagined in our meeting, annulling my gallantry and guilt in one blow. "I was," I admitted.

"Well why on *earth* have you *forgotten* me, sir?" she asked, affecting a Mason-Dixon accent with one hand propped playfully on her lower ribcage (other hand: melon) and a sweet sideways flex of her hip. "It's just not *right* to keep a girl waiting, you *heart*less man."

One of my knees buckled

"I've been busy."

"No more," Moira declared in her normal voice. "Come to my house at seven tonight for dinner. You remember the way, don't you?"

Every centimeter.

"I really can't," I said, steeling myself against my fantasies.

"Oh please do," she pleaded, lowering the attitude and shifting the melon flirtatiously in her hands. "I'll get a honeydew for you."

Naturally, I showed up at seven, armed with the best of intentions and the best bottle of wine I could find at the little liquor store near my apartment. When I'd visited the previous spring, the Flickingers were in the middle of a renovation that had completely taken over their home. Moira was obviously responsible for the overhaul, and the general disorder of the house was cause for apologies to me and recriminating glances at her husband. The lady of the house hadn't wanted to be receiving visitors *in medias res*, and her strong sense of etiquette—a side of Moira I'd never seen before—was in some way taxed by my awareness of such ungenteel circumstances. Of course her reaction was completely endearing.

Now, however, the renovation was finished and Moira's home was as tasteful as she. Though not large, the house was painstakingly decorated with ornamental accessories, couchant furniture, shimmering textiles, and drapery in smoldering earth tones. In the salon, recently refinished hardwood floors were covered with Turkish rugs, and enchanting plants hung from hooks in the ceiling. An exotic tree—not unlike the one in Pria's office—stood askance the north-facing bay window, and a rich intaglio portrait of a red-haired gentleman looked over a piano in an anteroom. It was definitely her work.

"Better?" Moira asked, a little self-consciously, though clearly ready for me to be impressed. "It's meant to be Moroccan-esque. I've always dreamed of living in North Africa."

"It looks amazing," I answered honestly.

Moira had prepared for an informal dinner in the enclosed back porch; she, barefoot, sat in a rocking chair across from me, one leg tucked becomingly under her lap as the sun set through magnolia trees, casting her remarkable profile in dim silhouette. The day cooled only slightly as the light faded. The Flickingers' back yard was now filled with late summer flowers, most which had been in early bloom during my first visit. As with the interior, Moira'd spared nothing in her garden. Before dinner, she took great pleasure in leading me through her little Eden planted with belladonna vines and bird-of-paradise, kudzu and devil's paintbrushes, each of which she appointed by name. She even plucked a few clean, bright marigolds, one petal of which caused me fantastic distraction by falling in the gap between her breasts.

For our meal, she made cheeseburgers of ground sirloin and Colby, along with a fresh mesclun salad topped with artichokes and grape tomatoes. Moira graciously uncorked the wine I'd brought, as well as a better bottle from her own collection. Her talent for making a special occasion from simple ingredients had me beside myself with envy. My only consolation was her admission of Kent's preference for domestic beer.

"I doubt he could tell a Pinot from a rhino," Moira said with a roll of her pretty eyes. "More Coors than connoisseur in that one."

As she leaned toward the table to refill her wine glass, I felt the warm glow of dusk, wine, and a beautiful woman. "I've always wondered about that," I said hesitantly.

"About what?" She favored me with a radiant smile.

"You and Kent," I answered, taking a quick sip, for courage. "Neither of you is really the type I'd imagine for the other. How is it that the two of you got together?"

Wine in hand, Moira threw her head back and laughed with unadulterated delight. "You mean: How did a guy like him get a girl like me."

Embarrassed at having been read so easily, I remained quiet.

"Oh, Dwight," she said fetchingly into her glass. "Don't you think I've been asked that before?"

"I suppose."

Moira gazed contemplatively out the back porch, easing deeper into her chair as she draped one knee casually over the arm, her pretty ankle dangling just inches from my hand. "He wasn't my first, you know... Love, I mean. There was someone else, in Westchester, where I grew up. Sort of, I guess," she said with a shrug, continuing to gaze into the middle distance. "Not a high school sweetheart or anything like that. He was definitely a man. I was sixteen, he was thirty-six."

She looked appraisingly at me. "Does that shock you?" she asked with a raised eyebrow. "You're always so proper. I can imagine you being shocked by such a thing." Her eyes were amused. "In a sweet way, of course."

Once again, I let the silence stand, and before long Moira rejoined: "My father was shocked, of course. Mad as hell, really." She laughed again in her wine glass, a trace of vino in her tone. "But there was nothing he could do, really. I was almost eighteen by the time he found out. And the man was rich, powerful," she smiled wistfully, "Dashing, charming, worldly. Irresistible, really."

"So what happened?" I asked.

She sighed, sipped. "His wife."

"He was married?"

"Widowed," she said. "Or widowered—I don't know what the hell you call it. Either way, I could never take the place of his wife. My heart was so broken."

"You were sixteen," I said.

"I was sixteen," she repeated. Moira sighed again and brought her leg off the arm of the rocking chair. "Anyway, after that my parents made a *great* effort to get me the *right* kind of boyfriend; set me up with every college-bound prep school boy they could find among their circle of friends." She looked ironically at me. "Just like that group I found you with, lo those many years ago."

She gazed sadly for a moment at the rising moon, sipped wine. "Yuck," she said at last. "I couldn't stand the sight of them. The last thing I wanted was some Yalie with perfect hair and a perfect trust fund."

"I know the type."

She smiled at me, a little teary, I think. "Of course you do.

"And then I found Kent, and he was the most sweet, simple, unaffected boy I'd ever met. I knew he'd never break my heart." She wiped her eyes and fought back a sniffle with a discreet knuckle under her nose. "And he won't."

"I'm sorry," I said, gently offering her a napkin.

"*God* no, *I'm* sorry," she answered, taking the napkin from my hand. "I can't believe I got all misty after three glasses of wine. I must be turning into a pathetic old woman."

"Um… no."

At that she laughed again, right through her tears. My heart soared.

Moira took a moment wiping her eyes before she settled back in the rocking chair, her leg draped once more over the arm. She eyed me playfully. "You're a sly one, Dwight."

"I have no idea what you're talking about."

She sipped her wine and continued watching me. "You come across all quiet and polite. But underneath it all you're a schemer, I think. Don't you have a girlfriend?"

"No."

"Why not? You're very good looking, you know. I've always thought so."

I was dumbstruck, of course, searching for a safe place to lay my eyes while shock and rapture ran me through. Moira let me squirm for an eternity.

"So," she said inquisitively, tilting her head to one side. "Why no girlfriend?"

"I just got here. I have a lot of studying to do. Maybe I'm waiting for the right girl to come along."

"Aha," she said, sitting back again as though all had been revealed to her. "A solitary romantic, that's what you are."

"Something like that," I answered, trying to place my déjà vu.

"I remember," Moira went on, holding her wine glass close to her rosebud lips, "The way you ate that cheeseburger when Kent and I took your class to dinner his last day at Urbana." She laughed, and sipped. "It was so charming; you spread ketchup on the burger with a French fry before every bite; it was like you were performing surgery. Such a fastidious young man, you were," she finished, wrinkling her nose exquisitely.

The young man I'd been beamed retroactively at the idea that she'd watched me. Moira laughed some more, a little bit tipsy from the wine, and the bulbs of her flower garden seemed to crane their necks in her direction.

"Well that's how my mother eats cheeseburgers," I answered at last. "And she is intolerably fastidious. But the truth is I prefer to use a knife."

"Oh, good," Moira sighed with exaggerated relief. "I kept imagining you sitting here, not sure how to proceed without the fries. I was afraid you'd go home hungry." She leaned forward, giggling like a girl—and the rocking chair creaked joyously in the sway of her laughter.

Beginning about halfway through the semester, Pria and I were joined at lunch by two other professors from Haber. Nelson Palanski had come to the Accounting Department from the private sector the year before my arrival. Apparently, practical accounting had been too stressful for him. Nelson had developed a corps of ulcers that were accompanied by fatigue, heartburn, and what he called "gold standard stomach pains." Notwithstanding his various ailments, Nelson brought an intensity to the table that was alternately disgusting and fascinating. I, for one, have never seen a man eat pork ribs—two plates, some afternoons—with the kind of vigor he brought to the task. Nelson was an eating dynamo, cutting through entrees like a well-oiled machine. Yet physically, he was a wreck, sweating, bursting, boiling over at the seams; he often lost breath from the exertion of lunch. He was also the first among us to begin ordering liquor with his meals, which he dispatched as avidly as the food. All that said, it occurred to me that Nelson's former job was not, perhaps, the only cause of his stomach pains.

The other new arrival was Dr. Gilbert Howe, a philosophically gaunt music professor I'd seen several times in the fine arts building on the west side of campus, where I attended my Baroque Art class. In appearance, he was dead ringer for a thin Richard Burton; in timbre he was magnificent. Howe's New England tenor was the most sonorous voice I'd ever heard, ringing crystal clear across the table, like a bell resounding in a nearby campanile; his mere presence at lunch made the occasion more dignified. I think he was also a composer. He and Pria often talked of music—obbligatos, arpeggios, oratorios—at abstract, almost metaphysical levels.

Nelson Palanski was lately separated from his wife.

"She started talking about divorce last night," he mumbled, wresting a piece of animal fat from between his teeth.

"I hope you changed the subject," said Pria. "Talk about the weather, the moon, debits, credits. Just don't let her get rolling too swiftly. It's Newton's third law."

"You bet I changed the subject," Nelson answered heatedly. "Jesus, we've only been separated a month. Isn't there supposed to be some kind of grace period? You can't start talking divorce until you've given the separation time to see if it takes, right? Christ, we were engaged for eight months before even setting a wedding date."

"Well, then," Pria mused, "If she hasn't given you a divorce date yet, you're safe for a few more months."

Nelson grunted. I passed him the salt.

"Oh God," he whined. "I can't stay in that hotel another night. I can't sleep. I can't eat."

There was a pregnant silence.

"Fast food in a hotel room. Who can live like that?"

"Please Nels," Howe crooned, "Can we talk about something else for a little while?"

"The weather, the moon, debits, credits…" Pria mused, gazing vaguely in the middle distance.

"You want me to make small talk while my marriage is breaking up?" Nelson asked, his voice rising. "You want to talk about current events? Baseball? Politics? My wife said 'divorce' last night. That means I have to talk about it. Not with *her*, damnit, but with *somebody*."

Howe beckoned the waiter over to the table.

"Yes, my friend here is getting a dee-vorce," he enunciated. "And a sherry please."

"Nice, real nice," Nelson grumbled. "At least Dwight here has some compassion."

"Maybe you should see a marriage counselor," I suggested.

Nelson threw his hands—knife in the right, fork in the left— into the air. "Yeah, there's a racket. Let them spike a vein before the lawyers come after me for alimony. Oh God," he moaned, as if punched in the gut, "Alimony."

"Four syllables. Sounds like *all your money*," Howe noted impassively.

"Oh don't worry, Nels," Pria said, dismissing the idea with a wave of the hand and crossing his legs with considerable physical aplomb. "In all honesty, alimony, in your case, won't amount to all that much. As for your blood…Well, *that* might as well be bacon grease."

There was muffled laughter around the table.

"Nels," Howe said mellifluously, leaning his sherry-drinking arm comfortably on the table, "Have you thought to ask *why* she would like a divorce?" He took a quizzical sip, raising his graying eyebrows in Nelson Palanski's direction. "I mean, I hate to be indelicate, but perhaps she's seeing someone else."

Nelson rocked back in his chair abruptly, as though stabbed, throwing his arms out at his sides. "Thanks Gil. That's just what I wanted to hear."

"What I mean is," Howe rejoined, "Is that if she's cheating, you might get out of the alimony."

"No," Nelson answered, waving a rib bone like a gavel. "That doesn't work anymore. That kind of reasoning is ancient history. Nowadays they take reparation notwithstanding infidelity. Trust me, I'm an accountant."

"Well then, you know what you ought to do, Nels," Pria said, leaning an elbow meaningfully on the table. "You should take a lover."

At that, our lunch party rose to all-out guffaws—the idea of Nelson having a romantic affair being too ridiculous for gravity. Dr. Howe even raised his glass, and we toasted the prospects of Nelson Palanski's unlikely infidelity.

But after a moment's distraction, Nelson quickly regained his malaise. "Whatever happened to vows?" he said dejectedly.

"As you said, Nels, that kind of reasoning is ancient history," piped Howe, half in his glass of sherry.

"I tell you what," Nels rejoined, "I never really understood it till now."

"What?"

"'Till death do us part.'" Nelson shrugged his shoulders. "That's the only good way; the only clean way out."

At that, Pria suddenly, but casually, pushed his chair away from the table. "Have to use the..." he said, gesturing away from the table. "Gil, put lunch on my tab." And Pria walked almost solemnly off toward the john, leaving a strange silence in his wake.

After several seconds, Howe spoke up. "Well that was a stupid thing to say."

"I know. I'm sorry," Nelson answered.

"What?" I asked, feeling suddenly like a child among adults.

Howe looked at me. "About the death of a spouse..."

"Why?"

"He was married once, you know."

"No," I answered, shocked. "Really?"

"Yes," Gil mumbled absently. "Ten years ago or more. Awful. Died of leukemia or some such horrible thing. She was in her thirties, for god's sake. Beastly experience." He glared at Nelson Palanski. "And anything but clean."

On the way out, Pria approached me and wrapped his arm warmly around my shoulder, leaning a bit heavily as he extracted a cigar from his opposite pocket, seemingly recovered from his momentary melancholy.

"I forgot to tell you, Dwight. We're going to a smoker this weekend. Your attendance is mandatory, so I won't stand for vagueness or mendacity, or vague mendacity."

"I have to wash my hair," I said.

Pria grinned famously. "Friday, eight o'clock, dress well. Ever been to Kimballs? Superb place," he said disengaging my shoulder and rolling his head to indicate the two men behind us. "Gil and Nels will be there too, so you'll have a cadre of familiars. I'll teach you to appraise a fine cigar, and you'll thank me for it."

That week, Moira and I were back at the farmer's market, as we'd been several times since the day she made cheeseburgers for me. As it turned out, Kent's letter had been in earnest—she really did seem to need companionship in her husband's absence. And for three amazing weeks I was the beneficiary of that absence, filling Moira's spare time with every ounce of lovesick charm I could muster.

In that short span, we took in just about every type of entertainment that part of Virginia had to offer, including minor league baseball, community theater, second rate war memorials and colonial landmarks, and a mediocre sculpture exhibit that left almost everything to the imagination. In addition, Moira and I enjoyed all the late summer activities that couples do in the country: picnics, biking, feeding geese, rowing dinghies along the calmer stretches of the Appomattox—and, of course, cooking dinner in the evening. Because of the last, we'd become quite familiar at the Haber farmer's market, virtual intimates of every garden enthusiast and small-time organic producer in the county. Naturally, Moira won each one over with her teasing wit and lovely face, and we always got the best pickings of the lot; sometimes it was even set aside before we arrived.

But that day the weather was colder, the wind brisker, the trees a breezy décolleté, having shed the leaves that now rustled along the riverbank. Certain it would be one of the last good vegetable batches of the year, Moira was determined to get everything she could at the market. And she wasn't the only one—a few rows down from us, Mrs. Nelson Palanski was eyeballing sweet corn with an epicure's discretion. Moira and I avoided eye contact with her while I relayed the news that Nelson and his wife were finally going to see a marriage counselor, as Pria had told me earlier that day.

She seemed unsurprised.

"Of course, now Pria's upset, because it means Nelson can't go to the cigar thing he's planned," I said.

"Guy stuff," she said in a mannish false bass while examining the shallots.

"I suppose. But I don't think we're going to watch porn or anything. Mostly spitting and crotch grabbing."

"Delicious," she said. "I meant the shallots." Moira smiled impishly.

I raised my eyebrows at her.

"So what's it going to be, really?"

"I don't know," I said with a shrug, feeling shallots of my own. "Cigars. Eats. Drinks. No Grabbing."

"Well it sounds like there's an extra place at your table. That's what I'm hearing isn't it?"

"You want to go?"

"All my life," she said desperately.

"Smoke and brandy, dirty jokes and glad-handing—raw testosterone on a Friday night," I explained.

"Grand," she answered. At that, Moira turned triumphantly toward the cabbage as if her plans had been realized.

Pria, for his part, was equally delighted I'd found someone to take Nelson's place at the smoker. He said he was relieved to learn I'd made at least one friend in two months in Virginia. He didn't, however, bother to ask who it was.

On Friday, I went to Moira's house a full hour early, partly out of sheer restlessness, but mostly because I'd taken it upon myself to rent an odd old calash a businessman in Haber kept to earn extra money in the summer, and I wanted to leave time for us to have a ride. It was a bit corny, I knew, and I really couldn't afford it—neither morally nor financially—but I'd decided that for one night I would allow boldness to take hold and let fortune follow where it may. I'd probably been talking to Pria too much.

When I arrived, I found the Flickingers' front door ajar, a crack of interior light beckoning me inside—not a great surprise, as Haber was the kind of town where an open door posed no threat whatsoever. I guessed that Moira was upstairs, most likely donning a black dress with sheer material and spaghetti straps, sure to knock men dead on sight. A shiver of anticipation and a wave of rough pride at the thought of escorting her combined to give me vertigo; my mind was going too many directions at once, and I had to put a hand on the banister to steady myself.

The flare of a match brought me back to earth. Moira wasn't upstairs at all. Rather, she sat the living room, her feet (in black wingtips, no less) resting on the arm of the divan in parody of masculine guile. She wore a high-collared white shirt, silver cufflinks, and men's suspenders that held up the pants of a slick black suit, the coat of which I noticed thrown over the back of the couch with a black felt hat resting atop it. Her smirk glowed like the thin panatela in the corner of her mouth. Moira laughed richly, and asked:

"Do I get to play?"

I nodded at her, half-cocked. "You're looking pretty butch."

"Too much?" she asked, crinkling her nose enough to remind me of herself.

"Don't sock me on the arm or anything," I said, taking a seat beside her on the divan. "My brother used to do that. I hated it."

"Don't be such a girl," Moira answered, showing her pretty teeth.

I took a draught from the cigar and returned it. We lingered in the darkness for a moment, amidst smoke floating slowly toward the ceiling in sweet, ghostly rings. A thought of Kent passed briefly across my mind, but vanished at a glance.

"I considered a mustache," she said thoughtfully, "But the glue held me back."

Puffing the cigar again, without looking at her, I answered: "You're perfect."

"Let's go," she said, rising and taking the cigar from my mouth. She put on her hat and even affected a mannish swagger, suit coat thrown over her shoulder as she walked toward the door. But when Moira saw the carriage parked on the street, she returned to pure girl.

"Oh my God!" she said, her voice filled with honest astonishment. "You didn't."

To which I nodded as suavely as I could manage. The truth is that I was struggling to keep my cool, for that moment—when Moira's eyes sparked with excitement and she clasped her hands to her chest—was the fulfillment of a long lost dream. I'd surprised the woman that I loved. She wasn't mine to surprise, nor to love for that matter, but I'd done it with style. Every man should, at least once in his life, feel that thrill—one of our gender's privileged pleasures.

"*Tres galant*, Dwight," Moira said coyly, aspirating the 's' for effect and taking my arm as we walked toward the carriage. Thankfully, she'd abandoned the swagger.

That night, an evening breeze had brought on a late summer chill, but Moira refused to let me put the bonnet up, preferring instead to brave the night and savor the scenery. So I poured two glasses of champagne and we went clop-clopping across Haber, Virginia—the long way—toasting the locals as we passed with boisterous voice and androgynous good will, a scandal in the making.

For my part, I felt high, and it wasn't the wine. Indeed, to this day I can recall the ride only like the tentative memory of a late night dream: Moira's dizzying smile and my excitement mingling with cool breeze, soft bubbly, and heavy hooves echoing through the trees—all punctuated by the touch of her hand as I helped her out of the cab.

At Kimball's, we found Pria leaning against the oak bar, a thick Diego already lit, making hazy circles as he parleyed with a patrician gentleman who, ominously, held a Spanish sword balanced steadily across his palms. The conversation waxed and waned between puffs of smoke and mouthfuls of brandy, all of which precluded greeting for the time being.

"You've studied Cannae, of course," Pria conceded to his counterpart, whose desultory nod seemed to take in everything under the sun. "The advent of the *art* of war. Before Cannae, warfare was simply bar*bar*ic."

"Double envelopment. Feint. Timing," the older man recounted.

"Choreographed like an opera."

"With a captive audience of forty thousand."

"Hannibal killed 'em at Cannae."

Both men smiled as the punning died short of laughter, cigars and brandy reining the scale of manly cheer.

"No battles like that anymore, Colonel," Pria noted.

"No indeed." The colonel took the sword's hilt in his right hand and executed a short, violent pantomime, felling some small phantom in the smoke. "It's not for men anymore," he lamented. "Honor's been cuckolded by technology. Men don't fight wars these days unless it's from an aircraft carrier a thousand miles away."

"That's a weighty statement coming from a man like you," Pria said, taking it in.

"No dignity in bombing across the sea, Dr. Pria."

"No *thumos*."

The colonel raised his eyebrows and nodded meaningfully. "Alexander fought hand to hand. Caesar. Napoleon."

"Satan and the angels of Hell made machines to face Gabriel and Michael," Pria said.

And just like that their rhapsody seemed to drift away like so much exhaled smoke, the colonel lost in a half-maudlin downward gaze that eclipsed further comment.

"Hello Dwight!" Pria exclaimed, turning and clapping me on the shoulder. "It's good to see you removed from the halls of academe. I feared you'd become a book rat, packed in your apartment with a volume of Livy." Of course he knew better, but he was performing.

"This," he continued, "Is Colonel Elias Stromvold."

"Retired," the colonel greeted me with a handshake like the grip of death (the sword still clutched in his other hand). Releasing me, Stromvold opened a long box on the bar at his right, retrieved a cigar at least a foot long, and ran it sensuously under his nose. He stubbed out the one he'd been smoking.

"Please, Dr. Pria," he said as he clipped and made to light the next cigar, "Give the young man a Churchill."

"Of course. And it's nice to see you again, Mrs. Flickinger," Pria said slyly.

At that, Moira peeped out from beneath the black fedora, which had until then been pulled down over her eyes. She offered him her hand, palm down.

"Don't be charming, Vincent," she said dismissively. "And do give me one of those."

Elias Stromvold's jaw dropped fifteen degrees as Moira's painted nails reached across the bar and into his cedar humidor. It didn't register as full shock, of course—the colonel was much too experienced a man to betray real surprise—but as the only female at the smoker, Moira did elicit mild surprise, at least. And her expression said clearly that she relished it.

When she'd retrieved a Churchill, Moira looked the colonel dead in the eye, smirking beautifully as she mimicked him sniffing the length of the cigar. Her eyes danced like diamonds as she bit the end and spit on the floor, then sucked a flame from the lighter Pria had produced from his pocket.

Blowing white smoke high in the air, Moira said enigmatically, "Save me a dance, Dr. Pria."

From there, the party got on splendidly. A jazz trio materialized in the back, playing a catalog of tunes that predated all but a few in the room; canapés and cocktails circulated like a polonaise; and of course, fire-red cherries glowed and dimmed intermittently in the fog like distant ships signaling in the night. As the evening wore on, Vincent Pria produced a box of Arturo Fuentes and flamboyantly ordered two bottles of Louis Quatorze for the house. Elias Stromvold introduced me to Haber's mayor, and Gilbert Howe sang a Scottish ballad, a cappella, for Moira.

Eventually every table in Kimball's supported half-empty glasses of brandy and piles of half-smoked cigars, many of rare and expensive pedigree, heaped like the papers I'd once seen on Kent Flickinger's desk in his little office on the west side of Myrna Hall. It was obscene.

And always at the hub I could hear Pria laughing and expounding—somehow even more voluble, more charismatic than ever. Moira, meanwhile, remained mostly a short distance from his side, bending her ear to listen above the din, her felt fedora still cocked modishly over one eye, veiling her face like a crescent moon beckoning onlookers for a better look. Later, she removed the hat, and for a time all eyes receded like the tide, taking time to acclimate themselves to her full, luminous beauty. For at that moment, Moira cut an awkwardly feminine figure in that sea of masculinity. Yet she quickly proved herself capable of matching their bravura, and was thus accepted with pleasure at the smoker.

Thereafter, of course, she was *the* attraction at Kimball's; by turns every man in the room came to make conversation with her, some politely, some vigorously, yet all in the spirit of the evening treating her (to a degree) with equanimity. All but Stromvold, that is, who stayed near, often speaking quietly to Moira and/or shielding her from the harsher racket that's bound to arise in a narrow congregation of men with drinks. He watched over her like a father figure, even when she was occupied with Pria or me. For this service, Elias Stromvold would be singled out at the end of the evening with a kiss on his regent brow.

At three o'clock, Kimball's was a wreck. The fumy air sparked remarks of Gettysburg from Stromvold; Howe was too hoarse to speak; the mayor and his cohort had long since left the premises. Pria declared the party an unqualified success. Of course, the handsome cab was also gone, so at her discretion Moira and I set out on foot, with the memories of a fine evening and the farewells of a dozen envious men trailing us from the doorway.

"You take care of our girl," Pria said to me before kissing her richly below the eye.

Leaving Kimball's, Moira and I sauntered through a park that ran along the southern bank of the river. We weren't five blocks from my apartment, both of us dead tired and quite drunk on brandy and cognac. Still, I knew that suggesting, even innocently, that we go to my place would be presumptuous as hell. Besides, Moira seemed to enjoy the walk, drifting along like a pantomime and swinging a snifter she'd pilfered from Kimball's in rhythm with the long watch chain that hung from her suit vest. We sat down in a gazebo, passed the glass between us, and lit a Perfecto I found lodged in my coat pocket. There wasn't a breath of wind.

"I'm going to hate the taste of these things for the rest of my life," Moira said drowsily, scrutinizing the torch end of the cigar.

She gave it back and shifted on the bench. I put an arm around her and her head fell on my shoulder. A half-moon glazed the river through a break in the clouds, recalling to my mind Moira's luminous beauty, and how the men at the party had fawned on her; they'd tried to treat her indifferently, but despite the suit, the drinking, the smoking, and all the manliness she'd put on for the evening, Moira was too essentially feminine. Inevitably, beauty shines through. Strange that I felt pride.

Not strange that I was lost in the moment, however, with lovely haired Moira leaning her pretty head on my shoulder, my arm draped easily round her; more than a touch, more than a smile, more than the last three weeks I'd spent almost daily in her presence—more than any moment I'd lived—that bit of intimacy in the gazebo felt true to me. No matter that it was all a fiction. I wanted the world to stop, and leave me there forever: true, sublime, timeless.

If not that, I wanted at least something to mark the moment, some piece of familiarity we could refer to when Kent returned—a stolen footnote marking this perfect moment on this inspiring night. I wanted my pieces of mythos.

"What was that you said about a dance with Pria?" I asked.

Languidly, she replied, "At my wedding…" Moira shifted, half in a daze, burying her head in my chest. "We danced for *hours*," she murmured. "After the wedding. You know, at the …"

"Reception."

"Certainly."

"You didn't dance with Kent?"

"Well, *yes*," she corrected. "But to be truthful, Kent isn't much of a dancer. Vincent," she said, raising the glass of brandy, "Is."

She took a drink, still resting on my chest.

"Dance, Dwight," Moira said drunkenly, "Is very important. Gets 'em right in the knees."

At that, she settled gently again on my chest and fell asleep for a few minutes, the soft moonlight shining on her hair. The best, the longest minutes of my life. Eventually, I woke her, and with an arm round her waist led her to a cab that would take us back to her house. I was prepared to say goodnight from the car, but Moira insisted I follow inside. She nearly fell through the door, tugging at the collar of my coat so that we lurched across the threshold like a couple of sailors on shore leave.

"Wait here," she whispered, her face so close that her breath warmed my cheek.

As Moira climbed the stairs, my heart almost burst in my chest, which suddenly seemed too small to contain its dashing beat. I paced a little, eyes blazing, blinking furiously, mouth dry, hands wet, nostalgic, anxious, drained of all hope and any judgment. I sat down on the divan to gather my thoughts, picked up a book of Georgia O'Keefe prints that happened to be sitting on the coffee table. No help there. I got up again and crossed the room, poured a drink from a bottle on the bureau, drank deeply to calm my wild nerves. Beside the bottle on the bureau sat a cherrywood cigar box, inside of which lay a plain paperback Penguin edition of *De l'Amour*, by Stendahl. Without thinking, I opened the book to its marker, where was underlined one sentence: "It is better to have a prosaic husband and to take a romantic lover," with the letters V-I-P written beside it.

Oh shit.

"Hey," she said behind me. "Flip that light on."

I lit an Egyptian-looking lamp to reveal Moira leaning against one of her home's faux-Oriental columns, wearing a strappy black gown that hugged each curve of her perfect shape—exactly the dress I'd expected at the beginning of the night.

"Do you like it?"

I probably nodded.

"It was a gift...from an *admirer*," she told me coyly, her eyes alight with drink and excitement.

"You're beautiful."

"Thank you," she whispered, looking in my eyes.

Moira took the glass and slipped past me. She put Frank Sinatra on the old turntable, and laid the glass beside the bottle on the bureau.

"Did you save me that dance?" she asked, extending a hand.

Of course I knew it wasn't me she'd reserved *that dance* with. And yes, I was aware of the layers of betrayal I was hazarding. But what could I do? After all, there was Georgia O'Keefe on the coffee table and an Egyptian lamp in the corner; there was Stendahl *On Love*, Frank Sinatra singing "Tangerine," and a face to launch a thousand ships asking me to dance—which she'd confessed herself not long before, in a moment of half-conscious candor, was how you "get 'em." I wasn't man enough to say anything but:

"Yes."

Then again, what man in his right mind *would* say no? Forget love, passion, myth, devotion. Forget a fantasy that had lingered since my adolescence. Forget all that crap. The truth is that any man would want her. *Every man did.* As long as I'd known her—and obviously longer—Moira Apple (Flickinger) had been the object of men's affections, desires, dreams. Was I really supposed to say no to such a woman just because the morality of her question was questionable? Could I possibly hold myself accountable to that pang of conscience ringing in my middle ear like a tuning fork?

After all, there's nothing earth-shattering about indiscretions of the flesh, nothing historic in an act of adultery. Quite likely, Nelson Palanski's wife did have an affair, and *everyone* at Urbana knew why Mr. Overton left the History class in Kent's hands—and even to schoolboys, the truth of the affair was nothing more significant than driftwood washed up on the shore. This is the world we live in, driven by impulses is as old as the seas. Georgia poses wantonly on the table, teasing with a rosebud, while Frank charms us a piece of fruit. Eve sins. Paris seduces Helen. Like Pria said, the story's not so old because it was the first; it was the first story because it's so old.

This what any man with a gram of pride—the ideated representation of the will to survive—would do. This is *thumos*. Paris didn't steal Helen. He won her from a man who didn't deserve her. And standing in the Flickingers' living room, just inches from Moira, I finally bucked up the courage to act on an impulse that had been goading me for years. I knew with certainty that this was the moment I'd been waiting for since Moira first stepped a lovely foot on that Urbana campus, ringed by the arm of her incredibly dull boyfriend.

I took her in my arms—because that's what a hero would do, that's what a prince would do. No matter that I wasn't the prince she had in mind. And for that delicious, eternal, urgent instant, I filled the role like a natural. I became the *tres galante* Moira had chided me as at the start of the evening—ten feet tall and glowing boldly, with Helen herself propositioning me in the parlor. We touched, we swayed to the music, hip to hip, breast to breast, hand to hand. Her cheek to my neck, her brow to my cheek, her temple to my chin, our mouths edging closer to their inevitable destiny...

"Oh god, Dwight!" Moira shrieked.

I staggered back.

"Oh no," she cried in confusion. "I'm sorry." Moira put her hands over her face, hiding the shock of catching herself with the wrong man. Indeed, with the wrong *other* man.

In a panic, I spun round and grabbed the needle of the record player, tearing the vinyl like a knife.

Silence.

"You have to go," Moira said gravely.

And go I did, taking but a moment in clumsy apology, bothering neither to cajole nor mollify nor put off the awkwardness falling between us like a curtain. Rather, I left as quickly as my failing dignity would allow, a wretch who'd reached too eagerly for someone else's fortune. Duped, suckered, burned to the ground—if only for a kiss.

As I left Moira that night, with a faltering glance at her downturned face lit significantly by the lamp—she still rooted to the spot of rug where I'd tried to kiss her—I knew without a doubt it would be the last time I'd see her.

In the weeks that remained till semester break, I delved deep into my studies, avoiding human contact wherever possible, blending into the shadowy scenery of autumn. It wasn't hard; everyone I knew was vanishing that season. Moira, for her part, faded into the ether, appearing neither at the college nor any of her usual haunts around town; eventually, I learned that she'd disappeared from Haber not long after the night of the smoker. Not coincidentally, Pria also became suddenly inconspicuous, leaving detailed notes and vague writing assignments rather than presenting himself for lectures.

Meanwhile, Nelson Palanski had taken to lunching with his semi-estranged wife. I saw them occasionally at midday when she picked him up outside his office, and if Nelson recognized me from the other side of the car window, he betrayed no signs of familiarity. Later, Gilbert Howe later told me, in passing, that she had Nelson in group and private marriage counseling, as well as two AA sessions a week. Perhaps under the governance of those communities, Nelson would finally find what he needed. In any case, it likely made him appreciate the few moments he could be alone with his wife—say, at lunchtime.

In December, when I'd finished my final exam in Dr. Pria's Greek Tragedies class, he took me aside in the hallway, leaving for a moment the remaining students still hunched over their tests. He put a hand confidentially on my shoulder.

"Dwight," he said, bearing for the only time I can remember an expression utterly drained of his endearing fustian. "I'm not coming back next semester."

"I understand," I answered.

He shook my hand and went back to the classroom.

That year, I Christmassed in northern California, where a cousin of mine was married in a secular ceremony in the Napa Valley. Even at that time of year, the hills were green and the air was golden; all the guests went barefoot, and the bride and groom exchanged vows of their own composition before a bohemian clergyman, while an accompanist played selections from the oeuvre of Nickelback. In all, it was a poetic setting for a counterfeit sacrament. But the wine was excellent.

In January, I returned to Haber. Kent Flickinger never did. Perhaps he found another teaching position, perhaps he stayed in Europe. I don't know when or if he ever retrieved his belongings from the house where he and Moira had lived as man and wife, but by the first of February the property had been resold.

For my part, I drifted through the spring semester like a lonely ode, taking classes in stride without seeking the advice or company of others, unmindful even of the breathtaking spectacle of the season, which held only dead memories for me now. Nelson was once again fully re-assimilated into married life, and Gil, a hoary veteran of academe, quickly fell in with another coterie of professors. I saw them at lunch sometimes, but never joined them. In the end, Pria's conjecture about my reclusiveness was fairly accurate.

One day in April, I drove past the house where the Flickingers had entertained me, only a year before, during my first visit to Haber. The marigolds were coming up.

I couldn't blame her, really. Nor him. In hindsight it seemed—as such things always do—that I always knew it would end that way, that there was no other way. That it was, in a queer way, what we'd all been waiting for, though without the slightest idea. After all, there was nothing surprising in it; it was what they were made for. Love animates myth and myth adumbrates life; heroes do and beauties move; and historians fill in the blanks while grasping at straws. For some—the solitary romantic fools, perhaps—all that's left is a poem. And maybe, somewhere amid the tangled ménage of love, myth, and history, some kind of meaning peeks through.

It seems odd that I knew each of them for no more than a season, really. Yet each taught me something of manhood, laden as it is with admiration and affection, pain and purpose, dread and love. They helped me translate life, piecing together a song of my own that, if not exactly immortal, is at least individual.

But more than anything, I learned in that stolen season that real people can shape everyday history and still embody eternal verities. There are those whose appeal is patent, simple, and assured, needless of explanation or excuse. They give form to our thoughts and contour to our lives. For them, time is a road much traveled, and a day oft-celebrated. Others call to mind the highest ideals, stirring emotions that make us at once fearful and ambitious. They polarize and inspire; they live in ether, thrive in the senses, conjure our dreams. From them there is no escape, and no denying their influence. And then there are people who attract us on an unconscious level, catalysts that color our lives without trying; just as undeniable, but evermore sublime. They are anachronism, myth, and psyche. They are what cultures are built on.

I knew them all, yet I can't tell you which was which.

What I do know is that there are, every day, places where the sublime and the defined combine.

The Italian Manuscript

For truth, I do not know what I would do without that
beguiling smile. It is the sun of morning, the hearth of home.
She is the most dear, the most intimate thing in my life.
—Francesco del Giocondo

*M*arriage presents a particular paradox for people who move to New York. On one side of the ledger, there are obvious financial advantages. Rent alone demands cohabitation of some sort for most the city's residents, and logic dictates that sharing a bedroom (and more significantly, a bed) confers greater fiscal efficiency than merely sharing a home. And of course, that economy trickles down through every other aspect of the city's inflated cost of living, from cable bills to the price of milk. It's just the reality of the market: New York is organized for couplehood.

On the other hand, the culture of the city is specifically engineered for singles—and not just because there are literally millions of eligible men and women to muddy the waters of long-term relationship. There's also something in the very character of New York that demands a radical sense of selfdom, especially from the vast class of young professionals who go there with nothing but their goals as collateral. These ambitious immigrants expend enormous mental, emotional, and physical will establishing a durable identity in what is, in truth, a pretty orthodox environment. Unfortunately, the qualities it takes to carve out some kind of psychic niche tend to be anathema to marriage. By the time we're ready for it, most of us are absolutely unsuited to that kind of commitment. Thus another piece of the paradox: In the world's most postmodern social fishbowl, a seem-ingly antiquated ritual like arranged marriage actually has renewed merit—though, of course, no self-respecting New Yorker could ever confess to such an opinion.

My wife and I married fairly late, having spent the first part of our thirties building distinct identities and somewhat public careers, she as the vice president of a boutique literary agency catering most-ly to cookbooks and memoirs, and I as an editor for a pharmaceutical trade magazine. When we wed, Miriam and I were typical middle class New Yorkers, neither rich nor inexperienced, neither promi-nent nor naïve. Yet neither of us regretted having waited. We were each established, we were both tired of dating, and we were eager to try a new kind of life in the city at the beginning of the 21st century.

Miriam's one regret was that her father, Tom, didn't live long enough to attend the wedding. In fact, I'd met Tom just a short time before he was diagnosed with the liver cancer that would kill him within six months. Yet he must have seen something in me, or sensed something about Miriam and me that gave him confidence, because before he passed he bought a two-week honeymoon package for us, including four days each in Rome, Florence, and Venice. It was almost like a dow-ry; we scheduled the wedding around it, nearly a year after Tom's death.

And so in late June, one week after the wedding, Mir and I ar-rived in Rome for the first leg of our Italian honeymoon. The Eter-nal City was majestic and seductive, a spectacle to stir the heart and beguile the mind. We spent a morning in the Forum, an afternoon at the Coliseum, a sunset on the Spanish Steps. Despite everything that happened afterward, I still remember those four days like a dream, a perfect parenthesis in the muddled syntax of love.

The next day we were on a train to Florence, speeding along-side the Apennines under a crystal sky. Miriam slept light against my shoulder while I watched Lazio shade peacefully into Tuscany. I basked in the glow of the summer sun and a new marriage, deeply pleased with my life.

"Where are we?" Miriam asked without stirring from my shoulder.

"Feels like heaven," I said.

"Oh God. You're getting poetic." She nestled deeper into my chest, her dark curls tickling my collarbone. "Pretend I'm still sleeping."

"I can't help it," I said, ignoring the request. "A beautiful woman beside me, a beautiful countryside around me; I just spent four amazing days in one beautiful city, and now I'm on my way to another beautiful city." I spread my hands to demonstrate the point: "Face it, life is beautiful."

"Wasn't that the name of a movie?"

"An *Italian* movie."

"Didn't everyone die in the end?"

"I don't recall."

"Well don't go all Pollyanna on me just because we're on vacation. I don't want to have to rehab you back in Manhattan. Italy is beautiful. Life is life."

Miriam still had not raised her head.

"God*damn*," I answered, shifting my shoulder a little. "You know how to ruin a mood. I thought you were supposed to be sleeping anyway."

"Saccharine makes me restless."

"You just don't know how to relax. That's what happens when you go two years without a vacation."

It was true—Miriam spent more time in her office than the desk. Of course, it went with the job. Her agency had only five employees, and the demands of a small, privately owned company are different from a corporate position like mine. Miriam's long hours were a mark of her dedication. And there was always a good reason: an editor dragging her feet on a contract, an author late in delivering his manuscript, bad copy editing, lost galleys, shitty art. There are a thousand little problems that can arise in the production of a book, and I'd heard them all at least twice from my new wife. I'd learned by that time to accept the hectic nature of her job.

But it also reflected a difference in our temperaments. At thirty-six, Miriam still attacked work with the vigor of a twenty-four-year-old. Any problem that needed solving needed solving immediately; any deal that could be made should be made today. She saw each contract as a battle to be won; she viewed each client as a cause to be championed. The truth is she was a damned good businesswoman, and her tireless efforts had transformed the agency into a million-dollar operation.

I, on the other hand, had long since settled in to the schedule of a monthly publication, with regular deadlines and datelines that divided my time neatly between professional obligations and personal interests. That meant I had time for a more active social life than Miriam's, as well as hobbies and avocations that occupied me away from the office. In particular, my interest in Leonardo da Vinci had become, of late, a minor obsession. Mir humored my dabblings in Vinciana the only way she knew how—she suggested I write a book about it.

Unfortunately, that was about the last thing I wanted to hear, as one unfinishable novel and an aborted ghostwriting project had left me bitter about a once-desired writing career. Writer's block had set in like rigor mortis. At first I was despondent, then philosophical, and finally ambivalent about the loss of my dreams. Eventually I reconciled myself to a mid-level editorial career. Maybe that's why I was good at vacationing.

Of course, Miriam never quit pressing me to work. And I knew that she was just trying to help. Indeed, if I could ever finish anything she was in an ideal position to help, what with her contacts at all the New York publishing houses. But the encouragement did me no good. On the contrary, it worsened the block. And hearing about her clients' publishing successes—such a large part of Miriam's life—only drove me deeper into doubt. By the time I got married, the thought of putting pen to paper made me perfectly nauseous.

As the train came to a stop, Miriam lifted her head off my chest. "Where are we?" she asked again.

"Arezzo," I said. "It's not much farther."

"What time is it?"

"About two. We should have plenty of time to get checked in and find a place for an early dinner."

Miriam sat up and stretched her arms high above her head; her breasts rose like a sea swell. I gazed brazenly at my wife.

"What are you thinking?" she asked, yawning and brushing the hair out of her eyes.

"I'm thinking we may not make an early dinner."

She smiled complaisantly, yawned and stretched again—my heart danced. "We don't have time for that, love," she said.

"Why not?"

Miriam cast a furtive glance in my direction and proceeded to a make a production of searching through her purse.

"Miriam?"

"Where's my hair clip?"

"I don't know dear." I watched insistently as she continued digging through her bag.

"Okay," Miriam said, succumbing to the weight of my stare. She sighed and looked vaguely at the ceiling. "We're seeing someone tonight."

"In Florence?"

"Yes. I think. Sort of."

"What did you do?"

Suddenly Miriam came up with the elusive hair clip; she seemed deeply pleased as she gathered her voluminous curls into a delightful mess atop her head. God help me, I loved her hair. Thus arranged, Miriam flashed a wide-eyed, gaping face at no one in particular. She was dissembling.

"What did you do?"

"It's no big deal... I just told Olivia we'd stop by her parents' restaurant for a while."

"Why?" I asked.

"Just dinner."

I stared at her still. There was something else, I could tell.

Miriam rolled her big brown eyes in a lovely, exasperated way and faced me for the first time since the business with the purse. "Fine. They might have a book idea."

"Miriam, this is our honeymoon, for Christ's sake. Can't you leave the office behind for a couple of weeks? You don't see me dragging my work across Europe, do you?"

All at once my wife's face turned hard. "No David. I don't see you dragging your work anywhere. In fact, you've got so much free time I don't know what you do for a living. I know you sit in your office and goof off for about five hours a day, then you come home and piss around for another four. Maybe your job is so easy it only needs three hours of your time, but I don't have that kind of job. I have to bow and scrape and coax and soothe and, yes, discover new clients in my spare time. This shit doesn't just fall into my lap, you know."

"And you seriously think Olivia's parents have a book in them? Jesus, the people must be in their eighties."

Miriam sighed, not happily. "Seriously? No. But Olivia is one of our most important clients, and her next book isn't under contract yet. I can't afford to lose her, David. I need to keep her happy. Even if that means going out of my way to listen to a pitch from her family on my honeymoon.

"I'm sorry," she said softening her tone. "I have to do this. And I could really use your support."

I looked at my bride, whose dark eyes glowed with emotion. I felt like a heel. "Of course," I said. "Of course we'll go to dinner."

At that I kissed her soft on the lips, both as an apology for being difficult and as a promise of whatever support she ever needed.

For almost twenty years, Olivia Wolfe (nee Bardani) had operated a modest Italian restaurant on the Upper West Side of Manhattan. Olivia's Kitchen, as her first restaurant was called, was strictly a neighborhood place, catering to a loyal clientele of off-Broadway actors and middle class professionals who'd lived in the neighborhood since the seventies or before. Everyone who knew the restaurant—and it wasn't many, by the city's standards—loved Olivia's for its palatable fare and simple, uncomplicated ambiance. And, of course, for the bonhomie of their Old World hostess. Reservations were never necessary, because a table was always available. To eat at Olivia's was like being with family, no matter where you came from.

One year, more out of her usual gentility than a hope for exposure, Olivia had agreed to appear on a local PBS cooking show produced by a longtime customer at the Kitchen. And as it happened, she'd loved doing the show. After all, cooking to her was a family activity, and for that half hour on the air, Olivia felt like all the world was with her in her kitchen. What's more, the natural warmth and gregariousness that had made her restaurant so inviting to customers showed through the TV like a beacon.

Within a month of her first appearance, Olivia was contacted by producers from a new cable station called The Cooking Network; they wanted her to host her own weekly cooking program—called, naturally, Olivia's Kitchen—bringing the tastes of Northern Italian cuisine to Americans from Amherst to Albuquerque. She said yes.

Olivia's natural charm and simple, delicious recipes made her one of the network's first stars. Before long, it was difficult to find a table at Olivia's Kitchen. Within a year, Olivia had plans for a second restaurant (Olivia's Garden, in Tribeca), as well as a cookbook manuscript awaiting an offer from Clarkson Potter. Lucky for her, she had a customer who just happened to be an agent in the cookbook business.

That was two restaurants and three cookbooks before Miriam and I got married. All of which is to say that Olivia Wolfe had—after a long, modest existence—become very famous, very quickly. Needless to say, a lot of the old bonhomie had given way to the narcissism of celebrity. Thus my wife was undeniably required to pay a visit to Olivia's family on our honeymoon.

So by seven o'clock we'd checked in, dressed, and arranged for a car to take us three miles up the hillside to Settignano, where the Bardanis had operated their restaurant for more than sixty years. Miriam and I arrived just in time to take in the sunset from Piazza Desiderio. For several minutes we watched quietly as the day's last rays warmed the hills with their loving touch, and for a time the feeling between us was as idyllic as it had been in Rome. Miriam filled my arms, her head laid gently against my chest, my hands straying below her waistline and over the knoll of her hips.

It crossed my mind to point out how utterly romantic it was for us to have that perfect moment in a place called Desiderio, almost as though the piazza had been created with no other purpose than for the planets to align at that instant, with the sun setting over the picturesque hills and the city nodding softly in the twilight, I with my love couched close against me—these being desiderata, one and all. But I knew, of course, that Miriam would just accuse me of being poetic again. I also knew that the piazza was actually named for Desiderio da Settignano, a Florentine sculptor who died right about the time Leonardo was beginning his apprenticeship in Verrocchio's workshop. Vasari includes a short biography of him in *The Lives*.

Miriam sighed sensuously at my breast. "We'll try to keep this short tonight," she said. "I want to be alone with you." She stepped gently from my embrace and kissed me on the lips before leading me to our appointed dinner.

The Bardanis' restaurant—called Lola's, after the matriarch—was just down the hill in a cream colored, one-story plaster building off Piazza Tommaseo. Inside, lamplight and candles lit a wood-beamed interior occupied by a mere six tables, each set simply with white linen and silverware beneath a centerpiece of lavender. To say it was cozy was an understatement. Indeed, it made Olivia's quaint New York locations seem opulent by comparison.

At eight o'clock we were the first customers of the evening, and Lola, Olivia's mother, was clearly caught off guard by our arrival. She jumped up from one of the linen-covered tables where she'd been smoking a cigarette with the day's *Corriere della Sera*. We were inundated with *buona seras* and embraces, having been identified at a glance as the anticipated *Americani* from Nova York.

Lola Bardani was a short, round, lively woman well into her seventies, with dark hair and bright eyes and pockets of loose skin around her jowls and under her arms that flapped and fluttered when she talked. And she talked. From the moment we arrived, Lola seemed to be in overdrive, rambling, wobbling, nodding, waving, touching, pointing, and not a few times kissing each of us separately and together in a perfect caricature of an excessive Italian mother. Still, I had no doubt it was genuine. In fact, in certain ways her performance reminded me of Olivia before she hit it big. Though even then Olivia had not half the brio of her mother. And even then, I always got a faint idea that Olivia might be putting on.

After several minutes of fussing and welcoming, Lola, who spoke no English whatsoever, ushered us to a table and disappeared into the kitchen—though not before taking my wife's face affectionately in both hands for a long moment. When she was gone, I gave Miriam a wide-eyed, inquiring look. She just shook her head, as much at a loss as I was.

Even then we got hardly a chance to ponder the strangeness of the situation, for Lola returned in a trice bearing a plate of carpaccio, parmesan, and olives, along with bread, oil, an open bottle of sparkling wine, and three threadlike flutes. Before I could establish how she'd managed to carry all that from the kitchen, our hostess had set the table and poured glasses all around.

"Auguri, cari miei!" Lola declared. *"Per tanto amore e felicità!"*

With that, the little woman saluted us both and threw back her glass, grinning the whole time. *"Mangiate, mangiate!"* she chirped happily, then turned her heels back to the kitchen.

Miriam and I each sipped the dry wine—which was excellent—for a few seconds, allowing the air to settle after Lola's conspicuous withdrawal. Finally, it was I who spoke.

"Jesus," I said deliberately. "What the hell was that?"

"I have no idea," Miriam giggled. And I too began to laugh, releasing the anxiety that the encounter had produced.

From there, the evening seemed to go forward of its own accord. Miriam and I both dug hungrily into the carpaccio, which was followed by a course of fresh sardines with sweet and sour onions, and a fennel salad served with more parmesan and the thinnest slices of pink grapefruit I've ever seen. For the pasta course, Lola brought us eggplant ravioli sprinkled in red wine and truffle oil, and for the main course veal scaloppini with wild mushrooms and marsala. We'd finished the prosecco somewhere around the grapefruit, and were delivered a bottle of garganega before the ravioli arrived. All of this, mind, without the first bidding to our hostess; the food simply came to our table, in perfect order and presentation.

At some point between the eggplant and the veal, a middle-aged man in jeans and a loose Oxford shirt materialized with a mandolin, on which he proceeded to play high, heartrending melodies to the furtive night. Of course by that time the other five tables at Lola's were occupied, all by Italians—and from Lola's demeanor, I guessed, all regulars. Before long several strains of bantering Italian conversation joined with the mandolin to create a lively atmosphere. And though I'd had misgivings, I had to admit that it turned out to be a very satisfying evening.

Later, as Lola returned to the kitchen, having just bussed the plates from our finished veal entrees, she was replaced at tableside by the mandolin player, who held a decanter and three short-stemmed sherry glasses in one hand. "Ciao!" he said exuberantly. "Everything is good, yes?"

"Delicious," Miriam replied.

Still holding the decanter and glasses, the mandolin player gestured to the side of the table, asking if he could join us. The invitation accepted, he put down his drinkware and pulled up a chair.

"I am Andrea Bardani," he said, offering me his hand. "Olivia's brother, Lola's son."

"Of course," Miriam exclaimed. "I should have known—Olivia told me her brother was a musician. It's so nice to meet you."

"*Piacere,*" Andrea answered, shaking Miriam's hand before pouring grappa into the three sherry glasses. "And how are you liking your stay in Italia?"

"It's lovely," Miriam answered. "The art, the architecture... The food, of course." She gestured to the table indicating the evening's meal.

"Ah, *grazie.*" Andrea held up his glass. "To love and long life," he said. Then just like his mother, he threw back the whole glass in one swig.

I, on the other hand, sipped gingerly at the liquor, which burned like kerosene going down. I've never had much of a taste for grappa, and I still don't understand the logic behind burning away the taste of a perfectly good meal. But of course, refusing it isn't an option—especially in Italy.

Andrea, meanwhile, had poured himself another glass and leaned back in his chair, his long legs crossed at the knees pointed slightly in Miriam's direction. "So you are the book maker," he said.

Miriam was taking a sip of her grappa, and all at once I saw the businesswoman rise inside her, as she realized that of course she would be speaking to Andrea about any manuscript—Lola didn't know a word of English, after all. "Agent," Miriam corrected. "The book makers are the people I negotiate with."

"*Si, si*, agent," Andrea repeated thoughtfully, running a hand through his wavy blond hair. Though in his mid-forties, he still dressed the part of a young man—long hair, shirt unbuttoned halfway down his chest, a two-day growth of beard that accentuated his lean, angular features. Andrea was a man with no corporate commitments.

"So the agent talks to the book makers about what, exactly?"

"Well, a lot of things," Miriam answered. "But primarily I find people like your sister who have an idea to sell, and I show it to a book maker—publishers, they're called. If the publisher likes it, they'll tell me how much they are willing to pay for it."

Andrea tilted his head to the side and rubbed his whiskered chin. "So you sell things that you find; things that belong to other people."

"Yes."

"And what good is this for you?"

"I get part of the money the publisher pays for a book."

"*Che?*" The last was lost completely on Andrea.

Miriam leaned forward and placed both hands on the table, explaining deliberately to the confused Italian. "Whatever amount of money the publisher is willing to pay for a book, I get 15 percent. For instance, Olivia's last book sold for $200,000. That means the publisher gave her $170,000 and gave me $30,000."

"*Madonna mia!*" Andrea exclaimed, sitting up straight in his chair. "*Che tipo di mestiere e questo! Stanna rapina, verimente!*"

"We don't understand you," I interjected.

Miriam said nothing, but looked squarely at Andrea as he settled back into his chair. "That's the way it's done," she said.

Andrea struggled visibly with this information for a long minute. Finally, he picked up his grappa and threw it back like a cowboy. "Maybe I speak with these book makers myself."

"You could try," Miriam answered, unfazed. "Do you have any contacts?

"*Che?*"

"Names, addresses. Do you know who to send your book to?"

"You can tell me this, no?"

"No."

"*Ma perche?* This I do not understand. You are friend of Livia, you are friend of us. You come here to our restaurant to eat, you do not have to pay—it is our wedding gift to you. This is what family does."

"No, we'll pay," I insisted.

But before I finished speaking Miriam had raised her hand from the table to calm me; she was completely unruffled.

"Yes, Olivia is my friend," Miriam admitted. "But she's also my client, and she understands that those two roles, while not completely separate, have to be separated in some ways. If you can't accept that, then perhaps we shouldn't work together."

Still hot under the collar, Andrea threw up his hands in a supremely Italianate gesture of frustration. At the same time, Miriam leaned back in her chair and crossed her legs at the knee, a mirror of our host's pose.

"But maybe since we're friends now," she went on, "You could just give me your recipes and I'll write my own cookbook." Through it all, my wife remained straight-faced.

Slowly, Andrea smiled and began to nod—his hair fluttered in the night breeze. The Italian pointed his right index finger in my wife's direction as he turned to look at me. "I like this. This is someone I can do business with. This is the kind of agent I need for this book," he said, grinning like a circus clown.

Andrea took up the bottle of grappa and poured another round, though Miriam and I were each only halfway finished with our first. "Okay!" he said happily raising his glass. "We make a book! *Salut!*"

I looked to Miriam, who smiled and calmly raised her glass. "*Salut,*" she repeated.

At that moment, Lola reappeared tableside, her face beaming with joie de vivre; she laid a hand lovingly on her son's neck. "*Ciao ragazzi, sta tutto buon?*"

"*Si mama, si,*" Andrea answered. "*Diciamo di fare un libro di cucina pergli Americani. Com' Olivia. Ha ragione?*"

"*Si, ho capito, caro,*" Lola said to her son. Then smiling at Miriam and me: "*Dolci?*"

"Would you like dessert?" Andrea translated.

"*Si. Certo,*" Miriam answered.

"Ahhhh!" Lola cried throwing her hands up happily at the sound of Miriam's Italian. She leaned over and kissed the girl warmly on the cheek before returning to the kitchen.

My wife's eyes glowed with delight; my heart swelled just looking at her. "She's wonderful," Miriam told Andrea.

"Mama? *Si.* She is the soul of Settignano. That is why there must be a Lola's cookbook."

"I agree," Miriam answered, still smiling, though obviously more for Lola than Andrea. "So what have you got?"

Andrea spread his hands, indicating the restaurant. "We have this. For more than sixty years people come here because they love this food. You eat, you know. Mama cooks food that makes people think they have died and gone to heaven."

"Yes, but what else do you have? You need more than just recipes to make a cookbook. You need to have an idea—a story that will make people want to learn the recipes."

Andrea nodded thoughtfully, chin in hand.

"You've got a good start," Miriam went on encouragingly. "Sixty years in business, your mother the 'soul of Settignano.' And with her personality, I'm sure there are plenty of stories she could mix in with the recipes."

"*Si, si,* you can do that."

"No," Miriam answered.

Once again, Andrea was at a loss.

And once again, Miriam sat forward, hands on the table, to explain. "All I can do is sell what you—and Lola—give me to sell. I'm not going to write it for you, and I won't tell you what to write. If we do decide to work together, I'll give you advice, I'll give you support, and I'll do my best to sell your book. But it has to be *your book*."

Andrea mulled this over for a moment; his face dropped as he considered the burden of actually producing this book that was going to make him rich. And suddenly, with his long hair and loose clothes, Andrea seemed less a free spirit than an overgrown adolescent.

"Maybe this time you do it different," he said finally. "You write this, this story…and we give you recipes. Instead of 15 percent, you take …" Andrea's hands went in five different directions as he visibly weighed his greed against the prospect of writing the book himself. "You take 30 percent of the money. That is $60,000 instead of $30,000." He looked at me and nodded in approval of his suggestion.

Miriam smiled indulgently. "I'm sorry. I just don't have the time, Andrea. If I were to do that, I wouldn't be able to take care of Olivia and my other clients who need me to do my job for them." She reached over and touched his crossed knee. "I hope you understand."

At that moment—mercifully—Lola returned with our *dolci*, and shooed her son back to his mandolin. Miriam and I made quick work of dessert and said brief goodbyes to both our hosts, my wife leaving her card with the number of our hotel in exchange for a bundle of biscotti from Lola. As we walked to the door, Andrea played a sad aria on the mandolin, as though determined to make the most of his disappointment.

Outside, Miriam and I collapsed into the back seat of a cab, completely wearied by wine, travel, and Andrea's company. "Good God," I said. "Are your clients always like that?"

"Not always," she answered. "And he's not a client yet."

"Do you think he's got a book in him?"

"I doubt it," Miriam said with a sigh. "He just thinks it's a way to make money. The ones with heads full of dollar signs are always the most annoying—and almost always a waste of time.

"I had one the other day insisting that I get him in touch with Steven Spielberg; said he had a $100 million idea. Mind you, he wouldn't tell me what the idea was. He said he'd only talk to Steven Spielberg."

I chuckled. "What did you tell him?"

Miriam shrugged. "I told him I don't have Steven Spielberg's number, but he could send something to me—an outline, a synopsis—and I'd be happy to take a look at it. Of course, then he got paranoid, said that if he told me his idea I'd steal it for myself. He went on ranting for another couple of minutes, always coming back to him and Steven Spielberg."

"So what did you do?"

"Eventually I just hung up on him."

She leaned across the seat and laid her head against my chest. Her far arm draped across my outside shoulder, my wife let out a contented moan.

"When did that happen?" I asked, still amused by her caller.

"About two months ago."

"That's crazy. Why didn't you tell me about it before?"

"Because I know you hate to talk about my work. I know it makes you jealous that people without half your talent get big advances for their books while you're stuck every day at a trade magazine."

"I don't know if I would say jealous."

"Yes you would," Miriam answered, still resting on my chest. "And you're right, David: you're a better writer than any of my clients. You just need to find something to inspire you."

"Maybe I could help Andrea with his book," I said.

Miriam gave a tired little laugh. "I don't even want to *think* about *that*," she said, nestling closer against me. "No more talk about work. I want to go home and have my way with you."

With that, my darling wife drifted off. When we reached the hotel, I paid the cabbie and coaxed her out of the car, then carried Miriam from the street all the way across the threshold of our room—

though she was awake the whole time. We undressed and got in bed, but fell asleep immediately, too exhausted to make love.

For the next two days, Miriam and I made a grand tour of Florence, which we learned is nothing at all like Rome. Dimension alone presents an almost unfathomable contrast between the two cities. Rome, with its wide avenues and massive monuments, offers seemingly unlimited space for animation both psychic and terrestrial. It feels irrefutable, modern and ancient all at once, a gift from God to the ages.

Florence, on the other hand, seems uniquely temporal, even quaint. Which is not to say it isn't beautiful; its beauty is just more fragile than Rome's. From the Boboli Gardens to Piazza Michelangelo, from the Duomo to the Ponte Vecchio, the jewel of the Renaissance has a delicate charm that reinforces mortality. It is a smaller, softer gem than the capital, a tender tribute to human frailty.

But unlike the four days in Rome, our time in Florence was anything but idyllic. Of course, that could be chalked up to the fact that Mir and I had by then spent more than a week in constant contact, with no separation longer than a trip to the public toilet. One must also recall that neither she nor I was particularly young, and neither of us had been married before. Therefore, we were each, in our own idiosyncratic ways, well-accustomed to a good deal of selfness. We were New Yorkers, after all, not Italians. And so predictably, by the third day of our stay in Florence, my bride and I were firmly on one another's last nerve.

Then naturally it got worse.

We'd spent the day at the Uffizi Gallery, the city's premier museum, housing arguably the world's best collection of Renaissance artwork. From Cimabue to Caravaggio, the gallery features some of the greatest works of confirmed masters—including, of course, Leonardo, whose *Annunciation* and *Adoration of the Magi* are there. And the mu-

seum is vast; to see the Uffizi in a single day is a daunting task, yet
Miriam and I had set our minds to it. As a result, neither of us had the
opportunity to linger with the paintings we most wanted to see (I, of
course, with the Leonardos; Mir preferred Botticelli). By the time we
finished, we were both exhausted and somewhat irritable from constantly prodding each other on to the next collection.

Back at the hotel, the silence between us was deafening. Miriam
flopped down on the bed while I went to the bathroom to enjoy the
splendid isolation of a long, hot shower. When I came out—much
improved for the experience, I might add—Miriam had a grave face.

"Andrea left a message," she informed me.

"About what?" I said incredulously.

"Apparently he's put together a proposal that he'd like me to see."
She bit the inside of her lip. "They want us to come to lunch tomorrow in their home."

"No," I said immediately.

"David."

"This is ridiculous. These people *know* it's our honeymoon, and
they're still acting this way?"

"They're Italians. They're just trying to be hospitable."

"Bullshit."

"Okay," she answered, rolling her eyes. "Lola's being hospitable."

"And Andrea's being an asshole. Call them back and tell them no."

Miriam didn't answer. She got up and walked past me to the
bathroom.

"What?" I said.

"You know I can't do that," she answered, poking her head out the
door. "I told you before: I need to do this to make sure I get Olivia's
next book. Believe me, she's using this as a test."

"But you said he's probably got nothing worth publishing."

"It doesn't matter," she answered with a shrug.

My wife gazed at me apologetically as she gathered her great
mane of hair into a rubber band. "I'm sorry," she said at last, then

disappeared into the bathroom, where the running faucet told me she was washing her face.

"But we have that trip tomorrow," I said. "Don't you remember?" In fact, it was the reason we'd rushed through the Uffizi in one day—the next day we were booked on a coach to ride the 40 miles to Vinci, the birthplace of a certain artist.

"I know," Miriam answered, her head still in the sink. "Maybe we can cancel the tickets."

I waited for her to come out of the bathroom. "I don't want to cancel the tickets," I said.

"What do you want me to do, David? I've already explained—twice."

This time I shrugged. "Maybe I should go alone."

"You would go without me?"

"Miriam, you don't even want to go to Vinci."

"I wanted to go with you."

"Just barely."

She stared at me for a second then went back into the bathroom.

"Listen," I said, "You were the one who turned this into a business trip."

"So we'll write it off," she answered from behind the wall.

"If your father hadn't already paid for it."

A long, hot silence permeated our hotel room, leaving a patina of sweat under my shirt collar. Yet I refused to move from the place I'd staked on the cold, hardwood floor—because there was no way I was going to sit through another meal with that man. Finally, my wife emerged from the bathroom, her hair still pulled back from her darling face.

"Fine," she sighed. "I'll go to Settignano alone. You take your trip to Vinci."

We went to dinner that evening, but the feeling between Miriam and I was something less than genuine. Having claimed separate kingdoms within our marriage—and that just halfway through the honeymoon—we eyed each other suspiciously over the risotto, both angling for the upper hand.

The next morning, I was out the door early and down to Via della Scala, alone, to catch the day's first bus to Vinci. I hate to say it, but I was blatantly relieved—both to have been spared another sit-down with Andrea, and, frankly, to have some time to myself. Though Miriam and I had been together for nearly two years before the wedding, and had even taken some short vacations together, never before Italy had the relationship seemed so meager to me. We needed space. I needed to concentrate on something other than the narrowness of my brand new marriage, which at that moment was straining my patience.

And Vinci was the perfect place to clear my mind, for I'd harbored a fascination with Leonardo since early adulthood, long before the potboiler novel and its movie adaptation made him a household name. Of course, I'm far from alone—there are scores of biographies of Leonardo, the model Renaissance man, whose studies in mathematics, anatomy, and natural philosophy were literally hundreds of years ahead of their time. What interests me most is his spirit. In his writings, Leonardo displays a zest for life along with genuine reverence for nature—all of which is reflected in his work, both artistic and scientific. And though his artwork is by far more prominent, for me it's the manuscripts that get closest to the heart of the man. Vasari wrote, "He might have been a scientist if he had not been so versatile. But the instability of his character caused him to take up and abandon many things." Which was, perhaps, another reason for my affinity with Leonardo: His penchant for leaving projects unfinished mirrors something in me.

Whatever the reason, I was on my way to his birthplace—and on my own, no less. Perhaps it was the lovely Tuscan morning or the sudden buoyancy of being alone for a moment, but everything about the trip to Vinci felt like a retreat. All during the 45-minute coach ride I brimmed with anticipation, excited by the idea that I was approaching a vital moment in my life.

As the bus crept up a narrow road through terraced plots of olive and vineyard, I gained new appreciation for Leonardo's intimacy with nature. On every side, golden hills swelled against a sky divided by fine green arbor. Every vista seemed artistic. No wonder the young man had developed such an eye—beauty lived in every atom around him.

Then all at once we emerged from behind a final grove into a small village nested like a bluebird's egg at the foot of the hillside. The coach lumbered into the piazza in the center of town and ground to a halt; twenty passengers disembarked beside the church of Santa Croce, where, according to our tour guide, Leonardo was baptized in 1452. From there we were led across the piazza to a palazzo that was once the seat of the local nobility, and now houses Vinci's principal tourist attraction.

But the Museo Leonardiano isn't like any of the other galleries that exhibit the maestro's work. The difference is that Leonardo didn't actually create any of the pieces there. Rather, the Museo displays more than 100 models of machinery created from Leonardo's extensive writings and scientific drawings. The collection is impressive for its ingenuity alone. But when you consider that in the 15th century science didn't exist as a concept, much less a discipline, Leonardo's machines defy the imagination—any, apparently, but his. The very idea of a helicopter or a parachute 400 years before Kittyhawk must have seemed like madness. Yet there they were: Leonardo's designs for both helicopter and parachute—along with a clock, a loom, a primitive car, even a tank—valid, tangible, viable, and brought to life from 500-year-old parchments like phantoms summoned from the ether.

I stayed at the Museo for several hours, marveling at these feats of engineering, and the fact that he understood abstract mechanics long before anyone else even conceived of such machines. In any man, such brilliance would have been admirable. When added to Leondardo's body of work in other media, the pieces in the Vinci museum were like a whole other world within the man.

I left the Museo Leonardiano in the late morning; the tour bus had long since gone to pick up another group of sightseers in Florence; the piazza was mostly empty. I decided to walk two miles up the hill before lunch to visit the hamlet of Anchiano, which features the second big stop on the tour of Vinci—Leonardo's actual birthplace.

Of course, little is known of Leondardo's childhood, but the facts we have paint a picture of a boy reared in difficult circumstances. He was the first, illegitimate son of Ser Piero da Vinci, a well-to-do notary, and a peasant girl named Caterina, who lived for a time on Ser Piero's lands in Anchiano. Shortly after his son's birth, twenty-five-year-old Ser Piero was married to Albiera di Giovanni Amadai, a young girl of good family.

Unfortunately, the couple was unable to bear children, and at some time in his first five years, Leonardo left his mother in Anchiano to join his father's household in Vinci. There, he was raised by Albiera as her own son until her untimely death at the age of 29. Thus, by the time he was 13 years old, Leonardo had lost two mothers. Many believe that those losses forever affected his attitudes toward the women in his life—and his depictions of them in his art.

It was almost noon when I reached the Casa di Natale, a simple stone farmhouse perched on the hillside among silver-leafed olive trees. As a site on the tour of Vinci, Leonardo's birthplace has been returned to an ostensible 15th century state: a single, large room with primitive fittings devoid of decoration or embellishment. The rustic farmhouse displays little more than the family coat of arms and a number of reproductions of the master's drawings of the countryside, as well as a map of the Arno valley traced by Leonardo himself.

Yet standing inside the house where Leonardo was born, surrounded by the sights he'd known as a child and reproductions of his own drawings of the Tuscan countryside, I felt as though I was suddenly close to him—both the man and the legend. Inspiration rushed through me. Examining the farmhouse and its contents, I took from my bag the journal Miriam had bought me before we left New York. My intention, and her hope, was that I would write in the journal throughout our Italian honeymoon, and perhaps rouse something in me that could become the seed of a manuscript. Of course, up till that moment I hadn't written a word, mostly because my attention had been occupied by Miriam. But with her attending to Andrea back in Settignano, I finally had the opportunity to let my mind wander. And for the first time in many months, words poured through me, as though my voice had been hidden in that old farmhouse all that time.

What was I writing about? Nothing of particular import. Descriptions of the map of the Arno; thoughts about Andrea and his cookbook, which Miriam would have to bust her ass to sell; random observations about a man playing a violin in the courtyard. But then I saw something astonishing. In the distance, beyond the violinist, a black hawk dove like lightning toward the ground. As it reached the surface, the bird gracefully changed directions, stopping just before touching earth and ascending once again with a thick snake flailing in its talons. It was breathtaking—elegant, brutal, heroic.

I looked to see if anyone else had witnessed this miracle of nature, but not one of the dozen souls at the Casa di Natale showed any sign of seeing what had happened. Even the lonely violinist played on without missing a beat.

And suddenly I remembered Freud's monograph on Leonardo's childhood, wherein he cites Leonardo's "memory" of a vulture coming to his cradle and brushing its tail feathers against his lips. Freud, of course, made much of this image, and even expanded his interpretation beyond the obvious phallic association to an odd iconographic argument that covers many centuries and a handful of languages. The funny thing is that the Viennese quack had taken a mistranslation of the Italian word for hawk (*nibbio*) from the German translation of a Russian novel about Leonardo. His misreading of "vulture" then led Freud down a tangled path toward the ancient Egyptian god Mut (a vulture), from which he made a further association with the German word *"Mutter"*—thereby concluding that the tail feathers in Leonardo's memory were not only phallic, but also a symbol of a mother's nipple. This naturally—in Freud's twisted, mother-loving purview—was the perfect explanation for Leonardo's supposed homosexuality. It's all fantastic crap.

Yet on the other hand, it's *fantastic* crap—the kind of thing novelists live for. I stepped outside of the farmhouse into the midday heat; below, Vinci blinked in the numinous sunlight of the valley. I sat down with my back against an olive tree and began writing furiously, compiling notes for a story about Leonardo, Freud, and that Russian novelist (his name had to be available somewhere) who misjudged a species of bird, and thus sent the famed psychoanalyst on a perverted wild goose chase.

I'd run through several pages of my journal before I noticed that a small shadow had risen on my right. I looked up—between me and the blue sky stood a little middle-aged man sporting a grin that seemed to eat his whole face. Then I saw the violin case at his feet and realized for the first time that the music that had accompanied my whole time at the Casa Natale had stopped some time during my writing.

"You are American," the violinist said in heavily accented English, still grinning like a hyena.

I shrugged. "Yes."

He pointed a finger at me decisively. "You are a writer, no?"

How many times had I been asked that question? Once upon a time, when I still had courage, I'd give a quick answer. But years of frustration and failure had dulled my enthusiasm, all but killed my will. Eventually, when people asked I hemmed and hawed and finally landed, gingerly, on the reply that I was an editor for a small trade magazine.

But then again, I was in Italy—and I *was* writing. In a split second I aggrandized the five pages before me, seeing them through critical accolades to bestseller fame. It was a pipe dream, sure, but a harmless one. Besides, the guy was nothing but a second rate fiddle player at a third rate tourist site. Why should I feel guilty about lying to him?

"Yes," I said, laying down my pen. "I'm a writer."

"I know this," he said, wagging his finger. "I can see. Is in the face. Is in the eyes." The old man continued to stand over me, hands on his hips, blinking in the sunlight.

"So, you are on vacation?"

"Honeymoon, actually."

"Aye!" he cried out, clutching a palm against his chest. "*Auguri, signore!* Congratulations!" The violinist stepped forward and offered his hand. "My name is Silvo."

I reached up and shook it warily. "David. Pleased to meet you."

"Is your first time in Italia, at Vinci?"

"Both," I answered. By then, of course, I knew there was no way I'd get rid of him without spending a few euros. But I was in such a good mood it didn't matter.

"Is a beautiful country, no?"

"*Bellissimo.*"

"Ah, *buono*," the old man answered, nodding happily at my Italian. He stepped forward again and gestured toward the ground. "May I sit?" He asked genially. "*Sta caldo,* no? Is very hot today. I need the—*come si dice—l'ombra.*"

"Please," I said. "Be my guest."

The old man picked up his violin case and settled on a big tree root. He took off his jacket and Windsor cap, folding one neatly over his knee, and laying the other atop it. No wonder the old man was hot; it had to be ninety degrees outside, yet he was dressed all in wool. He ran a hand across his brow and back over his balding head, smoothing the few grey strands that remained.

"Much better," he said with a sigh. "Thank you my friend."

"Not my tree," I answered with a shrug.

The old man chuckled. "So, you write about Leonardo?" he asked. "Americans, they love Leonardo, eh. *Da Vinci Code.*"

I smiled, but didn't answer.

"You have been to the Museo?"

"Yes. I went this morning."

"Leonardo, he was a genius, this man. A painter, of course, as well as an engineer, an entertainer, a scientist. A poet too. Did you know this?"

"Actually, yes," I answered. "I know quite a lot about his life and his work."

"Bravo," the old man said seriously. "So you know our Museo before today."

"No, not really," I said. I reached into my pocket and pulled out a five euro note. "Can I give you some money for your playing?"

Silvo deftly lifted ten fingers and tilted his head an inch in refusal. Like all Italians, his smallest gesture spoke volumes.

"I guess I knew more about the museums in Pairs and Rome and London," I said, trying to make amends both for my ignorance of the Museo and the offer of money. I was feeling a bit the ugly American. "He's all over Europe, really."

"Da vero," the violinist answered. "It is true. And nothing in Vinci, the place of his birth. We Vincians have been robbed of our treasures—and by the French! *Porca miseria!*"

"But you have this," I said gesturing toward the stone home where Leonardo was born. "You've got the history."

"Quest' e un scherzo," he said derisively. "My friend, let me tell you the truth, eh? What you see is an illusion."

"How do you mean?"

"I mean the Casa Natale." He nodded in the direction of the farmhouse. "Is not what you think. It could not be. Leonardo's mother, Caterina, was a peasant girl, maybe sixteen years old when he was birthed. It is not possible that she lived in a house of this size, with such a view of the valley. This is a house for someone of means. Most probably, Caterina lived in a small quarters in some—how do you say—out-of-the-way place. All Vincians know this."

"And you all just lie about it?" I said, trying to hide my insult at being duped. Suddenly, irrationally, my enthusiasm was sapped; my bestseller an illusion.

"Is not a lie," the old man explained. "Is a fiction—like much of Leonardo. No one can know where he was truly born, but this place fits his legend, so it is this story we Vincians choose to tell."

"Also you want tourists to come," I said cynically.

"*Certo,*" he shrugged. "Of course. But you must understand, this place is not like it was one hundred years ago, when people lived from the land alone. Now we must do other things to make money. We Vincians have to eat as well," he added with a smile.

"Speaking of which," I said, "I think it's time for me to head back down for lunch."

"*Va bene.* I will walk with you," the violinist answered, putting on his coat and picking up his bags. "I will show you a good restaurant."

"You don't have to do that."

"Please. I insist."

What could I do? I got up and, with Silvo in tow, started the walk down to Vinci in the hot afternoon sun. It wasn't long, of course, before the old man started talking again.

"You see Vinci, she is very beautiful. *Molta bella.* But her beauty is only on the surface. Is, as you say 'skin deep,'" he said with a reassuring nod. "These lands, they have no marble, no minerals. The soil grows only bad wine and worse olives. This is why Vinci never grows more than a few thousand people. Compared to the rest of Toscana, we have nothing to offer. Except we have Leonardo. And so the Museo. You know the story of Vinci?"

"I can't say I do," I answered.

"*Allora.* The castle was built in the *medievale*—maybe the year of Christ one thousand—by the Conti Guidi. At that time, all you see here was the property of the Guidi. That is why even to this day it is known among Vincians as the Castello Guidi. But in the Quattrocento—the 14th century, as you say—when Firenze became a powerful state, the county changed hands very many times. This is because she lay on the very edge of Firenze's influence, you see? Is true, Vinci had many governors, many wars, much bloodshed. Those were terrible times for Vincians. The county was taken by the Strozzi, then the Borghese, even the Chigi-Albani; all of them from Siena—*porche puttane!* Finally, during the reign of Cosimo III, Vinci passed to the family of the Masetti da Bagnano—a good family of Firenze."

"That's an amazing story, Silvo," I said, consciously quickening my step, hoping to leave the old man behind.

"*Da vero*," he answered, matching me stride for stride. "But is only the beginning, my friend."

"Of course."

"From then for two hundred years the Masetti da Bagnano ruled Vinci as a property—*feudale*. Like others, they live in Firenze and have money from the olives and other things of Vinci. They are not Vincians, but they are not bad lords. After many wars, Vincians are happy for this.

"Then at the start of the Novecento, all family lands near Vinci passed into the hands of Count Giulio Masetti da Bagnano." Silvo looked at me gravely as we walked, his index finger pointing straight up beside his temple for the utmost emphasis. "This was a different type of lord. Count Giulio, he was not *un straniero* like other lords. He lived in the castle many months of the year. He walked these hills, he hunted these *coniglio*, he smelled these vines with his own breath. He loved this place as much as his own life. And to these people, Count Giulio was not a man of Firenze—he was a Vincian.

"And like you, Count Giulio was a great admirer of Leonardo. He understood that there is no way to separate the brilliance of Leonardo from the light of Vinci. His greatest wish was for people throughout the world to know this place where Leonardo's genius was born.

"But difficult times were coming to Italia. *I fascisti* were rising at Milano. Count Giulio saw this, and he knew that once again the Italians were at the *precipizmo*. He saw that our people would once again tear Italia apart with war—and that once again Vincians would suffer in the struggle.

"Count Giulio had to find a way to protect Vinci. But the *paese* had no wealth, nothing to offer for this protection. *In fatti,* in those years the people had barely enough to live for themselves. The one thing Vinci had to trade was its name and the connection with Leonardo. Fortunately, Mussolini revered history almost as much as he loved power. Count Giulio was able to convince the Duce to make Vinci herself a tribute to Leonardo's genius. In that way, the *paese* would come under the safety of the *fascisti,* and Vincians would be protected when war came."

By that time Silvio was walking much more slowly, visibly fatigued by the close, warm air and burning sun, both of which must have hung on his woolen clothing like anvils. I could have easily left him behind on the hill, and lost him completely in the village. But my pace had slowed—not because of the heat, but because I was hanging on his every word.

"Yet even while Count Giulio was happy for the Vincians, his heart was troubled by the agreement he had reached with Mussolini. That is because in return for this protection of the state, the Duce demanded that Count Giulio donate the only building in Vinci large enough to house a museo in Leonardo's honor. In order to save Vinci, he would have to give up the Castello Guidi.

"Now it is possible you think, 'Why is this such a difficult thing for a count?' But you must understand, my friend, that Italia in the Novecento was not like Italia in the Quattrocento...or even the Ottocento. Is no longer nobles who own all the lands. *In fatti,* the lands of the Masetti da Bagnano had by then been broken up so much that the properties near Vinci were all Count Giulio had left of his *patrimonio.* That, and Castello Guidi.

"And so Count Giulio agonized over the decision he was faced with, for he knew that saving Vinci would mean the end of his *patrimonio*. If he did this, the Masetti da Bagnano would cease to be a noble family." Silvo shook his head sadly as he walked. "*Ma certo*, there was nothing he could do. He was a Vincian, in his heart, and so he was bound to protect the people, even if it meant ruining his own family. So in the year *novecento dicenove*—nineteen, nineteen as you say—Count Giulio gives the Castello Guidi to the *paese* for the making of the Museo Leonardiano."

At that, ostensibly the end of his tale, Silvo looked at me and shrugged as though the story was a lament as well as a retelling—both personal and historical.

"*Aspetta,*" he said, stopping for a moment in the road. The violinist put down his case and retrieved a handkerchief from the inside pocket of his coat. He removed his hat and wiped his bald head dry with the cloth. "Is very hot, my friend."

I was touched by Silvo's love for the city's patron. Yet at the same time I was puzzled by his intimate knowledge of this Count Giulio. I also recalled that I'd just been taken in by the ruse of the Casa Natale, so even though a part of me wanted to believe Silvo's story of the magnanimous count, I had my suspicions. I studied the old man closely for signs of deceit; he smiled comfortably back at me.

"There's just one thing I don't understand," I said. "How is it you know so much about Count Giulio? Like the fact that he agonized over the decision to give up the castle. Or is that just another story that fits the legend?"

At that, Silvo straightened; he folded the handkerchief neatly and replaced it in his inside pocket. "Because I am Silvano Masetti da Bagnano," he said proudly. "Giulio was my grandfather. I am the Count of Vinci."

There are many turns of phrase that have become so deeply ingrained in English vernacular that the literal meaning has been replaced by the figurative idea the words convey. For instance, a man might actually take a step back. Yet when someone says "take a step back," you don't think of the physical act. Rather, the connotation of deferral and reassessment takes precedence. As such, the idea of a man literally taking a step backward in a situation that calls for deferral and reassessment seems patently absurd.

And yet when Silvo told me who he was, my jaw literally dropped.

"*Piacere*," he said, offering me his hand once again.

"You're kidding me, right?"

"*Da vero,*" he answered with a cordial nod. "Is true."

"Then why are you playing violin for loose change at Casa Natale?"

Silvo sighed. "I need the practice."

He picked up his violin case and we continued walking down the hill at a slow, even pace, the Count of Vinci whistling Mozart at my side. "So all of this is yours?" I asked finally, gesturing toward the surrounding countryside.

Silvo flipped his free hand upward, as though swatting at a fly. "No. As I said, my friend, being a noble isn't like it was in the old times. When my grandfather, Count Giulio, donated the Castello, our fortunes were greatly reduced. Much of the Masetti da Bagnano land was sold in the years that followed. And of course then came the war." Silvo raised his hand to the landscape, much as I'd done, though there was something dejected in his gesture. "Is all gone now," he said. "All that remains is a small farm in San Silvestri and an enoteca in Vinci. I will take you there for *cena,* as my guest."

In another half hour we were at Silvo's restaurant off the main square in Vinci, which I now realized was called—what else—Piazza Leonardo. The Antica Cantina di Masetti was hardly larger than Lola's, in Settignano, and not nearly as well-kept, with tables of rough wood that had likely seen generations of service without refurbishment, and brick walls that seemed to be crumbling from their mortar. The doors were thrown open in the front and the back of the space, allowing a slight breeze to come off the piazza; several tables were occupied by European tourists in sandals and socks.

The lunchtime atmosphere of the Antica Cantina was also notably different from Lola's. In Settignano, the crowd of Italians had dined with vigor, their laughter and conversation rising above the meal. These tourists, on the other hand, ate quietly, paging through museum brochures or gazing vaguely at the light of the piazza.

Silvo directed me to a narrow staircase just inside the front entrance, gestured for me to climb. It emerged onto a recessed terrace ten feet above the street, with a single table set for two.

"*Benvenuto,* my friend," he said behind me. "Please. Sit." I did, as Silvo disappeared back down the stair.

In the few moments I was alone, I looked out over the piazza toward Castello Guidi, recalling all that Silvo had told me. Small as it was, the history of the place was awesome. I was inspired by its quaint intimacy. In Rome, every monument is a well-tread path leading back through millennia. Even Florence—the jewel of the Renaissance—has little novel to offer. But Vinci felt both historical and personal, especially with its count as my guide. For the first time that day, I was sorry that Miriam hadn't made the trip. She had to meet Silvo; I knew there was a book in this.

The old man returned with a carafe of gleaming white wine in one hand and two narrow tumblers in the other. Country glassware. Only city people drink wine with stems. Tucked under one arm, Silvo also carried a leather portfolio, which he placed carefully on the table without explanation before settling in the chair across from me. Both his hat and coat were gone; the Count of Vinci wore a collarless muslin shirt with unlinked cuffs and woven suspenders that crossed in the back. He basked in the sunlight for a long moment, and then poured wine to the rim of both glasses.

"*Salut,*" he said, leaning in to clink my glass. "Carolena will bring us food soon. First we drink, eh?"

The wine was dry and light and ice cold, perfect refreshment for a hot summer day. Before I knew it, my glass was half empty and

Silvo was reaching for the carafe to top it. "Drink, drink," he said cheerfully. *"Vino sta piu bono rimedio contro il calore."*

He laughed and refilled his glass. In another moment a girl arrived with a plate of meat, cheese, olives, and bread, still warm from an unseen oven. "Pancetta, pecorino, gaeta," Silvo said, pointing out the items on the plate. I listened politely to my host, though many nights at Olivia's restaurant had given me an adequate vocabulary for Italian food. Only the gaeta olives stuffed with sprigs of rosemary were a novelty on my palate. When that plate was finished, Carolena returned with another carafe of wine and another plate, this time arranged with fresh mozzarella, bright red tomato slices, and fennel leaves fanned around a full bulb in the center.

"You know this?" Silvo asked, picking up the bulb. "Is a plant that is native of Toscano; many people use this in cooking."

"It's a fennel, right?"

"Here we call this *finocchio.*"

"Finocchio?"

"Si. You know this word?" the old man asked, a hint of a smile creeping around the corners of his mouth.

I shook my head. Silvo cradled the bulb in his palm and pointed at it with his other hand. "When a person sees this plant, he thinks is a *cipolla*—an onion, no? But taste," he said, gesturing to the leaves on the plate.

I picked one up and bit; it was shockingly sweet, with hints of aniseed in the nose. "Sweet," I said without thinking.

"Si," the old man answered with a nod. "You see, the *finocch'* is the shape of a ball—*un palle*—like the onion, but has sweet flavor, not strong flavor like the onion.

"Now you can guess what *finocchio* means?" he asked, leaning forward puckishly. Once again, I shook my head. *"Ommossesuale,"* Silvo said with a grin.

I translated that for myself as my host fed a *finocchio* leaf into his smile.

"This is the Italian humor," he went on while chewing. "We take pleasure in things that are not what they seem. Like the Casa Natale. Like me: the count who is *un violinisto*. Things are not always what they seem. But you know, sometimes what appears to be false is more real than any truth could be."

"Americans like this kind of thing too," I answered. "Why do you think we're so interested in Leonardo? He left many mysteries."

"*Si,*" Silvo answered. "Is true. There are many mysteries about Leonardo. You know the mystery of *La Gioconda?* Mona Lisa, as you call it."

"Which one?" I asked with some little bit of savoir-faire. For the first time since talking to Silvo, I felt on solid ground.

The count smiled serenely. "The one about her *identita.*"

"Oh that," I answered. "I know a little."

"*Diceme,*" Silvo said, refilling my wine glass.

I picked it up and saluted him briefly before drinking. "Well, Vasari's account is the most famous—the one where he describes how Leonardo had singers in attendance while Lisa was sitting, in order to coax that amazing smile. But then again, Vasari couldn't have actually seen the painting, because from the time he was born, in 1511, to the time of his writing, the Mona Lisa had never been anywhere near Florence."

Silvo raised his glass and nodded happily. "*Bravo,* my friend."

"*Grazie,*" I said, and took a drink. "On the other hand, Vasari served in the court of the Medici, and could easily have met Francesco and Lisa del Giocondo, which means that the story about the singers could have come directly from the lips of the model." I rubbed my chin, considering. "Or, thirty years after Leonardo's death, it could have already been common knowledge—part of the master's legend."

"Ah," Silvo smiled. "You are a true *entusiasta.*"

"Just wait." I took another sip of wine; the old man eyed me merrily.

"Charles Coppier was the first person to suggest that the painting wasn't actually a portrait of Lisa Gherardini del Giocondo, but an idealized woman. Of course, later scholars objected that it could easily be both a portrait and an idealized interpretation by Leonardo. So that theory was quickly torn to shreds.

"Still, by casting doubt on the traditional identification of La Gioconda, Coppier opened a floodgate of 'interpretation,'" which I signaled with air quotes.

Silvo seemed amused.

"Since then, there have been a lot of theories, mostly from historians who want to believe that the Lisa was of nobler birth," I went on. "Isabella d'Este, the Marquise of Mantua, had tried to persuade Leonardo to paint her portrait for almost ten years. Other people think that the sitter is either the wife or maybe one of several mistresses of Giuliano de'Medici. But if that's the case, then the portrait was painted not in Florence, but in Rome.

"In all, about half a dozen women have been suggested as the real Lisa. But the evidence always falls short in one way or another. And then, of course, there's the idea that it's actually a portrait of Leonardo's mother, Caterina, and that's why he kept the painting for the rest of his life.

"Still most scholars lean toward the traditional view that *La Gioconda* is a portrait of Lisa Gherardini. But people will always speculate, because that's half the fun." I took a sip of wine. "Like you said, people take pleasure in mysteries."

The old man nodded sagely. "And what do you think, my friend? Who do you think is the real Madonna Lisa?"

I lifted my shoulders. "I don't know. I'm not a scholar, just an *entusiasta*."

"*Va bene,*" he said, fixing me with a complex stare. "Who do you want it to be? If you could make it be whoever you choose, who for you would be the real Gioconda?"

I considered Silvo's question for a minute, all the while fixed with his unblinking gaze. "Lisa Gherardini," I said at last.

"*Perche?*"

"There's something satisfying in the idea that the most famous face in the world is that of a merchant's wife, rather than a noblewoman or a nobleman's mistress. She was just a regular person, like you and me." I faltered there, of course, remembering of a sudden that I was sitting with the Count of Vinci. Silvo noticed, chuckled, and reached for the carafe of wine.

"Sorry," I said.

"*Sta niente,*" he answered with a tip of his hand. He proceeded to fill both of our glasses with the last of the second carafe, and leaned back, his legs crossed at the knee, hands webbed across his belly.

Finally, Silvo raised a single finger. "Do you know this, my friend: Lisa Gherardini's mother was a Del Caccio. This means her family was from the Val de Greve. This place is only—*boh*—ten *chilometri* from here."

"I did not know that," I answered.

"*Si,*" he said affirmatively. "This, I think, is the reason Leonardo put so much beauty into *La Gioconda,* and why he never parted with it: because the face of Lisa Gherardini is the face of his own people, his own home. Those other women —" he waved them away one at a time—"*da* Mantua, *da* Milano, *da* Roma. These were not women who could capture Leonardo's heart or inspire his hand. No. *La Gioconda* has a face that touched Leonardo very deeply. *Ha capito?*"

"It's a good theory."

At that the old man uncrossed his legs and sat forward, setting an elbow light on the table. "What if I tell you is more than a theory?" he said.

"I don't understand."

Silvo brought his hand down deliberately on the leather portfolio. "What if I tell you I have proof that she is the real Madonna Lisa?"

I glanced at his hand. "If you have that proof, why would you tell me?"

"You are a writer. And you are *entusiasta.* We can help each other."

I eyed Silvo skeptically; he smiled back without moving his hand from the portfolio. Inevitably, my pulse quickened at the thought of some new thread of evidence to add to the fabric of Leonardiana. After all, even a vague implication about the "real" Mona Lisa was the kind of thing that could make a career. I'd be a fool not to be thrilled. But I didn't want Silvo to know that—assuming he didn't already. Eventually I shrugged, trying to hide my excitement. "I'd have to see what you've got."

"*Certo,*" the old man answered, shifting the manuscript at his right hand to the center of the table. "I have the personal *diario di Francesco del Giocondo.*"

"That's not possible," I scoffed.

"Is possible, my friend," he said, sitting back and sipping his wine. "And is true."

I looked at the portfolio, about an inch thick. "It's awfully small."

Silvo grinned. "My friend, I would not carry such a treasure with me. This is just a translation."

"Your translation?"

"*Si.*" He remained back in his chair, watching me like a hawk. "Now you see why I need a writer, to make the words more— *simpatico.*"

"Not if you want to publish in Italian."

Silvo shook his head. "This is no good. I do not want to publish in Italia."

My hands rose automatically in a questioning gesture. I'd been in Italy for more than a week, after all.

"In Italia, Leonardo is a national treasure. *Allora,* all things that have to do with Leonardo are monitored very closely by the government." Silvo huffed with disdain. "Even to show this manuscript in Italia would bring a *mal' de testa* from the Minister of Culture. *Forse,* they tell me I have no right to publish. *Forse,* they allow me to publish, but they tax me for the right to publish what is mine. Either way, they find a way to steal the *diario.* And again, Vinci's treasures will be taken from us. No." The old man shook his head. "Of this, I want none. *Capito?*"

In fact I did understand. And my mouth was practically watering at the chance to get my hands on the manuscript. In Miriam's words, this was something to inspire me. "What's in it?" I asked.

Silvo grinned. "Francesco, he was a silk merchant. From a family of silk merchants. Some of the entries are about his business dealings in Italia and Francia: how much of this was sold to that man; what happened at the family's office in Lyon. Good for *un storico,* but a little boring, eh?"

A wave of disappointment swept over me. A minute earlier we'd been talking about La Gioconda—and now the trade secrets of a fifteenth century burgher. This was definitely not where I wanted the conversation to go. Silvo must have seen my face drop, though, because he moved quickly to reassure.

"Is more than that, my friend, don't worry," he said. "*In fatti,* Francesco del Giocondo was a man of passion. Let me ask: what do you know of the man?"

"Very little," I answered.

"Let me tell you," he repeated, "Francesco del Giocondo was an extraordinary man living in extraordinary times. Times of great turmoil in Firenze. He was a businessman, yes. But also a politician, a lover, even a poet of sorts. Not on the level of Leonardo, of course. *Ma dai,*" Silvo exclaimed, "Neither was any other man!

"Did you know this? When his father died, Francesco was made head of the family business, even though he was the youngest son. This is something very important in Italia." Sivo nodded his head gravely. "It means this man was a man of great substance."

"I understand," I said. "But is there anything in the manuscript other than business?"

"*Certo,*" the old man answered. "He lived a full life—sometimes happy, sometimes tragic. Francesco buried two women before marrying Lisa; he writes of both of them with great feeling. He also served in the Signoria during the conflicts between the Medici and Savonarola. He was faithful to the Medici, but at one time respectful of the friar. He was a very powerful man, and also a very thoughtful man. He was a patron of the arts, which is how he commissioned Leonardo, and he was a man of great honor. All of these are things that people do not know of the husband of Mona Lisa. In his own time Francesco del Giocondo was one of the great men in Firenze."

"And the painting?"

"*Si,* is in the manuscript."

"What does it say?"

Silvo smiled. "See for yourself, my friend."

An hour later I was rushing across the hot piazza to catch the last bus back to Florence—with Silvo's portfolio clutched in my hand. Though the early afternoon had dragged, once I started reading Francesco's diary the day melted like one of those awful Dali paintings. When I realized it was already half past four, I barely had time to tell Silvo that I'd meet him in Vinci the next day to discuss just what to do with the manuscript. In the meantime, I had to get back to my wife, the literary agent.

I clambered up into the bus just ahead of the accelerator and staggered down the aisle, woozy from the wine and heat, giddy with discovery and ambition. I flopped down in a double seat near the back, directly across from the same European tourists who'd been sitting in Silvo's restaurant when I arrived. The portfolio lay beside me on the seat; I was shaking with adrenaline. This was better than anything I could have imagined happening in Vinci—or, frankly, on my honeymoon.

Of course, it wasn't the actual manuscript, as Silvo had said. In fact, it might not have been the entire translation—but enough to give the reader (me) an idea of the man who'd commissioned the

Mona Lisa. And what a man! Thoughtful, practical, sometimes poetic, sometimes wry. Francesco came across as a man of commerce
and a man of politics, but also a lover of beauty and a passionate lover of women. Here was the untold story behind the world's greatest
painting, and I was getting a first reading.

All through that reading, I'd glanced anxiously at Silvo, who
quietly worked his way through the third carafe that Carolena had
brought to our table—as though it was the most normal thing in
the world to be reading a manuscript from the fifteenth century. But
when I told him that my wife actually worked in the book business,
Silvo sat forward with enthusiasm.

"You think this is something she will want?" he asked.

"It's possible."

I took a sip of my wine, and in the process glanced my watch.

"Oh shit!" I said, suddenly grasping that I was about to miss the
last bus back to Florence. "I have to go."

A look of concern swept Silvo's face; for the first time since I met
him he seemed at a loss as to what to do. There was no question that
I was leaving immediately, and I could see the old man angling for a
way to salvage the opportunity that fate had placed before him. All
at once he thrust the portfolio toward me.

"Take," he said. "Have your book business wife read this. Come
back tomorrow. We will talk again." I had no time to answer because
in that second I was off the terrace and scrambling across the piazza.

Now, seated in the back of the bus among the sandaled, bestock-
inged Europeans, I was the one who could hardly believe the opportunity that fate had given me. After years of languishing through
awful projects and writer's block, I'd finally discovered something to
move me again. At last, I knew the book I wanted to write; its impetus was sitting peacefully on the seat beside me.

With secret thrill, I picked up the manuscript and began reading
again from page one…

The Domestic Chronicle of Francesco del Giocondo, Merchant of Florence

February 21, 1495—In the name of the Father, the Son, and the Holy Spirit, praise be to Our Lady of Heaven, Mother of God, Matron of all the Earth and the Saints of Paradise. In this year of the Lord 1495, I, Francesco del Giocondo, being a descendant of Zanobi di Iacopo del Giocondo, whose son Bartolomeo del Giocondo was my own father, set out to write this diary wherein I shall put down a record of the secrets of my heart and the affairs of my life.

Being all my life a man who is principally concerned with business, I have never before thought of keeping record of my personal affairs. But the events of these last seasons are a trouble on my mind and a burden on my heart. I have been advised by my great friend, M_____, that a man who can divest himself of troubles in no other way may use the pen for refuge and release. For truth, I do not believe him. But my sadness has become so heavy that I am willing to endeavor anything to unburden myself. I pray to God that it will do good, for I can not conceive of living longer with such sorrow in my heart.

—————

March 11, 1495—Today, Antonmaria Gherardini gives me a farm in the San Silvestri as dowry for the marriage of his daughter. I make note of this bequest because my soon-to-be father by law has made a great sacrifice in granting this dowry, his second most precious possession in the world, along with his beloved daughter. And this despite the fact that the value of the farm is a pittance for a man as rich as me. It is a laudable, honorable thing he does, and for that reason I shall cherish this property for as long as I live. He is a fine man. There can be no doubt that I am gaining a wife of noble spirit. And beautiful too. Though barely more than a child, the flower of her beauty lies aching to bloom. I'm certain that within a short time I will be blessed with a beautiful wife. Why can I feel no happiness this day?

—◦∿◦—

March 20, 1495—The girl, my wife, Lisa, is established in our home on Via della Stufa since the day after the wedding. Once again, Antonmaria Gherardini acquitted himself with the utmost honor. From the ceremony at the Baptistry to the marriage celebration in his humble home, the day proceeded with strict deference to custom. This is not a trifle. These days in Florence, lack of decorum runs rampant, even among the noble families. This common lack of respect for ritual is a blight on our culture, even if the Signoria gives its consent. It is true that the Gherardini are not among the first class of the nobility, but the patriarch's manner is beyond reproach. I, for one, would rather have that than the best name in all of Italy. I think that I will come to love this man, my father-in-law, very much.

—◦∿◦—

March 25, 1495—Giovanni di Mariotto Rucellai came to my studio to offer his congratulations. He explained with earnestness that his family is related in a distant way to the Gherardini, a fact that I have been always aware of. This marks the first time I have seen Giovanni since well before Camilla's death. I recall now the dispute we had over Giovanni's wish to have my wife's portrait commissioned to Luca Signorelli. Like his grandfather, Giovanni has a fancy for artists that was, in my opinion, not entirely appropriate. I had seen Signorelli's *School of Pan*, which was commissioned by Il Magnifico, and it seemed to me heathen and obscene. Savonarola would disapprove adamantly of such a portrait, and at that time I was very much a devotee of the Frate. I refused absolutely to allow Camilla to sit for that man, especially with my child in her belly. I told Giovanni that no wife of mine would ever be painted thus, with such naked carnality. It is an offense against God, I told him, as Fra Girolamo says. Giovanni scoffed at me. He was never a follower of Savonarola, and in fact still seeks the return of the Medici. We argued, more heatedly than was necessary, and Giovanni left in anger. Months later, Camilla was dead without having seen her brother again. It has pained me to know that my prejudice against an artist, no matter how vulgar, cost Giovanni Rucellai the chance to see his sister. Though it does nothing to limit my shame, I'm happy he came to see me. Perhaps at least one of the wounds inflicted in my life, upon myself and others, can begin to heal.

April 3, 1495—Despite my doubtful expectations, Lisa's arrival has been a pleasing surprise, of a kind. I had anticipated a lengthy term of adjustment for the girl. It cannot be easy for the only child of a country noble to be delivered into a household such as mine, filled with two brothers and four sisters, my mother and my son. The poor girl faces generations of Giocondos! How terrible! And worse, as my wife she is assumed to be mistress of this brood. I envy her not.

Yet the girl has taken in with complete calm. Not once have I seen fear in her eyes. Rather, she proceeds wearing the same serene smile I noted on our wedding day. It is a face that beguiles all who look at her. Ha! This is a gift I wish I could teach to the city's diplomats. At the same time, Lisa listens intently, and she speaks wonderfully, in a clear, soft voice that expresses dignity and humility in equal measure. The quiet poise of her father is everywhere present in my new wife's demeanor.

Most impressive is the way she deals with Mona Piera. The girl
stands solid as an oak before my mother, even in a temper. And
I have no illusions but that my mother can be a terrible figure.
I remember well Camilla's first days here. Can it have been
three years ago? Mother of God, how quickly the time passes!
Camilla, at the same age that Lisa is now, was a frightened
dove among these people. Half a year must have passed before
she dared speak to Alessandra or Gherardesca, much less the
frightful Mona Piera!

—◆◆◆—

April 8, 1495—Camilla is much in my thoughts these days,
more than at any time since her death. I know that the reason
is because of my new marriage, as well as the visit paid me by
Giovanni some days ago. It is odd to be thinking of Camilla
once again, more tenderly than I ever did when she was alive.
Because I never loved my wife.

But at that time I knew nothing of love, only business. For
truth, my marriage to Camilla was more a product of business
than of love. She was chosen for me by my father and Mariotto Rucellai, who was not only a member of one of the best
families in Florence, but also a buyer of silks, even in these
dour times. I met Camilla on the day we were married, and
I impregnated her not long after because that was my duty as
a husband and a son, even as heir to my father's business.

What I was not prepared for was the joy I took in having a son.
Bartolomeo made me so happy that I was eager to have more
children, whether or not I loved their mother. But Camilla's
body was ruined by my son's birth, which had been long and
difficult. The women said it was madness to try again so soon,
but I would not be deterred. And so I made Camilla pregnant
again soon after Barto was given to the midwife. Neither she

nor my second child survived. This is my great shame. In my eagerness, in my selfishness, I killed the girl. She wasn't even twenty years old.

—⁓—

April 19, 1495—An unexpected thing has happened. It seems that Lisa has gained the absolute love of my son. I learned this not from the girl herself, for she remains a model of humility, but from my sister Alessandra, who treasures nothing more than spreading petty gossip. Lisa's behavior with Bartolomeo was not presented to me as the bonding of a mother and her new child, but rather as something less fitting. My vile sister claims that my wife and my son carry on unbecomingly, like a pair of playmates.

The next day I left my studio in the middle of the day to see just what was the behavior that had so offended Alessandra. What I saw filled me with cheer. Lisa and Bartolomeo were alone in the courtyard, the servants having evidently been dismissed by their mistress. My son, usually a boy of the strictest good temper and behavior owing to the fact that his upbringing has been supervised by Mona Piera, was chasing pigeons! And not just dawdling after them. Rather, Barto sprinted about the courtyard after the helpless birds like a wild fox at hunt, all the while emitting shrieks of pure delight. On my life, I have never seen that side of my boy. He was giddy with excitement, intoxicated with youthful pleasure.

What's more, it wasn't just my son who was bedeviling the pigeons. Lisa, too, had taken up the chase. And though she ran with somewhat less vigor, hampered as she was by the length of her skirts, she screamed with no less voice and smiled with no less joy than Barto. Needless to say, I had never seen this side of my new wife.

After several minutes of this activity, Lisa, seemingly exhausted by the chase, stepped off to one side. As I watched, she settled slowly to the ground, her skirts billowing like a puff of wind going out of a ship's sail, before gathering around. It was a movement of wonderful grace, revealing a femininity that I had not yet witnessed. I admit that it stirred me in a way that has not happened since Tomassa's death. And that brief, fleeting feeling was enough to bring tears to my eyes.

I began to turn from the courtyard, for I wanted to escape the incipient grief in Lisa's charm. But then something fantastic happened. Bartolomeo, my son, my child, seeing that his playmate had given up the game, let out his greatest peal of laughter and ran across the courtyard into Lisa's arms. She captured him and lifted him and spun like a dancer with my son against her breast. Both laughed with unbridled delight.

And I, in the shadows, who had just been near to weeping at the thought of lost love, suddenly burst in unrestrained laughter. It was the most euphoric type of feeling. Like being washed in happiness.

—◦◦◦—

April 22, 1495—Poor Barto. I did not realize until I saw him at play with Lisa, but my son has been deprived of love for his whole life. Camilla, God bless her soul, was never well enough after his birth to give him the natural love of a mother. And before the boy was two years old, his mother was gone. Thereafter his care has been left to the servants and my mother, and none can speak better than I for the lack of affection obtained in my mother's agency. She has been, as long as I have had conscience to know, a cold, hard woman, unforgiving in nature. I am sure it is the reason why I too have been deficient in showing my son the love he deserves.

And yes, there is the other reason. The one I keep hidden. Yet having merely written Tomassa's name some days ago in this diary, I am unable to escape the memories I have buried under a mountain of shame. My disgraceful acts are piled so high that I feel trapped in the dark. But I must speak of it, if only here. Perhaps then I will be able to dig myself from this grave I have created, and offer Barto the love a father owes his son.

Tomassa had come to my shop only a short time before Giovanni Rucellai came asking for a portrait of his sister. At that time, Camilla was only half of the way through her term. Her body was then beginning to show the signs of nativity, and I am certain that she would have made a beautiful portrait. In fact, Camilla was, by all opinion, a most beautiful girl, with reddish gold hair and fair skin and blue eyes that shone like the sky. In her fertile state, her face glowed like an opal. She was lovely, and I loved her not a bit, for I had fallen utterly under Tomassa's spell. I realize now that when I refused to allow Giovanni to have a portrait painted of his sister, I was answering more to the guilt in my own heart than protecting Camilla from the lewdness of Signorelli. Or adhering to the teaching of Savonarola. Had I not been so desperate to hide my shame, Barto would have some knowledge of his mother's beauty. Instead, he will never know the face of the woman who bore him.

That is enough. I can write no more today.

—◦◦◦—

"That's it?" Miriam asked holding up the whole manuscript, though she'd read only a part of it.

"There may be more, I have to ask Silvo," I said, tipping my shoulders an inch toward my ears.

"The Count of Vinci." Miriam reached past me to grab the wine bottle off the hotel bar, her expression heavy with skepticism.

"I know you think it's weird, but these kinds of things happen here."

"They do?" she asked sarcastically. "Counts come out of the hills with five-hundred-year-old manuscripts that no one has ever seen. Doesn't that sound a little farfetched to you, David?"

"Maybe. But certainly not impossible. And if it is real it's something like the find of the century." Frankly, I couldn't understand why my wife was quashing my excitement.

"More likely your friend Silvo is putting one over on you." Miriam held up the manuscript. "How much did you give him for this?"

"Nothing," I said, grabbing it out of her hand. "In fact he bought me lunch."

My wife rolled her big brown eyes beneath her browner curls. "What?"

"David, in this business if something seems too good to be true, it probably is. And like I told you, it's always the crazies who think they've got the find of the century."

"Like Andrea, I suppose."

Miriam took a thoughtful sip of wine, averting her eyes from me briefly. "Actually, Andrea has a pretty good idea for a cookbook," she said at last.

"Are you kidding me?"

"No," she said, though she looked as surprised as I was. "Of course, he still has to write it, or get someone to write it for him, and it's not so much his story as his mother's. But I have to admit, it really is a good idea."

"What is it?"

"Well, it's not a cookbook per se," Miriam explained. "It will have recipes, but it's almost a memoir. You have no idea what this woman, Lola, has seen and done. Her restaurant was open during Fascism, stayed open all through the war. She served food after the war, when there was almost no food in Europe. And she has all of the recipes. It's like seeing history through a menu.

"Not only that, but she served *everybody*. Picasso ate there; Toscanini, Fellini, Mastroianni. Andrea says that Victor Emanuel even

came in once, for coffee, after he'd abdicated but before he was ex-
iled. I can't believe Olivia never mentioned any of this."

"Almost sounds too good to be true," I said flatly.

"This is different," she said.

"I'd love to hear how." The first currents of anger were heating
my skin.

Miriam sat back and folded her arms beneath her breasts, making them rise perceptibly. "This is what I do for a living, David. Trust
me, everyone thinks they have a book in them, everyone thinks they
have a great idea. But there really aren't that many great ideas out
there, and pretty often the worst people are full of passionate intensity, as the man said. My job is to tell the difference between
the cranks and the real thing." She uncrossed her arms and laid her
hands palms-down on the bar. "I admit that when I first met Andrea
I thought he was a crank. But he came through with a great idea.
Why can't you just be happy that I found this?"

"I am!" I snapped. "Why can't you be happy that I found *this?*"
I held the manuscript by its spine above the bar.

"Fine," Miriam said, as if giving in. "If you're that excited about
it, I'll talk to some people when we get back to New York."

"I told Silvo you'd meet with him," I said.

"When?"

"Tomorrow. In Vinci."

My wife recrossed her arms and fixed me with a stare. "David.
We have a train to Venice at ten."

"So we'll get another train. Venice isn't going anywhere."

"It's sinking, actually," Miriam said saucily.

"By Friday?"

My wife took another long sip of wine. "You seriously want to
change our honeymoon—the honeymoon my father bought us before he died—for this *nonsense?*" She flipped at the edge of the manuscript with naked contempt.

That seemed a low blow. And finally I was mad. "I can't fucking
believe you," I hissed. "We've spent hours doing your business on

this honeymoon, but you can't give me one day for something that's important to me."

"Funny," she answered demurely. "I thought that's what I did *today*."

Miriam turned so her back formed a right angle with the bar, and I could tell from behind that she was trying not to cry. Since her father's death, any mention of him drove her to strong emotions. Yet my wife was anything but a crier; in fact I'd only seen it once, on the day her father told us he was dying. Thereafter, even at the funeral, she shed tears only in private.

"Mir, listen to me," I consoled. "You were the one who told me I had to find something to inspire me, something that would make me want to write again. This is something that makes me want to do that."

"No it's not," she said, shaking her head. Miriam turned halfway toward me. "Can't you understand, David, this is a hoax. Whoever this 'Silvo' person is, he's not on the level. He waits in Vinci for people, like you, who are fascinated with Leonardo, then he tells you this romantic story about his noble birth and his current straits, and oh by the way he's got a priceless manuscript that just happens to link him with da Vinci himself. On top of all that, Silvo is so generous he's willing to cut you in on the opportunity of a lifetime.

"It's a false hope, David," Miriam said seriously. "He's a con man preying on your poetic notion of the world. And it's only a matter of time before this Prince of Vinci asks you for some seed money to keep him going…against the millions the two of you are sure to get for the manuscript."

"Count," I said abashedly. "He's the Count of Vinci."

"Of course he is." Miriam reached up and touched my face; her sympathy made me foolish. "You have a romantic soul, David," she said flatly. "That's why you *should* be a writer. But you want it to be easy. You want a book to just fall into your lap. It doesn't work that way." She took her hand back.

At that moment I realized it was not my wife but my agent talking—and she was offering a vote of no-confidence in her writer. All at once tears welled in my eyes and rolled down my cheeks. I was too ashamed to answer, yet too humiliated to leave. So I just sat there staring at Miriam through tears till she wiped my eyes with a soiled napkin, and we went up to our room to pack.

The next day we were on a train out of Florence. Not to Vinci, of course, but east through the Apennines—a rather glum affair compared to our happy journey up the coast from Rome. Miriam sat across from me flanked by an enormous handbag she'd bought at one of the leather shops near Santa Croce, and for most of the trip remained preoccupied by email. I, on the other hand, suffered the morning wedged between a window and the huge suitcase of a Canadian teenager who was touring Europe for graduation. I felt no desire to read or write or even take in the scenery of eastern Tuscany, but contented myself with being distant and miserable, the perfect antithesis of my diligent, fulfilled wife.

Still, we proceeded without incident until somewhere around Ferrara, where the train came to a stop for more than an hour. I was beginning to wonder if we were going to be stranded in the countryside when suddenly the whole crew—conductors, ticket-takers, and serving staff together—came parading through the train waving signs and chanting something musical in unison. At the end of the phrase, someone yelled out, "Show pero!" and the others echoed in kind.

At the time, of course, I had no idea what they were talking about. But fortunately the whole show was over in only a few more minutes, and the crew resumed their posts as if nothing had happened. It was, I decided, just another cheap piece of Italian theater.

From there we got without further delay (though neither without hurry, it must be said), approaching Venice by shadowy, painstaking degrees. Whereas Lazio and Tuscany had seemed miracles of light, the Po Valley was a fairly dreary experience. Mist set in when crossed Emilio-Romagna and the rains arrived in earnest as we descended Veneto, where the wine-dark sea asserts its abysmal influence. Or maybe it was just me. In my bleak mood, I could practically feel the bad tidings lapping at my heels.

By late afternoon we were finally making our approach to the island via the long causeway that crosses the Venetian lagoon. Across the water, a line of deserted piles pierced the surface as though awaiting naval companionship, and a blonde boy shouted *"Aiuto!"* while his parents meticulously ignored his difficulties with his jacket.

By the time the train reached the terminal—a concrete monolith which modernist style seemed prominently out of place amid the Baroque stones of the Old Republic—my wife was obviously irritable. I did my best to gather our bags and hustle her out to something more pleasing. But when Miriam and I emerged from the gray light of the station we were greeted by a chill wind that seemed to foretell storm. I wanted nothing but to check into our hotel, grab a quick dinner, and put the whole awful day behind me. Little did I know what was waiting at the hotel on an unimposing three-by-five-inch notecard.

"Che la un messagio per la signora," intoned the elaborately mustachioed master of the hotel, whose name, it appeared, was Robert.

"English, please," I answered.

"Si," he said, adjusting his glasses. "There is a message for …" he hesitated a moment in looking for the right relation. "Your wife."

I shot a nasty look at Miriam that she ignored completely as she took the card from the maitre d' and made straight for our room.

The message, inevitably, was from Andrea Bardani, which fact Miriam revealed with a little bit of prodding. Funny that she seemed neither surprised nor annoyed. I was.

"How did he know where we were staying?" I asked.

My wife rolled her head in a gesture of blatancy.

"You told him?"

"It must've just slipped out," she said, retreating to the bathroom.

"How does something like that 'slip out' when you're talking about his big book idea?"

Her head poked back around the corner of the doorway, big curls in a top knot wagging like a poodle's tail. This was, of course, at a range of about five feet, as the whole room was no bigger than an albatross. Venice is perhaps the only city in the world where space comes at a higher premium than in New York. Thus, for a considerable sum we were letting what amounted to a glorified closet.

Miriam shrugged and went on. "It was lunch. There was wine. We talked," she said. "It's the kind of thing I do with writers all the time. Even writers I don't like. And Andrea is quite charming when he wants to be. That's not a bad trait in this business, believe it or not."

"What the hell is that supposed to mean?" I asked, getting, admittedly, a bit red in the face.

Miriam put her hands on her hips. "What I mean," she said sensibly, "Is that an engaging personality can be an *asset* to a writer who is trying to *sell books*. Kind of like having an interesting subject, or at least an idea that isn't completely obscure. You put a nice face on a normal story, give it some sex, a little suspense, a little humor. Those things aren't contingencies, David. They're essential."

"That's bullshit and you know it," I answered. "Tarting up crap just makes people stop and stare. You still have to hold your nose."

"Yeah. They stop, and stare, and *read*."

"It's still shit."

"Well, that shit pays the bills, sweetheart," Miriam said.

This was an issue that had only lately surfaced in our relationship, as Miriam's burgeoning client list began generating bigger commissions. Quite suddenly, my wife had leapt a tax bracket on me. Granted, this wasn't particularly my fault (at least not by my reckoning), as I was in a pretty fixed, 3-percent-a-year career, while she had almost unlimited opportunity to open new revenue streams, provided that she found the right clients. Hence the interest in Andrea Bardani.

And on a certain level I was happy for her. Hell, I even stood to benefit from the fact that she was making money. For instance, upon returning to New York we were scheduled to move in to a brand new condo in a doorman building on the Upper East Side—something we could never have bought on a double-dose of my salary. Even the trip to Italy (largely subsidized by her late father, of course) was more luxury than I could afford. So yes, I appreciated being able to share in Miriam's wealth and success, and I accepted the fact that she'd become the primary bread winner in our family. Still, I didn't need to be reminded of it on my honeymoon, for Christ's sake.

And Miriam, bless her heart, understood that too. "I didn't mean that," she said before I could answer. She took her hands off her hips and came out of the doorway toward me. "I didn't mean that," she repeated. "I'm sorry."

I straightened, trying to find the exact gist in her eyes. (In Venice, even four-star hotels are invariably dim, something to do with antiquity and superfluous water, I'm sure. Suffice it to say, there's no lighting anywhere and even in the daytime you end up straining for a bit of clarity. Nothing like Vinci, QED.)

"I know," I said, reaching out to take her in my arms. "I didn't mean it either."

"Yes you did," she muttered into my chest.

The Domestic Chronicle of Francesco del Giocondo, Merchant of Florence

April 30, 1495—Since witnessing Lisa at play with Barto, I am seeing her differently. Though she maintains an attitude of perfect obedience, I have noticed, on a few occasions, that there is an air of play in her behavior. To look upon her for more than a glance, one is presented with the notion that there is much activity behind that tranquil countenance. By Mary, I almost believe, at times, that she is mocking me with her eyes!

Far from insulting, I find this attitude delightful. More and more, I find myself watching her from afar, acquainting myself with the signature of her gestures and the footprint of her movements. In the back of my mind, I cannot escape the notion that she knows I am watching, and that she performs that clever smile for my eyes. I fear I shall be lost in fascination with the girl.

—⁓—

May 7, 1495—Long before she came into my life, Tomassa Villani was a scandalous figure in Florence. She had been married, at fifteen, to Antonio Cennini, a wealthy gold seller who was widowed at the age of sixty. The marriage was not supported by the Signoria, for it is not the custom for a man of such advanced age to take such a young bride. But Cennini was vain, and lewd. He also had the ear of Il Magnifico. Lorenzo approved the marriage in spite of the Signoria.

It is also true that Tomassa was not considered the most marriageable of girls. Whereas Camilla came from a noble family well represented in the Signoria, Tomassa's father was not among the Buonmini. Neither did Tomassa possess the type of beauty wealthy men look for. Rather, she was dark as an olive, with black curls that gathered about her head like a thorn bush.

Nor was she docile in the way of Camilla Rucellai. Even at an early age, Tomassa was passionate and quick-tempered, with a loose tongue that more than once caused her family scandal. And so, while the marriage was generally disfavored, no one in Florence blamed Villani for giving his daughter to Cennini.

But Tomassa was no great bargain, for rather than taming her, marriage seemed to inflame her further. Like any wild thing, Tomassa chafed under the yoke of decorum. She challenged Cennini at every pass, and took pleasure in rebuking him in public. For a man as vain as he, such behavior was too much to bear. He tried bribing her, but she refused his gifts. He tried beating her, but she defied him more passionately. He tried shaming her, but she was beyond disgrace. He even tried to have the marriage annulled, but the Signoria, flouted once, refused to grant it, and Il Magnifico withheld his support. Finally, there was nothing the old man could do but confine his wife to the palazzo.

When Cennini at last left this earth, Tomassa had been quarantined for more than a dozen years, with none for company but her servants and the friar who took her confessions. Still the years had done nothing to tame her. This I learned when, mere weeks after her husband's death, Tomassa came brazenly to my studio accompanied by none but her maid. Years had passed her by sartorially, for Cennini, out of meanness, refused to buy her new fashions. Thus she appeared before me in a dress that was many years old.

Yet despite confinement and the antiquated gown, the years had been kind to Tomassa. Her skin, still olive, had not wrinkled even a little, and her hair remained abundant as the lilies of the field. Because she was childless, and rich, her body had gained a ripeness not often seen among the women of Florence. She had never been pregnant, of course. Few believed that

Cennini had the courage to bed her, yet none could credit her a virgin at thirty. She was a woman of magnificent vigor. I blush still to think of the heat that came over me that day. I dare say I was in love before she spoke the first word.

—⁊⁊⁊—

May 17, 1495—I have had a gown made for Lisa. It is green satin, with a full skirt and short train and bodice inset with gold damask, all trimmed in golden silk threads. These come from my very own prized stock, reserved for only a few families in all of Florence. It is far too lavish for these austere times, as the Frate frowns on Florentines who take pride or pleasure in beautiful things. I paid the tailor handsomely for his discretion. When the gown was presented to her, my wife could not help but lose her usual calm. In fact, she lit up like a wild moon. It gives me great pleasure to see that reaction from her, and to know that I was the cause of it.

—⁊⁊⁊—

May 20, 1495—Despite his hatred of her, Cennini did a curious thing. He left Tomassa the majority of his fortune, more than enough to make her the richest woman in Florence. Though the old man's sons had preceded him to the grave, there were others among his family he could have made rich. Yet he chose Tomassa. Was it the old man's pride at not wanting to admit his mistake in taking her for his wife? No. It was revenge, in my opinion. In return for refusing him annulment, Cennini loosed Tomassa on Florence with his vast wealth. This, he knew, would be a force as uncontrollable as death itself.

So Tomassa came to me rich and in need of enough silk to make up for twelve years of neglected dressmaking. Her eyes burned through me. Her first words were, "So, Giocondo, I think we will be seeing much of each other."

We did. From that day Tomassa came to my studio every week for two months to select the best silks I had in stock, despite Savonarola's prohibitions. She wasn't to be cowed by a simple friar. Always, Tomassa appeared at my studio unannounced, at random times, as though hoping to catch me off my guard. First she was accompanied by her maid. This was a welcome thing to me, for whenever Tomassa was in my studio I found myself to be agitated beyond reason. It was only the presence of the servant, I was certain, that kept me from losing my senses completely.

Then one day Tomassa appeared without her maid. When I inquired after the girl, Tomassa didn't answer. She merely looked at me from the side of her eye and continued running her long hands across my fabrics. This was troubling to me, but I could think of nothing to say. Tomassa went on inspecting the silks for several minutes. After a time, she faced me directly, her dark eyebrows arched, a slight smile to one side of her lips. "Why do you ask of my girl, Giocondo? Do you lust after her?"

Though I had been anxious throughout her visit, when Tomassa spoke the last, brazen words I was made so ill at ease that I wanted to escape my own studio never to return. She, of course, was calm as low tide. I could not understand how she could speak to me thus, with outright authority. She was a woman, and in fact only a few years older than me. I was already a successful merchant, destined, I was sure, to serve in the Signoria in my time. Yet Tomassa spoke to me in the tone of a queen to her subject. I was both paralyzed and enchanted by her.

As she prepared to leave, Tomassa once more addressed me. "So Giocondo. Shall I bring my girl with me the next time I visit?"

I answered, "As you please, signora." I never saw Tomassa's maid-servant in my studio again, though her mistress came more often than ever. And within weeks she became my mistress as well.

—⁓—

May 25, 1495—Bernardo del Nero held a ball for the feast of Saint Zenobius. It was, by the standards of the day, a lavish entertainment, attended by all the knights and the Buonomi, as well as many great ladies and beautiful girls. Lisa was among them for the first time since we married. The girl was, in fact, dazzling in the gown I'd made for her, along with an emerald medallion and ear pieces that matched her eyes. My young wife comported herself with excellent poise, though I could tell she was nervous as a hummingbird. I have heard it said that Bernardo spent as much as 8,000 florins on the ball.

It was also the first time I was invited to dine with Buonomi since Camilla's death. My affair with Tomassa cast a dark shadow over me, particularly in the early days of Savonarola's rule. Tomassa's infamy was enough to exclude me from the company of the great families, to say nothing of the rumors surrounding her frequent visits to my studio. It was hardship for both my honor and my business to be so proscribed, but at the time Tomassa was there to soften the ignominy. When she was taken from me, it was necessary to marry Lisa immediately. My business and my honor demanded rapprochement with the friar and the Buonomi. This could only be achieved by marriage to a respectable girl of noble birth, to expunge the memory of my liaison with Tomassa. I did what I had to do. Now I am once again permitted audience and commerce with the great families of the city. My marriage is a success, though it is a betrayal of my love. Forgive me Tomassa.

—⁓—

As a northern city, Venice is notoriously *pronto*—which is to say that the dinner rush begins before sundown and ends during mid-evening. It's a pretty small window, really, and reservations are strictly required. You never go to a Venetian restaurant expecting to be seated after ten unless you want all you can stand of the local ill humor. Thus the sun was just fading when Miriam and I boarded a gondola on one of the inner canals, supposedly for a romantic trip to a someplace called Il Bacino, where a table had been arranged for us courtesy of Olivia Winters (nee Bardani).

The gondola was of course an extravagance, as the restaurant was barely a quarter mile away, but it seemed a necessary gesture at the time—both to soothe my wounded ego and to salvage a bit of the marital bliss that had frittered out of our Italian honeymoon. Therefore, I shelled out about a hundred bucks to have a rude oarsman pole us a whole ten minutes across the back canals, alternately cursing other gondoliers and singing what was, I was sure, a vulgar ballad in the general direction of my new wife. Like so many things in Italy—as I was learning—the reality isn't as romantic as its reputation.

Il Bacino, on the other hand, was impossibly romantic—a peculiar blend of Oriental sensibility and Old World charm that reflected impeccably its exotic setting. We were seated, immediately, at a table overlooking the Grand Canal, which cut the cityscape cleanly in two. In the middle distance, palazzos rose like basilisks against the sapphire sky while the last needles of sunset wilted over Lido Island, where, I recalled, Giacomo Casanova had once seduced a beautiful, bald nun. I mentioned this queer bit of trivia to Miriam; she smiled inscrutably and dipped a piece of bread in balsamic vinegar.

We ordered antipasti and secondi, forgoing for this meal, at least, the pasta dish. Miriam got a course of risotto di go and Fegato al Venezia (calf liver and onions, the signature dish of Venetian cuisine). I was a bit baffled by the menu, but started with sardines in soar and ended with Black Sepe—cuttlefish cooked in its own ink.

These seemed the kinds of things I ought to try, given the aquatic ambiance, though in the end I regretted both choices.

At some point between the sepia and the brine, my thoughts turned to an earlier dinner. Only three days past, the meal we'd eaten at Lola's in Settignano already seemed as quaint as ancient history. By comparison, Il Bacino was operatic—a bonfire of vanities inflamed by waiters as mannered as their mise en scene. Frankly, it was a little much, even for my poetic sensibilities. Lola's, by contrast, had been rough and rustic, a muddle of domestic chaos and mandolin charm. To my surprise, I found myself recalling that earlier supper with something like longing.

"What's going on with you *now?*" Miriam asked, eyeing me across our entrees. Of course she'd noticed my abstraction. "Is this still about Andrea?"

Was it?

"Just tired," I lied.

Miriam laughed, though not without sympathy. "You poor thing. That cuttlefish is going to do you in."

I laughed as well, though with less soul than my wife. "I don't know what I was thinking," I sighed. "Who the hell do I think I am?"

"It doesn't matter," she said, taking my hand atop the table. "I love you just the same."

With that, dinner at Il Bacino was pretty much over. From there, Miriam and I walked all of five minutes back to the hotel, and after a sad patch of cursory lovemaking, fell asleep before midnight—keeping veritable banker's hours on the first night of the third leg of our honeymoon.

The Domestic Chronicle of Francesco del Giocondo, Merchant of Florence

June 20, 1495—The silk trade is better than it has been for more than a year. Even with the Frate's restrictions on personal adornment, our business is once again prosperous. Giocondo and Giuliano are especially pleased, relieved even, as my brothers both had despaired that my behavior in the aftermath of Camilla's death would ruin us, at the very least. Other possible consequences were banishment, or worse.

Of course, Lisa is to credit for my remission, both in theory and reality. My marriage to her, after the scandal of my liaison with the widow of Cennini, signaled a return to respectability for myself and my trade. And Lisa has proved an accomplished wife both inside and outside of our home. It is not easy to assume the mantle of mistress of the house at only sixteen years, but she has done so with the assurance of a woman twice her age. She now runs the household completely, with little objection from any save Mona Piera, which cannot be remedied by God himself. She has also proved a fine society wife. Since the Neri ball, we have appeared in public together on several occasions, and always my wife represents me with the greatest propriety.

That was the problem with Tomassa. She had no esteem for propriety. Though our affair had begun before Camilla's death, once we were two widows there should have been a way to form a respectable marriage. The Signoria would certainly have approved, if only to end a scandal. My business and my honor would have been rightly restored with little hardship. Yet Tomassa would not consider it. Florence is not Venice, I said to her. The people would not tolerate us. But Tomassa refused to be ruled by any man. Twelve years of captivity were enough. She was a free, and would do as she pleased.

Worse yet, she did. Tomassa had the most lavish gowns hewn from the silks I sold her, and insisted upon parading in public thus adorned. On the street, Savonarola's holy tramps harassed her for her vanity, and once even assaulted her in broad daylight, stealing a string of pearls for the coffers of San Marco. None defended her. Still Tomassa would not relent, appearing the next day with the same extravagance enhanced by a gold-handled dagger. When the gamin came to harass her once again, Tomassa took half an ear from one in compensation for her pearls. By God, such a woman will never exist again!

—⁓⁓—

July 18, 1495—Today we celebrate Lisa's nativity. My wife is now seventeen years old, and grows more beautiful by the day. Barto is completely in love with her. He cries when the maids take him to bathe or bed, and will not sleep until Lisa comes to his room to bid him good night. She likewise has become singularly attached to my son. Her face lights with equal fire when he is in the room, and the attention of either never strays far from the other during the day. I am told that Lisa neglects everything when Barto is ill, taking his care upon herself above the servants and even Mona Piera.

Perhaps this is because Lisa also was the only child of her parents, raised without the amity of siblings. Though she is familiar and gracious with everyone in the house, as I am assured by the tenaciously verbose Alessandra, she and Barto have formed a discrete bond within the household. How strange and wonderful it is that my son and my wife seem to have found in one another the companionship each has sorely needed.

—⁓⁓—

July 19, 1495—Antonmaria Gherardini, my father-in-law, took me aside yesterday during the celebration for Lisa's nativity. Always a most tactful man, Antonmaria was at pains to introduce the subject of prospective grandchildren. I sense now that his daughter has informed him that I, her husband, have yet to summon her to my bed. Under the guise of a proud and happy father, Antonmaria pledged his honor upon his daughter's virginity, as well as her readiness for the marriage bed. Like Barto's, Lisa's mother died when she was very young. However, Antonmaria assured me that his servant women have tutored the girl fully on her wifely responsibilities. He assured me, furthermore, that all signs from the girl's birth indicate that she will be fertile and healthful in childbearing. In this last, I detected a note of understanding at Camilla's passing, now almost a year on. Once again my father-in-law marks himself, undeniably, as a man of honor and good faith. Though I do wonder what Lisa has told him, and how.

I was quick to assure Antonmaria that I had no questions about his daughter's honor or her fitness as a wife. I told him that I was observing a full year's mourning for Camilla, who died in July of last year. I did not know if he believed me, for it is almost certain that even a country noble like Gherardini would have heard rumor of my liaison with Tomassa. Yet true to his dignified nature, he betrayed not a hint of doubt. In fact, he commended my devotion to Camilla, and agreed that such a period of mourning is proper to observe. At that, something in his face told me he was thinking of Lisa's mother, who had been taken from him so many years ago.

After a short, quiet moment had passed between us, Antonmaria lifted his eyes and fixed me with a fatherly gaze. "But you must allow the mourning to end, Francesco," he said. My heart flooded with love for the man, because at that moment I knew he did not speak of Camilla.

—◦∾◦—

July 24, 1495—Today it is one year since Camilla's death. Accompanied by my mother, I took Barto to visit her grave for the first time. But the boy remembers nothing of his mother, and is too young to understand the solemnity of the occasion. He is nearly impossible to contain in such a situation, for these days he sees any excursion as an opportunity for play. His freedom with Lisa has awakened the child in him to both pleasant and trying ends. He bristles under the care of Mona Piera, and of course she bristles back with equal vigor. All this made for a rather pathetic outing, as none of the three mourners seemed to care a fig for the poor dead woman beneath us.

This anniversary brings another matter in my life to a head. My stated mourning period having passed, it will be ever more difficult for me to elude my husbandly duties with regard to Lisa, who despite her usual grace cannot hide her eagerness to be accepted as my wife. How can I be with this girl after all that has happened in the last year? Is there some compassionate way to explain to her that our marriage was arranged, by my brothers, for no other reason than to restore my reputation and salvage the livelihood of my family? How much does she already understand? And even if I can find some kindness to express these circumstances, I do not know what effect the truth will have on her. To be told that she is meant as the saving grace for a family, and a family of supposedly better standing than her own humble origins. It could crush her or enflame her, but there is no way of knowing which.

It is better, in the end, to uphold the charade, even to my wife. This week, or next, I must consummate my marriage.

July 28, 1495—After more than four months of marriage, I bade Lisa come to my bedchamber last night. For all the girl's charms, I did so with a heavy heart, for it was only slightly more time since I promised Tomassa never to love another.

The girl, my wife, was lovely and obedient, docile and fearful and eager. The act was not altogether unpleasant for her, nor for me, as it had been when I'd lain with Camilla the first night of our marriage. Lisa is very different from Camilla, a fact that I am understanding by small degrees. Yet after love with Tomassa, wedded or not, the thought of laying with another young wife chosen for her name rather than her person appealed to me very little.

Camilla, a Rucellai by birth, came to our marriage little more than a child. My father deemed it great accomplishment to have bargained such a wife for me. As did I, for in those times I too judged love less dear than business, and a connection to the Rucellais would ensure the fortunes of the Giocondos for generations. I lay with Camilla without delay to seal the pact that had been drawn between our families. We performed the act in the most modest fashion, either for tradition or nescience, or perhaps because of the then-novel yet powerful influence of the Frate, who preached vehemently against all earthly pleasure, even between spouses. She had come to my bedchamber clothed in a silken dressing gown, a gift, I'm sure, from my own family. This I raised discretely as I lay atop her fragile, childlike frame inserting myself with ungentle pressure. She clenched and sobbed through the act, trying not to cry out from the strange pain inside her. Camilla bled dutifully, and withdrew immediately after my spasm, to finally cry, I suppose. And I, no more satisfied, was glad to have her go.

With Tomassa love was very different. It was she, not I, who pursued and captured. When she first began coming to my studio alone, Tomassa made great display of following my movements with her keen eyes, like a hawk stalking prey. She was more carnal than any woman I have ever met. Inevitable as fate, implacable as inspiration. That is how Tomassa approached me. It was all too soon I found myself drowned in her gaze, and locked in her arms.

But being with Tomassa was nothing like the difficult nights with Camilla. For Tomassa was nothing of a girl, but a full formed woman, rounded and fleshly where Camilla had been lean and frail. So too, Tomassa was as fervent as the wind. In the act of love, she became if anything more free. Her whole body sought pleasure in mine, and she signaled her delights and gratifications with expressions arrayed between a mouse's squeak and the roar of a tigress. It was a paradox I had no way to anticipate. Camilla, as pure a girl as could be imagined, was vexing in the bedchamber. And though an utter devil of a woman, Tomassa was love divine.

Lisa is something between them, naturally, neither wretched nor wanton. And though I could not take her with my whole heart, I will admit that her graceful disposition coupled with this amenity in the bedchamber deepens my fondness for her. Am I so fickle that I can already love another, and Tomassa not six months dead?

—⁓—

Venice is a fantasy and a riddle, an endless fugue, an optical illusion, an orgy of vitality, a nightmare of echoes and ghosts and silhouettes and piss, all retreating beneath the ripples of the pitch black Adriatic. Miriam and I had a little less than three days to take in this chaotic, exotic abundance before we had to be back on a train to Rome and a plane to New York. By afternoon we'd dined at Harry's Bar and mingled in St. Mark's Square, crossed the Rialto and climbed the campanile, explored the Doge's Palace and wondered at the Bridge of Sighs. The rest of the afternoon was reserved for the Gallerie dell'Academmia, with its grand Bellinis, wastrel Titians, and Tintoretto's *Miracle of St. Mark*, just one of many works dedicated to the city's patron saint who seems to touch everything living and dead in Venice. And, like everything else, an object of sullen beauty cloaked in shadow.

Fortunately, I suppose, the Academmia didn't have the appeal of the Uffizi for either of us (no Botticelli for the lady, no Leonardo to hold my interest), and so we experienced none of the prior turmoil over where to linger—no small consolation given the previous day's contretemps. Indeed, Miriam and I found a kind of solidarity in our coldness toward Venetian art; by the end of our tour we were practically snickering at the sight of yet another gilded mask, another hazy seascape.

When we finally quit the museum, returning to the mayhem of early evening in Venice, it was like a resurrection. After all that gloom, the hurly-burly seemed to awaken a part of me that had laid dormant since Vinci. I was so put off by the Venetian School that I felt like I had a grasp on my own persona for the first time in days, and best of all, my wife was right there beside me—sharing my disdain.

I was so cheered by this sense of restored comity that I began to even feel a little of the charisma that is so famously part of Venice's allure. It is a place of writers and romantics, after all: Thomas Mann and Casanova, Henry James and Hemingway, Browning and Byron and Ezra Pound. At one time or another, many an author has supped of the inspiration in that mysterious city. The painting isn't nearly on par with Florence, but there's something definitely poetic about Venice. I started to feel a little of the old juices start to flow again; I wanted to get back to the hotel and write something in that stupid journal I'd been toting around for the last week.

With that hopeful sentiment in mind, I turned to my new bride and sometime literary agent—only to find that she was once again busy receiving messages on her ever-present Blackberry.

"Jesus, Mir," I said in disgust. "Can't we have a *little* time to ourselves?"

Miriam rolled her eyes in the direction of her phone. "It's Olivia," she answered. "She heard about my meeting with Andrea."

"Of course."

"Please, David." (Still typing furiously with her thumbs.) "This is important."

"Well, have you fulfilled your duties?" I asked when she finally stopped.

"Sort of," she said uncertainly.

"You mean there's more?"

Miriam pocketed her cell phone and proceeded to search for something that had fled to the furthest reaches of her new purse. This operation took up more than a few seconds during which time I could see the wheels in my wife's mind turning at top speed.

"Oh, this can't be good," I said to no one in particular.

Miriam didn't even look up. "She wants me to see Andrea again."

"We're not going back to Florence."

She paused for a moment, as if gathering resolve, then dove elbow-deep into her bag and came up with the inexorable hair clip. Miriam's eyes shined with vague satisfaction as she answered: "Olivia said he'll meet me here."

"Absolutely not."

"I know. It's out of the question," she said, shaking her head. "But you kind of have to respect his determination."

"No I don't. In fact, I think it shows a lack of common sense for this man to think he can invade our goddamned honeymoon. You, of all people, I would expect to be creeped out by this kind of thing."

"Yes," Miriam agreed coolly. "All I mean is that I can appreciate his persistence. He knows what he wants and he'll do anything to make it happen. There's something admirable in that."

"Admirable!" I screamed, now aghast at everything my wife was saying. At that point I noticed for the first time that we were making something of a scene on the crowded Venetian street—the American couple having a spat. I should have restrained myself. I didn't.

"Wait a minute," I went on just a moment later, "That note he sent to our hotel—did you know about this already?"

"No," she insisted. "He was only checking up. He wanted me to call him to say that we arrived safely in Venice."

"What business is it of his? What the hell happened at that lunch, Miriam?"

"Don't be dramatic, David."

"*Me* dramatic? He's phoning ahead to see that you weren't killed on the train to Venice."

Miriam huffed. "He's European, it's expected of him. You don't have the same excuse."

"Well he has no excuse to be here," I insisted. "And you need to make that clear to him, and to Olivia."

"I know," she said, raising a placating hand. "I will, don't worry."

We walked on a few feet in irksome silence until I piped up again: "I don't know if I want you working with this guy."

That brought her up short. She eyed me dubiously and I stared back at her like a stranger who'd forgotten his own name. "Listen," she said finally, "The whole thing is probably going to come to nothing. Believe me, if I had a nickel for every good idea that never gets to print, we'd already be millionaires.

"But if by some chance Andrea does finish this book and he does send it to me, then, yes, I am going to work with him and hopefully I'm going to make a sale and take a fifteen percent commission on every cent the book generates—just like I told him. This is what I do for a living, David. I told you that when I met you, and you knew it when you married me. And yes, all of my clients are incredibly self-involved, some of them are a bit neurotic, and most of them are needy as hell. But in my experience, that's no small part of what makes them successful."

I did my best to ignore the implication.

Miriam sighed and relaxed her posture an iota. "All the same, I know you're right: I shouldn't be doing business on our honeymoon. I didn't think it would get this far out of control. But what's done is done. I promise, no more Olivia, no more Andrea." She squared me with a strict expression. "Until we get back to New York. Then I intend to work with anyone and everyone who has a good idea to sell, just like I always do. You understand that, right?"

"Yes," I admitted with an irrefutable gesture of surrender. "I understand. I'm sorry."

"Are you?" she said, emotion glinting in her eyes like sunlight on the water. "Are you really? Because you know, my clients aren't the only ones who can seem self-involved sometimes."

"They're just more successful than me."

Miriam answered with a shrug and walked on, thus ending the modest detente I'd imagined in the museum.

The Domestic Chronicle of Francesco del Giocondo, Merchant of Florence

August 15, 1495—The Feast of the Assumption. It was last year at this time that Tomassa and Savonarola had their public feud. The Frate, of course, had heard of her immodest behavior. And with Camilla's death, rumors of our liaison came to light. In fact I had begun paying visit to Tomassa's home, coming and going at unusual hours. And Fra Girolamo's spies were everywhere in the city, on constant watch for signs of decadence among the people.

On Assumption Day, the Frate spoke his homily on the perfection of the Madonna, offering her chasteness and purity as the example for all women to live by. In comparison, he spoke of the perfidy of wealthy Florentine women, whose lack of morals led them to adorn themselves in lavish dress, brawl in public, and receive men after dark. All of Florence recognized the reference to Tomassa and I.

I felt ashamed for having been a supporter of the friar's teachings, if not as devoted as the piagnoni. Tomassa, though she thought Savonarola a trifling madman, was livid at the insinuation. That the Frate's claims were true meant nothing. The fact that a lowly friar felt he could address her character in such terms was more than Tomassa could bear.

Luckily fate soon intervened in the person of the French king, whose presence in Northern Italy gave Savonarola a suiting emblem of the divine wrath he had been calling down on Florence for years. In his excitement, the Frate all but forgot Tomassa's indiscretions.

And now, just one week hence, news from Parma that Charles has been defeated by the Pope's general, Francesco di Gonzaga.

The French menace has been turned away, Savonarola's divine wrath proven feeble. One can only guess what the Frate will say now that his visions have been proved blind. Perhaps Tomassa was right, Fra Girolamo is more madman than prophet.

—∞—

October 3, 1495—Barto is to have a brother or sister. I have this information direct from Mona Piera, so I know it to be scrupulously correct. And my mother, stern as the earth, intimated a taciturn happiness in the telling, a fact that proves Lisa more remarkable than I could have imagined. To have won my mother in such a short time can be nothing short of a miracle.

But how quickly these young ones become pregnant! As though their bodies are fields wanting seed. Yet I know already that the season can be harsh, and that in harvest danger is never far. I admit that I received the news of my renewed paternity with some hesitation. For my wife grows in my affection. Having been received frequently by me these last two months, Lisa is now very familiar. The cool smile I was afforded in the first days of our marriage now brightens on occasion, and warms my soul like brandywine. I now await the days she will come to my bedchamber with heightened eagerness, and receive her with a vigor that beckons passion. How Fra Girolamo would frown on my decadence! No matter. The madman is a dark spirit in Florence, while Lisa is a lustrous presence in my bed.

—∞—

November 2, 1495—Today the Feast of All Souls is upon us. Sadly, my family has many to remember. Camilla and my second son both dead more than a year, and my father who has now been gone nearly two years. A mother-in-law of Giuliano and an infant son of Giocondo, neither of whom I knew well, also number among our recently departed.

And not a week hence a dire event. Antonmaria Gherardini, the fine man who gave me his only daughter as wife, was taken from this earthly realm to immortal Paradise. A short service was held for him at San Spirito. I gave an oration that proved difficult, being more moved than I thought I would be by the passing of a man whom I had known for only a short time, but who always left me humbled by his profound dignity.

Lisa has been distraught. Her great regret is that her father did not live to see the child that is growing inside her. Indeed, by the day she plumps like ripened fruit. Despite her grief, the pregnancy agrees with her immensely. In the weeks before her father's passing, she was affected with such an ebullient humor that she seemed to impart greater light to our household, and all of Florence, by her presence. My selfish hope is that her mourning, albeit warranted, will prove brief, if only that we may once again be privy to the radiance that was her portion before her father's death.

In the afternoon, we went to the Priory of San Marco to hear the Frate give his homily to the dead. Despite the humiliation of the French king, his prophesied instrument of divine will, Savonarola remains as powerful as ever among the people. For my part, I said a silent prayer for forgiveness from Tomassa, who even in heaven is likely looking down with jealousy and contempt. I admit I think less often of her now, but on this day I cannot help but grieve. Lisa, for her part, gives no indication that she ever knew of my affair. I have no idea if this is true. But that is her way, and it deepens my affection for her.

For his part, the friar began a commanding sermon, eulogizing the dead with such potent emotion that the piagnoni wept in every corner of the priory. He even invoked the hallowed name of Lorenzo de Medici, whose children yet inveigh against the friar's rule in Florence. Then the sermon took a turn none had heard before. Savonarola progressed from his praise of Il Magnifico to a direct condemnation of the Pope himself. While Alexander's corruption is no secret among the higher classes, the Frate's invocation to the masses was shocking. As his sermon continued, the sound of weeping gave way to gasps of astonishment. In the eyes of the friar, a wickedness has advanced through Italy to the very heart of Christendom. It has infected the Vatican itself. Surely this was a sign of the end times.

I don't think any person left San Marco this day with a hopeful heart.

——✍——

December 15, 1495—Yesterday I arrived in Florence from Lyons, where I left Giuliano to oversee our business interests in France. I return to find Lisa weak with illness caused by severe cold. According to Mona Piera, my wife has been bedridden for nearly a week. She appears pale and weary, and has great difficulty eating. The doctor insists that she must try, for her sake and the baby's.

I cannot stop myself from fearing the worst, for I have learned all too well how fragile life can be. Experience is the father of us all. I do not know how I would have gotten through the last two days without Mona Piera. She does her very best to keep me from worry, for Barto's sake more than any other. She says that my son is disconsolate without Lisa. I pray, for his sake as well as my own, that she will recover and come back to us as she has always been, a light in the darkness.

——✍——

December 30, 1495—Praise be to God and to His Son Jesus Christ our Lord in the season of His birth! I am alight with relief! Lisa is fully recovered from her illness in time to enjoy the celebration of Natale with the rest of the family. The color and contours have returned to her features with all the delight and grandeur of a new day's dawning. She is now infused with a golden glow that emanates from that radiant smile. How different she seems now than the girl I married some nine months ago.

Indeed, it seems that the weeks I spent establishing Giuliano in Lyons were considerable in her pregnancy. For when I left, my wife was only beginning to show signs of nativity. Now, released at last from the grip of her illness, Lisa appears as fruitful as the arbor. The fullness of her figure, the richly rounded embonpoint of her features charms me as I have never been charmed. I do so dote on her these days, eager to grant her every whim. For Natale, I spoiled her with fine gems and opals gathered on my travels in France. Though I know the Frate's minions would threaten if ever she wore such jewels in public, I do not care. The pleasure elicited in giving them to Lisa is enough for me to risk the condemnation of that mad friar. I have never been so happy in my life.

—⁄∾∾⁄—

I should say here that despite a few detours and digressions that occurred during our two-week Italian honeymoon—and one big mix-up we really couldn't avoid—the trip was actually quite precisely planned. Miriam, after all, was a precise planner. From our first breakfast in Rome to the dinner at Il Bacino, every detail had been designed down to the hour. And with the exception of the day I spent (alone) in Vinci, we hewed rather closely to the course she'd charted. Even—I realized later—the trip to Settignano had been part of Miriam's delicately premeditated itinerary.

Thus it was that following our little dustup outside the Academmia, my wife and I had to double-time back to our hotel in order to

be ready for the next item on her agenda. This, actually, was something of a blessing because the need for exact navigation (always a
dicey prospect in Venice) followed by a period for proper outfitting
kept us from sniping at each other for a few hours. And in truth,
the next event on our schedule was one I'd been looking forward to
since before our arrival in Italy. For through the seemingly ubiquitous
influence of Olivia Winters (who, in retrospect, exercised a strange
sway over the whole honeymoon), Miriam and I had secured an invitation to a swanky masquerade ball set to take place at the Palazzo
Zenobio, a onetime noble residence that had lately become the setting for lavish entertainments of the Italian elite. Olivia's American
fame had given her a certain cachet in her home country, and because
the masquerade had something vaguely to do with the Italian publishing industry, she had no problem getting us in. Miriam, of course,
was intrigued by the business prospects of mingling with Italian literati, but in this instance I didn't care that she was mixing business
with pleasure because I was as excited as she to be at the masquerade.

For the occasion, I'd packed the suit I was married in just two
weeks prior (the masquerade, I had been assured, was not strictly a
period-specific affair), while Miriam got herself up in a sheer green
armless evening dress that hugged her hips and bosom and tapered
to a sleek pencil fit just below the knee. Black shoulder-length gloves
finished her outfit in a mode befitting either business or pleasure.
Of course, we each had Venetian carnival masks: she a golden Columbine that exposed her burgundy lips, and I donned a bright red
Plague Doctor that looked like nothing so much as a dog's hard-
on. I felt kind of ridiculous, but Miriam was stunning—which fact
helped ease the discomfort at the bawdiness of my costume.

Unlike the limitations on public life (viz., the early dinner hour),
private affairs in Venice tend follow a more dilatory timetable.
Which is to say that an event like our appointed gathering at Palazzo Zenobio was scheduled to start rather late, by the city's standards,
and had the potential to last into the early hours of morning. Thus,

it was already well past nine o'clock when Miriam and I boarded a
vaporetto to go to the masquerade.

As we traveled down the Grand Canal, Venice was in full glow,
a blue-tinted still-life saturated with shapeless ghosts dancing amid
the crooks and shadows of the labyrinth. The wind raised a smell of
methane off the lagoon, spreading a sense of macabre through the
cool night. Miriam sat along the rail of the water bus, clenching her
shawl against the chill and rocking gently with the low tide in the
channel. I, meanwhile, stood a few feet away under the vaporetto's
canopy, already masked in shadow as I watched the silhouette of
domes pass like strange celestial mollusks.

Despite the rough patch we'd gone through in the last few days,
I was, at that moment, hopeful and happy in my new marriage.
Though we hadn't really spoken much since the museum, when Miriam scolded me for interfering in her business, the air between us
seemed more or less clear, minus the sulfur of the lagoon. We were
on our way to an event that would make for an unforgettable night,
placing a perfect capstone on our honeymoon—then back to New
York to start a new life. I was feeling overly romantic, or poetic, as
my wife might say, and I wanted that life to start straight away.

At that moment, the woman in next seat got up and crossed toward the gangway. I took the opportunity to squeeze onto the bench
beside Miriam.

"Cold?" I asked

"I'll be all right."

"I know."

Mir looked less assertive than I'd ever seen her. "We don't have
to stay long if you don't want to," she said.

"What do you mean? I've been looking forward to this all week."

"Then try to have a good time, please." She turned toward me, her
quarter profile lit by the lamps along the canal. "And don't get uptight
if I start talking business. This is a great opportunity for me to develop clients. Olivia knew that when she got us invited to this thing."

"I understand," I said, stopping her with a gesture. "Strictly business tonight."

"No, David, it's not *strictly* business. But if a little business happens to come up, I don't want you getting all bent out of shape about it."

"Okay, I get it. I promise," I conceded, and gave a kiss on the side of her forehead to seal the truce.

Minutes later we disembarked at Ca' Rezonicco, the nearest stop to Palazzo Zenobio. From there, it was a ten-minute walk to the masquerade. Yet at just nine-thirty the streets of Venice already lay in a state of eerie quiet; as we left the exposure of the Grand Canal, the wind died like a memory and the stone architecture swaddled us to its bosom. Miriam grasped the crook of my elbow as we walked quickly across the cobbled stones, our footsteps echoing forgetfully in blind passageways. We didn't speak or look at each other, but moved through the darkness as though in a dream.

Still, in some weird way it seemed the most intimate moment of the whole vacation. Not intimate in a romantic sense, perhaps, but there's unquestionably something private—indeed, secret—about plumbing Venice's depths at night. And yet alongside that intimacy I couldn't quite stifle a feeling of isolation, not only from the world and my wife, but from myself. I began to feel like an accessory on holiday, a bit character in someone else's story. In fact, at that moment I was (literally and figuratively) just a supporting actor helping the protagonist across the stones. Not even when I was ghost writing had I felt so disconnected from my own destiny.

There's just something about Venice that makes you feel fleeting in its presence. Maybe it's the quiet. Maybe it's the dark. Maybe it's sound of the sea relentlessly splashing against its foundation, reinforcing a sense of impermanence. Whatever it was, I felt like an illusion. Of course, I wasn't the first person to get lost in that city. But I wondered, perhaps, if I was the first to lose so much of his *self* in the Venice nexus.

Luckily, we weren't literally lost, and soon emerged from the maze onto Fondamenta del Soccorso, a wide quay straddling one of the east-west anabranches of the Grand Canal. There, the city came subtly to life—a water taxi lolled quietly among the waves and a pair of bohemian lesbians strolled (as now did Miriam and I) along the smoother stones of a better-traveled footpath. We passed the Palazzo Foscarini and the Church of Santa Maria del Carmini before coming upon the vast façade of Palazzo Zenobio, which loomed like a tombstone over the narrow embankment.

The Domestic Chronicle of Francesco del Giocondo, Merchant of Florence

February 15, 1496—It occurs to me with sudden shock that this day marks the Roman Lupercalia. I know this only because last year this day became an obsession for Tomassa. She planned to throw a great ball in honor of Pan, and in that way to spite the Frate to the marrow of his bones. She relished the idea of feting a pagan god amidst the Christian severity of Savonarola's rule. In her final days it was her passion, a way to take revenge on the friar who had dared denounce her in public.

I tremble now to allow that I let the anniversary of Tomassa's death pass without note. Lisa's impending childbirth and the rigors of a difficult winter and problems already arising with Giuliano in Lyons have dominated my attention. I neglected to think of my departed love just one year after her death. For it was in the midst of planning Pan's great saturnalia, the thumb in the eye of Savonarola, that Tomassa was suddenly and cruelly stricken. She weakened so quickly it was scarcely believable to me. I attended her daily and publicly, rumors be damned. Yet she died before my eyes, a moment at a time, fighting violently with every breath. I all but died alongside her. I believed I would never be able to look at a woman with love again. My God, how could I have forgotten so quickly? How could I have marked Camilla's passing, and let Tomassa's pass unnoticed? But it is worse. For truth I am not beside myself with anguish. And I am shocked that my affections can have been exchanged so quickly.

It also occurs to me now for the first time that some relation to that satyr appeared in my life at both the beginning and the end of my love affair with Tomassa. At first in the request by

Giovanni Rucellai to have Camilla's portrait painted by Signorelli. And then in Tomassa's determination to celebrate Lupercalia. I can think of no other time in my life when the figure of Pan came to me in any significant way. What does this mean? I do not know. But for truth I cannot think on it any more. Shame threatens to open a wound that has all but healed. The hole that Tomassa left has been filled by Lisa. And though it makes me as variable as the weather, I refuse to dwell in that sorrow more.

—⁓—

May 17, 1496—Lisa has given birth to a beautiful baby boy who will be called Piero in honor of my mother's father. It was Lisa gave him this name. My gratitude for this generosity is more than I can describe, especially as I would have assented readily to naming him Antonmaria. I have never in my life felt such complete happiness. In nearly two years since Camilla's death, I did not think such happiness could transpire in my life. It seemed at times that I had fallen into a great abyss from which I did not care to be raised. So I lay musing in the darkness, thinking of the past. But my wife, my lady, Lisa, has recovered me from the depths, back to the world of men. Today I feel as new as my infant son.

And yet to realize that I love Lisa is a surprise to me. For I took her as an act of resignation. Worse, a negotiation. At the time I felt that my marriage was a betrayal of love. But now it is more precious than any treasure. What appeared to be false was in fact more real than any truth could be.

—⁓—

September 12, 1496—I have taken Lisa, Barto, Mona Piera, and the baby Piero to the farmhouse in San Silvestri which was the dowry that Antonmaria Gherardini presented me upon my marriage to his daughter. Lisa is filled with joy to be here, as it is a place of many happy memories for her. I wish I could say it is pleasure that has caused us to leave Florence, but it is not.

The finances of the city, now the Republic, as they say, have been in a horrible state for years. Payments exacted by France and war with Pisa have exhausted the public credit, and the Frate's thirst for taxes and alms has emptied even the deepest wells. This alone might have been bearable, for Florence is a city built on commerce. But famine has now struck the countryside. By day, peasants flock to the city, uttering cries of hunger and pleas for charity. In days past, during times of want, these peasants were turned away as strangers. Now, under Savonarola's new laws, they are received as brethren. The Signoria, controlled by Piagnoni, has ordered our homes opened to the immigrants, many of whom are sickened from the hunger and exposure. Already fear of plague spreads through the streets, bringing panic to every eye. Florence is a dangerous place. I will not keep my family there.

Giocondo and Giuliano and their families have retreated to our farms on the Montughi hill, along with Alessandra and Gherardesca. Servants were left behind at Via della Stufa to keep our peasant guests from plundering the house in advance of our return. But for truth I cannot imagine taking Lisa and my children back to that city in its current state. I thank God my father is not alive to see Florence today.

—∾∾—

September 28, 1496—Dire news from Florence. The Pisans have routed us in the plains of Castellina, driving our armies to retreat their fortifications. Had Manfroni any will, he could have cut us from Livorno completely and strangled our starving city once and for all.

Yet the worst news is that Piero Capponi was lost in battle. Felled by a ball at the siege of Soiana. His funeral, I am told, was even more extravagant than the rites for Il Magnifico, only four years hence. The body was sailed up the Arno on a barge to his home at Santa Trinita, the church ablaze with tapers and hung with the banners of family and magistrates while the Buonmini proclaimed his valor. That such a man can fall to Pisans bodes ill for Florence. For the first time since the war began, I despair of the possibility of Pisans at our gates, rather than the other way around.

I have told neither Lisa nor my mother of the disaster at Pisa, or the possibility of Florence coming under siege. I did send messenger to Giocondo and Giuliano at Montughi, advising them to be prepared to join us at San Silvestri should events warrant. For if the Pisans come, their proximity to the city will place the whole family in danger.

Meanwhile, Lisa and the boys have taken to the countryside as though we were on holiday. Even Mona Piera seems to be at peace in this arcadian setting. I must admit, San Silvestri is more beautiful than I imagined. The lush hills and clear sky mingle with a sublime harmony that quiets the mind while exciting the senses. I am overcome, in retrospect, by the generosity of Lisa's father, who gave me this farm as a dowry for his daughter. Seeing it for the first time, I now understand the value my father-in-law placed on this farm, and I am humbled by his gift. If only he were here, that I might express my gratitude anew.

—⁓—

October 30, 1496—I return from Lyons to find all of Italy in conflict. The war between Savonarola and Pope Alexander grows more bitter with each passing week, Charles of France once more threatens invasion, the Milanese Moor makes entreaties to Emperor Maximilian, and Venice has designs on Pisa. How Florence will survive is a question I cannot answer.

The latest news is that the Frate has returned to the pulpit, in direct contravention of the Holy Father's orders. It is no secret that Pope Alexander is allied with Piero de Medici, nor that late difficulties in Florence have eroded Savonarola's authority. So too, the Arrabbiati and Bigi factions within the Signoria have formed a powerful opposition to the Piagnoni. Clearly Rome sees an opportunity to rid itself of the friar. Under these circumstances, it is impossible to think that Fra Girolamo could have stayed silent much longer.

Happier news is that my son Piero is growing like a wild vine. Two weeks in Lyons, and I feel I have returned to a different boy. He has Lisa's smile and her fine demeanor. Even Mona Piera claims she has never seen a more congenial baby. My mother coddles him excessively. Barto is having some difficulty adjusting to a rival for Lisa's attention, but God bless my wife, her affection for him is undiminished. The two of them run and play in the meadows while Mona Piera dotes on Piero.

And yet the change in my wife is almost as great as the change I see in our baby. Lisa seems to have aged ten years since Piero's birth, to great advantage. Her features and shape are no longer those of a young girl, but the ample stature of a fertile woman. While she maintains the same poise she has exhibited since moving into my household, that assurance is now buttressed by an authority not previously evidenced. My wife shows signs of one day being every bit as formidable as my fearsome mother. Mother of God! That is a thing to note in one who stirs my passions as much as she.

December 14, 1496—I am to return to Florence to serve on the Signoria. I do not take this action with light heart, as I am happy here in San Silvestri with Lisa and Barto and Piero. Mona Piera has returned to the house on Via della Stufa along with Giocondo and Giuliano, for the threat from Pisa has passed.

Yet the state of affairs in Florence is far from peaceful. The Arrabbiati have gained influence since the Frate's dispute with the Borgia pope, and the Bigi plot at all times to return Il Magnifico's son to power. The two parties have formed an alliance that wields great influence within the government. Yet the Piagnoni still hold power over the masses, and none can forget how they drove the Medici from Florence. Relations among the Buonmini are more acrimonious than at any time since the Pazzi intrigue. Factions vie bitterly for control of the Signoria. The state is fraught with peril for any man who aspires to power. Though I have been a loyal Florentine all my life, I frankly would prefer a quiet country life at this time.

I would not even consider the charge were it not taken at the express request of Bernardo del Nero. For I cannot forget that it was he who supported my return to public life following the scandal of my affair with Tomassa. Honor demands that I answer the call of such a man, who for all of Florence is like a stately uncle, if Savonarola remains its dogmatic father.

I shall leave Lisa and the children here, on her father's farm, better to keep them from the intrigues of the Republic. I will miss them terribly. But I must go, if not for honor, then by the grace of God to make Florence a place they can return to safely some day.

The Zenobio Palace is itself a kind of paradox, both an archetype of the late Baroque and an atypical example of Venetian architecture—and like so much else I encountered in Italy, not what it seemed at first glance. For while the details of the stark façade blend perfectly with the rest of the city's Gothic *palazzos* and *tenementi*, the underlying layout is almost outrageously foreign in design. The broad, U-shape of the building's outline creates a large courtyard that opens to the internal garden, while two smaller courtyards are set off behind the first rooms on either side of the loggia. (The left room, as you go in, accommodates a small, hidden staircase that leads to the *piano nobile*, or second floor, of the palazzo.) Two large halls—named, respectively, the Hall of Mirrors and the Hall of Stucco, for the obvious reasons—flank the magnificent, two-story ballroom that resides just behind the balcony of the central loggia. (Much more about this later.)

In any case, the venue was ideal for that night's event. By the time Miriam and I arrived the masquerade was in full swing, with some 500 guests spread throughout the palace's various anterooms and courtyards (save the Hall of Mirrrors, which, as a precaution, was closed to the public), mingling at a congenial intervals while sipping champagne from tulip wine glasses. With few exceptions, guests were dressed much like Miriam and I: formal eveningwear along with designer masks to instill the glamour with a bit of mystery. A few had gone in for extra ornamentation such as a wig or a tricorn or some other piece of period finery, but only the staff were outfitted in full carnival regalia. Their costumes were embellished with heaps of silk and lace and crinoline and veils and feathers and tassels, along with enough powder and makeup to outfit a brothel or a circus.

Miriam took the opportunity to dislodge from my arm and make her way toward the alcove at the right of the loggia. As she did, I momentarily saw her surveying the gathering from beneath her golden Columbine eyepiece. (We had both donned our masks before entering the palace.) She moved easily through the crowd, as her small mask fit rather closely around her eyes, offering an almost unobstructed view of the assembled guests. Meanwhile, my more weighty headpiece hampered my vision severely, and I had to concentrate on my wife's backside in order not to lose her as we moved from one room to the next.

In that context, the masquerade didn't seem—to me at least—particularly fertile ground for cultivating clients. After all, if you can't make out who you're talking to it would seem a rather neat trick to close a deal. But maybe that was just my limited business instincts talking. Miriam, it must be said, appeared (as near as I could tell) completely unfazed by the ambiguity.

We exited through the alcove and into the courtyard on the west side of the palace, where a canvas tent had been erected against possible inclemencies. But inside the sheltered confines of Zenobio, the night was quite perfect—clear and cool with neither a trace of cloud nor a whisper of wind. The tent and trees where decked with white lights that glistened like diamonds, credibly imitating the dome of stars clearly visible against the violet sky.

Miriam plucked two champagne glasses from a waiter and passed one into my flailing hand. "You look hideous in that mask," she deadpanned.

"And you actually look quite fetching in yours."

"Fetching?"

"Give me a break. It isn't easy to be charming with this thing on."

"I can see that," she said, taking a sip of champagne. "It's going to be even harder to get drunk." The last was a reaction to my obvious confusion over what to do with my glass, as the Plague Doctor offered no clear means of ingress.

"On a related note," I replied, having given up, for the moment at least, the riddle of how to drink through a full-face carnival mask, "How do you intend to do business in this crowd? You can't see anyone's face and you don't speak Italian. Those seem like pretty big obstacles to me."

Miriam waved off such trifles with a flip of her gloved wrist. "These are book people. Eventually the masks will come off. Literally and figuratively. Besides that," she went on after taking another sip of champagne, "Olivia gave me a few people to look for."

"Jesus," I said, "Was there any part of this honeymoon that Olivia wasn't in on?"

"Don't forget what you promised," she warned. "Just try to enjoy yourself and not trip over anything in that mask."

"It's a deal," I said ironically.

For a brief moment, she measured me with an exasperated gaze that somehow showed plainly through her mask, then turned and, again, moved through the crowd with steady grace. I hastened to follow her retreating figure, prepared to meet my fate among the assembled Italian literati.

Miriam led me through the Stucco Hall, which was hung with dozens of paintings of naked women wearing ceramic flower pots on their heads. But my wife was in no mood for art, and sliced through the babbling hall as neatly as a clipper on the lagoon. Within a minute we emerged—she leading me at a close distance—into the landscape of Palazzo Zenobio's lush garden. A sudden puff of breeze carried with it the scent of methane. As in the courtyard, the garden was decked with glittering lights, though here rich textiles, carnival bunting, and polished brass added to the period aspect of the masquerade.

I mused momentarily about how happy I was—to be married, to be in Italy, to be experiencing a once-in-a-lifetime night in an impossibly glamorous setting, even to be moving to a great new apartment on the Upper East Side. After years in the wilderness, it seemed to me that my ship had finally come in, and in Venice of all places. It was a life that I could never, until recently, have envisioned for myself. And naturally, I had Miriam to thank for it.

So what did it matter, really, if she didn't believe in me as a writer anymore (if, in fact, that was how she felt)? That didn't mean she didn't love me for who I was, flaws and all. In fact, in some small way that seemed even more touching: She loved me for me, and I for her. And yes, I realized that I was being foolishly "poetic" again. But I went with it anyway.

"Mir," I said, lifting the mask enough to show my whole face. "Here's to us." I raised my glass.

She smiled but sipped without toasting. She was already in full-on business mode, surveying the crowd for signs that were neither privy nor visible to me. For my part, I downed the whole glass of champagne, which fizzed in my nose and fluttered in my gut like a butterfly. I pulled the grotesque mask back down and enjoyed the gentle hum of foreign banter in my ears.

Miriam, meanwhile, went on searching.

"Have you located your accomplices?" I asked sarcastically.

To my surprise she raised a gloved hand in the direction of one of the gas lamps. "See the one in the red dress with the leopard mask?" she asked without looking. "Juicy Viola." (Or at least that's what I heard.)

"Juicy? You've got to be kidding."

Miriam rolled her eyes. "G-I-U-S-Y. Short for Giuseppa. Her family owns an art house press in Naples. Nothing I could sell in New York, but it's not her clients I'm interested in anyway."

"What do you want then?"

"A meet and greet, my dear," fondling her champagne glass as she gazed across the garden. "Her writers aren't right for my agency, but she knows everybody and what they're working on and who they're working with. If you want to find out what's going on in Italian publishing, you talk to Giusy Viola."

"And how, exactly, do you know all this?"

"It's my business to know all this. Just like it's her business to know everyone who's anyone in Italy." She looked at me with a confidential tilt of her head. "It's all part of the plan."

"What plan?"

She took my hand. "Come on. Let's see what we can find out."

Never one to be shy, Miriam led us right up to the leopard mask and wasted no time inserting herself into the clique around her. "*Ciao tutte, buona sera. Che la Signora Viola?*" she asked in rather well-accented Italian. I sometimes forgot what a smooth operator my wife could be.

"*Si,*" announced the woman, turning toward us with rehearsed assurance underlined by the genteel angle of her chin. In a second, though, she seemed to recall a lost thought and burst her shell like a newborn chick.

"*O dio! Signorina Miriam! Sta lei?*"

"*Si,*" answered my wife with a small nod. "*Ma io sono gia Signora Miriam.*" She fluttered her gloved left hand slightly to indicate our conjugality, which gesture Giusy Viola noticed not at all having already launched into an explanation—in Italian, of course—of the identity of the incongruous Americans at the masquerade. Inevitably, the only words I could comprehend were "Livia" and "Winters." Yet in the brief interval I realized, despite the masks (both hers and mine), that this supposed doyenne of Italian literature was, in fact, a twentysomething socialite chirping excitedly to a coterie of contemporary hangers-on—not at all what I'd expected.

"*E chi e l'gentiluomo?*" she asked in my direction.

"This is my husband, David," Miriam answered, switching to English for my benefit.

"Charmed," said Giusy Viola with a subtle stroke on the "r" as she extended a downturned hand. "Thees ees my hos-band, Antonio Bonaventura," she went on in syncopated English. "He ees a pob-lisher at La Virgola Edizioni in Roma."

Giusy presented a suave-looking man in a dark suit and an expensive, open-collared shirt. He wore only a black eye mask, most likely so as not to interfere with his significant hair. Like Giusy, he seemed ridiculously sophisticated for someone in his twenties.

"Ciao," said Antonio with a tip of his champagne glass.

"Also," Giusy continued, "Here is Benedetto Maturi, of the European Ministry; Signorina Ileana Pouce, from Prada Milano; Carlo Brera who is *un direttore* at the Banco Populare; Cecco Del Guidice of the Universita of Bologna; and Hasmig Kacherian, who is a sculptor and writer."

Each of the people Giusy introduced fit the same mold as she and her husband: youthful, beautiful, impressively dressed, and impossibly refined for such a young age. In all, there was something hypercultured about the set, like a collection of modern mondaines grown in a petri dish.

"And there of course is your compatriot, Signore Barron," Giusy concluded.

Until that moment I hadn't even noticed the last of Giusy's group: a fleshy fortysomething-year-old hodgepodge of a man standing a little off to one side while fiddling disinterestedly with the wick in one of the gas lamps. This homely subject seemed to emerge unbidden from the background of the garden, for unlike the others he was utterly unexceptional—except for the fact that he was the only person who remained unmasked at the masquerade. In fact, the man was barely dressed for dinner: He wore a blue blazer, khakis with no socks and tassled loafers, and a white polo shirt which collars lay gracelessly atop the coat's lapels. Wide, wire-rimmed glasses and apparent hair plugs completed the ensemble of a middle-aged, middle-grade schmuck. What he could possibly be doing with that crowd?

"Tod Barron?" Miriam exclaimed.

At that the man turned and broke a big smile, spreading his foreshortened dwarf arms in a gesture of genial self-satisfaction. His smugness seemed to thicken as he took my wife's hand in both of his.

"You recognized me," he verified, conspicuously taking in the gaze of the gathered, glamorous Italians, as if to confirm his importance.

"You're Tod Barron."

"I am."

"It's good to meet you," Miriam said.

"Thank you."

I, too, recognized the name, though not so much the person answering to it. Tod Barron had made a lucrative trade for himself in one of those backwater genres of commercial fiction which seem to generate special levels of bad prose and customer loyalty. Specifically, he was a writer of historical mysteries—whodunits set in (mostly) Renaissance Europe featuring scandalous casts of aristocrats, maidens, and clergymen involved in one kind of conspiracy or another. His books, invariably published under garish paperback covers with raised lettering, included *The Holy Grail Consortium*, *The Alchemist Murders*, *Death of a Duke*, *The Queen's Agent*, *The Maiden of Bohemia*, and *The Parliament House Conspiracy*—all of which followed the same basic formula and closed with an agreeable denouement. Of course, the books also had a lot of double entendre and racy sex scenes, improbable plot twists, inevitable anachronisms, and brutal effronteries to history and verisimilitude. But, alas, Tod Barron was a bestseller many times over. Exactly the kind of client Miriam dreamed about.

Most likely, none of the Italians at the masquerade (with the possible exception of Giusy) realized that the dumpling in the corner was a bestselling author. If they did, they no doubt would have paid more notice, because cultured Europeans are invariably fascinated by rich Americans—even the gaucheries like Tod Barron.

For my part, I'd have never even heard of Tod Barron but for the awful novel I'd agreed to ghostwrite several years earlier. At the time I was about four hundred pages into a vagabond invention based loosely on the lives of Hugh Ferriss, Raymond Hood, and some of the other progressive architects who had looked to turn New York into the new Athens in the early years of the twentieth century. But that project seemed to be going nowhere and everywhere at the same time, and it just so happened that one of Miriam's clients (a self-help writer who specialized in repairing failed marriages through tantric yoga) lived in the same West Side apartment building as a certain diminutive 70s-era Oscar-winning actor who had fallen on somewhat hard times, having been mostly run out of the film business (for poor receipts) and the theater world (for poor behavior). The self-help guru got Miriam in touch with the fallen star who was looking for someone to turn a failed movie treatment about the Crusades into a full-length novel. At the time he was in the midst of a small-screen comeback of sorts—one of the networks had picked up his TV pilot—and so Miriam assured me that publication was guaranteed. I was feeling stuck on my other project and agreed to take a look. Thus was I dragged into the vast morass of *A Knight's Journey*.

Naturally, the screen treatment was crap, but for once in my life I held my nose and plunged headlong into the cesspool of celebrity advocacy. Over the course of the next year, we met regularly in his apartment on West End Avenue, where a mere fraction of our time was spent actually reviewing new pages. The majority of each meeting was given over to his exhaustive and repetitive exegesis of each character's psychological motivations. He was an actor, after all—character was the one facet of fiction he could actually relate to. But he had absolutely no concept of plot, setting, or narrative structure. Still, he considered himself an excellent storyteller.

Not surprisingly, the project wound up in disaster. Despite Miriam securing a $75,000 advance for the book, the "name" attached to it refused to cooperate with me or his agent or the editor assigned to getting the damned thing to print. In the end he just wanted to hear himself talk.

Anyway, while all that was going on I had devoted a good deal of research to the manuscript, pouring through numerous books on the Crusades as well as dabbling in the type of period fiction I had decided to mimic in *A Knight's Journey*. That's how I came in touch with the oeuvre of Tod Barron, each copy of which featured a one-inch-square headshot of the author smiling just as smugly as he'd done when Miriam recognized him at the masquerade. Though that was, frankly, where the similarities ended, as the flesh-and-blood Tod Barron was clearly more ample than his photograph suggested, with bad skin, puffy cheeks, and a neck that went directly from his chin to the bottom of his Adam's apple. So too, the picture's generous combover had given way to the aforementioned hair plugs which were pushed up with some kind of brilliantine dyed too dark a shade of brown. Clearly, Tod Barron had been using an old photo to mask his real appearance.

Seeing him for the first time in person, it occurred to me that the writing in those historical potboilers more closely resembled the man than his back-page persona. Which is to say that the figure at Palazzo Zenobio—half-bred of vanity and self-consciousness—called to mind the mincing prose I'd subjected myself to through three Tod Barron novels. I wanted to get away before he uttered another word.

But, of course, I'd promised not to interfere with any business Miriam tried to do that night, so when Tod Barron placed his chubby hand on my wife's back and turned her a bit too eagerly from the rest of the group, there was nothing I could do but grab another glass of champagne and find someone else to talk to.

That person turned out to be Giusy's dashing husband, Antonio Bonaventura, who joined me in conversation while Miriam was being taken aside by Tod Barron. Antonio was, as I had been told in introduction, a publisher at La Virgola press. But that was a bit of a gloss. In fact, like his wife Antonio was a scion of the family that owned the publishing house. Yet even though he'd grown up with the business, he told me frankly that had no real interest in publishing—which is why he'd been given a position in a rather remote area of the family business, as publisher of La Virgola's textbook division.

But his real interest, he told me, was entomology.

"Like, insects?" I asked.

"*Sì,*" he answered with enthusiasm. "Thees ees my passion."

I looked around at the other members of the group to measure whether or not Antonio was joking. The only two who seemed to be listening looked on with continued interest—as though our young Mastroianni hadn't just told us he was a big bug-lover.

But he was, and for the next twenty minutes Antonio held forth on all things *Arthropoda*, from the elegance of arachnids to the social dynamics of anthood to the miracle of the caterpillar and the genius of bees, with stops along the way to explain the intricacy of compound eyes and the subtle advantages of an exoskeleton. The man was obsessed. I don't think I've ever been as consumed by any subject (not even Leonardo) in the way that Antonio Bonaventura was obsessed with insects. I suppose it was charming, in some way, to see someone seemingly with the world at his feet preoccupied by the lowliest of subjects—but still, creepy. Eventually I had to beg off the conversation by indicating the emptiness of my glass and chasing off after a passing waiter wearing extravagant garters.

After snatching two drinks (ostensibly for my wife and myself), I digressed for some minutes in the garden in order to avoid further entomological observations. As I circled back toward the group, my wife was just unfastening the ribbon that held her mask in place, thus allowing her brown eyes to catch the light of a nearby gas lamp. My heart warmed like morning. She laughed casually with Tod Barron.

I gave Miriam a glass of champagne, and before I knew what was happening the bestselling author grabbed the second glass out of my other hand. My wife shot me a desperate look, beseeching me not to ruin this for her.

"Tod," she said, "This is my husband David." She signaled for me to remove the Plague Doctor.

I took off my mask as he offered me his lifeless right hand. "Tod Barron," he said with airy self-regard.

"Nice to meet you."

"Thank you."

"David is a magazine editor," Miriam said.

"Really? What magazine?" Tod asked.

"Pharmaceuticals."

"Ohhh."

"Tod is working on a novel set in Venice," Miriam interjected.

"No. Not *set in* Venice," said Tod Barron. "A novel *about* Venice. A novel that *embodies* Venice, that captures its exquisite beauty and its rich history. I want to submerse my readers in the city's waters. I want to breathe the life into her stones. I want to live La Serenissimma though my words."

"Wow. That's really poetic, don't you think?" I said, turning to Miriam.

"Absolutely—" without missing a beat "Can you tell us any more about it?"

He tipped his head, pouted his lips, and looked pompously across his mottled nose. "What do you know about relics, Miriam?" he asked my wife.

"Not very much, I'm afraid."

"They're…religious artifacts, if you will, that have been shown to have special, even miraculous properties. It's often a bone or a lock of hair or a minor article of clothing or some other possession from a saint or martyr that has been documented as an object of veneration. For example, there is the cup of St. Anne in Canada, or the heart of St. Vincent de Paul in Paris, or the remains of the Three Magi in Cologne. These pieces have traveled down through the ages, through wars and disasters, conspiracies and intrigues, and are now objects of worship and even sites for pilgrimage.

"Fascinating stories. Really compelling stuff," said Tod Barron, oozing expectancy. "Stories that are timeless and original at the same time. Stories that can almost frighten you with their freshness, and still make you feel like you've known them all your life. Stories whose sensibility just speaks for itself. Those are the kinds of stories I want to tell. And Venice is full of relics of the first order. I bet you didn't know that."

"I had no idea."

"Oh yes," Tod Barron explained. "Many churches in Venice are the resting places for the saints. Everyone knows about St. Mark in the Basilica, but there's also St. Stephen, St. Athanasius, St. Theodore, St. Roch, St. Magnus, St. Lucy—all lying in one church or another somewhere in the city. You can also find the arm of St. George, rib of St. Stephen, the foot of St. Catherine, the finger of Mary Magdalene, the skull of John the Baptist. Venice is almost the world's capital for Christian relics."

"And that's what you're writing about? These relics?" I said.

"Not quite," coyly touching the rim of his champagne glass.

"Can you tell us?" Miriam asked.

Tod Barron raised one trite eyebrow. "Have you ever heard of the True Cross?"

"No."

"The cross on which Jesus Christ was crucified. Fascinating story." He paused for dramatic effect. "It was first discovered in a cave by St. Helena, who was the mother of the Roman Emperor Constantine, in the 4th century. When Constantine converted to Christianity, he built the Church of the Holy Sepulcher in Jerusalem to house the cross. It stayed there until a Persian king took the city in the 7th century and carried the cross back to Baghdad. But the Persians only had it for a few years until their empire fell to the Romans, who returned it to Jerusalem. It stayed there until the Crusades.

"During the Crusades, it's said that the Templars carried the True Cross into battle before them. But it didn't do much good because they were wiped out by Saladin at the Battle of Hattin in the 12th century. It disappeared after that. Some say Saladin destroyed it. Some say he kept it. Some say the Templars spirited the cross away before the sultan could get it. But ever since then fragments of the True Cross have been seen all over the world, particularly in Italy. In Venice fragments of the cross were said to have performed miracles as late as the 1800s."

"The Mystery of the True Cross," Miriam mused. "That's fascinating."

"Don't you think?" Tod Barron agreed.

"Of course the real mystery is how one cross could have produced enough fragments to build a cathedral," I said.

"I'm sorry? What?" Same airy intonation.

"You know. All those pieces of the True Cross all over Italy—all over the world, really. They're frauds. There isn't possibly enough material from one cross to contribute thousands upon thousands of fragments. Besides, after two thousand years, most wood would turn to dust. Right Tod?" I said, grinning ambivalently.

Miriam glared daggers at me.

Meanwhile, the cherubic novelist seemed momentarily taken aback. It didn't take him long to recover though. "Then I take it you've never heard of the miracle of the five loaves."

"Sure…bread and fish to feed the masses. That's a miracle worth performing. This other thing seems more like a marketing gimmick."

"Excuse me?"

"You know, each church gets a little sacred trinket to help fill the offering plate."

"I can assure you it's nowhere near 'each church,'" Tod answered with a knowing look in my wife's direction. "Are you some kind of atheist or something?" Which question seemed to me to be entirely off-topic.

"Whether or not I believe in God has nothing to do with it," I said a little—perhaps a little too—heatedly. "What I don't believe is that an old woman could find a slab of wood half a world away after three hundred years. That's not like finding a needle in a haystack, it's like finding a needle in a haystack that doesn't exist anymore. Now that's a miracle. If Helena could do that, maybe she was the Messiah."

Miriam forced a laugh. "He's joking, Tod, don't even take notice. Darling," she went on, turning her attention to me, "Why don't you go see the ballroom. I've heard the murals are amazing."

That, of course, was a none-too-subtle signal for me not to get "bent out of shape" by the way my wife was doing business at the masquerade, as I had promised on the vaporetto ride over. I took the hint and kissed Miriam demurely on the cheek, nodded to Tod Barron (who seemed pleased to see me leave), and re-donned my carnival mask to go see what all the fuss was about in the ballroom. Along the way I grabbed another glass of champagne, which I downed in a swift gulp under the Plague Doctor—a feat that made my head spin like a Turkish dervish—and lurched across the garden toward the palace's main courtyard, which was by then more crowded than when we'd arrived and bristling even more persistently with emphatic chatter. And yes, as Miriam had predicted the masks were coming off the assembled literates, not all of whom, I was relieved to see, were as youthful as Giusy Viola's set. With a few more moments and a little bit of gentle jostling (and, I might add, one more tulip plucked from a passing garcon), I finally reached the rear entrance to the palace, which opened directly onto the ballroom.

The Domestic Chronicle of Francesco del Giocondo, Merchant of Florence

February 10, 1497—What relief it is to return to San Silvestri, far from the dangers and vanities of Florence. My home city has become a nest of serpents eager to devour one another for profit or piety. Even Bernardo del Nero, whom I had credited as a man of dignity, plots continuously against the Frate. But his zeal to restore Piero de Medici is as futile as it is deliberate. Why a man of such venerable age would stoop to do the bidding of an arrogant fool is something I cannot understand. I can only guess what Il Magnifico's son must have promised in return for his support, for I am sure it was Bernardo arranged Piero's return. But they had too kind a view of their influence. The people refused Piero entrance at the city gates. A fine scene it was to see a Medici beg welcome of the masses. I have no love for this Republic, but I cry neither for a humbled tyrant.

For truth, I would prefer to quit the city for good. Give the house on Via della Stufa to Giocondo and live the rest of my days a gentleman of the country. Having returned to my wife's ancestral home, I know that there is no other place I want to awake with my family at my side. Lisa is now fully a woman, radiant and supple as the orchard. Barto has transformed from a baby to a young boy with a mind and will of his own, to the consternation of the servants. But Lisa is still his greatest love, and Barto will do anything to secure her favor. Piero, too, grows apace. His head is now downed with the same golden brown tresses as his mother's. Lisa refuses to have them shorn, for she loves to feel his soft curls against her cheek when they are sleeping. I accede, for to see them sleeping that way fills my heart to its limit. It occurs to me that almost without my knowledge I have acquired a very fine family. I should be the most contented man in the Republic.

But the politics of Florence abuse my satisfaction. In their foolishness, Bernardo del Nero and his allies have aided the cause of the Piagnoni, who once again seized control of the Signoria after the repudiation of the Medici. Worse yet, the impetuous zealot Franceso Valori was elected to be Gonfaloniere. And so at the very moment when there was opportunity to reconcile Florence, Valori instead passed measures to punish the Buonmini. His scaled tithe would have been improvidence enough for one year. But when the Piagnoni outlawed all balls and feasting, in advance of carnival no less, it was certain to unleash a new wave of bitterness. As well it did. The Arrabbiati, once humbled by their role in the attempt to restore Piero, became emboldened to resist the laws against feasting. And a new faction of wicked Compagnacci took to the streets at arms, promoting most vainglorious behavior in spite of Valori and the Frate.

In response, Savonarola sent his gamin through the city to collect every instrument of earthly delight, not only the dresses, masks and ornaments of carnival, but also mirrors, powders, perfumes, books, paintings, musical instruments. The children and their masters confiscated all signs of worldly pleasure to be sacrificed on their altar of austerity.

And so on Shrove Tuesday these vanities were taken to the Piazza della Signoria and gathered into a great pile. To see the wealth of Florence thus arranged, thrown together like a mélange of beggars' goods, it was almost too much to bear. And what wealth it was! Savonarola's tower of proscribed goods rose thirty meters, and covered half the span of the piazza. At the appointed hour, Dominicans appeared with torches to set the pyramid ablaze, and the riches of Florence, her tapestries, books, artworks, and sundry other fineries went up to the heavens in smoke. I recognized within the conflagration much of the silk that I had sold over the years. It was sickening to watch. Yet fire has a way of mesmerizing the eye. So while I was appalled at the sight of such treasures being burned in the name of piety, I could not, for a long time, turn from the harsh beauty of the flame. It seems now a strange contradiction that the friar's endeavor to purge pleasure from the Republic should have caused a spectacle of such striking beauty.

Thus I was still in the piazza when the artist Alessandro Botticelli made his way through the crowd carrying several canvases of what appeared to be his own work. Without the slightest indication of remorse, Botticelli stepped toward the bonfire and threw his paintings into the inferno, as if to cleanse himself of their pagan subjects. As he did this, another man of roughly the same age emerged from the crowd. He too, held a painting. He was small of stature, with a slight build and delicate, almost fragile features. The man I did not recognize. But the painting he held was immediately familiar to me. It was the same *School of Pan* that I had seen in the home of Lorenzo de Medici years before. From the murmurs in the crowd, I understood that the man was Signorelli, the artist whom Giovanni Rucellai had proposed to have paint Camilla's portrait. My refusal to allow the portrait had been based, in part, on my fidelity to Savonarola. Yet here now was Signorelli consigning to the pyre that artwork I had used to impugn him. And I, once a devotee of the Frate, looked at the spectacle with disdain.

———

August 25, 1497—Bernardo del Nero is dead, executed with Lorenzo Tornabuoni Gianozzo Pucci, Niccolo Ridolfo, and Givanni Cambi for their part in a conspiracy to restore Piero de Medici to power. My heart breaks and my hand trembles at this happening, for now certainly the city of my father is gone. How can I ever again be content in Florence?

And how could good Bernardo, a man of august disposition, have allowed himself to be influenced by Piero and implicated by that scoundrel Tornabuoni? It can only be the abiding love Bernardo had for Il Magnifico. But it is misplaced love, I say, for the great man's progeny all together are not worth the sacrifice of one del Nero.

I know that he was guilty, for I myself have heard him speak agreeably of such actions against the Signoria. That fact alone could endanger me if Valori knew. Bernardo's refusal to prevent such plotting was worse yet, for he held the gonfalonerie at the time. He was sworn to protect Florence. Instead, he took part in a plot to bring back a tyrant. What did a man of his age have to gain by returning the vicious young Medici to power? For all I know of Bernardo, and I have come to know him well in the last months, I cannot understand his actions.

Yet even for their guilt this punishment was too severe. Exile, and confiscation of properties was enough to disgrace and vilify the conspirators. They did not have to pay with their heads. It was not justice, but vicious politics that killed Bernardo. This is the swamp in which I have been sunk this last year. That is the cause served by five severed heads. With these executions, Valori secures his power over Florence. He alone lusted for the conspirators' blood, even cried out before the Council that either he or Bernardo must die. With the Signoria in the hands of the Piagnoni it was no question who would be sacrificed.

And what of Fra Girolamo, the prophet of God, scourge of the Church, savior of Florence? He alone could have stopped this injustice. Yet when given an appeal for mercy the Frate is said to have replied, "Let them die or be expelled. It makes no difference to me." This is the man who condemns the Borgia pope as a fraud. Where are the agents of God? If not in Rome, then surely not in Florence.

If only I could leave in peace. But all of Florence knows that I was Bernardo's man. If I flee now, it will be taken as a sign that I was involved in this conspiracy, and I will lose everything, perhaps even my brother Giocondo. Yet if I go back, I will have to guard myself against the vipers evermore, and without my strongest ally. That, and my former attachment to Tomassa will surely pit the Piagnoni against me. My position is more perilous than I could have imagined when I agreed to attach myself to Bernardo. But I have no choice, I must return no matter the danger.

I am here in San Silvestri only to prepare my wife and sons for the journey they must make. I have already sent word to Giuliano about the executions and the dangers for my family. Tomorrow, Lisa, Barto, and Piero will travel north to Lyons, where Valori cannot touch them. Then I shall return to Florence, where my fate will be decided one way or another.

—⁓—

At a height of two stories and the length of a prospect hall, the grand ballroom of the Zenobio Palace was a bona fide spectacle, a yawning chasm in the imagination decked in gold Baroque and mosaic filigree, with a marble floor that shimmered like a long mirage and an arched serliana that floated like a corona below the orchestra gallery, where a string quartet was playing a sonata that washed the entire chamber in somber timbre and tone. But the real highlights were the frescoes: a series of murals that had been created by different artists at different periods in the palace's history. The three landscapes along the short portego were painted by Luca Carlevarijs, the father of the *veduta* style of large-scale landscapes; the walls by Gaspare Dizani and Giambattista Tiepolo represented, respectively, allegorical depictions of "virtue and nobility" and "peace and love," while above the portego doors, high-relief golden medallions illustrated the contest between the god Apollo and the satyr Marsyas.

And yet all of this was figuratively eclipsed by the ceiling, where plaster and paint took elegance to a new level (a new dimension, almost) in a series of trompe l'oeil frames depicting magical and mythological scenes, dancing cherubs, mocking dwarves, frolicking nymphs, and nude statuary, all articulated with rich oriental fabrics and Rococo garlands to produce an impression of intense depth. Sweeping reds, constant gold, and pale stucco combined to create a kind of orbit in situ, a pretense of dimension, an illusion both immutable and fluid.

This protean creation was actually the work of a French artist, Louis Dorigny, who settled in Venice in the late 17th century and remained for 50 years, unable to free himself from the enchantment of the waterlogged Republic. I understood something of the sentiment, because for the next 20 minutes I remained glued to the marble floor while Dorigny's grandiose trickery excited every fiber of my imagination.

I should admit here that prior to that moment I'd never seen any of these artists' work (nor heard their names, for that matter) and it was weeks, in fact, before I could identify the paintings that had so moved me at the time. This was because all of the artists who'd worked on the Zenobio ballroom lived after the Renaissance, whereat my art interests were firmly grounded. Frankly, at that time in my life, if it wasn't created within about a hundred years of Leonardo, there was no chance I'd have heard of a given work of art. Indeed, Vasari's *Lives of the Artists* is still my principle source of knowledge in that realm. This is not a point of pride, but an admission of how narrow my margins are where art is concerned.

And yet, upon seeing this work—especially the Dorigny—I felt the same kind of mystical insight that had gripped me when I first witnessed Leonardo, like a light shined on some strange place in the soul usually reserved for religion and love.

Of course, thinking thus of Leonardo brought me quickly back to Silvo—the supposed Count of Vinci. Had it really only been two days since I met him? For some reason it seemed much longer. I wondered what he was thinking of me, the American "writer" who had absconded with his 500-year-old manuscript. Was he, at that moment, sitting on the balcony of his little restaurant along the piazza, waiting patiently for me to return with my agent/wife? Or had he lost hope? Was he cursing my existence? Did he think, finally, that I had tricked him out of the last remnant of his birthright? Or was Silvo—like Leonardo's birthplace and Dorigny's ceiling—just another trompe l'oeil himself?

For her part, Mir had assured me that Silvo was a fake and his manuscript a scam, one too eager to be good and the other too good to be true. Yet somehow I still had hope, or faith, or just some desperate desire to believe his story, if only to validate something I'd done in the eyes of my agent/wife.

It wasn't always that way. When I first met Miriam, I was still an aspiring writer and she a fledgling at one of the bigger literary agencies in New York. One summer night, we both attended a screening for an incredibly low-budget movie made by an equally fledgling and aspiring Indian American filmmaker from Queens. Miriam, obviously, was there on business—searching for properties among young artists was her thing in those days. I was there with my girlfriend at the time, an equally Indian American woman who was part of the quasi-Desi community in Jackson Heights. The catch was that even though we were sharing a bed and a lease—as well as a six-month-old cocker spaniel named Sanjay—her parents upstate knew nothing of my decidedly Caucasian existence.

At some point after the movie ended, when Reena (my girlfriend) was with the other Indians congratulating the filmmaker, both Miriam and I found ourselves at the small card table where a preteen Hindi girl was pouring guests red wine in even redder plastic cups. As was usual at those gatherings, I had been consigned to my own society while Reena mingled with her subcontinental peers. Miriam seemed even more alone—though no less at her ease for that fact and somehow much less obscure than me, surveying the crowd with the same kind of explicit significance I would see when we walked into the garden of the Palazzo Zenobio.

As always, she made easy conversation, and before I knew what I was doing (and before I knew what she did for a living, I might add), I was telling Miriam that I was a writer. Nothing exceptional in that, really; in those days I told everyone I was a writer. Soon—but certainly *after* she told me what she did for a living—she and I were discussing *The Skyscraper Theorists*, my long, dense novel-in-progress about architects in 1920s Manhattan. And she loved it: the theme, the setting, the context, the characters, even the bald phallic overtones of the title ("just like the city," she said approvingly). And she was literate and articulate and funny and caustic and completely comfortable in her own skin, even in a place where she didn't know a soul. We talked for a long time —not just about my book—and for the first time at one of Reena's Desi get-togethers I didn't feel completely invisible. Though Miriam left early that night, she encouraged me to send my manuscript when I finished.

I didn't wait. Within a week I'd sent her the first four chapters and within a month she'd read the first ten. For the next few months, Miriam and I were on the phone practically once a week talking about *The Skyscraper Theorists*. In addition to being funny and bright, she was legitimately interested in the book; her comments were generous and her criticisms spot-on. I'd not only found a reader for my work, I thought I'd found an agent who could get the damn thing published.

But then one day Miriam informed me she'd gotten a better offer to join a smaller agency, and would be leaving within a week. Though I wasn't officially a client, she said she couldn't in good conscience take my manuscript with her, and would be passing *The Skyscraper Theorists* on to another agent with her best wishes for its future. Of course, the other agent didn't like the book and didn't think it would sell, so after several months of waiting I was abruptly cut loose.

At about the same time, Reena and I finally flamed out. She took Sanjay and moved into a flat in Jackson Heights.

It didn't take long after that for me to call Miriam at her new office, though this time the conversation focused less directly on my book. I told her, of course, about the snub from her former colleague. She apologized and offered to meet me in person, and soon we were having dinner at Olivia's Kitchen on the Upper West Side, where Miriam had only recently become acquainted with the rustic fare and the hostess' laudable bonhomie. A couple dozen dates later I was meeting her soon-to-be-terminal father and—albeit unknowingly—being gifted a honeymoon in Italy. In fact, it all happened so fast that I practically forgot about *The Skyscraper Theorists*.

Miriam didn't, though. She continued to coax and criticize and encourage, just as she had done since our earliest conversations, just as I would see her do with other clients through the years. Despite its rejection by another agent, her confidence in my manuscript— and me—was unwavering. She claimed that mine was the kind of manuscript she'd always wanted to sell, the kind of book that made her become a literary agent in the first place. I was flattered and infatuated.

But I was also lost. My story had grown so unmanageable that I hardly knew where it began and ended anymore; voices died in empty rooms, characters disappeared down vast rabbit holes. Some days I'd sit down at the keyboard and be adrift in the backstory before I could finish a sentence.

Miriam, bless her heart, understood that I was blocked and wanted to do something about it, so she got me a writing gig that should have been a surefire publication and payday. That, of course, was *A Knight's Journey*, which (QED) turned out to be a soul-sucking disaster. After that I pretty much gave up on novels and concentrated on my tedious magazine job. Miriam also stopped looking for the kinds of manuscripts she'd "always wanted to sell," focusing instead on the type of books that made money.

All that was about a year before we got married. Now she was wooing the likes of Andrea Bardani and Tod Barron while I was literally staring at the ceiling in search of something to inspire me. But, alas, there was nothing there but fancy paint. Instead, I managed to find another glass of champagne—they seemed to be everywhere—and staggered off toward the north door of the ballroom, passing in my flight divers mistresses, aristocrats, politicians, plutocrats, ingénues, European film stars, and Italian athletes, masked and unmasked, as well a gaggle of middle-aged gays whose aggregate flamboyance practically echoed off the walls.

I exited at the anteroom opposite where Miriam and I had entered the palace. My purpose there—having witnessed several guests on Zenobio's *piano nobile,* which balcony surrounded the ballroom—was to find the stairwell by which I might gain access to the second floor and get a closer look at those frescoes. At least, that was my plan. Suffice it to say, I was in no condition for such explorations, what with several glasses of champagne and the lack of oxygen beneath the Plague Doctor. In fact, by that time I was so dizzy I could barely see straight.

I rambled round the corner in search of a way upstairs. This took me into a niche that seemed to be blocked on three sides—that is, until I stumbled into one of the stucco walls and it gave way slightly, yielding the promise of undiscovered territory. I put my shoulder to the door and opened a gap large enough to squeeze through, provided I removed my phallic mask.

On the other side of the door was a darkened hallway matching exactly the one I'd just come from. To my right it came to a dead end, but to the left a faint glow summoned my slightly drunken attentions. Though I still intended to find the stairway by which I might continue my reverie with the Dorigny ceiling, this new and unique prospect (mostly for the fact that I was, suddenly, alone) was too intriguing to pass up. I went toward the light at the end of the passage.

The corridor opened into a gallery with high ceilings and arched skylights. From above, the moon gazed down on the empty hall, creating a pale radiance that whispered through the narrow space, illuminating motes of dust cast like statues in the still air. In the dim glow, I could see that the walls were hung with dozens of antique mirrors made of silver and copper, tin and steel, curved and flat and framed with gilding, carving, varnish, leather, stained glass, matte, and stone in all shapes and all sizes arrayed along all points to make a veritable kaleidoscope of the moonlight. This, of course, was the Hall of Mirrors, counterpart to the Stucco Hall that Miriam and I had passed through on the other side of the ballroom earlier that evening. In order to protect these various precious objets d'art, this part of the palace had been sealed from guests at the masquerade. Thus I was unaccompanied among the mirrors—that is, unless you counted the hundreds of small doppelgangers that materialized the moment I entered the gallery.

The contrast between the ballroom and the Hall of Mirrors could not have been more striking. There, the frescoes and marble blended with the gaudy trompe l'oeil to create something greater than mere plaster and paint. The mirrors had almost the opposite effect, as any image that passed their purview suffered such exponential reflection that it was instantly reduced to oblivion. As my own image bounced through a thousand steadily smaller repetitions, I couldn't check a feeling of diminishing integrity, as though duplication served to reduce me. Once upon a time I'd assumed that I contained multitudes, but to see those multitudes scattered about the gallery like so many tokens and trifles just made them seem sad and shattered.

It was only after turning, in aversion, from those frightening little apparitions that I happened upon the paradigm for Zenobio's collection: At the far end of the gallery, just beyond the area where moon beans cut through the skylights, stood the largest mirror I'd ever seen. It covered the entire eastern limit of the gallery from floor to ceiling (at least twenty feet) and wall to wall except for a small, draped aperture at the very bottom middle, through which, presumably, visitors usually entered.

This glass giant was simultaneously a miracle of engineering and a complete failure of agency. As to the first: It covered some 300 square feet in a single, unbroken plane without seam or graft, yet somehow accommodated a four-by-six-foot portal at its base without supports. Gravity alone should have made it splinter like a spider web, but the surface appeared smooth and even throughout, save for the beveled edge that ran the perimeter at a width of six inches. Beyond that border was a heavy iron frame wrought into a kind of vinery that projected toward the reflecting area. The whole deranged behemoth hovered above the doorway like a magician's crystal ball, threatening to crash into a million pieces—though through some unknown alchemy of art and construction the damn thing held fast to the wall.

It was a miracle.

The failure lay in the fact that the mirror's amalgam was either poorly made or poorly applied, and was thus deteriorating unevenly behind the glass. As a consequence, the reflection it gave had as many gaps as a birdcage; whole portions of the mirror simply swallowed all visible light, never to give it back. This gave rise to a curious phenomenon that truncated the reflection in areas where the amalgam broke down, causing the Hall of Mirrors' mirror image to have a queer Escher-esque aspect—corners went unmet, walls stopped mid-climb, and the floor buckled uncomfortably as though it had been rift and restitched by a madman.

Likewise, my own image twisted and broke and eventually evaporated in the foggy glass—only to emerge (if briefly) intact from another part of the mirror like a ghost from the ether. I've never, before or since, seen anything like it. But suffice it to say, these repeated reincarnations were enough to give me the willies. I'd never really appreciated until then how much we rely on mirrors to cement our sense of self. From the time we're old enough to understand their device, mirrors are an instrument to situate us as individuals in the physical world. Take away mirrors and you've removed a central plank of your identity: how you appear to other people.

Thus to look into an unreliable mirror strikes one as a kind of betrayal. This is best understood in the surrealist aspect of the funhouse mirror, which grotesques our features for amusement. But because the funhouse only *distorts* the reflection, it represents a minor betrayal. It's another thing altogether to have an entire reflection disappear before your eyes. That's just creepy.

It's also the kind of thing that can plant deep, existential doubt in your mind—the kind of doubt that leaves a blemish on your soul and gives an uneasy inkling of the great cosmic void and whatnot. Or I was just drunk, I didn't know which. In fact, my doubts were multiplying like reflections in a chamber full of mirrors; I was disappearing down a vortex of a faulty alloy. Worst of all, I was getting poetic again. In addition, somewhere along the way I'd lost my carnival mask and I had no idea—nor any desire, really—where to look for it.

Whatever the case, I was done with all that reflection. I turned and scurried out of the Hall of Mirrors like a frightened bug.

The Domestic Chronicle of Francesco del Giocondo, Merchant of Florence

February 27, 1498—I come to San Silvestri to make preparations for the return of my wife and children, who have been these last six months living in Lyons with Giuliano while I was enmeshed in the malicious politics of Florence. For truth, I had despaired of ever seeing them again, for the climate at the time of their departure was so fraught with peril that I had little hope of surviving.

In contrast to my expectations, the conflict between factions in the city cooled with the air of autumn. In the end, Valori's execution of the conspirators served its purpose. The Bigi lost their captains, the Arrabiati were cowed by the killing of such prominent citizens. Even the vile Compagnacci ceased to campaign for a return to the luxury and license of the Medici. The Piagnoni ruled unopposed throughout the winter. For all these months, the Frate's only opposition was from Rome.

But the Borgia pope is enraged. He has twice threatened interdict against the city, as well as confiscation of Florentine property in Rome, in addition to excommunication for Savonarola. Still the friar does not cease speaking against Pope Alexander. Now, only yesterday, comes the final brief from Rome. Savonarola is forbidden to preach, and the Signoria is ordered, upon pains of interdiction, to deliver him into the hands of the Vatican.

Pope Alexander has a great army at his disposal, and an even greater hatred for Savonarola. Yet the masses love Fra Girolamo, and would not stand by should any man lay violent hands on the friar. The Signoria is trapped between the Church and the people, with a likelihood of violence on either side. I had thought the danger passed. I shan't have sent for Lisa and the children had I known of this new threat on the horizon.

—*ww*—

March 3, 1498—What joy it is to be with my family once again! For truth, I had awaited them with great anticipation, and yet I was little prepared for the happiness our reunion produced. Tears flooded my eyes when Barto rushed from the carriage to greet me. I knelt and caught my boy in my arms, hugging him and weeping without shame for my heart leaped with the enthusiasm of a child.

Yet at the same time a feeling of quiet sadness was creeping through me, for the boy I held is not the boy I had expected to see. Barto has become lean and dexterous and heavy, so much so that I had to put him down after only a few moments of holding. I realized with self-pity that I would never again be able to throw him over my head as I used to, for I could not guarantee his safe return to earth. Ah, how my son has grown. Even the way he leapt from the carriage to greet me seems bittersweet. Gone is the poor clumsy boy who was forever stumbling because his limbs could not meet the demands of his excitable mind. Barto is now a boy of five years. Only last week I pictured him as a babe in swaddling clothes.

So too, Piero is less an infant. He walks now, to better effect than his brother at that age, and talks an incessant stream that only his mother and brother can comprehend. Indeed, both of my children now have vocabularies spotted with French phrases. And they share secrets that none other is privy to. Lord, how did I allow this time to go by unnoticed?

Lisa, thank God, remains unchanged, the same lucid beauty who greeted me when her father brought her to my home. She warms me to the bone, and seeing her in these last days, I know that the long winter is over. I shall stay in San Silvestri. No more of Florence for me. For truth, I do not know what I would do without that beguiling smile. It is the sun of morning, the hearth of home. She is the most dear creature, the most intimate enthusiasm in my life.

Now that I have a moment to reflect, it is remarkable to contemplate the change that has happened in me these last years. For thirty years, my life was consumed by thoughts of business and politics, and building my position in the world. Love and family held no rank in the hierarchy of my life. So while Giocondo and Giuliano, my older brothers, married and bore children, I focused all my energies on making the family silk trade one of the most envied ventures in Florence. At length, and ahead of my elder siblings, I became de facto head of the family. And a believer in the severities of Savonarola's teachings. And for truth I looked down on my brothers for their dependence upon women and children for happiness.

But I was wrong. For in all that time I never once felt the happiness of these last days with my family in San Silvestri. Now politics and business seem nothing but a burden to me. I would sooner leave Florence altogether, pursue a life of penury and irrelevance, than ever be separated from Lisa and my boys again.

———

March 18, 1498—Incredible news from Florence. In obeisance to the papal bull, Fra Girolamo has retired to the priory of San Marco. The Borgia pope is appeased. Florence is, for the moment, saved. Oh Lord, I pray that this is the end of such unfavorable relations. And please let it be the beginning of more peaceable times.

———

April 9, 1498—All night to San Silvestri. My mind is shambles, Florence is in frenzy. Savonarola is jail; Valori and his wife torn to pieces by the mob. In Rome, the false pope laughs at the carnage. Is this the friar's prophecy come to pass? Is it the end of days? But it cannot be, for here, an arm's length from me, my wife lies in lovely repose, more perfect than anything in God's creation. Amidst the day's madness my heart fills with abysmal love. I do not want an end. No matter if Paradise awaits, I do not want to leave this earth if she is here. God grant me another day another week another year that I may look upon her beauty and know that I am a man.

—⟡—

After leaving the Hall of Mirrors and steering my way through the haute monde in the ballroom and the courtyard, I made it back to the garden where Miriam was still engaged with the novelist Tod Barron, who was at that moment simultaneously holding forth and biting down on a napkin-wrapped petit four. My wife attended him with professional gestures and a pursed mouth that said she was ready to deal. As I approached, Miriam looked up and found me with a kind smile, which, after my recent bout of spiritual anomie, was bracing to say the least.

"I was beginning to think you'd disappeared," she said when I met them. "Where's your mask?"

"The mask has *come off*, literally and figuratively," I said, echoing my wife's prediction from earlier in the evening. My voice, alas, seemed thick and inept, as though I'd just learned to use it.

"Are you okay, darling?" Miriam asked.

"First-rate. And you?"

She took my hand firmly in hers and pulled me to her side. "Tod was just telling me something about his method."

"His *method*?"

Miriam squeezed hard.

Tod Barron finished chewing the pastry and crumpled the napkin in his fat, rheumatic hands before letting the paper drop randomly on the ground. He inhaled visibly and spoke in the same airy tone as before, "Why do I get the feeling you don't respect what I do?"

Miriam squeezed even harder to forestall my reply.

"Have you ever read one of my books?"

"Several, in fact," I answered, retrieving my hand to avert further pressure.

"Oh," smugly, "You're a fan."

"Well I wouldn't say *that*, exactly."

"David wrote a book," Miriam broke in. "He used your books as...inspiration."

"Well I wouldn't say *that*, exactly."

Tod Barron nodded pompously. "Now I understand: You want to be a writer."

"Excuse me?"

"That explains your confrontational attitude toward me. Don't worry," to Miriam, "I see this kind of thing all the time. An aspiring writer encounters a successful artist and immediately he feels he must try to measure up. But sometimes the only way to bring things equal is to tear one side down."

"I'm sure he doesn't mean it, Tod."

"It's perfectly alright."

"It's *perfectly* alright?" I gasped, taking a step away from my wife to form a more equal triangle between us. "Perfectly alright. What a delightful locution, Tod—a categorical platitude modifying a vague cliché. Tell me, how do artists such as yourself come up with these ingenious bon mots?"

"David!"

"Miriam, I'm simply trying to learn from a successful artist. Certainly Tod has valuable pointers that could help me create a literary masterpiece like *The King's Vendetta*."

"That book sold probably 50,000 copies."

"More like sixty," Tod Barron corrected.

"What was this king's vendetta anyway? Can kings even have vendettas? Isn't that pretty much a plebian idea? Kings don't take revenge, do they? They're supposed to be instruments of God and all that."

My wife stared daggers at me.

Tod Barron smiled again, though somewhat less comfortably this time. In the lamplight, a little bit of color had actually broken out on his papier-mâché forehead. "I think I'll be leaving now," he said delicately.

"Not on our account, I hope."

To which the novelist uttered a noncommittal murmur and minced off in the direction of the courtyard. Miriam shot me an absolutely poisonous look and rushed after him, initiating contrition mid-stride. "I'm so sorry Tod…"

Meanwhile, I took the opportunity to acquire another glass of champagne, for courage.

Within a few minutes I spied Miriam cutting back through the crowd at a steady clip. The bottom part of her mouth was twisted like the rictus of a small bird, an expression that represented (I knew from long experience) the absolute height of my wife's consternation. For good measure, she avoided eye contact while I attended her arrival, and made a great show of assaying the entire garden before returning to me.

"That was quite a performance," she reported.

"You or me?"

She put a hand on her hip and inclined her eyes toward the moon. "You didn't have to insult him," she said.

"Well, you didn't have to humor him," just as bluntly.

"Actually I did," she confirmed, pitching her head at an aggressive angle for emphasis. "I keep telling you that, but somehow it doesn't sink in. Tod Barron is a commercially viable writer with a book to sell."

"Tod Barron is a horse's ass."

"Well his readers think he tells exciting, compelling stories that are easy and enjoyable to read. Have you ever seen the reader reviews? I have. They love him. More importantly, they buy him."

"I can't believe you're defending this. The man is walking schmaltz."

"Fine, he's not exactly a *literary* writer."

"Not *exactly?*" I asked, aghast. "Jesus, when did you get so indulgent? Tod Barron has all the eloquence of direct mail. I've heard limericks that are more original."

"So what am I supposed to do, ignore him? Or mock him, like you? If I dismissed every writer who didn't live up to your standards, David, I wouldn't have a single client. And we wouldn't have any money."

"Again with the money?"

"Yes, again with the money! What the hell did you think I was doing? His last book sold 60,000 copies. Do you know what kind of commission that would mean for me?"

"Do you know what kind of crap you would have to read for the payoff?"

"Of course I do. Don't pretend you're telling me something I don't know. I usually have to read through piles of that kind of crap for something an editor *might* be willing to take a chance on publishing. The difference is that with Tod Barron the deal is guaranteed."

"Really? Like *A Knight's Journey?*"

"That was *not* my fault," Miriam insisted, her voice wavering a little on the negative. "Don't you *dare* try to lay that on me."

"That was supposed to be guaranteed."

"It was, as much as anything can be. I did everything I could to save that book and you know it. I couldn't help it if the front author pissed the whole thing away."

"If you couldn't help that, you shouldn't have gotten me involved in the first place. Instead you *sold* me, and I wasted a whole year on that piece of shit. You were supposed to be my agent too."

"I *was* your agent and it was the right thing. That book should have launched your career." She threw up one hand in a gesture of helpless contempt. "Sometimes these things just don't work out, even if they seem guaranteed. I'm sorry."

I realized at that point that I'd been glaring at her with gritted teeth for about the last minute and a half. I made an effort to temper my expression.

"What happened?" I asked. "You used to want to sell real books. Now you're coddling Tod Barron and touring Italy at Livia's beck and call."

"I told you: That's my job. I do what I have to do to make money for my clients, my company, and myself. That means selling a lot of crap and bending over backwards to do it. Of course I'd like to represent only clients whose work I love. But those projects are, if not one in a million, then one in a hundred or one in a thousand. The rest of the time, in this business, you have to get your hands dirty. And, yes, my hands are dirty.

"But this isn't about me," she went on. "Tod was right: You do have a problem with successful writers. Every time you meet one of my clients, you have this huge chip on your shoulder, like you have to prove that you're better than them. And you know what? You might be. *The Skyscraper Theorists* is a wonderful book—thoughtful, funny, even moving. And *A Knight's Journey* was good for what it was, which was a perfectly serviceable page-turner.

"You're a lovely writer, David. The difference between you and my clients isn't talent or opportunity. You've got both of those. But you don't have any ambition, my dear," she said unsympathetically. "You used to, but you gave up. So you had a bad experience. That doesn't mean you abandon everything. You need to get back in there and be excited about writing, like the guy I met three and a half years ago. You can do that. I believe in you. I always have. The only reason I brought that project to you was that you were drowning in your own novel. You needed to come up for air. And you did. Like I said, *A Knight's Journey* was a very good book."

"Thank you."

"You're welcome." Miriam came closer. "Come on. How many writers have written a book that didn't get published. Most of them, right? So write another. And if that doesn't sell, write another. Get over yourself; you're not the only person who's afraid of a blank page. But there aren't any shortcuts. You have to pour out all the shit that's in you and then sift through it to find a few little shitty pieces of gold you can polish up and use. Then you get up the next day and do it again. You have to get your hands dirty too. I tell all my other clients: The only way the work gets done is to do the work. That might sound trite, but it's a stone fact."

My wife let out a sigh, shook her curly hair, and looked at the ground. "You know the old cliché about writing what you know, don't you?" she asked.

I nodded.

"Well it's wrong," she said flatly. "You'd do better to write what you love, or at least what you like, or what really interests you. Write something *you* want to read about. That's why Tod Barron sells—because he dives into every one of his lousy books with something like love. Don't think about *finishing* a book, for god's sake, concentrate on *writing* a book. Because unless you find something that inspires you, then the whole thing is just a lot of drudgery, and you're never going to see it through.

"But first you're going to have to decide whether you want to be this poser character you've created as a way to mask your insecurities, or if you want to become a real goddamned writer. Because right now, that's what you are, David. You're one of those people who talks a good game but can't back it up. And until you get off your ass and write something, that's all you're going to be."

We stared at each other for a long moment, like strangers on a bus. After nearly three years together —and not yet three weeks of marriage—Miriam suddenly seemed something untouchable, as distant as the gulf between life and death. The gap between us felt almost physical, as though describing clear differences in space and time, underlining doubts about the future and present, giving voice to the gray ghosts of days gone by. In truth, I barely recognized my wife, and in her naked face I could find no hint of intimacy, no reflection of my *self*.

It then occurred to me for the first time that we might *not* have gotten married. Not that we didn't get married, as though some alternate reality had taken hold; or that we shouldn't have gotten married, as if passing judgment. But that, indeed, there had been another choice. That we simply might not have wed and yet have gone through with the other arrangements of our early middle age: *viz.*, finances and amusements, jobs and books, a new apartment on West End Avenue.

But was it really possible to have all those amenities without the nuptials? Case in point: our trip to Italy. Was this merely a timely opportunity for travel, or was it contingent upon something bigger? Was it conceivable that Miriam and I might have accepted her father's intended wedding gift if, indeed, there had been no wedding? Not likely. In even the best of circumstances, such a thing would appear crass. The stark fact of Tom's passing between purchasing the gift and its itinerary dates would have made taking the trip as an unmarried couple an unpardonable indulgence.

Which suddenly suggested something weird about the patronage we'd received from Miriam's father—in his waning days—with (admittedly) scant cause for his faith in us. For the first time I wondered whether, in fact, there was an ulterior motive behind the gift. Whether, in fact, he'd not so much seen something in Miriam and me that gave him confidence in our future together, as he had wanted to push that future in a definite direction. Thus the perfect honeymoon package slated for a date that allowed for a more or less normal courtship. In short, it seemed entirely possible that Tom had arranged my marriage to his daughter, and done so with such subtlety that I failed to grasp that fact till the honeymoon was almost over.

At that moment, from the direction of the palace, a rhythmic commotion rose over the courtyard like déjà vu, and within seconds the masquerade crowd parted to give way to a parade of persons waving signs and chanting something musical in unison. At the end of the phrase, someone shouted, "Show pero!" and the rest echoed in kind. Of course, this whole rigmarole was exactly the same thing we'd seen when our train came to a stop outside of Ferrara. As then, the group was made up of people dressed in the attire of train personnel—conductors, ticket-takers, serving staff—leading me to guess was that we were being followed across Europe by some kind of weird railroad cult. This version was even more bizarre though, because the odd conga line was now snaking its irksome way through the crème de la crème of the Italian literary world.

As if on cue, Giusy Viola emerged from the throng—still, for the record, wearing her leopard print mask—shuttling a drink in one hand while the other cut the air in a near-caricature of Italian animation.

"What's going on?" Miriam asked.

"Aiii," Giusy moaned, throwing her free hand in the direction of the chanters. "*Lo sciopero.* Ees the—how you say?—the strike for the train."

"There's a train strike?" Miriam turned a concerned eye toward me.

"Si. *Domani:* Tomorrow." Giusy sipped carelessly at her drink. "*Madonna mia!* They are noissy, no? They only can come in here because Vittorio, *il diretorre,* was a *communista* in the 70s."

"Show pero?" I asked.

"*Si. Sciopero,*" Giusy answered matter-of-factly.

"Tomorrow?"

She looked at me like I was an idiot and glanced conspicuously at Miriam before answering again: "*Si.*"

At that, Giusy made an excessive gesture of greeting to someone on the other side of the garden and begged off with a short ciao and staccato kisses on each cheek, leaving Miriam and me in the crater created by her strike bombshell.

"What are we going to do?" I asked.

"I *have* to make my plane in Rome on Monday," Miriam insisted.

"Then we have to leave now."

"Right now?"

"We might still catch the last train," I said with a shrug. "If we don't there's no telling how long it could take to get back to Rome."

Miriam bit her lower lip and I could see the scales balancing in her head. On the one hand, she hadn't accomplished anything at the masquerade (no thanks to me), and clearly wanted a few more hours to see if she could make some contacts. On the other hand, any delay could jeopardize our return to New York—which, in turn, meant further issues with clients and colleagues.

"Fine," she said at last. "Let's just go."

So without further ado Miriam and I turned and hurried out of the garden, across the courtyard, and through the ballroom with its tempting frescoes, exiting hardly a minute later onto the Fondamenta del Soccorso where, luckily, a line of water taxis had begun gathering in the canal to ferry the masquerade's early departures. By the time we pulled off the quay, Miriam had already ascertained that the last train out of Venice was scheduled for 11:56 p.m., which meant we had less than 30 minutes to get our bags and reach the station. It was impossible, of course.

Happily, at that late hour (at least by Venetian standards) the water taxi met no traffic, cutting up the canal some hundred yards in just seconds before ducking into a narrow cranny between two palazzos. We were plunged into darkness so thick I lost track of my wife at my side, and once again by some magical factor of the labyrinth time seemed to linger and die within the architecture. Less than ten minutes later, we reached the hotel, slashing the trip to pieces by way of our boatman's saturnine shortcut. There, we packed in a flash and, aided by the same graciously mustachioed maitre d'—Robert, who, incidentally, asked no questions about our hasty departure—threw the suitcases back in to the waiting water taxi, then swept definitely up the Grand Canal as midnight approached. In minutes we were in view of the still-lit monolith of the train station, into which I could see the conga line of strikers dancing and hear their rhythmic leftist mantras bouncing off the concrete. The water taxi didn't bother with a jetty, instead approaching the quay directly and disgorging us and our luggage on the coldish pavement. I paid the taxi man handsomely and (as there were no porters at midnight) Miriam and I gathered the bags and scrambled after the protesters, who were just then embarking. The train's lights flashed and a pill-boxed conductor wandered down the platform, glancing disinterestedly at the two would-be passengers literally sprinting down the concourse—me in my wedding suit, she in her evening dress—toward his steel vehicle. He blew a whistle and the train uttered some ominous, preparatory resonance. Miriam and I were just twenty feet away, straining for the door. We needed only a few more seconds. The conductor poked his head from a coupling two cars on, looked us over once again with Mediterranean disdain, and disappeared back into the gap. I knew we were doomed.

And yet by some miracle of temporal and physical will we made it, leaping onto the rear landing of the last car just seconds before the train pulled out of the station.

Miriam and I both sat stunned and exhausted for several minutes, aghast by our mad dash to catch the last train from Venice. Then all at once we collapsed into hysterical laughter born of some parts solidarity and relief, and in another moment we were embracing away the absurdity of the situation. When we'd caught our respective breaths and recovered from the excitement, Miriam and I once again gathered up the bags and entered the train proper, which by that time was already crawling across the dark margins of the lagoon.

The most surprising thing was that the train was, in fact, practically deserted. Here and there a few solitary souls dotted the landscape, usually sprawled across several seats for better sleeping, but for the most part each car that Miriam and I passed through was astonishingly vacant. To New Yorkers, this was something of a shock. My best guess was that the last train out of Venice—or anywhere, for that matter—before the strike hit would be packed to the rafters. Italians, it seemed, where much more sanguine about the prospects of being stranded.

The upshot was that as Miriam and I went further toward the front of the train, we found several sleeper cars that were unoccupied.

"Should we?" she asked, stopping at one of the open sleepers.

"Yes. I don't care what it costs."

Together we shuttled the bags inside the compartment and I flipped on a small overhead lamp that barely lit the cabin. Miriam splashed onto the far bench, arms raised and her hair cascading round her face like an aureole. Thus arrayed in the yellow light, my bride called to mind the Botticellis we'd lingered over in our hurried tour of the Uffizi in Florence.

I perched on the seat opposite and watched her, almost literally, unwind, elongating her body from toes to fingers, arching her back, and twisting her hips to exert her torso, still sheathed in green satin—all this in a way that, just then, struck me as almost unsuitably sensuous. After all, only an hour earlier Miriam and I had been at daggers-drawn in the middle of a garden party. Every quarrel has its own a perspective; some are conducted at long range, striking lightly along broad lines of contention, while others are performed in close quarters, where every thrust and parry engages a hard emotional target. What Miriam and I had done at the masquerade was a knife fight. And with the exception of our brief, cathartic embrace when we made the train, there'd been no attempts at amends since then. But seeing her there, limned in the dim light like an artist's model, all the hostility faded away. Instead, I found myself smitten with her tousled beauty and amazed by the strange alchemy that translates ire to ardor and conflict to conjugation. It didn't make sense, but that didn't matter. Love rings truer than reason, creating its own source of light. And for me, for the first time in days, everything seemed brilliant.

Miriam opened her eyes and a warm sentiment swept through our small compartment. "Turn that off and get over here," she said amorously.

I stood and switched the lamp, throwing us into dark save for the pale moon just then at climax over the fens. Miriam became a vision in black and white: hair fanned and her cocktail dress stretched tight across the bust, extending herself erotically on the odd chaise-lounge.

I stepped across the small gap between our benches and Miriam's hand rose like a lily toward the sunlight. I guided her to a sitting position and took her face in my hands. She gazed up; the moon shone in the corners of her dark eyes. Maybe it was the champagne, or the train, or maybe it was just the blue light of midnight in Italy, but at that moment Miriam looked more pliant, more yielding, than I'd ever seen her, somehow absolved of all her professional skepticism.

My hands slipped softly down the sides of her neck and across her shoulders. She dropped her head against my chest, letting her curls fall opulently around her face. At the same time I leaned over and undid the clasp on her dress and she let out sigh of approval. I steered Miriam back to an upright position, and she, once again, met my eyes with that incongruous innocence that had aroused something unusual inside me. Kneeling, I coaxed the satin dress over her breasts and bent forward to place my lips against her nipple. Miriam gasped and sank back against the couch, taking my eager mouth with her.

After a moment I let go of her nipple and laid quiet kisses along the outer curve of her left breast, gradually working down her side, nibbling her ribcage, nuzzling her stomach where it met with the top of the depended dress. At the same time my hands ran up her legs and under the hem. Miriam sighed again while I kissed my way back up her chest and neck, finally meeting her parted lips, accepting me with eyes wide open and that mysterious, submissive air still lingering in shadow, as though awaiting my next movement.

I separated myself and took hold of her dress where it met her skin. She leaned back and surrendered her body, eyes still fixed on mine, while I pulled the dress down over her hips and thighs and her toes that pointed like a gymnast's as the fabric came free. For a moment I stood back and admired my wife's near-nakedness, the green dress draped in front of my erection. Miriam then stood up and with one plain turn of her wrists shimmied out of her underwear, leaving herself gloriously unclothed before me. She raised an eyebrow and bit her lip.

I dropped the dress on the floor.

Miriam stepped toward me, shameless in her nudity, and pushed me back onto the couch. She stood over me for a willful minute, hands on her hips and one leg forward, her ankle raised at an impish angle that exposed her sex to my appreciative gaze. Seeing her like that, as naked as the daylight, awakened sense of sexual privilege in me, the idea that I, as her husband and master, had absolute right to the pleasures of her flesh—a kind of droit du seigneur, though with less chauvinist overtones merely for the fact that she was, after all, my own wife. Miriam, meanwhile, had lost the strange veil of innocence she'd put on the last few minutes. In its place was a frank sexuality that expressed its own clear intentions. I pulled her to the couch, basking in her naked grace before my (still) suited person.

Miriam leaned between my legs in order to engage her breasts once again with my mouth, gathering my face to her bosom with a gentle pressure on the ridge of my neck. She let out a moan as my tongue and lips coaxed her nipples to erection. I drank in her odor—a mixture of sweat and lavender perfume—awash in the cascade of hair that engulfed my head and neck, evoking further prurient yearnings on my part. (And, I might add, my *part*.)

This time it was my wife who took a step back, as though deliberately repeating my earlier movements in an amorous dance. Miriam bent forward and undid my belt and zipper, then grabbed my waistband and pulled my pants past my knees, all the while considering me with her particular, professional air—though in this instance the look was spiced with something more lusty than usual.

Miriam carefully mounted the couch, placing her knees on either side of my body while guiding me inside of her with an expert hand, then delicately descended until our hips met. For a long moment neither of us moved or spoke, but sat in motionless silence absorbing the first frisson of penetration. Then, gradually, Miriam began to pitch her hips back and forth by tiny degrees, caressing my base with her labia while the tip remained fixed inside her. After a few minutes of these excruciating ministrations, my wife planted her hands onto the couch over my shoulders and started rocking her body in earnest, massaging me and pivoting her hips to increase the pressure against her pelvis. Thus intently pulling on my cock, Miriam worked herself into a harder rhythm, drawing up slow and coming down hard enough that it nearly took my breath away each time she thrust onto me, and I into her.

As Miriam continued to maneuver in my lap, I closed my eyes and tried to concentrate on the two inexorable mechanisms moving me—my wife diligently pistoning my shaft and the train steadily eating up miles of northern Italy—if only in an effort to prolong the vicious ecstasy of the moment. Thus disposed, I began to feel a welcome tension increase through my midsection, which, combined with the severe rearward velocity (I was laying/sitting on the forward bench in the train compartment), created the sensation that my body was actually floating in cold space, drifting out of time and place while anchored only and intimately to my anxious groin. This spot of erotic nirvana seemed to go on for an inordinate amount of time (and distance, I guess) while Miriam, invisibly, brought each of us closer and closer to crisis.

When I finally opened my eyes, my wife was no longer leaning over me but now was kneeling upright on my lap, hands tangled in her thick ringlets, eyes locked shut in concentration, features rapt, lip bitten, and her breasts billowing with the elegant gyration of her hips. Seeing Miriam so completely immersed the act of passion, I suffered a torrent of love (or something) that threatened to spill beyond the confines of my body.

Then all of a sudden a deep rumbling came up through the train's wheels and chassis, vibrating into me and out my extremities, and flashes of light brightened the cabin at half-second intervals creating a slow strobe of white and gray candescence. Of course, this was merely the train speeding through a nonscheduled station in the dark countryside, but in my compromised condition I think I can be forgiven if it felt to me a little like the onset of death.

I looked up one final time at my wife fucking me in slow Kinetoscope and gasped my last breath before diving into the breach. My hips clenched and my groin flexed and I let out a groan of anguish. At the same time, Miriam opened like a rose and gave a scream of her own just as the train whistle blew high and hard, signaling its indelicate passage through the vacant station.

The Domestic Chronicle of Francesco del Giocondo, Merchant of Florence

February 28, 1500—Today, I return to San Silvestri for the first time since the events of two years ago, when it seemed as if all was about to come to an end. Looking back at the last words that I wrote here then, I can still feel the echo of that dread, still sense remnants of the fear that nearly conquered me. These things linger like the ash of the great fire lit in the Signoria that day, which caused the end of Savonarola's rule of Florence.

But despite the terrible horrors of that time, all seems now to have happened for the best. As though coming through its own ordeal of fire, Florence has survived desperate days and become stronger. Pisa is for the moment quiet, the black Duke of Milan has been driven from power by France, and the Borgia pope was appeased by the immolation of Fra Girolamo. Without Savonarola, the Piagnoni cease to exist as a political faction. A new Signoria, composed almost completely of Arrabbiati, now governs the city peacefully, without the rancor that affected the better part of the last five years. Piero Soderini has established himself at the head of the faction, and now serves as gonfalonerie of the Republic. He wields much influence in Florence, yet does so moderately and judiciously. His power is credited more easily than a Valori or a Medici. Even Piero de Medici seems, for the time being, to have given up his ambition of regaining his father's seat of power. All is well in Florence for the first time since before the death of Il Magnifico.

The downfall of the Piagnoni has been good for me as well. With Fra Girolamo's strictures loosened, hunger for luxury is greater in Florence than any time in the last decade. Silks are once again in high demand, and I have had so much business that I can hardly keep stock. So too, the end of bitter rivalries among the Buonuomi has made politics tolerable once again. I was recently elected a Lord Prior for the first time.

But none of this has anything to do with why I am here. In fact, I am in San Silvestri because of a series of happy and sad coincidences. The first, sad fact I learned several weeks ago is the death of Giovanni Rucellai, brother of my first wife, Camilla. Thrown from a horse in Campania, he died instantly of a wound to his head. He was a younger man than I am. May God have mercy on his soul. Upon hearing this news, I could not help but think back to our quarrel over Giovanni's proposal to have Signorelli make a portrait of Camilla in the time of her second pregnancy, and my later guilt in having denied him his sister in the last days of her life. It is an act of selfishness I have never been able to absolve. To this day, my heart heaves with shame. I never apologized to him for the wrong I did. And yet upon my marriage to Lisa, after the scandal of my affair with Tomassa, Giovanni was among the first to come to me with wishes of congratulations. I am humbled by his goodness.

The second, happier fact is that Lisa is once again with child. It is our first child since Piero, who is now almost three years old, and the very image of his mother. Mona Piera guesses that my wife is almost three months with the child, as her bosom is beginning to show the fullness of nativity. I confess that I find her startlingly beautiful this way, and have often times found myself gazing at her with the ardor of a supplicant before the Holy Mother.

And yet, though it feels wrong to think it, a part of me wishes against this pregnancy. For I confess that I fear for my wife's safety in childbearing. I have, in these last years, come to know no greater pleasures than love for my boys, but was it not Camilla's second birth that took her from this world? And she was but a fraction of the wife to me that Lisa is. I could not endure her loss. I would surely never have another child if it means losing the light of Lisa's smile. But now it seems I have no choice but to take that risk.

The third event in this series of coincidences was made known to me just more than a week ago, when I visited the notary Ser Piero, the same man, in fact, who notarized the dowry of this San Silvestri from Antonmaria Gherardini upon my marriage to his daughter. Ser Piero told me that his son, the artist Leonardo, has left Milan and is now returned to Florence. Upon hearing this news, the idea came to me as clear as matins from a campanile. I determined at once to have a portrait of Lisa painted by the great Vincian, whose work I have of course seen and know to be brilliant. Images arise as though breathed to life by his genius. Lazarus rises blithely from oblivion. This is a man who makes pictures become alive. This is the man to paint my wife.

It was Lisa who insisted that the portrait be done at San Silvestri, as a tribute to her good father. I see absolutely no reason to disagree. And Leonardo, in fact, pronounced himself pleased to come to our farm, as it is so near Vinci where he was a child. In a few days, the great Vincian will be here to give me a gift far greater than gold or jewels or the scepter of the realm. He will paint me another Lisa, forever young, forever invulnerable. If Leonardo recreates her, I will never be without my love.

―――∽∾∽―――

About four hours after boarding, still in the small hours of predawn, the train from Venice was making its final approach to Rome. Miriam and I had managed to sleep for several hours following our (mutual, complementary, simultaneous!) orgasms—she in her blessed state of nudity and I with my pants still gathered around my ankles. Not, perhaps, a dashing image, but under the circumstances there wasn't much I could do: She had passed out on top of me immediately after climax.

Luckily, the striking crew members seemed every bit as nonchalant about their work stoppage as the Italian passengers. As a result, no one had come round to check our compartment. So even though we were basically stowaways—and had, by the by, made a pretty good ruckus with our semi-public lovemaking—we encountered exactly zero supervision from the train's authorities. Sleeping in varied degrees of undress presented no particular problem on that particular night, and by the time we disembarked in Rome we were both fairly well rested.

Just after sunrise, Miriam and I arrived at the hotel where we were due two days hence to stay one night before boarding our plane to New York. It was only then that we learned the truth about the Italian *scioperi* from the rather amused—though none-too-amusing—maitre d'hotel. He explained to us that Italian "strikes" were less general work stoppages and more like a pro-union formality, an essential gesture for the little socialist that lives in the pink heart of every working class European. The strikes, which can be local or national, are scheduled months, if not years, in advance, and last anywhere from a few hours to a day. There's even a calendar published to inform travelers (and strikers) of the upcoming *scioperi*. In other words, the whole thing was just another species of *scherzo*, or as in my initial estimation, a cheap piece of Italian theater. (In fact, that strike ended before the dinner hour had passed.) Whatever the case, Miriam and I had sacrificed our last two days in Venice to the collective conscience/sense of humor of the union establishment. As a result, we would have to stay two more nights in Rome, at considerable expense.

Not that I complained. After all, Venice was the darkest part of our honeymoon, whereas the first three days in Rome had been the most lighthearted by far. There was no question which city I'd rather be in.

And ironically, the return trip turned out to be just what we needed. Being absolved of the usual touristic obligations to sightsee, Miriam and I were able to get some of the coveted "space" that long-time New Yorkers so crave, even from a significant other. She spent the majority of those two days in the hotel, corresponding with clients and editors she'd been out of touch with for more than a week, as well as those she'd kept abreast of her travels. That included Olivia Winters and Andrea Bardani, who, of course, offered to come down to Rome for another meeting. My wife politely demurred. Meanwhile, my time was spent mostly in Piazza Navona and Campo de' Fiori, drinking endless espressos and observing the currents of the Roman *giornale*. For the first time on my honeymoon, I took time to sit down and spend real time writing in my journal—though in truth most of those pages ended up being fed to pigeons.

Granted, it wasn't as blissful as the first tour of Rome, but after the difficult days in Florence and an almost hostile day in Venice, culminating with open combat at the masquerade, a tranquil interlude was about all one could ask for. And frankly, bookending the honeymoon that way in Rome suited me just fine. By the time Monday morning rolled around, we were both ready to get home.

As the plane taxied down the misty morning runway, performing painstaking turns and queuing for interminable delays, I turned to Miriam, who was just then thumbing her last emails before our six-hour flight.

"Well, I guess the honeymoon's over," I offered with what I felt was the requisite irony.

"Yep," she said without pausing to look up from her Blackberry.

The Domestic Chronicle of Francesco del Giocondo, Merchant of Florence

March 20, 1500—The Vincian has now been with us for four days, and he is not as I would have thought. Of course, I had heard stories of his peculiar and mercurial behavior, of the unfinished works and the perhaps too intimate relationships with his assistants. For truth, even Ser Piero was conscientious enough to warn me of his son's eccentricities, though not without recommending that I commission him. Still none of it prepared me for the idiosyncrasy of the man who has come to San Silvestri.

Foremost, Leonardo's appearance is shocking. Though I have heard often of him, and have seen his work on more than one occasion, until four days ago I had never laid eyes on the man in person. And what a sight he is. The hair of his head and face falls long around his shoulders, making for the visage of lion wrapped in a great mane. Were it not for his elegant dress, one would think the maestro little more than a barbarian from the furthest reaches of civilization. Yet despite his leonine appearance, the Vincian's bearing is as gentle as a mouse, and as capricious as a sparrow. All day he wanders the grounds of San Silvestri in a perfect fit of curiosity, examining now a rock, now a bird, now a flower, never able to focus his attentions on one object for more than a short time. In this way, he seems strangely distracted and obsessive at the same time. If his intellect is limitless, as people say, then certainly his interest is finite as a knife.

Only Lisa, it seems, has the ability to compose his disorderly mind, for when he is with her, whether walking in the hills or sitting in the parlor, the erratic conflicts of his thoughts are all quelled for the moment, and his senses focus completely on her. When she speaks, he is rapt. When she is with the children, I find him watching her with such ardent concentration that it is as if he were absorbing her every gesture. Indeed, if I did not know of Leonardo's proclivities I would think the man quite obscene for his interest in my wife. As it is, I can only hope that this is the method of his particular genius.

——❧——

March 26, 1500—Today, Leonardo informs me that he is to return immediately to Florence to attend to business there. In all he was here for ten days, and not once did I see him touch brush or pencil. Already I worry if this commission will ever be finished.

——❧——

April 28, 1500—A strange thing has happened. I return today to San Silvestri to find the house teeming with people. Not only Leonardo and my family and the servants, but all manner of actors, dancers, musicians, and fools. It seems that Leonardo has invited a troupe of traveling players to stay at the farm for some days. Lisa explains to me that he instructs them to sing and dance and go about their merriment while she is sitting for the artist. It is, he tells her, to make her face more natural for the portrait. I have never heard of such a thing being done before, but I am so happy that the man has finally commenced work on the portrait that I am willing to forgive almost any eccentricity to that end.

——❧——

April 29, 1500—It is, as my wife said, a regular spectacle in the parlor where Leonardo has her posing. Behind the artist, the troubadours play harpsichord. They dance and mimic and throw balls into the air, catching and tossing them again with intricate symmetry. Barto and Piero clap and sing and play along with the youngest of the troupe. Meanwhile, before the

Vincian sits my Lisa, facing all that jollity. She is now some five months with child, and her smile is as radiant and peaceful as moonlight on glossy water. Neither Salome nor Helen of Troy ever glowed with such allure.

To my great fortune I am finally allowed to glimpse this portrait for which I am to pay twenty gold florins. I have not the eye of an artist, but I can begin to see Lisa taking shape before Leonardo, rising from the wood like an angel in animation. It is a thrilling thing to behold. And though it be unchaste, I admit that already her painting stirs my blood as its model did when we first married.

For his part, Leonardo remains modest about the painting. He took some time in explaining to me that it will take many applications, layering paint by the smallest degree, to get the effect he is creating. Yet when this is done, he says that my wife will come fully alive, and I will have Lisa in all her beauty forever. This is my wish, and I am very pleased.

As for the Vincian himself, he is completely changed when sitting before his panel. He is, for the first time in my seeing, a man of singular purpose. I must return to Florence in the morning, but now I am confident in the direction of this enterprise. I know that Lisa's portrait is in the very best hands.

—⁂—

July 1, 1500—Once more, the summer smolders in Florence. The air feels close, accumulating every self in the city's hot population and making the streets a swamp of infirmity and disease. With Lisa still in term, we retreat once again from the city walls, and from the plague. If nothing else, San Silvestri is excellent respite from the heat, though I quite doubt it will be relief enough for my wife, who is heavy of limb and huge with child. It devils her terribly. She was ill for a time during her term with Piero, but Lisa never appeared as strained, as burdened by the toll a child takes from a woman's body. I worry for her. This is another reason for us to be at San Silvestri, for I know that there is no other place in the world where Lisa feels so happy. My hope is that this happiness will aid her through the coming labor.

I lately spoke to Lisa of my fear for her impending labors, those arising from the memory of Camilla's second, fatal childbearing. I confessed as well that the impetus for my commission to Leonardo was the fear that she would be taken from me. But my dear wife is a pillar of strength. She received my confession with humor and compassion, and assured me that she plans to bear me many more children in her lifetime. In her great generosity, she even suggested that if it be a girl child, we shall name her Camilla. I do not know what I have done to deserve such a woman. God has rewarded me far beyond my merit.

———✦———

July 18, 1500—I return from a trip to Florence at an emergency meeting of the Signoria. The worst fears are realized, plague has struck the city. Already dozens are dead, many more expected. Measures will be taken to quarantine the city, grain will be rationed before harvest, the city gates will be closed to strangers. I have ordered Giocondo and his family to retreat to the Montughi farms with our servants. The house on Via della Stufa will be placed in the hands of a caretaker. I have done all I can do as a citizen and as the head of my family. Now I can only pray to God for the good of my family and my people.

While at Florence I also paid call to Leonardo, who has lived these months at the priory of Santissima Annunziata. I have not seen Lisa's portrait since the spring, and I had hoped that it would be finished so that I could bring her this gift along with such dire news from the city. Leonardo informed me that he too will be leaving Florence, having been summoned to Rome by Pope Alexander. When asked of the progress on Lisa's portrait, he seemed to grow anxious of the question, and spoke instead of engineering projects he expected to undertake for the Borgias. Still I persisted, asking him when he expects to be finished with the painting. To this, the Vincian gave a strange answer. He said to me, "Art is never finished, only abandoned." For truth, I do know what this means, but I think it does not bode well for this commission.

Here in San Silvestri, Lisa is close approaching childbirth. In fact, she is as pregnant as a vineyard in autumn, heavy with the fruit of her womb. She can hardly rise from the bed, where she lays in stately beauty for most of the day. Yet despite the summer heat and her advanced condition, my wife maintains the same tranquil pleasure that has been her fashion ever since she entered my household.

She told me she hopes for a girl child. I join her in that hope.

———— ⚬⁄⚬ ————

Miriam and I returned to New York a married couple, and life got on as it had before our fortnight in Italy. I went back to my droll job at the magazine, marking time against a schedule that was set years in advance, and Miriam returned to her office, where she put in sixty hours a week nurturing writers whose work she believed in. Her business was growing by leaps and bounds. Soon enough, Olivia Wolfe re-signed with the agency, selling her fourth cookbook for a quarter of a million dollars, and within eighteen months her brother, Andrea Bardani, published *60 Years in Italy: A Life in Food*. It remained on *The New York Times* bestseller list for more than ten weeks. Andrea had since moved to New York, and was an intermittent presence in our lives; successful, social, full of obsequious gratitude. I hated him more than anyone I'd ever met.

On the bright side, Tod Barron was never heard from again.

As for my writing, I made several attempts at the Freud/Leonardo/Dimitri Merejovski manuscript I'd made notes for at the Casa Natale—the book I was so hopeful for that afternoon in Vinci. But each time I tried, I put it aside in disgust, unable to maintain a coherent voice or story beyond a couple dozen pages.

I even tried, once, to ascertain the location of Silvano Massetti da Bagnano, the supposed last count of Vinci, but neither he nor the Antica Cantina di Massetti were listed in the Italian directory and no one at the office of the *comune* spoke enough English to understand what I was getting at. By the end of the conversation, I could tell that the civil servant on the other end of the line was beginning to think I was crazy. Indeed, that minimal effort to find Silvo made me feel so foolish that I couldn't help but concede that Miriam might be right about the old *violinista*.

The last straw came on a cold night in September, some two years after Mir and I were married. I was alone in our dark apartment on the East Side, as Miriam was once again out of town seeing to the needs of her growing client list. We'd been having trouble for months; I was almost certain she was seeing someone else, maybe even Andrea. That, plus the death of my writing life—my most personal pleasure—had me so low I couldn't fathom a way out of the depression.

I went back, for perhaps the twentieth time, to the box where I kept the notes for the novel I was "working on"—only this time my plan was to get rid of them for good. I took all the papers, including my honeymoon journal and two years' worth of bad drafts, and stood over the waste basket feeding them aimlessly to the void, my feelings of abdication and despair growing deeper with each sheet that drifted into the bin. I was all but finished when I found myself holding a page that read, "The Domestic Chronicle of Francesco del Giocondo, Merchant of Florence." It was Silvo's manuscript, which I hadn't seen since the day Miriam and I returned to New York.

As I read Francesco's first journal entry—if that's what it was—I couldn't help but sympathize with his despair, which seemed much more real to me than the first time I'd read it. Knowing what he'd been through, recalling the trials to come and his eventual triumph and happiness, I was moved near to tears by the hopeless tone of the first entries in his diary. If, in fact, that's what it was.

Yet at the same time my nerves trembled with the same excitement I'd felt two years ago, during a sunny afternoon on the terrace of an old restaurant overlooking Piazza Leonardo—a sensation ancient yet novel, strange but familiar, something utterly false and completely real. Where had I heard that before? From Silvo, of course. "Sometimes what appears to be false is more real than anything could be." That, he told me, was the Italian humor.

Did that mean Silvo was a forger, a hoax, a con man as Miriam had thought? Or was really the last Count of Vinci? Was I a dupe, was Savonarola a madman, Francesco a poet, and Lisa Giocondo the most famous face in the world? Could it be that I was sitting in my dark, lonely apartment reading the find of the century? I had no idea.

What I did know—perhaps all I knew—was that I finally had something to inspire me.

Oral Sex in the Communication Age
or
The New Pygmalion

9-22-02 13:47
Singles Sexchat Social Network
Type: Private session
Users: albertsprag1972, Ruby_Bottom00
(partial transcript)

albertsprag1972: *You like it?*

Ruby_Bottom00: *God yes. A girl can't go wrong with dick.*

albertsprag1972: *Not sure all girls agree.*

Ruby_Bottom00: *They should.*

albertsprag1972: *They don't.*

Ruby_Bottom00: *They don't know any better. It's an acquired taste, like brandy or haggis.*

albertsprag1972: *I don't get it.*

Ruby_Bottom00: *The first time you taste haggis you're not thrilled. But once you get around what you've got in your mouth and let yourself enjoy the texture and roll it around for a while, it's a treat. Girls get scared by WHAT they're tasting.*

albertsprag1972: *Did you? The first time.*

Ruby_Bottom00: *Nope. Liked it right away.*

albertsprag1972: *What do you like?*

Ruby_Bottom00: *The taste, the smell, the wet on my chin, pressure at the back of my throat. All aces. I could suck cock all day.*

albertsprag1972: *How do you do it?*

Ruby_Bottom00: *Are you looking for pointers?*

albertsprag1972: *I want you to write it.*

Ruby_Bottom00: *It turns you on.*

albertsprag1972: *Yes.*

Ruby_Bottom00: *You can't just swoop down. You've got to nibble around the edges, blow on it a bit.*

albertsprag1972: *Yes.*

Ruby_Bottom00: *I start by running my hands up your thighs, under your boxers, up to your crotch and tickle your sack. I want to see you squirm, bring your hips up to my breasts, my mouth.*

albertsprag1972: *What next?*

Ruby_Bottom00: *Bite your nipples. My lips over your stomach, grazing the skin till my chin comes to a rest on your pelvis. Bone to bone. look you in the eye and take the waistband of your shorts in my teeth. It may take a tug or two, but that's part of the fun. As I pull past your pubes, your hair tickles my nose and I laugh right on your dick. Can you picture that, Albert?*

albertsprag1972: *Yes.*

Ruby_Bottom00: *Now we get to work. Your cock is sticking up like a candlestick. My mouth waters. I lick my lips and swallow deep, tracing the veins with my eyes, blowing the stray hairs on the underside of your shaft. I get butterflies in my belly and a tingle where your dick will hit bottom in my pussy. Not yet though. First my mouth. You want that baby?*

albertsprag1972: *Yes.*

Ruby_Bottom00: *I lick you from balls to tip. When I get there, there's a drop of wetness for me. I catch it on my finger, like taking the icing off a cake. Then I dip the finger between my lips. That taste is in my mouth, I want more. I'm torn between needing you in my pussy and wanting you in my mouth. What should I do?*

albertsprag1972: *I don't know.*

Ruby_Bottom00: *Neither do I. But then I look up, and you answer my question, because you're staring at me with your mouth half open, wanting me to go down on you. And how much you want my mouth turns me on more than ever. I look deep in your eyes one more second, then take your dick to the hilt in one gulp. You gasp and I moan on your cock and my pussy lights up the fourth of July. I'm all over you, baby—my mouth is on your shaft, my tits are on your knees, my hands are on your balls, milking, massaging, coaxing your come up through your thick penis. Every second you're getting harder in my mouth, your legs are bucking, your hands are pulling my hair, your hips lift to fuck my throat, you're writhing, you're panting. The tip pushes against the roof of my mouth as you rise that last fraction of an inch. And at that moment, I stick my finger all the way in your ass, so deep it touches your soul. You scream and come in my mouth. I swallow every drop.*

Ruby_Bottom00: *Did you like that?*

albertsprag1972: *Yes.*

Ruby_Bottom00: *Good boy.*

The moment Albert Sprague walked into the Love Grotto—a place he'd been about a half dozen times, though never as a customer—he was caught short because Delaney Bowles was staring straight at the doorway, grinning his best shit-eating grin, as if he'd been expecting the visit. This though the two hadn't spoken in almost a year.

"Sandwich?" Delaney asked blandly, gesturing to the uneaten half of a cow tongue sandwich that lay on the counter in front of him. Albert winced, recalling Delaney's exotic tastes. Delaney laughed his usual laugh, tinged with mockery, and rolled the well-sucked pit of a queen olive audibly about his mouth.

"Didn't think so," he said, and proceeded to spit the olive pit three feet into an open wastebasket. "What'll it be? Business or pleasure?" Same shit-eating grin. Same old Delaney.

Still Albert couldn't help but laugh, and even hope that Delaney's invariable need to make light might ease what was to come. The Love Grotto was their unofficial nickname for the adult video store where Delaney Bowles worked as manager.

Albert took a chair along a narrow stretch of unused slatwall, making space for himself between a price gun and a double-sided glass dildo. He grimaced.

"Make yourself at home," Delaney said.

"I'd like to make this quick."

"My God, Albert, you've even started to sound like Sally."

Albert frowned but smiled—a borrowed expression Delaney recognized with a pang of regret.

"You've created an empire of smut here," Albert said glancing uncomfortably around. "A person can't turn around without a… something in his face," He tipped the package of a rubberized anus. "It's like you crawled back into the womb."

Delaney ate his sandwich with his back against the cash register. Albert swallowed hard, his mouth was bone dry.

"How can you eat that?"

"It's an acquired taste," Delaney explained, his mouth full of tongue. He grinned.

"You're disgusting."

"Oh come on," he said, offering the sandwich. "Just a taste."

"I'll be sick if I put that in my mouth."

Delaney sighed. "God, I miss her. Sometimes it's like she's right here in the room." He looked around thoughtfully. "Of course, Sally would never be in *this* room, but you know what I mean. I guess it's true what they say about couples, you know, becoming *like* one another. Osmosis and all that shit. It's touching, Albert. Sally and I never had that kind of thing."

"She wants me to marry her."

Delaney took a big bite of tongue and chewed for a long time; Albert sat stiff as a statue, inspecting sex toys with a peculiar frown. The Love Grotto seemed small indeed.

"So?"

"So."

"You got an answer?"

"Not yet."

"You want a soda?"

"Yeah."

Sally O'Malley was exhausted. After hours of listening to patients' problems, she wanted nothing more at the end of the day than to fall into a deep, dreamless sleep—the sleep of the just; the sleep she deserved.

Our Father, who art in heaven...

Even this, the prayer she'd said every night since she could remember, was difficult to remember through the first fog of sleep. She stumbled between clauses, lost the thread.

Our Father...

The words got lost between consciousness and her subconscious. Yet even in the fog, Sally was aware of her conscience. How could she forget *these* words?

Hallowed be thy name...

What?

There was a shift. She felt him against her; warmth, weight, comfort; his body stretched along her back, over her margins, down her legs. What?

Hallowed be thy name...

His hand slid up her t-shirt, over a breast, and pinched a nipple. A shock shot to her groin.

"Oh God," Sally gasped. Her guilt doubled. What? No. Shit.

Hail Mary, full of grace, thy Lord is with thee. Blessed art thou amongst women, and blessed is the fruit of your womb—

"Come on, baby."

"Oh *don't*. You know I *hate* it when you call me that. I'm a grown woman with a mind of my own and serious need to sleep. So just quit, you pervert." Sally wrenched his fingers from her throbbing nipple.

"Jesus Christ. What did I do?"

"It's nothing, Albert. Just go to sleep."

He huffed and rolled away.

But now, of course, Sally wasn't tired. Or, despite how tired she was, she couldn't clear her head for the rush of hormones and the whiff of anger he'd given her. And now she felt guilty for having snapped at Albert. He wasn't a pervert. Sally reached back and gave him a placating pat on the hip.

"What."

"Come here. Spoon me then."

He rolled back and there it was, proud and stiff, burrowing her panties into the cleft of her ass.

"Albert!" Sally jumped. "Are you naked?"

"Yes?" he said through a laugh that bubbled up from his throat. He danced a finger along the outside of her thigh.

Any other time, Sally would have found such an awkward come-on simply ridiculous—and therefore charming, in Albert's bumbling way. But not now. "Why? What? No," she said. "I can't tonight, Albert. Let's just sleep."

"*Tonight?*" he answered, the tone changed to pure complaint. "How long has it been? Two weeks? Three? What's the matter?"

"Nothing's the matter."

"Are you sleeping with someone else?"

"Oh God, Albert. I'm tired. All day people want me to help them, to fix them, to mold them into better versions of themselves. You don't know what it's like being a therapist. It's exhausting

"And of course I'm not sleeping with anyone else. Where on earth would I find the time? Why is it men think sex is the test of a relationship? Just because I don't want to have sex with you all the time, it doesn't mean I love you any less, Albert. You should know that. I'm *just too tired.* I'm sorry, okay." She ended with a hand on his cheek, placed a kiss between his eyes.

Sally lay back down and turned around. But within minutes he was back at her, all hands, but gentler now, as though cajoling; wet breath in her ear, pushing between her thighs, creeping down her back, dipping past the waistband of her panties. It wasn't all bad.

"Please. I have to sleep."

More hands.

"Albert, don't. You don't want to go there, Albert. *Albert, I've got my period.*"

The hands stopped.

He was still for a moment and Sally began to doze. But she could tell he wasn't sleeping. Eventually he spoke up: "Well…" he said, chin slithering over her shoulder. "There are other things we could do." He bit her gently on the neck.

"*What?!*"

Albert retreated again to the other side of the bed. "I thought that maybe…you know…since you have your period. You might… *do something for me.*"

"Stop right there, Albert."

"Just for a minute. It's not a crime, Sally. And I want it. You're the shrink. What would you tell me if I was your patient?"

"I'd tell you you're a pig, and you should seek help elsewhere."

"Oh bullshit. You'd tell me to talk about my feelings. You'd tell me that I owed it to my partner to discuss problems in our relationship."

"You're saying that's a problem in our relationship?"

"No. Not that exactly," Albert shrugged. "But it's a symptom, isn't it? I mean, look at us. We never have sex. And okay, the sex was always a bit routine…"

"Excuse me?"

"But now I long for routine."

"Well you'll have to keep on longing tonight."

Albert stared at her a long moment, caught between frustration and excitement. In another second he lay down and rolled peevishly away from her, murmuring to the other side of the room. Sally's heart warmed—she loved him most in his childlike moments.

"You hate sex."

"I love sex."

"Well, not as much as me."

9-22-02 13:47
Singles Sexchat Social Network
Type: Private session
Users: albertsprag1972, Ruby_Bottom00
(partial transcript)

Ruby_Bottom00: *Tell me what you like.*

albertsprag1972: *What do you mean?*

Ruby_Bottom00: *Tell me what you like sexually. Give a little back. Come on, Albert, let your zipper down. Give me a peek, baby. Do you like it when I call you baby?*

albertsprag1972: *I guess so.*

Ruby_Bottom00: *So what about it?*

albertsprag1972: *I'd rather you go on.*

Ruby_Bottom00: *You like to listen?*

albertsprag1972: *Well it's not exactly listening.*

Ruby_Bottom00: *Stop right there. If you want to play, there are rules.*

albertsprag1972: *Okay.*

Ruby_Bottom00: *First, don't tell me what you look like, not even if you're a fucking Adonis. Nothing about appearances, unless it's requested. And in that case I prefer you lie. That's what fantasy's about.*

albertsprag1972: *You want me to lie to you?*

Ruby_Bottom00: *Yes. Save sincerity for your girlfriend.*

albertsprag1972: *I don't have a girlfriend.*

Ruby_Bottom00: *Yes you do. But thank you, baby, you're trying.*

albertsprag1972: *Why do you want me to lie to you?*

Ruby_Bottom00: *Because I don't want Albert. Not the way the world sees him. I want an Albert that I can mold to my mood. One day I might want you to be a Marlboro man with a moustache that tickles my clit. Another day I might want to take a strapon to a drag queen, or have my ass fingered by a French pastry chef. Baby, I might ask you to be a farm animal. I'll create the image, if you don't want to. What I want from you is intercourse. That way you'll always satisfy to me. Understand?*

albertsprag1972: *I think so. It excites you to make me what you want.*

Ruby_Bottom00: *Yes baby.*

albertsprag1972: *What else?*

Ruby_Bottom00: *If I say we're on a gondola in Venice, don't ask me how much the ride cost. Play along. Don't question the logic. Ask for details, but don't ask them to make sense. Fantasy is about acceptance. It's one of the perks of being fictive—you can't get hurt no matter what you do. You'll ruin your fantasies, and mine, if you insist on being literal.*

albertsprag1972: *Are there any other rules?*

Ruby_Bottom00: *Yes. Don't ever ask to meet me.*

albertsprag1972: *Yes ma'am.*

Ruby_Bottom00: *Mmmm. Now you're getting the hang of it. You make me wet when you talk like that. I want to tie you down and ride you like a stallion.*

albertsprag1972: *Do you like horses?*

Ruby_Bottom00: *Honey, all women like to ride horses. You want to be my stallion? I'll work you into a lather, my sex pressed against your back, hot tears running down your cheeks. You like that?*

albertsprag1972: *Yes.*

Ruby_Bottom00: *Shame on you Albert, you dirty pervert. There may be hope for you yet.*

"So when's the wedding?" Delaney asked, breaking the silence in the Grotto.

Albert didn't answer.

"You're not going to speak to me now? Why'd you come here? Surely it wasn't for the anal beads." The shit-eating grin returned.

Albert said nothing.

"I'm invited to the wedding, right?" Delaney asked. "You can't *not* invite me, Albert. Neither of you. Don't let her do that, Albert."

Albert said nothing.

"Albert, how long have we been friends?"

"I didn't say there was going to be a wedding."

"Then there's *not* going to be a wedding."

"I didn't say that either."

"Then what the hell are we talking about?" Delaney straightened against the counter, bracing for the worst. "Albert, are you and Sally getting married?"

Albert wringed his hands and shifted in his chair, his face was bloodless as a ghost. He looked guilty. He looked horny. He looked lost. "I don't know."

Delaney brooded and nibbled at the olive pit he'd been moving round his mouth for the last five minutes, grinding it into sand. Meanwhile, he bounced a medium-sized rubber penis along the countertop till it bumped randomly against the cash register. There seemed no reason under heaven that Albert wouldn't marry Sally O'Malley.

"Don't you love her?"

"Of course I love her!"

Delaney winced, recognizing the tone he'd used in the last days of his relationship with Sally, and a lump rose in his wicked throat. It was the same lump that had nearly choked him when he left Sally, when he thought he might die of regret.

But that was a different time. He was different now. Stronger, perhaps; worse, surely. Delaney Bowles pushed that goddamned lump back down where it came from. "Why?"

"I can't tell you."

"Well thanks for stopping by then," Delaney said.

Albert looked pitifully up at him; he seemed tethered to the floor.

"No." Delaney grinned indecently down at him.

"Don't say it," said Albert.

"It's the sex."

Albert scowled.

"Oh my God," Delaney said with genuine surprise. "My God, Albert, this must be really embarrassing for you. After the tongue-lashing I got. After your *indignation,* for christsakes, when it was none of your goddamned business anyway."

Albert said nothing.

"After you stole my girlfriend, Albert. You're telling me that *now* you under*stand?*" Delaney laughed scornfully. "This is rich. You're nothing but a pervert, Albert. A freak like me. On the lookout for a real tongue-lashing, eh?"

"Don't be disgusting."

"Suckle the puppet. Pull the bull. Wank your crank."

"Enough!"

Silence.

"Why do you think I feel so shitty?"

"I know. The last thing you want to be is like me."

"I didn't mean it that way," Albert answered evenly. "I know you love to watch me suffer."

"Oh Christ," Delaney hissed. And though he wanted very much to love watching Albert suffer, it just wasn't the fun it should be.

He realized what an almost indecently decent person Albert was. And of course, what happened with Sally had nothing to do with Albert. It was all awful—especially the decency.

"You want the rest of my sandwich?" Delaney said.

Albert laughed, fussed, struggled, almost cried, and ended laughing again.

"I've got to tell you, Albert," Delaney said with his mouth full of tongue once again, "I'm at a loss."

"You're not going to gloat?"

Delaney scratched his chin and rotated the olive pit—which had somehow survived the cow tongue—between his front teeth. "I should," he said. "But I can't. I mean, honestly Albert, is that the *real* reason."

"I think so."

"I can understand it coming from me. But is that the real reason for *you?*"

Albert hesitated, as if considering privileged information. He looked up at Delaney. "She didn't want me to tell you."

Delaney's heart raced. "She mentioned me? What's going on?"

Albert shrugged. "She was offered a job in Boston. She wants me to come, but says we need to make our relationship 'official.'" He looked helplessly at Delaney. "And, of course, there's the Catholic thing."

Delaney huffed. "You've been living together for six months for God's sake. Sally won't do a lot, but she does plenty the pope won't approve."

"Don't be nasty."

"Look around, Albert. We haven't touched nasty."

"Well you don't have to say it about Sally."

"Fine. What else is wrong?"

Albert thought for a moment. "Nothing. She's perfect, except in bed. But you can't talk to her about that."

"No. You can talk to Sally about God or politics or family or philosophy—anything really," Delaney said almost wistfully. "But you can't talk about sex."

"That's what I don't get," Albert answered. "Isn't that what she talks about all day? It confuses the hell out of me."

"So tell your shrink."

"Sally's my shrink."

"So don't." Delaney made a vague gesture of uncertainty and finished the tongue sandwich, licking his fingertips singly after the final bite. "Listen," he went on, "It takes balls to tell anyone they're lousy in bed."

"I wouldn't put it that way."

"Yes you would."

"Well I wouldn't say it to her."

"You're right on that one," Delaney answered. "When I brought it up, it was a goddamned shock."

"I know," Albert said painfully.

Delaney nodded. "Granted, she knew something was wrong. Hell, she used to sit me down almost daily for a dialogue about where *we* were headed, trying to crack my nut and all. You remember. She practically had me on the couch.

"She figured it had to be that daddy never loved me, or some awful trauma in my past—all the fantasies shrinks make up. Never occurred to her that all I wanted was for her to suck my dick."

Albert nodded absently.

"Not her fault, really, it's the way she was raised—all those Hail Marys and rosaries and nuns and such. That's what happens when you make a goddess out of a virgin. Fantastic nonsense. It's fucked up I tell you."

"Delaney," Albert pleaded.

"No. She told me herself. When we started dating—when she told me she loved me and she'd *let* me sleep with her—she explained the whole thing. Trust me, my friend," Delaney went on, forcing Albert to look him in the eye, "I wasn't the first person to have an audience with her holiness, if you know what I mean. Always rationalizing, that one.

"Yet you wouldn't believe the look on her face when I donned a condom. Never mind the sex, she was convinced she'd go to hell for *that*." Delaney huffed, twirling the rubber penis ruefully in his hand. "Imagine, all hell and brimstone over a Trojan. You can't live like that man. The world just ain't the same place as when Mom and Dad O'Malley were popping 'em out one sacred fuck at a time. Sex is a condiment, Albert. Discretion is dead."

"You don't say."

"I don't want to talk about it."

"That won't make it go away."

"Why don't you just pick something up and help me," Sally said. "Nothing needs to go away."

"Fine. Then let's talk about you and Delaney."

"I said I didn't want to talk about it. Can't you just leave it at that?" She creased a dryer-fresh towel and turned to reach back into the basket. Albert, meanwhile, continued to stare at her empty-handed.

"This is neither the time nor the place, Albert," Sally said, folding a pair of his boxer shorts. "We're in *public*." She didn't whisper; the Laundromat was practically empty.

"It's nothing to be ashamed of," Albert said. "So it doesn't matter that we're in public, baby." He held out a hand for Sally to give him something to fold. "All I asked was if Delaney was your first."

"Don't call me baby," Sally answered, concerning herself with a blouse. "What does it matter anyway?"

"If it doesn't matter then why won't you tell me?"

"If it doesn't matter then why should I?"

"Fine," he said. "It matters."

"Just like that."

"If that's what it takes," Albert said, bargaining a laugh and reaching behind her to get another piece of clothing.

Sally put down the blouse and glared at him for a long moment. "Yes." She turned her eyes from him to the laundry.

"There. Are you satisfied?"

Albert shrugged. "I don't think it's something to be satisfied about."

"Then why on earth did you need to know!"

"Shhh," Albert said under his breath. "We're in *public*." Sally managed to smile and frown at the same time; it was a look that said she was not amused.

"It's not an uncommon question between couples."

"Oh, and you're the expert now."

"No. You are. You're the psychologist for God's sake."

"Believe it or not, Albert, people have plenty of problems that are not necessarily about sex. In fact, most people with real problems don't have time to obsess about their sex lives." She gave an exasperated shake of her head. "You think that because characters in movies talk nothing but sex with therapists that's what real people do?" She looked back at him. "That's not real. It's just an image, it's a fiction.

"Real therapy is all about communication. It's about breaking down barriers and getting people in touch with their innermost feelings through sharing and understanding. By doing that, they can strengthen themselves and enrich their lives—and the lives of their partners."

"So they never talk about sex?"

"Rarely."

"And you think that has nothing to do with you?"

At that moment a young man walked into the Laundromat. Sally picked up another towel, purposely avoiding eye contact with Albert, who fidgeted as he refolded a t-shirt he'd been holding for the last minute or more. The young man checked his machine, which was still running, and promptly walked back out the door.

"*What!?*" she screamed under her breath.

Albert flinched. He coughed and hesitated, but kept on: "You don't exactly like to talk about sex."

"That is not true," Sally hissed.

"You certainly didn't want to talk about sex with Delaney."

"And how is that any business of yours?" she snapped. But immediately she knew that was wrong, and when Albert turned to leave Sally reached out to stop him. "Don't, please, I'm sorry." She put down the laundry and wrapped her arms around his waist from behind, laying her cheek against his back. "I'm sorry."

Albert stepped out of her grasp and turned to her. "You certainly didn't want to talk about sex with Delaney," he repeated.

"Goddamnit Albert!" Sally snapped again, breaking his gaze and going back to the laundry. "What is your obsession with Delaney today?"

"It's not about him. It's about you, and why you find it impossible to talk about sex."

"With Delaney? Are you kidding? I didn't talk about that with him because I knew how vulgar it would be. Albert, Delaney is a pervert."

"Yet you dated him for two years."

"That was my mistake."

"You still get defensive when I talk about him."

"I want him out of our lives, that's all."

"He was my friend too."

"That was your mistake."

Albert shook his head. "That's not what I'm talking about."

"Isn't it?" she asked. "Like I said, you seem to be obsessed with Delaney today. What's that all about?"

"Don't analyze me, Sally."

"Then don't interrogate me, Albert."

"I'm not interrogating you," he insisted. "I just want to talk."

Sally sighed. "About what?"

10-1-02 15:55
Singles Sexchat Social Network
Type: Private session
Users: albertsprag1972, Ruby_Bottom00
(partial transcript)

albertsprag1972: *What are you wearing?*

Ruby_Bottom00: *A black corset and high heels with leather straps pulled tight around my ankles. That's all. And I'm lying on a bed covered in red satin sheets, handcuffs dangling from the headboard.*

albertsprag1972: *What are you doing?*

Ruby_Bottom00: *I'm nibbling my index finger the way my lover used to do when he knew I was in the mood. My other hand is busy lower.*

albertsprag1972: *How are you typing?*

Ruby_Bottom00: *Don't interrupt, Albert. And don't be literal.*

albertsprag1972: *Sorry. What are you thinking about?*

Ruby_Bottom00: *My lover. He liked to tell stories. Create fantasies. He wanted to take me to the airport, he got off on strangers. We'd sit at the far end of the arrival lounge watching travelers come and go, looking for signs of heat amid the boredom and gloom. Lovers reunited. Businessmen's wives. College sweethearts. Or just the odd pair looking for a quick fuck. It's easy to spot the ones waiting for it. They keep checking their watches even though the flight isn't due for another hour. Men push their hands in their pockets, like they're reaching for something, the women cross and recross their legs ten times a minute just to feel the friction between their thighs. They all sip small drinks. Some pace, some roll their shoulders, some fidget till you think they'll explode. The sex is building up inside them and they need some kind of release. My lover and I sit in a dark corner watching, making up stories about them.*

albertsprag1972: *What kind of stories?*

Ruby_Bottom00: *His favorite was long lost lovers who decide to meet for a weekend to rekindle an old lust. Not love, lust. Love might die hard, but it dies. Real lust, on the other hand, is timeless. The one you cheated with, not the one you cheated on, is more likely to be the one who gives you the fidgets in the airport lounge. With all that hankering, the air of the place is charged. You can almost hear them thinking: What will it be like? Will it be fast? Will I recognize him? What if he's fat? I could lose the last, best fantasy I have…the one that gets the capsheaf every time.*

albertsprag1972: *What the hell is a capsheaf?*

Ruby_Bottom00: *It's a finishing point, baby—a climax. I like the word. Sounds dirty.*

albertsprag1972: *Okay.*

Ruby_Bottom00: *My lover pushes me into the corner where no one can see us, and slides his hand under my skirt while he describes the woman at the end of the bar. On the outside, she's common. Pretty, but common. But on the inside, she feels wild. She's the girl with steady work as a secretary, who took the job as a temp, always planning for better things. But now she finds she can't afford to leave. And she's scared that everything got too big for her while she wasn't looking. Scared to find out that she actually can't remake herself. Scared that she's finished, and life isn't as beautiful as it was supposed to be. She left something once, when she wasn't so old. But now the cocktails and anticipation remind her how brave she was, and— my lover whispers wetly in my ear—you can almost see the inhibitions slipping off her like a silk shift. It's in the way her hands caress her glass, and the way she moves a cherry around her mouth as she watches the door. She's waiting for it.*

albertsprag1972: *And that's the kind of thing you like?*

Ruby_Bottom00: *Very much so. Why? Don't you like it?*

albertsprag1972: *Yes.*

Ruby_Bottom00: *What do you like?*

albertsprag1972: *I like the action in the corner, though the girl at the bar sounds nice too. I like the whisper and the friction. I like the hand beneath your skirt and the cherry in her mouth. I hope that the wet breath, the hand on your thigh, the girl at the bar, the airplane, and the capsheaf, of course. Can all arrive at the same time.*

Ruby_Bottom00: *Mmmm. Good answer.*

"Are you going to tell her?"

"How can I? It'll break her heart. It broke her heart when you told her." Albert looked up at Delaney, bitterness and sympathy mingled on his face. "When things got serious between us, I swore I'd never…"

Delaney waited. "Never what?" He spit the olive pit. "Never dance with the devil in the pale moonlight? Never eat where you shit? Never eat where *she* shits?"

The bitterness took for a moment, but Albert couldn't hold out, and in another second his eyes rolled around like a child's toy lost in the street.

"You swore you'd never be like me."

"Yeah."

"Then you're going to marry her."

"I'd be a fool not to," Albert answered. "If I let her get away, I'll spend the rest of my life regretting it. Right?"

Albert slouched in his chair. Delaney stood against the counter chewing his bottom lip with restless teeth. The room seemed uncommonly hot.

"No good waiting for a second chance," Albert said coldly.

Delaney's throat tightened again. It took a minute to regain his sense of resignation. "Of course you should marry her," he said in a voice like a dying quail.

To which Albert answered: "I think I'm having an affair."

At that moment the door opened and a young man came in; he and Delaney exchanged a familiar nod as the man walked casually to the back of the store. Meanwhile, Albert squirmed in his seat, as though apologizing for his presence. Within a few minutes the young man made a selection and left the Grotto with the circumspection of a specialist.

"*What?!*"

Albert shrugged. "There's this woman" he started with a gulp. "There's this woman I talk to every day on my lunch break I can't stop thinking about her. I can't stop thinking about the things she says to me. When I'm at home, I'm talking to Sally but I'm thinking about this other woman."

"So what. You have lunch with this woman and you think about her sometimes."

"I don't have lunch with her."

"You said you talk to her at lunch."

"Yes, but she's not there."

"Then where is she?"

"Well," Albert said, "She's there but she's not there."

"Is she real?" Delaney looked at askance. "Albert, is this some kind of delusion you're having?"

"No. She's on the computer. I guess I don't know where she *is*, but she's still *there*. Get it?"

"You spend your lunch break on a chat line?"

"Yes."

"What the hell do you talk about?"

Albert hesitated. "Sex," he said finally.

Delaney laughed. "Cybersex? That's not an affair."

"Isn't it?"

"Albert, you and I are talking about sex right now. Hell, we talked about nothing but sex the four years we lived together. Shit, if talking about sex is just like having sex, I'm Wilt fucking Chamberlain."

Albert rolled his eyes.

"It's not an affair, Albert."

"This is different."

"How?"

"It's like we're having sex on the computer."

"Do you *satisfy* yourself, Albert?"

"Of course not!"

"Hey, a guy's got needs."

"Yeah. And a job is one of them."

"It's not sex, Albert."

"Is it?"

Albert glanced over his shoulder to assure that they were alone, then reached inside his jacket to retrieve a sheaf of papers. He smoothed them across his lap before handing to Delaney, who read them with the air of a scholar. The pages contained fragments of the "conversations" Albert had just mentioned, all frankly, if not graphically sexual in nature.

"I like this girl," Delaney said nodding. He read for several seconds. "But it's not sex, Albert. And it's not an affair. It's all in your head."

"Is it?"

"Yes." Delaney paged through the sheets one at a time, skimming with appreciation. "This is just a bunch of dirty talk from someone with a filthy imagination. And from what I see she's the one doing most of the talking. This is pretty good stuff, very literate smut," he said, gesturing toward the Grotto. "I should know."

"Thank you," Albert answered acidly. "Thank you for that."

"Oh get over it. There's no cause for guilt, Albert. In fact, in your situation, it's pretty damned understandable. Better do this than go out and find a real woman to have a real affair with."

"And you know so much about relationships?"

Delaney shook his head as though chastising a child. "I know porn."

"You say that like you're proud."

He shrugged—with satisfaction.

Albert shook his head. "Four years of college and you know porn. Don't you think that's kind of a waste?"

"I see it as graduate work."

"You're joking."

Delaney considered. "Listen, Albert, what do you think porn is?"

"Disgusting?"

"It's narrative," Delaney answered with outstretched hands. "It's art. Okay, it's crappy art, but that's because it's more human than any other. Porn is interactive, after all."

"It isn't art. It's vulgar."

"Of course it's vulgar. That's what makes it popular. Listen, all art coarsens with time as its latent sexual function becomes manifest. Sex is integral to art. You start with Venus de Milo, Lysistrata, Tristan and Isolde; you end up with centerfolds, pole dancers, and *Penthouse* letters. Same purpose, really; it's just that the mores are stripped away. Adam and Eve beget Debbie Does Dallas. The Birth of Venus becomes chicks with dicks."

"But it's not real."

"Neither is the Mona Lisa."

"The Mona Lisa is a work of art. Watching people have sex is nothing like that."

"The Mona Lisa is wood and oil. The woman is an image, and the way it's presented is very sexual. Like porn, it's about fantasy."

"You're saying the Mona Lisa is just like porn."

"More or less."

"You're twisted."

Delaney tipped his head thoughtfully. "She's a fantasy Albert. Only in the fifteenth century there was more left to the imagination, because the recording equipment was less sophisticated and the rules were more stringent. Still, at bottom, it's sex." He raised his eyebrows. "You don't think anyone ever jerked off to the Mona Lisa?"

"Why would anyone do that?"

Delaney raised his eyebrows. "Is she warm? Is she real? Or just a cold and lonely, lovely work of art?"

Albert rolled his eyes. "Not everyone is obsessed with sex."

Delaney held up the printouts. "It's nothing to be embarrassed about, Albert. Everybody does it. *This,*" he gestured to the Grotto, "My friend, this is the great undiscovered country at the end of the sexual revolution—something for everyone and no one's to judge. You like boobs? Aisle two. You like Asians? Aisle five. You like transsexuals? Aisle nine. You like nothing but big-boobed Asian trannies? There's an endcap. It's all here."

"Except the real thing."

"The real thing is everywhere else, man. And out there in the big bad real world, you can't get what you want anyway. Out there, you have to compromise. But leave reality behind, and the world is your oyster. So to speak."

"It's demeaning to women."

"That's what they want you to think," Delaney scoffed. "Listen, Albert, for the last million years females have been making males jump through hoops. And what for? Sex, man. All the fucking red bellies and rainbow feathers in the whole world have just one use: to get laid. And it ain't any different at this end of the food chain. *We* have to impress *them.* Meanwhile, women sit back and choose.

"But here—in our Mecca—the male *Homo sapiens* gets to shop for *his* orgasm, instead of the other way around."

"But you can't fall in love with a video."

"Jesus, Albert, I'm not talking about love. I'm talking about sex."

"Of course. How foolish of me. Sex always comes first with you."

"Sex comes first ninety-nine percent of the time. That may be vulgar, but it's why porn works—because it's so damned frank. Life isn't high art, Albert. Like porn, it has very little drama. It's the other stuff—

the pie-in-the-sky love-at-first-sight nonsense—that's got it back to front. In any decent porno, the sex comes before love, both in sequence and order of importance. No one's got time for love precisely because it's timeless. Sex has an agenda." Delaney held up the printouts of Albert's noontime chats. "And there's nothing wrong with jerking off, Albert," he said. "Look around: It's damned good business."

"I feel like I'm cheating on Sally," Albert said.

"Don't waste your time. Shit, you don't even know who Ruby Bottom is. She could be a man for all you know."

Albert's terror showed so plainly even Delaney could not enjoy it. "Oh, don't get shook up, Albert. I'm sure your mistress is a woman. But it's not sex. And you're not cheating. It would be different if you were thinking of leaving Sally for this woman."

Albert shrugged.

"You're not that kind of person, Albert."

"Is that a compliment?"

"That's an appraisal," he said "Look at you. You're giving yourself an ulcer over this. You think she is? Do you think that 'Ruby Bottom' is wondering what you're doing this moment?"

"I told her I was coming here to talk to you."

"And she's probably got another guy on the line right now."

"You don't know her!"

"Neither do you," Delaney said flatly. "Listen, I know you, Albert. This is about all the kink you can take. Jesus, you've been squirming for the past half hour just being in this room. A Ruby Bottom—*this Ruby Bottom*—wouldn't flinch in a sea of dildos. Don't get wrapped up in this, Albert. Let it pass."

"What if I don't want to?"

"What do you mean?"

"You know the feeling when you fall in love? Do you remember that feeling?"

Delaney hesitated. "Yes."

"I get sweaty palms for crying out loud."

"This is different, Albert. It's not real."

"Love is never real till you believe in it."

"You have to have something to believe in."

"I do."

"You don't."

"I know what I'm doing."

"I don't think you do," Delaney answered. "Take home a few movies. Diddle yourself for a while. Do it at lunch if you have to. But take some time off from this before you do something you'll regret."

"I know what I'm doing," Albert insisted again.

Delaney huffed. "Albert, why did you come here?"

"I don't know."

"I do." Delaney held up the sheaf of papers one last time. "You came here because I'm the one person you know who might say this is all right. Right?"

Albert sighed. "So what do I do?"

"Suffer," she said.

Once again, Sally lay awake a half hour after she'd crawled into bed; she was cross. So when Albert asked for perhaps the sixth time *What am I supposed to do?* she finally dropped her clinical demeanor and let him have it—or not, as the case may be.

She'd have liked to add, *And get the hell away from me,* but Sally O'Malley was too polite for such things.

"Maybe I should just satisfy myself."

"Not in this bed, you won't," Sally commanded without turning around.

"*What?!*"

"If you need to do that, take it in the bathroom, Albert. I don't want you making a mess of the bed."

Behind her, Albert flicked on the lamp. "We need to talk."

"Don't *start*, Albert."

"We need to start."

"What does that mean?"

"It means I don't know if I can move to Boston with you."

Sally finally turned around. Albert sat against the headboard, looking churlishly at his hands folded on his lap. She felt no shock. She felt no concern. She felt only annoyance at having to solve this problem—whatever it was—*right now*.

"Can't we talk about this tomorrow, Albert?"

He shrugged. She hated it when he shrugged. Still, it was reassuring; probably he would let her get some sleep.

"No," he said at last.

At that, Sally pulled herself up in bed, and was immediately aware of the downward heave of braless breasts beneath her t-shirt. So was Albert; when he looked at her, his eyes went immediately to her chest.

"I don't think you should talk to Delaney," she sighed. "I don't want you to become like him."

"That's not the issue."

"Then quit pawing at me, Albert. How many times do I have to tell you that just because we don't have sex all the time doesn't mean we don't love each other."

"I want... I need something else."

"What?"

"Something else.

Sally sighed. "What?"

Albert turned away. "I don't know."

"No, come on, Albert. If you say there's a problem, then we should talk about it." Sally folded her arms across her chest and wagged her head condescendingly. "And apparently we have to talk about it in the middle of the night."

Sally looked past Albert; she saw the clock change. Albert looked at his feet under the comforter.

"Did you ever have an idea in your mind of an ideal mate? Like the perfect person that you should fall in love with?"

"I suppose," she answered with a quiet smile. "But Albert, that's just a childhood fantasy."

"You're everything I ever wanted," Albert said, looking Sally in the eye for the first time since turning on the light. "I knew it the first moment I saw you. You're exactly what I imagined."

Sally smiled. "I love you too, Albert."

"But I can't live like this."

Suddenly Sally thought she understood the problem—and she couldn't help being pleased. She felt guilty for her anger, and was touched by Albert's embarrassment. Certainly *this* was worth losing a night's sleep.

"Do you know what I mean?" he asked.

"Are you saying you want to make an honest woman out of me?"

"No," he snapped. "I mean no." Albert fidgeted. "You're right about childish fantasies. I can't live with an ideal. I need something real. Something human."

"What?" Sally demanded, losing a good part of her resolve.

"Human."

"What does that mean, Albert?"

"I mean a guy's got needs."

Sally's jaw dropped and a sick feeling rose in her stomach. "Do you really mean to tell me that this is still about sex?"

Albert shrugged.

"Oh God, don't do that!" Sally snapped. "At least try to act like a grown man, Albert."

"I'm acting like a child?"

"I'd say so."

"No, Sally," Albert said. "I'm acting like a man. You're the one that needs to grow up a bit."

"Why? Because I don't want to fuck all the time? Is that it? Is that what you want, Albert? You want to do your business, and then we can get some sleep? Is that it?" She lay down flat with her arms locked at her sides. "Come on, Albert. You've got needs, don't you?" She stared at him or a moment. Albert didn't budge—and yet the comforter began to tent in his lap.

Sally looked down at his erection growing beneath the covers. "Oh Jesus, Albert."

"What?"

"You're serious. You just want a whore."

"It's not like that!"

"What's it like?"

"It's like being in bed with a woman who doesn't know what she's doing."

"What the hell does that mean?"

"It means you're old enough to like sex." Albert paused. "And old enough so that I should like it too."

"Albert!"

"It's the truth."

Sally pulled the covers over her breasts. "I can't believe I'm hearing this—not from you. I never thought that you would reduce women to sex objects. You can't make a woman into what you want her to be just to get off, not in a healthy relationship. You have to show respect. You have to compromise. You can't get everything you want."

"Neither can you," he said.

10-7-02 12:11
Singles Sexchat Social Network
Type: Private session
Users: albertsprag1972, Ruby_Bottom00
(partial transcript)

albertsprag1972: *Why do you talk to me?*

Ruby_Bottom00: *That's a terrible thing to ask. Are you trying to hurt my feelings?*

albertsprag1972: *No. I'm sorry.*

Ruby_Bottom00: *Apology accepted. Now, tell me what's on your mind, baby—especially if it's kinky.*

albertsprag1972: *I was just wondering what you and I might have in common. What kind of food do you like? What's your favorite color? What would you say if you saw me on the street? Would you let me hold your hand in public?*

Ruby_Bottom00: *I don't think it's a good idea to ask those kinds of questions.*

albertsprag1972: *I have to. I have all kind of thoughts about you, but they're all reflected off this one side of you I get to see. Which I like, but I wonder about the other parts of you.*

Ruby_Bottom00: *Don't. Concentrate on that one side of me and create the rest from that. I told you, Albert, that's what fantasy is about.*

albertsprag1972: *But I wonder what you're really like. And I wonder why you talk to me. I'm probably not the most exciting guy you've ever talked to. You could do this with someone else who'd do better than anything I come up with. You could be doing this with someone better than me.*

Ruby_Bottom00: *I guess I should be flattered.*

albertsprag1972: *I guess so.*

Ruby_Bottom00: *Are you hard, Albert?*

albertsprag1972: *Maybe.*

Ruby_Bottom00: *Are you being a tease?*

albertsprag1972: *Maybe.*

Ruby_Bottom00: *You want your tongue in my ear? You want your hand in my pants? You want your tongue in my pussy? Don't you Albert. Come on, tell me what you want.*

albertsprag1972: *Like what?*

Ruby_Bottom00: *Half-mooned over a park bench, Levi's wrapped around our ankles, thighs slapping against my ass; wet, hard, public fucking. You like that? You like the risk of getting caught?*

albertsprag1972: *Yes.*

Ruby_Bottom00: *Have you ever done it in public?*

albertsprag1972: *No.*

Ruby_Bottom00: *Why not?*

albertsprag1972: *I usually do it in the dark. Actually, I used to have dreams that I can only get an erection in the dark. In the dream, I'm with a woman with the lights on, but I can't get hard. So I go to turn out the lights and the woman disappears. Then I go to turn on the light switch again—to find her—but I can't find the switch. I think I have an exaggerated inhibition. My mother once caught me masturbating. I can't believe I told you that.*

Ruby_Bottom00: *What are you, a shrink?*

albertsprag1972: *Not really.*

Ruby_Bottom00: *You are kind of a mamma's boy. You want to please me, I like that. You want me to tell you how to please me. You want me to give directions, especially in bed. Albert, you're a boy toy and a perfect gentleman all in one. The kind of guy a girl can take home to mommy then fuck him in the linen closet. You like that?*

albertsprag1972: *I want to meet you.*

Sally O'Malley met Delaney Bowles in the late summer of what was to be their junior year at Haber College, at about the same time Delaney and Albert Sprague—a nondescript but thoroughly genial friend of long standing—moved into an apartment above the Scottish deli downtown. Not surprisingly, that was the same year Delaney developed his taste for exotic fare.

Sally was anything but exotic. She was a respectable Catholic school girl from a prosperous middle class family on the outskirts of Boston, with a solid sense of right and wrong and a healthy respect for her reputation. She was a good student and a good person, though certainly no saint. She'd had her fair share of fun, including several boyfriends with whom she'd been intimate, one of whom had given her something resembling an orgasm.

Sally wasn't a prude. But she wasn't a slut either. Still, she was a woman, and she liked having a man's hands—along with lips, tongue, and other body parts—on her body. Did she feel guilty about this? A little. But being a psychology major had given her the tools for dealing with such feelings, tools that differed completely from the things she'd learned at St. Catherine's. In all, she was an eminently self-possessed girl, in the process of becoming a woman. She was normal—not exotic.

When Sally arrived, the party was already well into its third hour, and a half dozen conversations filled the room with a warm social buzz. Sally and her girlfriend picked up cocktails and looked around through the thin haze created by cigarettes, incense, and pop music. Sally was looking for a suitable niche to slip into the fabric of the party. The widest, most vibrant swatch of that fabric belonged to a voluble young man standing at the corner of the kitchen's banquette table; he spoke in big gestures connected to a half full glass of liquor—so big, in fact, that the girl listening to him seemed bowed by the force of his speech.

There was something appealing about the young man—something almost Romantic in his manner: the wildish hair and patchy beard across his cheeks and chin; the long, expressive fingers that never rested, even as his glass came to his mouth. In the half light, Sally could see something lecherous in his eyes. It turned her on.

Just over his shoulder, another, unimposing boy listened interestedly while sipping on a bottle of Heineken.

Sally marched over to make her presence felt. Or so she thought.

By mid-evening, Delaney had managed to corner a semi-pretty grad student whom he was entertaining with a story from the oeuvre of Manny Gubatz, the shoe shine guy who worked around the corner from the video store. And even though the girl—whose named seemed to be Jane—appeared to have lost interest, Delaney kept talking. Maybe it was the liquor. Maybe it was the atmosphere. Or maybe he kept on just because he was caught up in the spectacle of her lips, which appeared eerily overwrought against the dull background of her face. Delaney wondered what had made her (Jane) make them up that way. He wondered what those lips could do. What, in fact, was she suggesting?

That kind of trampish affectation never failed to remind Delaney of his mother's too-prominent beauty. He was aware of the Freudian inference in that line of reasoning, but frankly he considered Freud a crank and a creepy old motherlover anyway. Delaney's mother had been a voluptuous—which is to say not-quite-exotic—dancer on the Vegas to Reno circuit in the early seventies. At one time, she'd hoped to end up on Broadway. But she got knocked up by a choreographer, and missed her window. Eventually, she got her figure back, if not her form, and managed to find small-market fame as a minor television personality at a Vegas network affiliate—which guaranteed an income and no end of suitors. As a result, Delaney's childhood home featured a revolving retinue of men.

And he realized the experience had shaped his libido, which was generally considered monstrous. Yet that didn't mean he had an abnormal, or God forbid, Oedipal drift to his sexuality. In fact, he liked to think that his upbringing had given him a good outlook on sex. In his experience, too many people made a mystery of it. He liked sex, goddamnit, and wasn't afraid to admit it—even if the only person listening (sort of) was a rather plain, perhaps too painted girl in a tight shirt. But by God he'd talk that average-looking girl clear across the hall and into his bed if that was what it took to convince her of his self-image.

"So you get my meaning?" Delaney asked, waving his drink in front of him in a vague effort to ascertain if this Jane was still listening.

"I don't know," the girl answered with half-assed condescension. "It all sounds kind of Freudian to me. I've got to pee," she added, and walked past Delaney to the far end of the room—opposite, one might add, from the bathroom.

Albert hadn't wanted to come to the party at all. He was still in the process of moving into the new apartment, and the thought of everything he owned sitting in boxes across the hall put the ants in his pants.

But Delaney had insisted. And basically when Delaney put his mind to something, Albert was helpless to resist. Anyway, after a day's worth of moving, Albert didn't have the strength to fight. Besides, experience told him that within a couple of hours Delaney would be distracted enough by something—almost surely something with breasts—that he wouldn't notice if Albert slipped away to finish the work of moving in.

And by mid-evening it seemed he was about to get his chance. Delaney had taken up with Jane Tetley, a graduate student in the English Department whom Albert had actually met during his freshman year, when she was finishing her Bachelor's at Haber. Of course, Jane had no recollection of Albert, but that was just as well. If he could just blend into the background for an hour or so, surely he'd get away when Delaney made his move.

But his plans fell through when she walked in the room. Of course, at the time he had no idea who *she* was. Yet from the moment he saw her, Albert felt he'd known Sally for years. He'd never really thought of love at first sight as something that existed in real life. That was a fiction, something for storybooks and cheap romance. It was also a gambit that people like Delaney used to further their sexual exploits. Then again, how could it not be love at first sight if she seemed so familiar? Indeed, Albert felt he'd seen her a million times in his mind's eye; he know the curve of her neck, the shape of her face; he knew the color of her eyes, and was sure he would recognize the timbre of her voice with the same intimacy that he knew his own heart. She was as real as dirt—the girl of his dreams made flesh, standing ten feet away holding a red plastic cup against her lips.

It was like one of those old-fashioned myths they talked about in Lit 101, where the Greeks or whatever said that people were once both men and women joined together, till they were separated from their mates. Of course, Delaney would know the story, though the idea of a soul mate was as foreign as Portuguese to him. But suddenly it seemed possible: Maybe this girl was the other half of Albert's soul, torn from him a million years ago. How else could she seem so familiar?

He could hardly believe she was there, or that he was there. Only Delaney's incessant, ascendant voice assured him that he wasn't dreaming.

Now there was no way he was leaving the party.

Sally had no misgivings about her own sex appeal. After all, she was fair-skinned and high-necked, with light green eyes and fine blonde hair that was inevitably called flaxen by the men she attracted. And beyond her physical appeal, Sally had cultivated a stone cold hauteur completed with the gravity of sun. She pulled men like a magnet.

Therefore, as she crossed toward Delaney Bowles, she was prepared to steal his attention. But to Sally's surprise, he cast hardly a glance at her. In fact, he looked her over with brevity that cut like a knife. Instead, he kept talking to a plain-looking girl with short red hair and too bright lipstick that distorted her features like a funhouse mirror.

Miffed but undaunted, Sally struck an interested pose and tossed her hair lightly in his direction. Yet still the young man talked on, unfazed, ungained, uninterested, apparently, in her.

Meanwhile, in the background, Albert Sprague nearly choked on his Heineken.

At that, Sally was about finished. It wasn't often she made such an advance, and almost never that she was ignored. She turned to leave. And if she'd been one step quicker, she'd have never spoken Delaney Bowles again—and probably never met his unassuming roommate either.

But courtship, love, heartbreak, and all the other traumas and dramas were salvaged, in fact, by that bored, plain, overly decorated graduate student (named Jane) to whom Delaney was speaking. Because at that moment she said: "I've got to pee," and walked brusquely past Delaney toward the far end of the room—opposite, one might add, from the bathroom.

"Was it something I said?" Delaney asked no one in particular.

All at once, Sally asked: "What was it you were saying?"

Delaney turned toward her, this time taking her in more fully as he lifted his drink in the general direction of his mouth. Unfortunately, when it got there he missed the mark, and spilled a little bit of whiskey down his shoulder. Sally laughed.

Delaney raised his shoulders and eyebrows in a pantomime that immediately eased the introduction. "I was just telling a little story," he said.

"What about?" Sally asked.

Delaney sighed. "Oh, all kinds of stuff. Trains, adultery, destiny," he said with a grin.

"All in one?"

"You got it."

"Indulge me."

At that, he went on, not briefly, to describe a story about someone named Manny Gubatz—a story that did, indeed, include bits about a train, mirrors, destiny, and adultery, though Sally wasn't really listening that closely.

"But you know," Delaney said at the end, trying to appear honest as he carefully raised his glass to his lips again, "I can't really remember why I was telling it now."

"You were trying to get that girl to go to bed with you," Sally answered.

"Really?"

"Oh please. It was all in your body language—those big gestures and leering stares. You might just as well have unzipped your pants."

"I can if you'd like."

Sally tipped her flaxen head and smiled again. Meanwhile, Delaney's gestures had settled; he stood still before her, cradling his drink near his navel.

"Is that a real name," Sally asked, "Or just part of the act?"

"Manny Gubatz? Of course."

"Seriously."

"Yes," he insisted. "One of the great raconteurs of our time. I once heard him tell a joke that lasted three days. Also, he shines shoes."

"Oh Christ," Sally said, flipping her head again. "That's got to be the most Freudian thing I've ever heard of."

"*What?!*"

"Manny Gubatz? Mirrors? A love story on a train? It's classic. Please tell me there isn't a cigar in there." She laughed as she drank.

"Excuse me?"

"You heard me." Sally was enjoying herself immensely.

Delaney grinned. "You know, I see your lips moving, but I can't hear a thing you say."

At that moment, the other boy—the one who'd been lingering in the background, stepped forward. "Hi," he said. "My name is Albert."

"Was it something I said?"

"What was it you were saying?" asked a girl with honey-colored hair, who'd been lingering for a few minutes in the near distance.

Delaney turned from the retreating girl and appraised this other one. This girl was certainly beautiful: petite, pale skin, pearlescent green eyes that glowed like marble in the dim light. Along with the shoulder length, honey-colored hair, her looks actually had a touch of the spectacular. In short, she wasn't Delaney's type at all—too beautiful by half. He tended, instead, to go for girls with sketchier looks. The classic beauties rarely had to work for anything. As a result, they rarely had the stamina to be good lovers. Whenever he'd taken time to speak with one of those perfect girls, Delaney inevitably got the impression he was talking to a statue. He'd never fucked one, though his guess was that it would be much the same.

"I was just telling a little story," Delaney answered.

"What was it about?"

"Nothing really." He was looking for a way out of talking to this girl. Where was Albert when he was needed?

"Indulge me," she said with ruthless charm. And at that moment her face changed from being merely pretty to something much more interesting, as though this beautiful girl was challenging Delaney to enliven her evening. Of course, that was one of his favorite things to do.

"It's actually a story about a fellow I know named Manny Gubatz," Delaney began. "See, some years ago, Manny took a train trip from Philadelphia to Chicago, to see his family for Thanksgiving. At that time Manny wasn't married or anything, so he was traveling alone."

Delaney sipped his drink and leaned on the banquette. The honey-colored girl (as he'd already come to think of her) followed his lips with her eyes; she was looking better than ever.

"Well, dinner time comes around and Manny decides to go down to the diner car to get something to eat. He sits down and orders, and he's waiting there for his food to arrive when two women come in and sit at the table right next to him. Of course, the women start talking, and because Manny's alone, he can't help but overhear what they're saying." Delaney made a gesture of understanding with his hands; the girl returned the gesture along with an expression that was something between a smile and a frown.

"So a few minutes go by, and to Manny's surprise, the two women, who it turns out are sisters, start talking about, well, adultery. For his part, Manny's a little embarrassed—he's looking out the window at, you know, *Ohio* going by, trying to seem inconspicuous and all. But at the same time, of course, he's listening to everything these women are saying."

Delaney took a sip of his drink. The honey-colored girl watched him impassively.

"The older sister—who Manny soon realizes is the married one—is telling the younger sister that adultery in itself isn't necessarily the end of a marriage. Of course, it's not good, but it's not the kind of thing that has to automatically mean divorce. In fact, she says, adultery ought not apply equally to men and women, since women are by their nature—this was in, like, the sixties, you understand—better able to keep more than one partner satisfied." Delaney raised his eyebrows for effect.

"After all, says the older sister, if women are in the home 90 percent of the time while men are out working, they simply have more time and more energy for extramarital affairs. And so long as they keep their men satisfied, what should it matter to the men that their wives were finding fulfillment elsewhere…fulfillment that husbands couldn't provide by themselves.

"'For instance,' the woman says, 'If a wife gives herself to her husband, at all times and as often as he pleases, what is she to do when her own needs rise over and above what he is incapable of providing? What if he's out of town on business? What if he's serving overseas in the Army? What if he's just too damned busy to do what she needs?'" Delaney nodded his head in sympathy with the character in his story. "'Isn't it better for her to give herself to another man, rather than let herself go to ruin?'

"And then she says this: 'A woman's got needs, after all.'" This time, Delaney raised his eyebrows and nodded suggestively—conveying the suggestiveness of the woman's remark.

After a moment, he went on: "Now by this time, Manny can hardly believe what he's hearing. He doesn't want to look directly at these women, because he's embarrassed that they'll know he was listening to their conversation. Still, he's curious as hell about these two.

"Lucky for Manny, it was about the time when it starts getting dark outside, and the windows were beginning to mirror the inside of the train car. So when he looks outward, Manny can see the older sister—the married one who's going on about her 'needs'—in the reflection beside him.

"But at that very moment, she too is looking at the window, fixing her lipstick in the reflection or something. And when Manny looks out the window on his side," Delaney pointed his right index finger to the right, "And she looks out the window on her side," his index finger pointed left, "Somehow their eyes meet in the middle." He switched directions with both index fingers and crossed them at the midpoint of his body.

"And I'll tell you what," he went on, fingers still locked. "To this day, Manny swears up and down that that woman winked at him." Delaney, of course, pantomimed a wink.

"That's it?" Sally asked, chin raised boldly.

"No." Delaney raised his glass to his lips, keeping eye contact with Sally. When he was finished, he replaced it on the banquette table.

"So she winks at him." Delaney nodded to Sally, to remind her. "When Manny sees this, he's shocked. So shocked, in fact, that without thinking he turns to look at the two women sitting beside him. And when he does, he sees the younger sister for the first time. Beautiful, this girl. Long, auburn hair, bright blue eyes, lips like rosebuds. In an instant, he's smitten. What's more, when he turns, she turns and looks right at him. Their eyes meet, and it's like a flash of lightning. Pow!" Delaney slapped his hands together.

Sally cradled her drink, listening.

"And now Manny realizes that *she knows* he was listening to their conversation. He's mortified. Immediately he's looking for the waiter so he can pay his bill and get the hell out of there.

"But while he's hemming and hawing and squirming in his chair, suddenly the girl—the younger one—turns back and answers her sister. 'Sister,' says the younger girl. 'I have to disagree with you.'

"'How's that?' the older sister says, still fixing her makeup in the window.

"'A woman who's found a man she truly loves doesn't need any other, no matter what the circumstances. She will be happy with him, and him alone. And that doesn't mean she should have to go to ruin, as you say, if she can't have her husband with her at all times. If a woman has greater capacity for lovemaking than a man—for whatever reason—then she should enjoy him doubly when she's with her husband. It isn't the quantity, but the quality of lovemaking that binds men and women.

'A woman who can't get satisfaction from her husband alone doesn't truly love her husband. Because any woman who gives herself entirely to the man she loves—physically and spiritually—couldn't possibly need anything else from another lover.'

"At that, the girl folded her hands peacefully in front of her," said Delaney. "Manny was so heartened by what he'd heard that he was able to look over at the two women without embarrassment. And do you know what he saw?"

Sally shook her head.

"She was smiling," Delaney answered. "And Manny knew that smile was for him."

At that, Sally unconsciously raised a hand to her own mouth; she, too, was smiling. "What happened then?" she asked.

"Well, before they got to Chicago, Manny introduced himself to the auburn-haired girl. And six months later, she became Mrs. Manny Gubatz."

"…And they lived happily ever after."

"No," Delaney answered flatly, waiving his drink in the air. "Two years later she left him for another man."

All through Delaney's story, Albert remained glued to the floor, and completely stuck on the girl who'd crossed the room to talk to his roommate. And for the moment it didn't matter that all her attention was focused on Delaney; Albert felt happy just being near her.

In fact, he watched Sally as closely as Sally was watching Delaney, zeroing on her light green eyes. In those few moments, Albert learned her movements and expressions, and extrapolated her character and qualities—and the intimacy he'd felt upon seeing her increased exponentially. By the time Delaney was finished, Albert was in love.

Of course Delaney, who wanted nothing but to get in the girl's pants (Albert was sure), had slipped easily into conversation—something about a man on a train. Meanwhile Albert, who wanted to make this girl happy for the rest of her life, turned to stone, standing idly by while his roommate seduced his dream girl. Soon she and Delaney were standing much closer than necessary, their knees almost touching as her eyes followed the progress of his gestures, her face changing in concert with his voice.

Albert knew he had to do something before Delaney made off with this girl, or worse yet broke her heart. "Hi," he said, stepping forward. "My name is Albert."

"Sally," she answered, presenting her hand to Albert. "And you are?"

"Ben McCockiner," Delaney answered, his glass raised for theatrical effect.

"Of course."

Albert, too, was shaking his head against Delaney's incessant persona.

"I take it you two know each other."

Before Albert could answer, Delaney slid an arm heavily around his shoulder, simultaneously dealing him an open-handed whack in the chest. The impact took his breath for a moment.

"This fine young man happens to be my roommate." Delaney released Albert from his grasp and touched Sally on the arm. "If you'd like, I can show you where he lives."

"His name is Delaney," Albert said, his breath recovered—though he was already wondering why he'd said that. Truth was, he couldn't think of anything else.

Luckily, Sally seemed to take the whole act in stride. "Finally, a straight answer," she said. "Thank you Albert."

"Oh Albert is a fine straight man. And he is a straight man, in case you're wondering." Delaney leaned conspiratorially toward Sally. "*Hung* like a *mule*," he added in a loud whisper.

Albert turned red.

Sally felt sorry for him and shot back at Delaney: "Watch it, Romeo. I just might take you up on that offer."

For a moment, Albert's spirits rose; Sally was giving him a look halfway between flirtation and pity. He couldn't decide if he should take her in his arms or lay his head on her breast.

But before he could decide, her gaze switched to Delaney, who had straightened and sobered. His eyes, heretofore hooded with drunkenness, widened, and he looked at Sally with a modesty Albert had never seen before.

"So boys," she said, "Where do we go from here?"

The Confectioner's Mistress

*sol•stice n. **1.** either of the two times a year when the sun is at its greatest distance from the celestial equator: about June 21 and about December 22. **2.** either of the two points in the ecliptic farthest from the equator. **3.** a furthest or culminating point; a turning point.*

*D*ecember twenty-second. The shortest day of the year. The winter solstice.

What does this mean, thought Tannenbaum. It was still, even after the years, difficult sometimes to yoke words in English to their meaning—the words that were not heard every day. He had been thinking about this word since early that morning. That morning, while he made his sack lunch in the dark, as he did every other morning when the days were longer, and listened to the radio announcer tell him the weather. He looked for the word in his tattered Random House dictionary.

In all his life, Tannenbaum had never been the kind of man to watch the sun very closely, for it seemed there were always other things to do. Was there such a type of man? There must be, he thought, because there is a word for this solstice. He had once heard that on the equator the sun rises and sets at the exact same time every day of the year, but he was not sure what to make of that. Tannenbaum resolved that he would try to pay more attention.

He was still considering the solstice later, as he aligned ceramic statues on the shelves along the back wall of his candy store, picking each up, dusting beneath it, and wiping the bottom gingerly, as if they were little children. He thought of Christmas. Christmas comes soon after the solstice, soon after the shortest day of the year. This struck Tannenbaum as odd, for when he was a child in Germany the days before Christmas had always seemed, much to the contrary, to be the longest. And this year too, the days of December stretched out like old eternity in his store. For the first time he could ever remember, it seemed that there was not enough for him to do. He finished cooking early in the morning, which was his habit of many years, and cleaned up around the store. But by afternoon Tannenbaum was left idle, humming to himself, doing crossword puzzles.

He picked up an elf figurine displayed specially for the Christmas season, and examined its imperfectly rounded base. That was the style of all of the ceramics made by Mrs. Block: round bottoms, but never perfect circles. In fact, when he studied them closely, as he had done in fallow moments during the last week, Tannenbaum found that the base of each figurine was unique, worked closely by hand.

"Too hard to make," he said to himself.

Square bottoms would be more practical. Uniform. Easy to mold and reproduce. Then Mrs. Block could mount her elves on pedestals, like figures from the Greek mythology. It would make them more dignified, Tannenbaum thought. And still his methodical hands continued cleaning and replacing, trying to stack the statues in even rows, like a company of little soldiers.

"Hmmm," he sighed.

But what he was thinking was that these things were not of him anyway, and so it was not for him to judge. Mrs. Block was probably correct in the way that she made her little people, with their uneven and sometimes unfinished bottoms that would not line up no matter how precisely Tannenbaum nudged them into place. Who was he to say what was the best, or most beautiful (for Tannenbaum's wife had often remarked how beautiful the statues were) way to shape ceramic elves? They were, perhaps, like Mrs. Block's several children: As no two children could be the same, then no two of her figures would be exactly alike.

But Tannenbaum was a candy maker, not a sculptor. His wife, Reathel, had once wanted him to make molds for his candy—Santa Clauses for Christmas and rabbits at Easter, to catch the eye of the customers, she said—but Tannenbaum did not like the idea.

"Candy does not catch eyes," he had said. "One does not even need eyes to be a—what is it called—*connoisseur* of candy. My grandfather, in his last days, when his eyesight grew so cloudy that he could hardly find a chair to sit, still knew by his nose alone how many cups of butter had been added to the peanut brittle. Candy is not eyes. It is nose and mouth that judge the talent of the confectioner."

Of course, he did not say the real reason. The real reason was that one Christmas, Reathel had made gingerbread men, and Tannenbaum cringed every time he had to bite an arm, a leg, or finally—horribly—the head of one of her pastry figures. That, too, was like the Greek myth: eating his wife's creation. It gave him chills. Tannenbaum had to convince his wife that he no longer had a taste for gingerbread. The truth was that he missed the nutmeg and spices, but would just as soon bite the head off a ceramic elf as a cookie with a smile frosted on it. As for Santa Clauses and bunnies, it would not do for anyone to be horrified by his candy.

The clock told Tannenbaum that it was eleven-thirty. He pushed air out of his mouth, making a sound that was something in between a groan and a scoff.

"They are ruining my business," he said to the empty store, imagining that there was someone there to speak to.

Eleven-thirty already, and not yet one customer. Damn them. For all of December it had been this way because of the orange cones and the flashing lights outside his window. MEN AT WORK the signs said. But there were never any men in sight. The only movement that Tannenbaum could see was steam rising around that manhole cover that was always out-of-center (and, he insisted, always in the exact same place), and the blinking arrow that pointed away from his store, directing his customers somewhere else. Three times he had called to find out what the matter was that the city had blocked the street in front of a candy store at Christmas. He asked the sanitation department if they knew what they were doing to his business, if they realized that most of his profits came in this season, and that by laying siege to his store they were starving him and his wife, who was three years older than he and not of so sturdy a constitution. They told him to eat candy. He called the mayor's office and was put on hold indefinitely, listening to Christmas carols without the words. He told Reathel that he would like to march down there himself and get an explanation for such an infringement on his rights. But then who would make the candy?

True, Reathel had laughed at him when he spoke of this. She told him that he would do no such thing to embarrass her.

She said, "We will be just fine, you crazy old farcas."

This was a word that Tannenbaum could not confirm the meaning of, but he did not think that it was English.

"Your father, perhaps, when he came here and opened the candy store, would have had to worry about a bad Christmas," she said. "But your business and your house will survive."

Tannenbaum could not confirm the stability of his finances, though he had grudging trust in his wife's accounting. Reathel took care of all the money as well as the house. Without children, his wife had needed to learn a trade. This accounting was as good a thing as any for her to do, and also it helped with his business. This was not of him anyway. He was a candy maker.

But at present he was making candy for no one. In the beginning of the siege, though he saved no complaint, Tannenbaum had been privately optimistic. His customers would still come, he thought, because they loved his candy. Orange cones were not obstacle enough to deter them from his walnut clusters in the season. Tannenbaum did not know them by name, but he imagined their happy faces as he handed white paper bags over the counter, smiling and apologizing for the inconvenience. And in his mind they would shake their heads and tell him that it was "No problem at all."

But that was before, at the beginning of December. It was now the winter solstice, for heaven's sake, and the store was still empty most of the day. Eleven-thirty already, and not a single customer. And crossword puzzles.

Even if he did have enough money to last through this winter, or if he had enough money to last through the next five winters without any customers (could they dig in the sewer that long?), or if one of the lottery tickets that Reathel bought brought a million dollars, a candy maker still needs customers. What does a candy maker do if he is not making candy? His life becomes as empty as that store had been for the last three weeks. Tannenbaum's father died seven months after he retired. If you are making the candy and no one is tasting it, what use is the making? This was not the idle hobby of an old woman whose children have gone away, a woman who refuses to go south like the birds—as were Mrs. Block's ceramic people. This is what a candy maker is, thought Tannenbaum. Someone must eat the candy to complete the candy. It was like that question that people ask: If a tree falls in the woods and no one is there to hear it fall, does it make a sound? That is why one does not put faces on candy.

Tannenbaum looked up; the clock said it was twenty minutes until noon; the anise candy would be ready. The anise was the last he must make that day. Then, if no customers came, Tannenbaum would be left searching for something to keep busy.

In the kitchen, he retrieved the sheets of anise from the oven and brushed them to bring out their deep red color, just as his father had taught him long ago when he was learning the candymaker's craft. He stood back and took a deep, satisfying breath. Breaking anise was the one task that Tannenbaum, as a confectioner, reveled in the most. It was the only time when he agonized over the presentation of his wares. And his work was masterful.

He turned the cookie sheets upside down over wax paper and deftly tapped a mallet on the bottom of the pan, at first at the edges to loosen, then converging on the center from all four corners with light taps as he listened to the hard candy peel from the surface of the sheet. First one, then the second sheet of anise emerged from its pan faultlessly whole, without crack or a crumble, with Tannenbaum beaming over them like the proud father of healthy children. He then took out a long, fine carpenter's nail and the smaller mallet that he used for shaping the candy. Though other confectioners he knew used long knives to quarter the sheets (certainly it was more efficient that way), Tannenbaum found true joy in chiseling from the block, piece by piece. And despite what he said to Reathel about the appearance of candy being insignificant, he took great pride in the way the anise was displayed in his candy case.

No one cracked anise the way that Tannenbaum did. First, he measured its thickness with his eyes before leveling the nail. Always he would start with light pressure to let the candy open up and tell him where to go next. But as he progressed he worked into an efficient rhythm, splitting the candy with single incisions of his chisel, as though the pattern had been divined to him. With each tap on the nail he could predict with near certainty the length and direction that a crack would crawl through a particular sheet, forming beautiful icicles of candy. When he was through with the cutting, Tannenbaum staggered the edges in crystalline arrangements, the pieces packed so tight one against another that they stood vertical on the tray without any need for prop or crutch. The marvelous oblique (that is the word) angles gave the candy a star-like appearance. No two pieces overlapped completely.

As Tannenbaum was finishing, the bell over the door finally rang, and the confectioner rushed to the front of the store humming "The Ride of the Valkyries" with a tray of freshly made anise, ready for sale. Pride and excitement made him want to skip a little, though he was a man who usually did not skip.

There, in his store he saw a small girl standing just inside the high arch of the doorway. She shook all over, from her head to her toes, causing big snowflakes to fall from her hair and coat, making a misty ring like a halo on the floor around her. She stepped back to consider the ring of snow for a moment, and for some reason Oscar Tannenbaum thought of angels, like the ones that he had made with his sister when they lived on Hillshire Street, newly arrived in the United States. He had not made a snow angel for half a century.

"Very *wintery*," the girl said, placing special emphasis.

She stepped around the ring and began unbuttoning her coat, quietly twirling her muffler from around her neck as she inspected the candy on display. Tannenbaum leaned his elbows on the top of the glass case. He studied her face. It was a mixed bag of features that teased his interest. She had black licorice eyebrows and skin the creamy white of Jordan almonds. Her nose was full and long and broad in the middle like a marzipan bar, and overshadowed her thin mouth that was almost invisible, but pursed slightly now in apparent amusement. Where her cheekbones should have been high and defined, matching her arch eyebrows for the look of classic Teutonic beauty, she was soft and rounded like a child. Rather than unattractive, the strangeness of her features was altogether bewitching.

Das ist gestalt, thought Tannenbaum in his mother tongue.

"I love it when the snow comes down all *fluffy* and *velvety* like that," the girl said, looking up from the candy case. "See?" She held out a gloved hand to Tannenbaum. "The snowflakes are *huge*."

Indeed, on the back of her hand was a flake at least an inch long, and against her black glove Tannenbaum could well make out the latticework of ice, each branch stacked into a beautiful crystal.

"Would you like to come outside and make snow angels with me?"

Tannenbaum was surprised by her. "I cannot," he said, bringing his elbows off the counter. "I must mind the store."

"I bet you haven't made snow angels for *years*," said the girl. "And you know, there are only so many days for it. I assure you, Mr. Tannenbaum, today is the *perfect* day.'

"Have you come here before?" he asked, wondering if she knew him.

"The name on the door is yours."

"I made snow angels with my sister when I was young. I was only ten years old then. The snow was so deep that I thought I would lose Martha when she laid down." Tannenbaum was smiling softly, lost in nostalgia.

"Get your coat."

"The store will be empty."

"It's not a problem today. You can take a break."

Tannenbaum did not move.

She rewrapped her muffler and buttoned her coat, gazing at him crosswise with silent encouragement.

Tannenbaum hesitated. He looked at the tray of anise on top of the candy counter; he checked the clock. "I will have my lunch break now," he said, abandoning the anise and taking his coat off the tree.

The house was already dark when Tannenbaum got home from work. It was the solstice, after all. He shook himself from head to toe as he stepped through the door, sprinkling flakes from his coat and hat onto the floor around him. He had never done that before.

Inside, he could hear the chop, chopping of Reathel at work in the kitchen, accompanied by the sounds of her favorite radio station, KXBG, the big band channel. Tannenbaum slipped out of his boots and tiptoed on stocking feet, stepping as lightly as a man of his size could manage, moving in time with the beat of the chopping, which, it occurred to him, kept time with the music on the radio. So much harmony on the solstice, he thought. He peeked around the corner. Reathel's back was to him, standing over the counter, her right elbow moving up and down in a regular motion. With a silly, excited feeling in his belly, Tannenbaum crept up behind his wife, and, with his finger... poked her bottom!

She leaped and shrieked, reflexively pointing the knife at him. Luckily Tannenbaum, in his inspired mood, was ready and was well out of harm's way when she turned, he all the while giggling like a child who has played a winning prank.

In the midst of his merriment Tannenbaum heard a sniffle and noticed the red around his wife's eyes, which also were filled with tears. He stopped short. A wave of guilt ruined completely his giddy mood. Crying? Certainly she could not know, he reassured himself. But what was there to know? Nothing at all. Tannenbaum thought that the girl was pretty, in a way. Yes, he even went out into the snow with her to make angels—something that he had never done with Reathel. But this was nothing to be ashamed of. There was no one in the store. However, there was a moment—no, not even a moment—when Flora had rolled out of her angel—it was not his fault at all—she put her hand on his thigh to get up. It was nothing. Balance, gravity, that was all. No one could have noticed the flush on his neck or suspected the rush of adrenaline (is that the word?) that he felt. He had even kept it, he was certain, from the girl.

"I should slice you in two!" Tannenbaum's wife exclaimed. And then the confectioner realized that there were onion fumes in his nose, and that his wife had screamed at him through laughter.

Tannenbaum washed for dinner and put on his favorite sweater that he liked to wear around the house, even though Reathel complained that it was an eyesore and would make him take it off when they had company. They rarely had company.

The meal was very pleasant, almost uncommonly so. Reathel noted that Tannenbaum was in unusually good spirits even though he remarked that it had again been a very slow day at the candy store.

"Mrs. Block came for a visit today," she said.

"This is a good thing."

"Yes. But I feared she would kill herself in the walking. It is just so icy out there, and none of us are as thick-skinned as we used to be."

"We get along."

"Well, except for you of course, Oscar. You are immune to the common cold. You are immune even to the uncommon cold. But the rest of us have concerns about the weather and our bodies. Mrs. Block is thinking of moving to Florida."

"The world of ceramic elves will never be the same."

"Don't make fun, Oscar. It is something that we might be wise to think about as well. You know, I could slip on the sidewalk just as easily as Mrs. Block. God help us both if I should fall and break my hip."

"This is nonsense," said Tannenbaum. "Mrs. Block is an old woman. She is having the fears of an old woman. If she begins to fear that she will break a hip, eventually it will happen to her."

Silence.

Realizing his mistake, Tannenbaum made quick to cover. "This will not happen to you at all. Do not let an old woman pass her fears on to you."

"They were not her fears. They were mine when I saw her sliding across the street."

"Perhaps you should visit Mrs. Block in her house."

"Perhaps I should visit her in Florida."

"Say hello for me."

Instead of going to sit in his chair after dinner, where he would normally doze off until Reathel woke him to take to bed, Tannenbaum tried to pacify his wife by helping her clear the table. He found her implacable.

Reathel picked up the yellow pages.

"What are you doing, lemon drop?"

"I am looking for the numbers of private nurses, you bumpa gog, so that when the time comes I will have someone who can rightly take care of me. God knows that when I have an accident you will not be able to care for an old woman in traction. Will you pick me up and dust underneath me as well? Ha. You will still go to your beloved candy. I will be alone all day and then get a tray of gumballs for my dinner."

"Wife, what is a bumpa gog?"

"A stubborn old man who does not care about the safety of the wife who cooks and cleans for him."

"I have never met one."

"Who does not even realize that he too is growing old and will become fragile. Mrs. Block is seventy-two years old. That is just ten years more than you, husband."

"Eleven."

"Florida."

Reathel got up and stormed into the parlor, leaving Tannenbaum to wash the dishes alone. She was paging through a magazine when he rejoined her. He pushed back into a reclining position in his easy chair.

"You would have me retire and die like my father. Is there a word for that kind of woman?"

There was no answer, only the turning of pages.

"Who can live in Florida? There is nothing but the same, every day of the year. The same weather. Same green grass and palm trees. The same length of days every day of the year. There is no solstice in Florida."

"You said that Mrs. Block should move to Florida."

"When did I say that?"

"When her husband died."

"So you do want me dead." He said it in jest, hoping to turn her around.

"Eh," she answered.

Tannenbaum huffed and leaned back in his chair, not at all insulted, but defeated by her wit. He saw no reason to go on with the conversation. He would lie back and fall asleep to end the argument. But he would not quit making candy.

"I'm not asking you to quit making candy," she said, "Just to move. You could still make candy in Florida. Then you will live, I suppose."

Rising, Tannenbaum gasped, "And sell my father's store?"

"He has died—remember?"

"People do not eat candy in Florida. Chocolate melts. They eat bean sprouts and this tofu to keep them healthy and beautiful."

"You are thinking of California, husband."

"Ah yes, Florida is oranges and all-bran."

Reathel stormed out, muttering "bumpa gog" under her breath. Tannenbaum soon fell asleep in his recliner, and woke up at midnight still in the same place.

Because of pride, Oscar Tannenbaum did not join his wife in the bedroom on the night of the winter solstice; it was not right for her to leave him there, like a relic in his own house. After all, Reathel knew, did she not, how early he got up every day to go to the candy store—the same candy store that had provided for her needs all these years, even in the slow times. This was his livelihood. And so this was also her livelihood. There was no reason, Tannenbaum thought, that he should be left to sleep in a chair, and by she who was so worried about the health of Mrs. Block. She might as well move to Florida if this was the way.

Tannenbaum didn't pack a lunch the next day because he woke up late. He heard nothing of the weather or the sunrise from the radio announcer. In the twenty years since his father retired, he had never once been late to the candy store. Then again, he had never spent the night on the couch either.

The good news was that for the first time in many weeks, when Tannenbaum approached the store he was not greeted by a flashing sign. The orange cones had disappeared. Men were no longer at work. Despite his grogginess, a lingering sourness in the mouth, and a strange crick in his left side, Tannenbaum found the energy to hop two steps across his stride, satisfied by being rid of the nuisance. Perhaps finally someone would taste his season's sweets.

And so it happened. There was no time for dusting that morning, for shortly behind him customers began streaming through the door, declaring their relief that they had managed to stop in before Christmas, for the holiday would not have been the same without his brittle and peppermint and Scotch kisses. Tannenbaum received their compliments with gracious smiles, apologies, and thanks, just as he had envisioned doing during the previous weeks' long hours of isolation. Frankly, he beamed. In truth, Tannenbaum was never one to make much conversation with his customers; many he recognized from years past, though he had never exchanged a word with them outside of candy. But on this day he thought himself excessively cordial, approaching charming, and was sure that they felt the warmth of his appreciation.

Throughout the morning and into the afternoon, Tannenbaum was kept busy retrieving candies from the case. He even sold some china and baskets, as well as one or two of Mrs. Block's strange little statues. He did not think of his wife when he sold them. The store was teeming so much with people that once when he thought he saw Flora browsing quietly in the back of the store he did not have time to get a second look for her, and when he did she was gone.

At two o'clock the store was finally empty for a moment, and Tannenbaum could, though reluctantly, hang the CLOSED sign and lock the door for a short break. He had a long day ahead of him. There would now be much cooking to do. So much, in fact, that the candy maker, for the first time in his life, knew not where to start.

As he was trying to decide, there was another knock at the door, and Tannenbaum did not hesitate to jump up to answer. Through the glass he saw Flora's black button eyes peeking in beneath the sign, and when he saw her, Tannenbaum got a shiver down his back—

the same cold tingle as when he had laid down to make snow angels the day before.

"Merry Christmas," Flora said, pushing a vase full of chrysanthemums through the doorway ahead of her.

Tannenbaum fairly sparkled. "Oh no, you shouldn't have."

"But I *have*," she said. "To *brighten* the store for *all* of your customers. It's already cozy, but some bright color will go well. And these are *completely odorless*, because I would *never* want to do *anything* to change this smell." She drew a deep breath through her marzipan nose. "Mmmm, like Christmas morning."

Tannenbaum, in turn, sniffed absently at the chrysanthemums (they were, in fact, odorless), forgetting for the moment his many responsibilities on such a busy day, forsaking his usual diffidence once again in the presence of this pixie girl.

That was how it had also been the day before, on the solstice, when they made angels in the snow and Flora stayed with him all afternoon, talking and twirling a stick of saltwater toffee into an endless spiral. Tannenbaum loved to listen to the lilting way she talked. She talked like no one he'd ever met. At one point, Flora had crawled up on a chair to pluck the mistletoe from above the door. She told him that mistletoe was an old solstice totem from northern Europe—from the time before there were countries. People believed it caused the sun to shine, the trees to thrive, the crops to flourish, and that it warded off the wicked arts of fairies and witches and trolls. She explained that the word "solstice" came from the Latin word that meant "the sun stands still," and told him about the celebration of Sol Invictus, the unconquered sun (also Latin, Flora had said), a great celebration of the earth's fertility. And there was something called a saturnalia, which ended on the twenty-fifth of December—the solstice of the Roman Empire and also the birthday of their god called Mithras, the god of light and truth.

"Because the saturnalia was a celebration of beginning and ending—both a *culmination* and the annual *rebirth* of Mithras—people were encouraged to engage in *licentious excesses.*" Flora winked at Tannenbaum and nodded her head once. "Deliberate release of *erotic energy.*" She giggled. *"Liberal sexual activity,"* she whispered.

Tannenbaum blushed.

"And that began the tradition of kissing under the mistletoe. Then, when the whole lot was absorbed into Christianity, only an *innocent kiss* remained."

"But I do not understand," Tannenbaum had said, trying very much to distract from the flush in his cheeks, "How something can be both a beginning and an ending."

"You just have to think in circles rather than a straight line," Flora said, making a ring with a piece of red licorice. "Then every ending is a new beginning. Like the sun goes around the earth. Before there were watches and calendars, people looked to the sun for times and dates. You can do it even now. If you *look closely* and listen to what it's telling you, *then* you'll under*stand.*"

Flora had then dangled the mistletoe over his head and gave Tannenbaum a nice peck on the cheek.

Tannenbaum finally pulled his nose out of the scentless chrysanthemums. "You must excuse me please," he said, "But there is now so much candy for me to make that I should not, as they say, stop and smell the flowers."

Who was this silver-tongued confectioner?

"You *must* have *loads* to do," Flora said with a bright smile, motioning with a flower to the glass display case, in which every type of candy was wanting. Tannenbaum followed her gaze with a sort of beleaguered pride. "And only *yesterday* there was *nothing* to do."

Just then the door swung open, ringing the bell above. Tannenbaum had forgotten to re-lock it after Flora came in, and now yet another familiar, nameless face was returning after a long absence. The candy maker stood frozen and flustered, already twice-assured that he must close the store for some time, yet unable to turn away the appreciation of another smiling customer.

"Why don't you let me take care of that?" Flora said, placing her chrysanthemums on the counter. "Go make your candy."

Tannenbaum did not understand.

"I'll stay here and help you," she said.

That day and the next, Oscar Tannenbaum was feverishly occupied making candy from morning until night, to the point of exhausting the stock of ingredients that had accumulated during the weeks of flashing lights and lonely days. It was a constant effort to satisfy the line of customers that at times trailed all the way around the walls and out the door of his candy store. Truly, this was unprecedented. And although the sudden lust for his sweets was exhausting, it made Tannenbaum's heart swell. It was the culmination of the art that he—just as his father, and his father's father—had spent a lifetime perfecting.

His penuche, pralines, and licorice were harvested in big brown shopping bags the moment he brought them from the kitchen; the last of the lemon drops and bonbons once nearly caused a scuffle among the customers. And as for chocolates, Tannenbaum had to institute a ration—one could not even think of leaving the store with more than a pound on his person. Strangers who claimed to be from distant cities were asking for him by his first name. Others, the familiar faces of his longtime customers, would entreat special favors when informed that their requests were unavailable. One and all appealed to him not only as customers, but as friends, his loyal friends.

It was since that first day, when Flora had told Tannenbaum to go cook while she manned the cash register, that the madness for his candies began in earnest. Naturally, Flora had to be retained. Though he had never before trusted anyone, not even Reathel, with the smallest step in the process of his confections (from the choice and measurement of each ingredient to making the change and handing over the white paper bag), this time Tannenbaum simply could not do it on his own. Besides, in some strange, magical way it seemed that Flora was almost the cause of his good fortune, as if she was a beacon for candy lovers everywhere.

And Tannenbaum liked having her there. She brought more flowers into the store, and placed the ceramics and china in more lively arrangements, so that they looked less like an afterthought and more like decoration. She was dear with customers and chatty with Tannenbaum himself. After she had locked the doors for the evening, Flora would—and this was unheard of—venture back into the kitchen and get her hands in whatever sweets he was making for the following morning. Reluctant only at first, Tannenbaum began to teach her all of the secret recipes passed down from his family in the Old Country. He even showed Flora how to break the anise, carefully at first, but with tenderness and precision. Indeed, Flora was a source of rejuvenation (if that is the word) for both the confectioner and his business.

But he did not tell Reathel that he had taken an assistant. He knew that his wife had been concerned the first day of his business boom—the day after the first night that Tannenbaum had ever spent on the couch—when he came home so late from the lately empty candy store. She was only quietly apologetic for not waking him. All the same, Tannenbaum's good humor and news of the revived business helped to make the previous night's argument pass without need of consolation. On hearing of the crowds waiting outside the store, Reathel offered to help, but Tannenbaum declined even the slightest assistance, because (to her mind) he was so protective of his precious candy. The fact of the matter was that Tannenbaum did not want to tell Flora to leave. Besides, there was something exciting for him in the fact that Reathel did not know about her.

Tannenbaum and his wife always exchanged gifts on Christmas Eve, though the holiday was, like many other things in their lives, now a dull habit rather than a celebration. Every year, he and Reathel ate turkey with canned cranberries and mashed yams, then withdrew to their sparsely decorated parlor to enjoy the gift-giving ritual. Sitting in their accustomed separate chairs, they opened each two gifts, though for a few years neither had really bothered with wrapping, and it had been more than a decade since a tree and lights showed in their home. Afterwards, Tannenbaum would fall asleep in his chair like every other night, and she would wake him to go to bed when the time was ready.

But this year was different because, at Reathel's insistence, the widowed Mrs. Block would be joining them for Christmas dinner. For his own reasons, Tannenbaum had offered no complaint about the change of their holiday habit, which, however dull, was still the way of life for him. He was too satisfied by the business and his new arrangement with Flora to ruin his mood with a confrontation, even after he found out that he had been obligated by his wife to guide the old woman across the winter street so that she could safely join in the festivities (if that was the right word). Also on this occasion, for the benefit of her friend, Reathel had wrapped all of the gifts— even those from her husband to her—and brought out some of the old Christmas lights for holiday cheer. Tannenbaum was strictly forbidden to wear his favorite sweater.

And Mrs. Block had news to tell. The news was laid out in the form of a tract for the housing development at Vista del Sol, even before the settings for Christmas dinner were on the table. Mrs. Block was moving to Florida. Reathel thought that this was wonderful. Tannenbaum was indifferent until it was mentioned that there was an extra pamphlet in Mrs. Block's oversized purse.

While Reathel served the dinner, she and the widow chattered all about plans for Florida. Tannenbaum ate in silence. After dinner, they all retired to the parlor with their gifts in hand. Mrs. Block joined Reathel on the couch while Tannenbaum, already a little sleepy from the turkey, sat in his chair. All three savored the divinity that Tannenbaum made special for home every Christmas Eve, even if his store was running over with customers.

As guest, Mrs. Block unwrapped her presents first. She received from the Tannenbaums (gifts that Reathel bought and signed her husband's name to) a parasol and a wicker basket—just the kinds of things one would need for the countless sunny days in her new home. Next, Reathel opened her gifts from Tannenbaum: a fine new frying pan and a stylographic pen with which to do the books for the candy store. Tannenbaum was very proud of the pen that he had picked out many months before. And although Reathel had wrapped it herself for the occasion, he thought he saw a certain gleam in her eye after she had opened it, and was picking up the gift from Mrs. Block. This from Mrs. Block was a big white sunbonnet of the type that vacationers wear. Tannenbaum thought this an odd gift for his wife, but since his gift also was a hat (a Panama hat, Mrs. Block said), he decided that the old woman simply had hats on the brain. Finally Tannenbaum reached for the gifts from his wife, wrapped together in one box. Maybe it was seeing wrapping again after so long, or maybe it was the lights, or maybe it was the strangeness of Mrs. Block being there. Whatever it was, Tannenbaum felt an old excitement for Christmas gifts, the excitement of his childhood and family, as he had not known for many, many years.

But what was this? White cotton short pants (they were called Bermuda shorts, Tannenbaum recalled) and a pair of white canvas shoes.

The evening ended shortly thereafter. Mrs. Block thanked them very much for their hospitality, and Reathel said it was wonderful to have had some company on the holiday for a change. Both women agreed that they should make a new tradition of Christmas dinner together—a plan which raised Tannenbaum's eyebrows no little bit—as they hugged one another goodbye. Then Tannenbaum, carrying a wicker basket and a parasol, escorted Mrs. Block back to her home on the other side of the street.

When he returned, the big band station was playing, and Tannenbaum's wife sat at the kitchen table reading through the pamphlet of Vista del Sol. He stood at the sink for a minute, two minutes, looking at her without speaking.

"There is much washing to be done, wife."

"There is much of much to be done."

"Will you wash or dry tonight?"

Reathel did not answer him, but kept reading the pamphlet, making notes on a separate sheet of paper with an old ballpoint pen. Tannenbaum stood over the table, fidgeting with the ceramic salt and pepper shakers; picking them up, brushing the bottoms, and carefully nudging them back and forth across the tablecloth. He waited for her to look in his eyes. He wanted her to know how much he disapproved of the show that she and Mrs. Block had made of their Christmas Eve. He wanted her know that he did not appreciate short pants and canvas shoes. He did not need a Panama hat.

"Did you like the gifts that I bought for you?" Tannenbaum asked his wife.

"Eh."

Not this time. Tannenbaum would not let that stand. "And?"

"These are not the gifts of a man to his wife. These are the things a man gives to his cook and his secretary, for their work. These are not even gifts. Should I have given you, husband, a pound of sugar and a stick of butter for the gifts of my heart?"

"That would be more to my taste than these gifts that I have, Panama and Bermuda. You would have me wear the whole ocean. This is sunny-day clothing that a man cannot wear if he wishes to make candy."

"Again to make candy," she said. "Are you nothing of a man and only of a candy maker? Then what am I of your wife? I say that candy is your mistress in the day. But remember, husband, I am the wife you come home to at night. I am your home. And I am more of a woman than cooking and booking. I have my wishes that have been second to your candy all these years. And now I am finished with your candy."

"I am not."

"Then truly you will lose your home."

Tannenbaum shuffled the ceramic pieces into a row.

"Wife, what can I do? You say that my home and my business cannot survive together. I say they cannot survive apart. I have no choices."

Reathel held up the pamphlet to his face.

"This," he said. "And who will make the candy?"

"It was made before you were born and will be made after you die."

"Again my wife wants me to die like my father. But on a beach. I will tell my customers when they come that this is the wife that I go home to, and they will beg me to stay."

"Then you will stay."

"I will stay."

Reathel and Oscar Tannenbaum stared at each other across the table in the kitchen of their home. He was red-faced, nervously picking and replacing the condiments. She fidgeted with shaky hands at the pages of Vista del Sol.

"You are not what your father was," she said. "He left his candy store at a younger age than you are now, husband. And he did not leave to die. He left to live. He left to begin. That the life didn't last long was only an accident of time." She put down the pamphlet on the table. "Why can you not give up your mistress and begin your life with the wife of your marriage? Your father was made of courage. Your father, even in the end, was not so afraid as you. He was a man. Why, husband, can you not be a man?"

Tannenbaum stood for a long moment looking down at the salt and pepper shakers in his hands while his wife glared at him across the kitchen table, waiting for an answer.

"Because, wife, my father had me, as his father had he." He looked at her coldly. "Who have I to give my store to? To give my candy to?

To give my life to? Perhaps, wife, I am not a man because you could not be a woman."

Reathel turned pale. This was the last. The unspeakable. The thing for which his wife had no answer, no words. She began to cry. It was the first time in many years that Oscar Tannenbaum could remember seeing his wife cry. And the first time ever, he believed, that he made her cry. Reathel retreated from the kitchen with her hands covering her face.

Again that night, Tannenbaum slept on the couch.

December twenty-fifth. Tannenbaum had made better sleep that night on the couch from the turkey and the gravy and the cranberries, but it was still fitful, and an insult to his pride. Yet he made better sleep probably than Reathel. She was always a tosser and a turner, he thought. She needed him to provide—what is it called?—ballast on the other side of the bed. Tannenbaum went to make a sack lunch as usual, but quit when the man on the radio reminded him that the stores would be closed today, on Christmas day, the solstice from before there were countries. The pamphlet for Vista del Sol still lay on the table where Reathel had left it the night before. Tannenbaum inspected it with a pained expression. He left the house without looking in on his wife.

It was snowing again, but in a strange way, for to the east Tannenbaum could see blue sky above the line where the sun had risen into the clouds. And the snowflakes, he noticed, were not like those on the solstice, fat and soft and stacked in a hundred crystals all at once. Instead they were small and sharp and bit his face in the wind that blustered him from the first step out the door. It would not be, he thought, a good day for making snow angels.

Tannenbaum walked methodically through the snow and ice, mindful, for perhaps the first time in his life, of every patch of ice that stood in his path. When he arrived at his destination, there again, like something magical, stood Flora in the doorway, coated and mufflered and sheltered in the alcove of Tannenbaum's Candy Store, looking strangely alike to one of Mrs. Block's elfin statues. She was, it seemed to him, a nice surprise.

"I knew you would be here," she said.

Tannenbaum pawed at the snow with his shoe; he grinned like a younger man. "This is where I am always. This is what I am. One day is like the next. Day to day, as they say."

"It's not what you are."

"Yes," he said. "This is how life builds. You are young. Someday you will also know that the days of a life stack up like bricks, one after the next, until the life is made sturdy, like a home that you would be proud to live in."

"Really, Oscar," said Flora, laughing through her words, "Do you think that a stack of bricks is all there is to life? Do you think that a day in the spring is so much like a day in the winter? That a day in the future must be so much like a day in the past? Life is no more a stack of bricks than peanut brittle. And a real home is more than just bricks, just like candy is more than a list of ingredients and language is more than a dictionary of words. Your life, anyone's life, is much more than the sum of your days. That's only the start. Those are only the ingredients, Oscar. How you put them together is living."

Tannenbaum was quiet for a moment, taking in everything that she had said. "This is quite a speech for a young girl," he said finally, a little bit sensitive, though still merry enough in her company. He had felt wonder and delight when she called him by his first name.

"Merry Christmas," Flora said, taking a package from beneath her enormous coat.

"Oh, no. I have nothing to give you."

She did not answer, but gestured eagerly for him to open the package. Inside was a pair of bright orange plastic sunglasses, with little palm trees shooting out of the corners of the frames. Tannenbaum laughed. He put them on. He looked ridiculous, he knew.

"So that you will be able to see the sun, wherever you go," said Flora with a bright smile. Then she grasped his lapels and pulled his big face down to hers, so small and clustered and muddled. She gave him a sweet kiss on the cheek and whispered: "Open your eyes, Oscar Tannenbaum."

With that Tannenbaum, wearing his brand new sunglasses, looked up into the dappled sky to find that the sun that had escaped him that morning was just then peeking out above the clouds. It was his first view of the sun that day. When he looked back down, Flora was gone. He did not look for her.

Tannenbaum placed the sunglasses back in their box and tucked it under his arm. He faced his reflection in the glass door of his father's candy store, a smiling face set just above the sign, TANNENBAUM'S, that he had added after the store was passed down to him. He saw an old man in that mirror. And it seemed to Oscar Tannenbaum not his own refection, but the face of his father, smiling back at him from the glass of the candy store. His father, older than he ever was before. Than he ever was at all.

Could he have been so senseless?

His wife was right. Flora was right. The time, at last, was right. If Tannenbaum had failed to listen before, now, standing before his father's reflection in the door of the candy store, he knew without words that his love affair with candy had reached its end, and it was sad for him. Indeed, neither his house nor his business would survive.

Yet at the same time Tannenbaum felt a faint glow, like the moment before dawn. He felt the exhilaration—if that is...yes, yes, that is the word—of a new beginning, such as he hadn't felt in many, many years. He thought of his sister Martha making angels in the snow, and of Mrs. Block retiring to a warmer climate. He thought of stars of anise and marzipan noses. He thought of the lengthening days of January, and of his children he would never meet. And somehow the reflection in the window made Tannenbaum understand that he was free to be his own man.

It was a new day, with a new year lying just behind the horizon. And now, without delay, he would go home and make love to his wife, if she would still have him. They two would make their own private saturnalia—then gradually, and with dignity, he would let her convince him to move to Florida.

Ibid., a Symposium

To be loved at first sight, a man should have at the same time
something to respect and something to pity in his face.

—Stendhal

$\mathcal{G}$reetings, dear Reader! Welcome to the last story—the coda, the grand finale, the epilogue, if you will. Please do make yourself comfortable; pull up a chair or settle on the grass or flip on the bedside lamp if that's the kind of thing you do, because the three of us are about to get started. Don't worry, this won't be long—there aren't that many pages left, after all.

And yes, you read correctly: There will be three voices here. Naturally 'I' will be the first person and 'You' will be the second person. We'll be joined by that rather affable old fellow in the corner; you don't recognize him, of course, but you've heard of him. 'He' is the aforementioned raconteur and shoe shine guy, Emmanuel Gubatz. Manny for short.

"Hello."

May I say something?

As a matter of fact you can.

What's going on here?

A symposium. Didn't you read the title?

Yes. But I didn't think it would be like this.

What did you think it would be?

I don't know. I don't start out expecting anything in particular. I just read and the story sorts itself out along the way.

And so it shall.

"Come, my friend, be comfortable. Have a glass of wine."

Yes, by all means, dear Reader, have a glass of wine. For this should be a symposium in the classical as much as the modern sense. Did you know that originally, the word 'symposium' simply meant a drinking party? But of course, the Greeks, being the talkers that they were, inevitably turned such occasions into rhetorical contests, forums for debate, deliberation, and general boasting. Soon any event where people made multiple speeches on a given topic became known as a symposium. That's where we get the meaning we have today. And yes, we will have a topic on the agenda. But it should also be a social occasion, a celebration of the time we've spent together.

And what are we discussing?

Helens, of course.

The book?

Yes.

It's a bit odd to discuss the content of a book while you're still writing it.

"I think so too." (drinking from his wineglass) "Always in a hurry, this one."

I don't know what you mean. And I don't particularly like your tone, Manny.

I mean it seems a bit presumptuous. Normally one takes care of publication before worrying about a review.

Okay, maybe it's not normal. But what's wrong with that? What are you, some kind of Babbit? Can't you try to look at the subject from a different perspective?

Your perspective.

Perhaps. But haven't I—haven't we—deviated from 'normal' at times in these pages? You have to admit I've played a little hell with form from time to time. But I promise there's a premise. Besides, dear Reader, you've just opened our discussion on the very topic I suggested—these stories, herein.

Well that's hardly fair, seeing as I'm as much a construct of your imagination as he is. No offense.

"None taken."

You don't know that. You could be real, the image of someone who has read the book. Or you could be more than real, in the Platonic sense. Just think of yourself as my Ideal Reader.

"Be careful. He's starting with the flattery."

Shut up, Manny.

(Raises his hands deferentially)

Okay. If I'm as real as you say, maybe I want to leave.

Well, that wouldn't be ideal...

Hence the difference between a real reader and an Ideal Reader.

But you're free to do as you choose. Thanks for stopping by, sorry you couldn't stay longer.

(Manny has begun rummaging through the record cabinet with one hand, his wine wobbling precariously in the other) "We need music. That will make everyone relax. Where is Fats Waller? Artie Shaw. Pee Wee Russell. Why do you have nothing to listen to?"

Because I wasn't born in the thirties, Manny. You're lucky I have vinyl. Now put down that wineglass before you spill it all over.

(Sets his wineglass absently on the empty turntable) "What vinyl? All I want is a record I can listen to."

There's plenty to choose from.

(Harrumphs, still rummaging) "I tell you, when I was a young man, even before I was married, I understood better how to entertain guests. You give them music and drinks and make them comfortable. You do not call them rabbits and tell them to sit down and talk about this symposium." (Shakes his head and takes up the wineglass) "I do not care what Greeks do. Never have. Greeks, feh!"

Good for you, Manny.

I thought you were leaving.

"Ach! Remember: welcome."

I decided to stay. You two seem to need me around.

You couldn't be more right; Manny and I absolutely need you. Without readers, we authors and characters just go round and round, reaching no conclusions, signifying nothing. Without you, this whole operation is like a tree falling in the woods; whistling in the dark.

Didn't I read somewhere that "whistling in the dark" is a euphemism for masturbation?

Maybe you read too much... But the point is taken. Achieved *tout seul*, climax is a poor, amorphous, amor-less, simulacrum of sex. Likewise, without a conscience to read the words I write or imagine the actions Manny performs, his existence and mine—qua character and author, respectively—are vain, empty, and sterile. We need you, you complete us.

Jesus, you make it sound like love.

Of course. Love and writing are inexorably linked. The whole concept of the love letter is built on the idea that it's easier to express romantic feelings in print than in voice. And it's not just letters. Affairs of the heart always figure prominently in personal diaries. Lovers use writing both to record and comprehend their feelings; it's liberating and reifying to write about love.

Now you sound like Francesco del Giocondo.

That wouldn't be an accident.

"Aha! Now we're talking!" (Manny is holding up an album of Benny Goodman's greatest hits.)

Are you trying to tell me you love me, need me?

Maybe. But you need me too. (Manny ahems) Okay, you need us. Because without authors and characters, readers are lost in an ocean of erratic facts and fickle opinions. Nonfiction, ugh. Every writer of nonfiction has his own version of the facts, and everybody—everybody!—has his own opinion.

"Like assholes."

Thank you Manny. Yes, like assholes: Everybody's got one. Yet with all those facts and opinions in the water, you'll drown before you find a hint of truth in nonfiction. The truth, dear Reader, is that you need fiction to arrive at any kind of certainty, because only in the rarified world of a finely composed narrative can you distinguish the cant of attitude from gems of insight. Fundamental truth can only really be expressed through fiction.

Are you saying that love is just a fiction?

(Manny's eyebrows rise like a turgid penis.)

"Ach! Why do you write such things? It's disgusting."

Then don't look at me that way.

You didn't answer the question.

Well not completely. But like I said, in some several ways love is a construct of fiction. All that stuff about fate, destiny, kismet, and the rest owes a debt to narrative. And you'd certainly agree, dear Reader, that fiction can be inspired by love. More to the point, love is the essence of fiction, the force behind every story ever told. It's no wonder that Helen of Troy is the animus of Western literature: She's the embodiment of love and all its awful contingencies. Her mother was raped by Zeus; she wed Menelaus and cuckholded him with Paris; Achilles waged war for her honor and his own glory; Homer sang her beauty for undying fame. She is a link to antiquity—bred in the bones, coursing in our veins, alive in our conscience; she's the mother of history, the queen of literature, the epitome of love. As Vincent Pria says: Every story is about Helen.

Don't you think you're laying it on a little thick?

Now you're a critic?

Maybe. And if this is a symposium, in the Platonic sense, there really should be seven speakers instead of three.

Not necessarily. Plato's is a symposium in the tradition of the seven sages, each representing one of the styles of Greek rhetoric. We three, on the other hand, are conducting a symposium on narrative fiction, in which there are only three voices available. Therefore to include four more voices in our dialogue would serve no formal purpose, and it would complicate the matter beyond all understanding.

Now you're a strict formalist?

I'm always a formalist, never strict.

I think you just want to argue with me, like you argue with Manny.

An author always argues, in a manner of speaking. I've been arguing with characters and readers for more than three hundred pages, surely you don't expect me to stop now.

"That is enough the two of you. No one should be arguing here. We will have this symposium, and the subject will be what our host has suggested: We will talk about The Helens…"

It's just 'Helens,' Manny. That's the name of the book you're in.

"Whatever. Each of us will make the best speech he can about the book, moving from left to right as Greeks do, though that will make it most difficult for me, as I must be the last to speak. But I will not complain, because as long as the other speakers do their jobs, I will have plenty of things to say.

"Is it agreed?"

Yes.

Yes.

(Manny gets up, refills each of the wineglasses, and returns to his couch, settling with a look of auspicious calm)

Well then, I guess it's up to me to begin. To start, I want to go back to something that was said earlier about the relationship between truth and fiction. Our author explained his theory that fundamental truth can only really be expressed through fiction.

What, no quotation marks?

You know what you said. What I find interesting is the way that theory is expressed in the book. Throughout, we see characters telling stories for a variety of plot purposes, be it to explain, cajole, seduce, entertain, or educate. But that's only half of what's going on, because these narrative plot devices work on another level—at another remove—by communicating between the author and his readers.

Like you.

Yes. Please don't interrupt. The meaning of the frame story usually has some metaphorical relation to the embedded story told by a character. It is, in fact, a metafiction. I'd be tempted to say that these stories are 'literally' metafictional, if that kind of thing didn't sound like tautology. What's more, the characters' stories are almost always about love in some aspect, which reinforces the author's thesis that all narrative is simulacrum of the Helen of Troy myth.

Yet at the same time there's a different process at work in the embedded stories, as signified by the types of people who tell them. In story after story, embedded stories are narrated by the most dubious or deceptive characters in the book. For instance, the first story contains a nameless narrator who calls himself a faithless bastard; Francis Tuckwell is a thoroughly untrustworthy narrator at the coffee shop, while at the same time, in footnotes, he professes his fondness of irony for irony's sake; Vincent Pria, who goes on at length—directly—about the Helen myth, is sleeping with his friend's wife; Delaney Bowles is a perfect font of falsehood; Ruby Bottoms wants only fantasy from her online lover, forbidding him to engage in any kind of truth-telling where their relations are concerned; there is express doubt about the veracity of Franceso del Giocondo's writings; and Flora, the confectioner's muse and/or mistress, seems questionably extant within the narrative itself. So while truth and fiction are ostensibly linked within the six foregoing stories of 'Helens,' fiction and falsehood are almost always related in the embedded stories told therein.

"That is very interesting. But what does it mean?"

At the very least it means that the author presents a very different concept of fiction within the confines of the story than the one that was given as the basis of fiction. Between author and reader, fiction signifies truth. But between characters in the story, an act of narration denotes falsehood. Taken figuratively, that suggests a pretty bleak view of human nature. The world—or worlds—created in this book are filled with deception and unreliability.

May I respond to that?

Be my guest.

The worlds created in these stories (as you have it) are meant to bear a theoretical resemblance to the world of the Iliad, if only as a facsimile of the ur-fiction. Like the characters in 'Helens,' the characters of the Iliad deal with conflict, competition, deception, and frustration, all instigated by love. Even Zeus, the greatest power in that fictional universe, is powerless to resist his feelings for Leda, and by fathering Helen on her has set the whole awful drama in motion. Gods and humans alike struggle to reach their preferred ends, which remain, in the fictional world, in doubt. But Homer and his readers already know the outcome. The mythology precedes the poem, after all. So Homer doesn't just retell the story of Troy, he imbues that story with imagery and style that brings each passage to life. And that's important, because this is the first time that the retelling is not being performed by a live person. The fact that the plot is predetermined and that the poem is written instead of acted means that the words must be that much more compelling, the ideas conveyed from author to reader that much more valid. In short, it's the poetry, with its vivid imagery and formal beauty, that makes the Iliad the first written work of literature to survive.

Is that why you're all caught up on form?

I told you there's a premise.

"But these two things are not the same form. One is a long poem and the other is short stories."

Thank you Manny. My point, again, is theoretical.

"Of course." (Manny raises his glass)

Because the Iliad is a poem that was originally performed, it retains aspects of the oral tradition. Meter and rhyme were originally part of the format, as are character epithets—ox-eyed Hera, lovely haired Helen, and the like—which help facilitate the structure of the stanzas. Not only the epithets, but also certain tropes and motifs are common to oral poetry. That's why there tends to be a great deal of repetition in the Iliad. For instance, way back in 1948 a man named James Armstrong identified what he calls the 'arming motif,' a formulaic passage that occurs and recurs several times within the poem, specifically in chapters 3, 11, 16, and 19 (arming passages for

Paris, Agamemnon, Patroclus, and Achilles, respectively), when one or another of the heroes of the Iliad is preparing to go into battle. You can see that Homer is working with a pretty fixed formal structure, no?

(Manny nods)

The artistry of the Iliad derives from the way that Homer manipulates structure to augur ends and impart emotions. With the arming motif, Armstrong writes that prolix introductions to battle scenes generate a sense of suspense for the reader, while the repetition of the formula—I quote—'creates an atmosphere of smoothness' within the framework of the narrative. However, each time Homer presents the arming motif, he changes certain elements of style, such as utilizing negative turns of phrase when describing Patroclus' arming for battle. Armstrong explains that this is a foreshadowing device on Homer's part, as Patroclus is the only one of the four heroes described in an arming motif who is going to be killed in the upcoming battle.

I don't see what this has to do with you playing hell with form.

Well, as I said, in telling the story of Troy, Homer is tied to a well-known plot. He can't, after all, have Patroclus defeat Hector in battle, because that wouldn't fit the story his readers know. So his variation—his artistry—reveals itself in the internal style of his poetry, while remaining true to certain motifs that ground the Iliad in the oral tradition.

Similar to the Iliad, the stories in 'Helens' create a variation, but on a different element of narrative. It's like playing the same melody in different keys. The stories are not tied to structure or plot, but the theme I offered you earlier: That all narrative is derived from the Helen of Troy myth. If the theme is fixed, it's the structure or form of the story that varies. These 'Helens' are variations on the theme. And like Patroclus' death being foreshadowed by negative turns of phrase in his arming scene, the form of each story corresponds to the style of storytelling.

Therefore, 'The Unfinished Work' is composed of two parallel, elliptical narratives linked by the central icon of an unfinished portrait. 'En Passant' offers flirtation and verbal jousting, with much of the exposition related in the fleeting style of contemporaneous footnotes. 'Helens,' the story, is a pretty straight allegory of the Paris/Helen element of the Iliad, with plenty of allusions to the love-war motif sprinkled in for dramatic effect. 'The Italian Manuscript' is a classic found-document story, in which the reader (pace, dear Reader) remains as uncertain of the provenance of the manuscript as he is doubtful of the love between David and Miriam. 'Oral Sex in the Communication Age' analyzes the backward status of romantic relationships vis-a-vis pornography and cybersex. And the 'Confectioner's Mistress' offers a bit of magical realism as the solution to the obstacles of lasting love. In each story the structural variation—that aforementioned formal hell-playing—is a necessary element of the fiction.

It's just pretentious. You could do the same thing without resorting to tricks.

Then I'd just be telling an anecdote; it wouldn't be fiction.

What's the difference?

When form follows content, a narrative becomes more than description. There's resonance in a story that comes to a sympathetic end. That's the difference between fiction and anecdote.

I wouldn't use the word 'sympathy.' None of these characters seem very happy in the end.

This sympathy has more to do with agreement among the elements of the story, not compassion toward any character's end. Resonance derives from a feeling that the story's development and end seem fitting. When all the elements of plotting and character are in agreement, the reader feels that the story can't have ended any way other than it did. There are no curveballs or bombshells, as reality throws you. That's why fiction is truer than nonfiction—truer than life for that matter.

Truer than life?

Certainly. Fiction needs traceable motives and plausible causation as its bedrock and framework. If the development of a story doesn't logically follow its premise, a reader won't suspend his disbelief and will toss the book aside. Authors have to build a narrative on credible elements in order to guide readers to the conclusion they're trying to reach; subjects, characters, events, setting—all have to be believable in order to maintain a clear image in the reader's mind.

Life, on the other hand, is completely random. That's why life isn't fair. There's no guarantee that rational causation governs the passage of time. In fact, it's not a good bet. Fiction may be cruel, it may be capricious, it may even be indifferent in certain events. But in a broader sense fiction is fair, or it's not viable. That's why fiction is truer than life.

Let me give you an example.

I never believed in love at first sight; it's too complicated, too multi-sided an emotion to take in all in one glance. That is, of course, why it's the great spur of literature: Love bends the mind to abstraction while it focuses the heart in one direction. It's far too intricate to credit at first sight. Or so I thought.

Then one October, I found myself at a little hotel in San Juan, where I'd gone to get away from my life. More specifically I was there to nurse my bruised ego, having lost my second job, my first book deal, and yet another relationship for which I'd had real hope. All that within a matter of months. I was 32, and I was thoroughly depressed; I was starting over from scratch without the strength I'd had the last time. I lay on my back beside a pitiful swimming pool, fully clothed against the overcast, looking through the leaves of a banyan tree at a few low, dark clouds that swept across the grey background.

Then, I don't know why, but I turned. There was no sound or movement, mind you, no reason for my change of focus; it was just a random redirection of attention. And there was a girl looking right back at me. She wore a loose cotton dress over her swimsuit, the straps tied behind her long brown neck, and floppy shoes in a gaudy shade of green. Her hair was streaked with blonde, and tossed by

the breeze, except for a few thick strands that had been braided—
by herself, I was sure—behind her left ear. Her eyes were brown.
For a second the earth stood still. Even the clouds seemed to stop
their mad dash for the horizon. Then in another second a man came
from behind and ushered her toward the door. Our gaze broke and
I was left with the echo of something both too vast and too brief to
take in. It's what he Italians call 'il colpo di fulmine'—the lightning
bolt—a flash of emotion that imprints itself on your soul.

You didn't even talk to her?

Oh yes, I met her and the man she was with. Over the course of
the weekend we talked a few times at the hotel bar. And every time
I saw her she was charming and genuine and lovely. Every time she
smiled I just melted.

That's nice, but it doesn't quite sound like love at first sight.

There's more. The last night I was there, I stopped by the hotel
lobby to pay my bill. And there was this girl—let's call her Rachel—
alone, talking on her cell phone. She proceeds to tell me that the
guy she's with is her ex-boyfriend, with whom she'd booked this
trip months before they broke up. Furthermore, Rachel tells me that
she's been trying to get me alone all weekend, even going so far as to
slip notes under the door of what she thought was my hotel room.
She says she's been on the phone to her mother and her friends all
weekend talking about me. She tells me that even though I live in
New York and she lives in Miami, she really needs to talk to me because something happened when she first saw me. She says—and
I could never actually write this if they weren't her words—that she
thinks I'm her soul mate.

Okay. That's a bit more like it.

So she went back to Miami and I went back to New York, and
Rachel and I talked to each other every day, and she was amazing.
I felt like a schoolboy. Somehow I'd gone from being as low as I'd
ever been in my life to feeling like I was the luckiest guy on earth—
just because I'd turned my head at the right time.

In November, we had our first date: a weekend in Vegas at her stepbrother's wedding. No kidding. She looked gorgeous in periwinkle (no small feat); her family liked me, and I them. We saw a burlesque show; she held my face in her hands while she kissed me. We took a helicopter over the Grand Canyon; Rachel got airsick and laid her head in my lap the whole cab ride home. She told me about her late father and her time teaching English in Tokyo. I told her about my lost book deal and the vacation I'd spent in Italy.

Rachel came to New York in December; I picked her up at the airport. We had a romantic dinner and went to a Broadway show. We made love for the first time, and the second time, and the third. I bought her a piece of lingerie, she tried it on right there (Manny laconically follows the direction of my finger); the light from the window outlined her thighs through the shift. She called me from the airport to say she missed me already. Two days later, a plane ticket arrived in the mail; she said she loved being with me, and couldn't wait for me to come to Miami. Rachel said all the things I was thinking. I started scouring want ads for a job in Florida.

Then one day soon after New Year's, Rachel called to tell me she got married to a Swedish friend of hers. Kind of thing they do all the time in Miami, I guess. He needed American papers and she was going to spend a year in Spain, as a European citizen.

And that's it: no development, no climax, no resolution. A perfect anecdote. Real life. What could possibly be 'true' about that story?

"Horseshit." (laying a hand consolingly on the Reader's forearm) "I am sorry to use such harsh language. But when I see a pile of some disagreeable thing in my path, I find it best to call it by name. And this (waves his wineglass in my direction) is horseshit, Matthew."

Thank you Manny.

"No problem."

Is it that anecdote in particular, or my life in general you find to be horseshit?

"The antidote is perfectly fine. Your life is shit."

Manny!

"I am sorry. But you must forgive me if I am confused. I have heard many strange things this day about truth; one says that truth is what is not at all true, and another says that a falsehood between two particular people is a truth between two other people. Maybe I am naïve, but I thought that truth is to be made by telling facts. Maybe I am wrong about this. Maybe this is not the way to make a symposium. I do not know. I am not Greek, after all."

You can say anything you want, Manny.

"May I ask you a few questions first? Then I can deliver my speech with a clearer understanding."

Of course.

"Earlier you said that love is the cause of all fiction because it is the force that creates conflict and competition and all of those things that make a story. You also said that characters in fiction are powerless against this love that makes them do things. Even Zeus, who is the king of the gods, cannot resist the force of love, and so it causes him to conceive Helen of Troy, and this sets the story in motion. Is that correct?"

Yes. That's what I said.

"You also told us that what makes this Iliad such a great work of fiction is the way that the writer, Homer, uses the different elements of his poetry to create expectation and stimulate emotion. This, you say, is the manipulation of form that makes a story fiction instead of just a story that one person might tell another. No?"

Yes, I think I said something like that. I used the word anecdote. That's anec-dote.

"As you say. But it seems to me that you put the writer at a higher level than the god. After all, the writer controls every part of the fiction, and also knows what the outcome of the story will be, not only for the humans but for the gods. In this way, the writer is even more powerful than the god. Do you think that is correct?"

I guess within the confines of a story like the Iliad, where the gods are characters, yes, the writer is more powerful than the gods.

"But in fact the writer controls everything about the story. As you said, in a fiction that is well made, all elements are in agreement, and for the reader and the characters, the story can end in no other way than it does."

Yes, I said that too.

"So you admit that in the process of writing the story, the writer deliberately takes for himself the role of a kind of god."

Fine, Manny. I suppose it's true that all writers have a bit of a God complex. That's why we enjoy creating our own worlds.

"And that is why you say that fiction is truer than life, because you as a god have created the whole picture of life in harmony, or agreement, as you say, for the reader to see."

Yes.

(Shaking his head, now, with mock modesty) "Maybe it is because I am only a shoe shiner, and not a writer-god like some people, but to me this idea of 'truth' and 'life' as you call them have nothing to do with what is true or what is alive. Life cannot be contained within a frame, as can be done with art. What you show in a stack of pages breaks with the most basic element of life—the fact that it is miscellaneous and unlimited. And in the same way, life by nature forbids this restrictive idea of 'fiction.'"

What I mean is that events in fiction make more sense than they do not in real life, from a certain perspective.

Your perspective.

Yes again.

"So if this fiction is a thing that serves to gratify only the perspective of the writer-god, then it does seem to be… What was the thing you said earlier?"

Whistling in the dark?

"Precisely."

So my life is shit and my writing is masturbation. Is that what you're saying Manny?

"Almost. Your life is shit BECAUSE your writing is this masturbation. Tell me: do you have a girlfriend now? No. Have you had a girlfriend since Rachel Love-at-first-sight ran off and got married to the Swedish? Of course not. Instead you sit here in your little room writing about love that never ends right, and you tell yourself that you are being true. Well, these stories may be very true, as you say, because all of their parts are in harmony. But they can never be real. Fictions, like me, may be true, but only life can give you what is real. And life is somewhere outside these fictions.

"Now, let me tell you a story to show what I mean…"

AND NOW, WITHOUT FURTHER ADO, THE WORLD FAMOUS CLOWN JOKE OF MANNY GUBATZ:

"Once upon a time, there was a young boy who lived in a village somewhere in the middle part of America. Let us say it was Kansas. I am not saying for certain that it was Kansas, but things like this are always better when you can be specific about details, and I have always found that the word 'Kansas' has a very specific meaning. Even if it was not where the boy was really from.

"Now this was a very long time ago, as you can tell by the fact that the boy lived in a village, because no one in America has lived in a village for many, many years. This was before television and computers brought the world to your doorstep, and people were not so worldly as they are now. As a result, people were not so crude as they are now. It is sad to say, but worldliness is not often a polite quality. It is not, as they say, familiarity that breeds contempt, but sophistication, if you will allow me to state an opinion. In fact, for most people in Kansas, the world was bordered by the limits of their own village. And so it was a more simple time. This is how many people lived once upon a time, and this particular boy was no exception.

"One of the few times when the world did come to Kansas was when the circus came to town. But you must understand that this circus was not like the glitzy Ringling and Barnum thing you think of today. No. This was a spectacle of marksmen and magicians, snake charmers and goat boys, strongmen, bearded ladies, contortionists, clairvoyants, and hermaphrodites. This was an old-time traveling carnival unlike anything that has been seen in this country for many decades.

"So one year when the circus came to town, the boy's father decided that he would take his son to see this spectacle. And though the boy had no idea what a circus was, he was thrilled when his father told him they were going, because he was at that age, maybe six or seven years old, when boys idolize their fathers. The fact that he and his father would be spending the day at this circus filled him with pride and happiness.

"And on the day the boy went to the circus, his happiness turned to pure joy, because the circus was ten times more amazing than he'd imagined. There were men breathing fire and men walking on their hands, men taming lions and men pulling rabbits out of hats. It seemed that everywhere you looked there was something incredible going on. But for all the feats of amazement he saw, the boy's favorite part of the circus was the clowns that came out between acts to make everyone laugh. The boy loved these clowns so much that he could not take his eyes off them, even when the laughter filled his vision with tears. Near the end of the show, it got to the point that he couldn't wait for certain acts, like the bearded lady, to be over just so that he could watch the clowns once again.

"This is exactly the way the boy was feeling by the time Mandrake the Magician finished cutting his assistant, the Lovely Lillian, in two pieces with a shiny saw. As the two of them took their bows, out from behind the curtains came the two clowns: Toots and Mr. Jingles. The main clown, Mr. Jingles, had a white face and a bright green suit. He wore red shoes and carried a big tambourine that gave him his name. Toots had a striped suit and a wide straw hat and carried a little horn on a belt around his waist. These two had appeared throughout the performance, playing tricks on one another and doing foolery with members of the audience. The boy hoped very much that at least one of the clowns would come to play with him before the show was over.

"Now Mr. Jingles marches into the circus ring carrying a water bucket and a long-handled ladle. With a very dainty hand, the tall, white-faced clown dipped the ladle in the bucket and served himself some cool water. Behind him, Toots waited anxiously for a drink. But instead of giving his partner the ladle, when he was finished Mr. Jingles carried it to a young girl seated in the front row. He then proceeded to serve water to other audience members, walking twice, three times past Toots, who was growing more frustrated and thirsty with every pass. As Mr. Jingles continued to pass water out to the crowd, the boy wished desperately to be the next person who would be served. Not because he was particularly thirsty, of course, but because he wanted to be included in the clowns' play. But so far Mr. Jingles had not chosen him to be part of the show.

"Finally, the fourth time Mr. Jingles filled the ladle and passed by his partner, Toots had enough. As the taller clown raised the water-filled ladle toward an audience member, Toots pulled his horn—which was attached to his waist by a long piece of twine, by the way—he pulled his horn up to Mr. Jingles' ear and gave it a loud honk. Mr. Jingles jumped at the sound and spilled the ladle full of water all over the front of his green suit. The audience laughed along with Toots as Mr. Jingles walked angrily back to bucket to refill his ladle. But once again, when he walked toward an audience member and raised his arm to dish out a drink, Toots honked and wet Mr. Jingles front again.

"Now this time when Mr. Jingles went back to the water bucket, he didn't fill the ladle. Instead, he picked up the whole bucket, turned, and looked right at Toots, who quit laughing pretty quick when he saw the look in Mr. Jingles eyes. All at once Mr. Jingles ran at Toots, who took off like a shot.

"For several minutes the boy watched with laughter and excitement as Mr. Jingles chased Toots around the circus ring carrying the bucket of water. But every time Mr. Jingles got close, Toots somehow escaped from his drenching. Then, finally, Mr. Jingles cornered Toots on the far side of the ring. Toots couldn't move anymore because he was so tired from running. Mr. Jingles reared back and ran straight toward him, bringing the bucket forward with all his strength, but at the last minute, Toots ducked and the bucket poured out on the audience behind him. The boy held his breath because he expected the crowd to get the drenching that was meant for Toots. But what came out of the bucket wasn't water. Instead, the audience was showered with thousands of tiny pieces of paper.

"The crowd broke into wild applause because no one knew how the water had been replaced with paper. Still, everyone was happy and amazed by the trick the two clowns had played, none less than the boy, who stood and clapped until the clowns were replaced in the ring by Golda the Dancing Bear. And it seemed that that was the last the boy was going to see of the clowns, because after the bear act the circus' ringmaster returned to the ring to say that the show was over. The boy got up with his father and started making his way toward the tent entrance, feeling sad. It wasn't of course, a terrible sadness; not a sadness of loss or misery. It was the sadness of knowing something wonderful had ended. It was the sadness of time, the sadness of age.

"But then out of nowhere Mr. Jingles burst through the tent entrance at a dead run, followed closely by Toots, who, this time, was carrying the bucket. The boy laughed and clapped his hands, and he was so happy to see the clowns that he didn't even notice that even though he had stopped, his father had continued walking toward the door. The two clowns circled the ring once again, this time with Toots in hot pursuit. And as Mr. Jingles came around the near side of the tent, he looked straight at the boy. In fact, he was running right toward him, and every second the boy's excitement was getting bigger and bigger. Finally he would get to be part of the show.

"And indeed, Mr. Jingles ran right up to the boy, who was still clapping and laughing, and who could only assume that Toots was behind, because by that time the clown was so close that his big green suit blocked the boy's view of anything else. It didn't matter though, because the boy knew exactly what to expect. But he was to be amazed one more time by the circus, because when Mr. Jingles stepped aside and Toot's emptied his bucket, instead of being showered with a thousand pieces of confetti the boy was hit in the face with a bucket of ice cold water.

"Needless to say, the boy was hurt and angry and sad, as well as many other feelings that he didn't even have words for. And worse than that, the whole audience, which had been filing toward the doors, stopped and began laughing at him. But not like they were laughing before, when the clowns were playing funny tricks on each other. Now they were pointing and cackling. Now they weren't laughing at the show, they were laughing at him as he stood there drenched to the bone, his lips quivering, his chin curled like a gerbil, tears coming to his eyes.

"'Awww, what's the matter little boy, are you gonna cry?' Toots said, leaning right into the boy's face. 'Come on, ain't you got nothing to say?'

"The boy felt all of his anger rising up like a fire, and it burst out of him straight into the Toots big painted face. He screamed: 'Fuck you clown!'

"And just like that the laughing stopped, and the boy looked up through teary eyes to see that his father was standing beside him with a look of shame and amazement on his face. For neither he nor his father, nor anyone at the circus for that matter, could believe what had come out of the boy's mouth. That night, for the first and only time in his life, the boy felt his father's belt. And from that day on, there were no more private days for just the two of them. From that day on, they never went to the circus again. From that day on, he was no longer as much of a boy as he had been.

"But that wasn't even the worst part, because in a village like that there is no escaping such an event. Forever after the day at the circus, he was known in the village as the F-you boy in polite company. In private, he was called much worse. And the incident followed him through the years, from childhood to high school, affecting every relationship, or possible relationship, he had in his village. After all, who wants to sit next to the F-you boy on the bus? And surely no girl would ruin her night by allowing the F-you boy to take her to prom.

"Since this event made his life so hard, it should come as no surprise that when the boy grew up he made a decision that few others in his village did. He decided that he would leave Kansas. And his goal in leaving Kansas was even more revealing, and even more related to his experience at the circus. The boy would set out to perfect the art of the comeback. He would become the expert of the rejoinder, the gibe, the wisecrack, or as the French call it, the Mott juice. He swore that by the time he was done no clown would ever again catch him at a loss for words.

"So when he finished his schooling, the F-you boy, who by this time was a young man, kissed his parents goodbye and walked right past the border of his village, and the next village, and the village after that, all the way to Chicago, which as everyone knows is the home of the fastest talkers in all of the Midwest. Quite naturally, the young man found himself a job working in the rail yards, because everyone also knows that wisecrackers are to be found among men who work side-by-side all day long with no one to talk to but each other. And soon enough, after listening to the rail hands exchange their pleasantries and unpleasantries, their banter and mockery, the young man developed an apprentice's repertoire of comebacks that would work in almost any situation.

"He started off out with some basic, everyday quips like, 'Whatever,' and 'Here we go again,' and 'Keep talkin' buddy.' These weren't the most witty remarks. Still, any one of those comebacks would have sufficed that day at the circus. And as he worked a little longer, he picked up some better things, like 'What am I, flypaper for freaks?' and 'I'll try to be nicer if you try to be smarter.'

"After maybe a year or so, the young man found that the rail hands really didn't have anything new to show him. In fact, they seemed to use the same tired old comebacks again and again, without ever realizing that their words were getting old. So once again, he picked up and left, this time heading east to New York, where he had heard the people could talk up a blue streak. In New York, the young man got work as a busboy at Mo Ching's Fabulous Shalimar Lounge, a dingy basement in Chinatown where there were plenty of watery drinks and lots of watery eyes. This was the place, he was told, where all the smart alecks and fast talkers gathered. They went there mostly to see Shecky Burlap, the king of the insult comics, who performed three shows a day six nights a week, and four on Tuesdays.

"Shecky Burlap had a very unique act, because part of his routine was to take on all the hecklers in the audience, and give them back better than he got. So people did not only come to hear Shecky's show, they also came to hear what he would say to anyone who dared to speak up during his performance. In fact, many people came just for that reason. They were there to heckle the great comic, and feel the pleasing sting of his brilliant comebacks. For New Yorkers, it was an honor to be insulted by such a genius. But New Yorkers have always been a strange lot. And so every night from six till one, while he was cleaning up plates of duck orange and moo shoo this-and-that and general so-so's chicken, the young man got to hear all of Shecky's best stuff.

"If a bald man in the front row spoke up, Shecky would ask him, 'Is that your head, or did someone plant a pumpkin on your neck?' Or if he had a big nose: 'This fella's got a Roman nose…It's roamin' all over his face.' If he was hairy, Shecky might just call him 'King Kong's cousin.' And the women were not exempt, especially if they sat with a man who heckled in the middle of his act. 'You're lookin' lovely tonight, miss,' he would say, 'For an elephant.' Or: 'She's a light eater, that one. As soon as it gets light, she starts eating.' 'Beauty is obviously in the eye of the beer-holder.' 'A closed mouth gathers no foot.' Or Shecky would just mumble under his breath, 'I see the welfare checks came in today.'

"He had a thousand of them. The young man hardly ever heard him use the same line twice in a week. And the people loved it. They would shout over one another trying to be the next one to bring Shecky's insults down on them. Every night the young man would go home, back to his little one room boarding house with the bathroom down the hall, and he would write down everything he could remember that Shecky had said. And when someone gave him guff on the street, he was always ready with one of Shecky's gems. 'If ignorance is bliss, you must be the happiest guy on the planet.' Then the young man would chuckle to himself, just like Shecky did.

"One day, when Shecky was eating his general so-so's, just like he did every day before performing, the young man got up the courage to go over and ask him how it was that he always knew what to say, and that he knew so many things to say. Shecky chuckled, of course. Then he said he wasn't always like that. There was a time when he used to get tongue-tied. 'How did you get over it?' the young man asked. 'You just gotta get out there and live,' Shecky told him. 'Once you've done a bit of livin', it'll just come to ya.'

"So that night the young man quit his job at Mo Ching's, and the next morning he was aboard a slow boat for London, where he would spend many months among the West End cockneys. After that, he went on to Paris, and listened to all the great wits in the salons and cafes, and then he spent a year living with the pickpockets and con men of the Roman

Travertine. For years, the young man followed Shecky's advice, traveling to India, Morocco, and Brazil, seeing all there that there was to see in the world and learning all about how to read people, so that he would always know what to say when someone challenged him.

"Finally, after so many years of traveling, the young man returned to his village in Kansas, where everyone still knew him as the F-you boy. But now, when anyone spoke to him he answered in quips and retorts so clever that they were silenced by his eloquence. And even when one of them mocked him or teased him for his former nickname, calling on the shame of his former speechlessness, he mocked them back with such cool authority that they stood open-mouthed with shock. The young man, no more the F-you boy, was admired by everyone in his village. He went back to his parents' home and was received with all gladness and honor. He was a lost love, a prodigal son returned to the fold.

"As fate would have it, soon after the young man returned to Kansas, the circus came passing through his village. His father thought that it was fitting that they should go together to the circus, as they had on that day many years before. The young man agreed. And even though he had been all over the world, had seen sights that people in Kansas could only dream of, the circus still had the power to amaze him. The snake charmers and clairvoyants and strongmen and bearded ladies were still all there, and still as incredible as they were when he was a boy. Sitting at the circus, the young man felt the old innocence of his youth. And of course there were also clowns, playing and teasing and making trouble the way they always do. Although it took some time, before long the young man was laughing along with them just as he had done the first time he came to the circus.

"The clowns were up to all of the same old things like pulling down pants, squirting water with fake flowers and slipping on banana peels that the other clowns had thrown on the ground. All of the usual clown stuff, which they did while the main acts in the circus were preparing for performance. And though he'd seen it only once before, the young man remembered every trick and trip in the whole act. So when it came to the end, and he saw one of the clowns come out carrying a silver bucket and a ladle, he knew exactly what was about to happen.

"But then the young man noticed that the clown carrying the bucket was different from any of the clowns he'd seen that day at the circus. This clown had a striped suit and a wide straw hat and, yes, he carried a little horn on a belt around his waist. The young man peered in closer, straining to make out some difference from his memory, because it couldn't possibly be. It had been more than twenty years. He would have to be an old man by this time. But the more he looked, and the harder he tried to find something that didn't match his recollection, the more the young man became convinced: It was Toots.

"This time, Toots was doing what Mr. Jingles had done twenty years before, taking ladles of water to the audience while the other clown, a short, skinny thing with a yellow suit and a blue face, stood by in thirsty frustration. And just as the young man expected, after the third or fourth time Toots passed by him, the blue-faced clown took action. As Toots offered the ladle to a young girl with pigtails, Blue Face stood on his toes and blew into Toots ear, causing him to splash water all down the front of his shirt. Toots was angry, but he just went back to the bucket and refilled. But each time now that he tried to give a bit of water to the audience, the other clown snuck up on him and made him spill again.

"Well anyone can guess what happened next. After the third time that Blue Face made Toots spill, Toots had had enough. He picked up the bucket and pointed straight at the other clown. For just a moment, Blue Face froze. Then he took off like a shot, running around the ring with Toots right on his heels. The crowd, especially the children, ooohed and aaahed each time Toots reared back with the bucket. But each time he got close, Blue Face somehow managed to escape getting drenched.

"And then all of a sudden Blue Face was running straight at the young man. It was like déjà vu all over again, as the clown became bigger and bigger in his vision, his yellow suit blocking any view of Toots coming after him with the bucket. And once again, he couldn't help it, the young man felt his excitement rising as he was about to become part of the show. Not like the last time though. Because this time he knew exactly what to expect. As Blue Face stepped aside and Toots came into view, the young man smiled his biggest smile of the day, waiting for the shower of confetti.

"But that's not what he got.

"Instead, he got hit clean in the face with a bucketful of cold water that drenched him from his eyeballs to his pants pockets. And this young man, who had spent the better part of ten years traveling the world, learning to read people, perfecting the art of the comeback, sat perfectly still in his seat, his eyes closed, water dripping from the tip of his nose into the lap of his brand new wool trousers. The whole circus fell silent for a time.

"Then the young man opened his eyes. He looked Toots dead in the face and he said: 'Fuck you clown!'"

THE END

(Manny raises his glass and takes a short sip.)

Are you kidding me? That's it? After ten pages of Chicago and New York and France and India and dock workers and thieves and night clubs and Shecky Burlap for crying out loud, you're telling me he comes back and all he's got to say is the same thing? That's it?

Yep. That's it.

About the Author

Matthew Kalash is an alumnus of the graduate Creative Writing Program at New York University. He currently works as an editor in Palm Beach County, Florida.